North

The Wolf Trial

The Wolf Trial

Neil Mackay

**FREIGHT
BOOKS**

First published May 2016
Freight Books
49-53 Virginia Street
Glasgow, G1 1TS
www.freightbooks.co.uk

A CIP catalogue reference for this book is available from the British Library

ISBN 978-1-910449-72-1
eISBN 978-1-910449-73-8

Typeset by Freight in Plantin
Printed and bound by Bell and Bain, Glasgow

the publisher acknowledges investment from
Creative Scotland toward the publication of this book

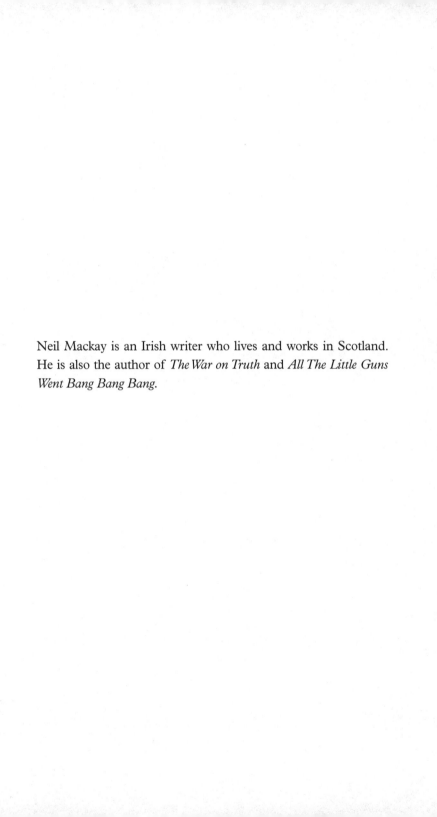

Neil Mackay is an Irish writer who lives and works in Scotland. He is also the author of *The War on Truth* and *All The Little Guns Went Bang Bang Bang.*

For my beloved little werewolves,
Niamh and Caitie

Handy dandy, change one for another
and both are the same.

A folk saying

Prologue

The solemn and avowed testimony of William Loos, known as the Dutch Master of Glasgow.

My story is so old now – because I am so old – that remembering my own role in it is like remembering a character some other writer invented in a tale from many years ago. I am not now the man I was back in Bideburg. In fact, back then, I was a boy. Like the long-travelling ship of Theseus – its mast replaced, oars changed, boards renewed, figurehead switched – there is not one part of me remaining today that was part of me then. The boy is gone, this old man sits in his place – and this is sad as I was a good-looking youth; though, of course, I am not just speaking of change in the face and body alone. Even the ground I walk on is different, and the language I speak, and the nature of the people I live amongst. Perhaps the spirit of the times remains a little the same though – history does not really change: a thesis my pupils would have taken trouble making sense of, if I was still of an age to teach, or in an age where teaching and learning still matter, rather than glad-handing and affectation – though I did plenty of those foolish things too when I was young, proving my point that nothing changes. My own teachers thought me shallow and full of pride, and perhaps I was, to my dishonour.

My home now – though home is too rich and precise a word – rather, the place where I have lived these sixty years or more is Scotland, cold and rocky. As far from the roots of my youth as I could get back then. I could have run to Muscovy or the Maghreb, but life among the Rus or the Moslem would have killed me, I thought. Too brutal and foreign. The Britons are as savage as I can bear, and I felt comfortable with their language, so close to my native German. The Rus speak the language of the forest and steppe, and the Arab of the desert. English and German are sister tongues of the fields and woods and small towns of Europe. We share blood going back to the time before history and civilisation.

What my dear, dead parents must think in Heaven, looking down and seeing their only son in Scotland, I pity to think. My mother would laugh, and turn to my father saying I had proved him wrong, for the old fool always swore when I was a boy that I was tied to my mother's apron and would never venture into the world. Though he loved me by his side as well. He taught me maps when I was a little boy, in the back room of his printing shop, and I remember him showing me Britain and Ireland on the page. He smelt of ink and the sweet vinegar of new paper, and told me the islands looked like a long-legged witch cradling a baby bear. I now sit in the brim of the witch's hat – in Glasgow, where I write, in my rooms in the Auld Pedagogy – for so the Scots, rough and quaint in the same instant, call their academy; a fine institution, though the teaching body has little grasp of modern disciplines such as state governance and political philosophy. In law, languages, mathematics, rhetoric and history, the university excels, and as such I was well suited to the staff – though mathematics is not my strength.

My old quarters have been pensioned to me. Now almost eighty, I teach rarely, if ever. My world has closed in – at most, these days, I will walk the few hundred yards from the head of the town and Rattan Row where my rooms are, to the old Dominican Hall at Blackfriars on the High Street to hear a lecture if a celebrated professor has come to visit. But that does not happen more than once a month. This town is a long way for anyone to come who is not looking to be left in peace and isolation. The rest of the time I keep to my rooms, and I have grown bored – and boredom is the sire of wickedness, and the child of ignorance. I have read all the books I will ever need to read and mastered every discipline that interests me. My body is too old for women and sport and drinking. If I stop, I will die. And so, to save me from dying I choose to write – but the only story I have to write is made from the fabric of my life, for I am not a man of fantasy or imagination. This life of mine, though, it is a patchwork coat – most of the material is dull and brown check, made of sturdy English wool, but of no interest to the eye. One patch though, over my heart, stands out. It is woven with silks of the best reds and golds and indigos, patterned and stitched by Persian craftswomen with hands as deft and precise as moving stars. That patch tells the story of my time with the lawyer Paulus Melchior in Bideburg and the trial of Peter Stumpf, as a werewolf – of which I will here bear honourable and true testimony.

I was a boy of sixteen when Paulus took me to Bideburg. I had been his apprentice four years and was excelling. Paulus had known my aunt – my mother's sister – when he was a boy and she was a girl. My aunt had died in Munster along with Paulus' family – but not side by side. Their losses came in the last days of the city rebels when killings happened on every corner. She died in the market square, and Paulus lost his family on the steps of his own father's printing shop. It was not for old family friendships or shared trade, though, that Paulus plucked me up and sent me to his college, as he did with many other boys – just as he secured many girls from poorer backgrounds with jobs, or even marriage, at court, if he could arrange it. He took me on as I was clever – and knew it – and he could see I was not meant for whatever drudgery of work my class and family had set aside as my fate. In those days, the poor moved more quickly to wealth and status, by dint of a brain and personality, than they do today. By the time my teaching days wore out, I had not seen a boy from a poor home come to my college for twenty years or more – prevented by money and snobbery. And so, society degenerates – because it must uplift and raise others to rise itself. But I am too old to fix that.

I do not hold with the fabulae of astrology – that dates fix fortune and character – but Paulus was sown into my own fate by whatever moves in the universe under the name of Destiny. I know that this moving force is not God, or a god – but a mechanical part of the existence of infinity. The proof that life harnessed me to Paulus lies in numbers, not superstition. I am not sure what these numbers mean, but there is an answer in them somewhere just as there is an answer to everything in the known and unknown world through the use of numbers. I may be no mathematician, no Pythagoras for sure, but I can read, and Augustine of Hippo said it well when he had it that numbers are the universal language which the deity uses to confirm truth to humans. As such, take this as evidence: my mother and father were married on June 24, 1535 – the numbers six, twenty-four, fifteen and thirty-five if the date is rendered in numerology terms. They were wed on the very day that Munster fell – though my parents were a week's walk away from the murder, living in a little village called Kirchborn near the Rhine, quiet on their wedding day as Munster thundered to the ground in fire and ruin. On the day that Munster fell, Paulus walked out through the city gates onto a field of blood and into a new life. He was raised up by others on a whim too – as he did for me – noticed for his brain, and given an education and a chance to be refashioned. And numbers play their part here too: he was twelve, just as I was twelve when he chose me for college. Twelve years to the day, after Munster fell, I was born on June 24, 1547. The date June 24 repeats and repeats. If the numbers for June 24 are broken down numerologically they become six, two and four – add these together and you have the number twelve, once again. A magical number, itself, it is said – think of the tribes of Israel and the disciples, the months of the year, the constellations; to the Hebrews who forged the supernatural study of numbers twelve represents perfection, government, heavenly order. A web of figures, therefore, seems to lie over my life linked to Paulus, yet it is too dark and heavy a veil to see past it, to establish its significance – beyond the fact that it must point to significance. On the numbers go: it was April 26 – four, two, six, an inversion of the numerological casting of June 24, as six, two, four – when Paulus took me under his charge.

The numbers do not hold for Bideburg, though, and I take significance from that also. I came to Bideburg aged sixteen. We rode into the town on July 8, 1563 to undertake the trial of Peter Stumpf. No mixing and adding of these numbers bears any pattern in the rest of my life. Seven, eight, one, five, fifteen, six, three, sixty-three – they say nothing to me. From that, I read, that my time in Bideburg was a time of corruption and distortion – a time that did not accord with the patterns set for me by my destiny, or the mechanics of the universe – that my time in Bideburg tried to assault the rhythms and repetitions of my life and ruin me, but it failed, because the numbers returned, as did I.

Many months after Bideburg – the numbers and the date are back again: six, two and four; on June 24 the next year, I had made it to London in England and kept my life. A year later to the day, I was in Scotland. I have come to dread the date June 24, though, for now that I am as old a man as there is to be found in Glasgow – certainly in the university – I believe that the date of my death will be June 24, though as to the year I hope never to have foreknowledge of such a fact. One more facet of the numbers fills my heart with fear as well, however; if I calculate that first key date – June 24 1535, the fall of Munster and the day my parents wed – and add it up in numerological terms as six, twenty-four, fifteen and thirty-five, then I reach the number eighty. That will be my age next birthday.

My story is not of numerology, though, nor of my flight from Bideburg, nor of Munster, though Munster changed the world; nor is my story of Paulus, though Paulus changed my life. My story is of Peter Stumpf, the werewolf of Bideburg – who, if you are as old as me, you may remember from pamphlets published in the last years of the decade of the 1560s. One, from a French printer's in Paris, even mentions me in passing. Titled 'The Full Account of the German Werewolf, Peter Stumpf, and the Massacre at Bideburg', it says on page twenty-eight that 'among the company of the lawyer and magistrate, Paulus Melchior, the chief delegate of the Prince-Bishop, there were some others, including a Sergeant-at-Arms Luther Karfreitag, church delegate Father Carolus Fromme, his subordinate and seminarian Aesop Jodel, and a student and notary-secretary to Paulus Melchior, Willie Lessinger'. That German student, Willie Lessinger, who only exists in that one pamphlet, on that one page, in that one sentence, has never been joined in the minds of any other living soul with the Dutch teacher in Glasgow, William Loos, who sits here, writing his poor life onto paper to pass away the time before death.

I am the only soul on Earth who knows the true story of the werewolf Stumpf, and so here I have put together a narrative of the events in Bideburg, from the scenes I saw with my own eyes, the facts as gathered by my master Paulus, the time I spent among the people of that town, most specially Greet – a young woman who rides with me in my heart every day, on every journey I take – and Divara, the daughter of the werewolf, and her mother who was married to the wolf. Lastly, the little girl Rosa – a lost moth in the night. This is a story filled with many men, but I give the story to the women and girls in it. They did better, as you shall see. Men clatter and make noise, but when women sing – though they seldom get the chance – the sound rings loud and pure. Most of all, though, my knowledge of this history comes from the words I spoke with Stumpf himself, for I became not his keeper or his friend, but his watcher during the days before the trial and grew to know the werewolf, or whatever manner of creature it was that sat within its double-bound cage before me, and talked.

Chapter One

The history begins of the lawyer Paulus, who oversaw the trial of the werewolf, Peter Stumpf, which resulted in the massacre at the town of Bideburg.

I had heard of the werewolf of Bideburg long before we set off for the town. Everyone had – a squadron of guards had been sent to Bideburg seven years prior to catch and kill the creature, they spent two weeks in the town but found nothing.

The wolf hunted in the forests and mountains all around Bideburg – many folk had gone missing, and some twelve or so had been found dead, torn to shreds and eaten on the heathland, it was said. I had met no-one though who knew of the town first-hand, having been there – it was presumed a quiet little hamlet, terrorised by this creature that stole its children and ate people by moonlight, for that is the habit of werewolves, according to the stories. People do not know of werewolves in this country I live in now – they have shape-shifting creatures, for sure, such as women who turn from fish into female, but nothing like the werewolf, which is a man under curse of the Devil and wolf's blood to run by night and kill and eat the flesh of human beings. Some say there are special means to kill these creatures – silver in a blade or bullet – certain magic which can protect you from them, but those are children's tales. We had consulted texts, law and doctrine before we left for Bideburg – seeking fact not superstition – and so far as I knew when I rode off with Paulus there was only one way to kill a werewolf, and that was the way you would kill a man or a bull or a horse or a leopard: the right shot to the right place – the heart or head – the right stab wound, or fire or drowning, strangulation, decapitation. All these would kill a werewolf as they would any other creature, for a werewolf is living; but it is not as easy to kill a werewolf as it is a man or a leopard, or bull or horse, as a werewolf has the body and strength and power and ferocity of a wolf, with the cunning and brains of a man. The Devil's combination.

All we knew, when we left for the town, was that the wolf had been caught and had turned back into a man – so the message said, which came from Bideburg calling on the attention of the court and law. The tales of werewolves have it that man or woman cursed with wolf blood – or child, for that matter, for that can happen too, according to the stories – only change after dark, though some say only by the moon as well.

When Paulus got his letter of order and told me I was to accompany him to set up a people's court for the trial of the wolf in Bideburg, he said that such creatures did not exist – that we were going to try a man.

I asked him, 'Sir, how can you know that?'

'Because such creatures do not exist,' he said.

'We do not know of everything that exists,' I said.

'If werewolves existed, Willie, I would have seen one by now.'

'You have not seen England, sir, and it exists.' I was allowed to be forward and some would even say rude, but Paulus encouraged it, and would rip on me hard if I grovelled or played the servant too much.

'I have seen England,' he said. 'I was there for a month. Try a better example.'

I reddened up a little. For every act in life that I had not experienced, Paulus had done it twice over. I had no way of ever beating him in any discussion we had – it was a process of yielding, with as little shame as possible, though he did not want to hurt in the process, and so it was like your father teaching you to wrestle when you are a boy and pinning you down without breaking your neck.

'You have not seen…' and I paused, thinking of a way to trip him up and throw him. 'You have not seen – my best friend Dolphie, from back home.'

'No, but he exists.'

'But you haven't seen him, so how do you know?'

'Because you have told me of him and you are a reliable witness – and it is credible that you have a friend called Dolphie – though he sounds quite dull.'

'He is not dull. And I might be lying.'

'If you are lying then he doesn't exist.'

'Aha,' I said, and I growled it all low at him.

'Aha, nothing, Willie. You have lost, you dog – do I have to send you back to logic class?'

'But,' I said.

'One last go.'

'You haven't seen God – he exists.' Trap sprung, I thought – I had held this back as my last weapon.

'Have you seen God?' he asked.

'No.'

'Thank you then, Willie. I think our little dialogue has come to its natural conclusion.'

'Sir, I can not think you are saying what I think you are saying.' And I shook my head at him, mock scolding.

'What kind of garbled grammar is that, Willie. You can think what you like – I am not here to tell you what to think. You are here to follow me around and do what I say and learn what you like or do not like.'

He sat at his desk and made me a list of chores – what supplies were needed, books required, where to send them once they were packed for collection when we left. The university was a hubbub outside, and he raised his voice to be heard. It was too hot and the air too thick to shut the window. He told me to roster the rest of the party – there were other scholars to accompany us, a priest and his boy – and the small squad of guards assigned. I had to compile an itinerary, check lists, ensure warrants and passes. Lastly, he wrote a list of instruments needed from the city jail – of torture and execution. Paulus said we would need a separate wagon to carry these, and weapons and ammunition. We needed six pack mules, as well as our own horses, to take the supplies up through the mountains, once the wagon and carts could go no further. If we used dray horses alone from the start of the journey they would die going up through the mountains, Paulus told me.

The university grew even rowdier as night came on – some players were in town – and Paulus told me to hurry as he did not want me to miss the performances. I was still trying to calculate the wine needed for the party.

He had been drinking while he gave me my instructions and was a little happy, though not drunk. The quadrangle below the window of his apartment began to fill up with students as the actors set up stage.

Paulus looked out of the window. 'I would have loved to have been an actor,' he said.

I asked him how he came to be him – though not in such a blunt way, rather I asked him, why he had not become an actor and run away when he was young. He started, then, to tell me about his life as a child in Munster during the rebellion and the days of Jan van Leyden and Knipperdolling, and the holy poor and the community of all goods among the people as one – life everlasting on Earth as a soldier of the risen Christ.

He told me his story, though, in fits and starts, a little bit that night, some more the next as we rode over the plain outside the city – more of the story when we camped in the mountains and still more during our days in Bideburg, and our last night, with our little group.

His story should have scared me. On first listen, it was the story of a heretic who lied and pretended to embrace Christ but remained a heretic in his heart. But it was not the story of a heretic. It was the story of a man who embraced nothing. Not that he was empty, but he could not hold to the truth of others or believe in what they believe because of the shape Munster had imprinted on the soft part of his heart, or his soul, and I know and now affirm that my friend Paulus had a soul, and it flourishes as I write.

★ ★ ★

I will tell you something now, though, before we go further, before Bideburg comes: Stumpf claimed he was no werewolf. Stumpf told me square that werewolves kill by moonlight, and he never killed by moonlight. A man could be seen killing by moonlight. Instead, by moonlight, Stumpf said in his sing-song country-soft voice, 'I race through the forest alone – in the deepest runs of my timberwoods and hills.'

He would strip, he said, at the great rock by the river in his forest, leave his warm workday clothes and put on a patchwork girdle of skin and hair – then he'd run barefoot till his legs grew heavy, and that took a long time of pounding blind strides in the night.

At his tree – the giant oak that lolled over the centre of his woodland – he would climb to the top, and there, tucked into the highest boughs, he would hunker before the moon. On the tree, the wind rocking the leaves, he prayed to the great moon, with its god-face grey, ancient and granite. He would not tell me the secret words of his prayer, and I was not the kind of boy to have him tortured to reveal them, though he did say he asked for endurance – and I considered this an honest enough offering of the truth. He said he felt the moon talking in his heart. Stumpf told me that he asked for endurance so he could live on this world below the moon. To suffer life among people. To accept never walking on its silver surface and being with it, alone. I asked him if this was his way of saying that as a sinner he would forever be turned away from the face of God and never allowed the Lord's love. He said, 'No, Willie. I have not spoken of God. I have spoken of the moon.'

Stumpf said that when he prayed, he would look out over the shaking stalk tops of his forest, to Bideburg below in the shadow of the Steipplinger mountains. He would stand and clutch the trunk with one arm for balance, and then he would shoot shards of his own warm water, long and hard, and deep from within, towards the town, silvering the night air, wet drops on the leaves and the tree tops beneath.

He would climb down, and return slow to the great rock by the river where his clothes lay – stroking the soft hair of his girdle as he walked. He dressed as the moon set and the sky pinked up and purpled, and then he would walk home to his bed, and his wife and family, and work and life in the morning, tomorrow – his girdle tucked safe inside his shirt, and patted for good luck. If I think on it, I have come to reckon that the werewolf believed in one thing only which he could not see with his eyes: luck.

Chapter Two

A comedy and a tragedy are performed by visiting players in the courtyard of the university before the party leaves for Bideburg.

A story such as the one I am now about to tell should open on a snowy scene, to match its mood, but mine does not, for it begins in high summer, in the month of July – and the weather was hot.

A troupe of actors had spent the end of term at the university, and the night before we left the city for Bideburg, they gave their last performance. The quadrangle filled up with students, standing and shuffling around, waiting. I watched them from the window of Paulus' office as I readied all we needed for the journey – packing up books, and money, paper, ink, weapons, clothing, food and drink – and then left our supplies at the city's south gate with one of our guards, so we could collect it all in the morning on the way to Bideburg, with the rest of the men. I walked back to the university, to the square courtyard, cramped now, as a hundred or more students had come to watch the actors perform. Their stage – two high heavy carts locked together – sat where it had for the last two weeks, throughout the death of the term: at the centre of the quadrangle, so spectators could see the performances from all sides.

Nearly all the crowd stood to watch, though the professors and administrators had seats, placed high on a platform against the quadrangle's far back wall – so they could see over the heads of the students to the stage. I walked to the platform – it had been constructed the day the actors arrived in town – and up the steps to the benches and seats that were laid out upon it. There were three rows of seats and Paulus sat at the front, just off from the middle. He was leaning forward and talking to one of the students on the ground below, laughing and joking with the boy. He held no more than two classes a term but still had a coterie of boys who flocked to him for their betterment. I made my way to him, and waited until I caught his eye

– it did not take long, a moment maybe – and I told Paulus everything was arranged. We only had to rise at dawn and meet the rest of our party at the south gate. He slapped me on the back, and said 'good lad', and then asked the professor beside him – a gentleman who taught mathematics and logic called Kluge, if I remember rightly, it is that long ago – to shift up a fraction so I could sit beside him. Kluge looked disgusted at having to move for an inky little student like me – especially one known to have to work as a skivvy for Paulus while he studied – but it was Paulus asking, so Kluge hoisted his backside along the bench, and I sat down between them.

Paulus patted me on the leg and said again, 'Good lad, good lad. Now let us watch the play.' He lifted a little flask of wine from the floor between his feet and offered me a sip. 'And enjoy yourself.'

The light had faded, and it was night, lit by torches and candles, when the opening actor jumped onto the stage – and he did jump, right from the floor of the quadrangle onto the boards above, the height of a man. The crowd was cheering already as he rolled, stood, and took his introductory bow. He was dressed like a Fool, in multicoloured patch-worked clothes, torn at the elbow and knees, but with an expensive and elaborately decorated hat, full of feathers and flowers, like something an old Landesknecht veteran from the Peasant Wars would wear on his head. His boots rode up to the thigh, and looked as if they would have cost most men a year in earnings.

He spoke a monologue which moved from thanking the city for hosting his troupe, to jokes at the city's expenses – which everyone took in good stead, for who hasn't heard one thousand times over that men here would mate with anything that moves, and all the women are drunks. Paulus had stood sponsor to the actors – both into the city, and to the university – so as their friend it was time for them to take some liberties with him, which he expected and was excited about, and so had taken his seat at the front of the platform the better to take part in the entertainment. He nudged me, and laughed like a child of ten.

The Fool spoke to the audience, 'And we must thank our patron, Paulus Melchior. We know that though a holy man, he is still a scholar, and as such has little time for relics. However, I have learned that he does have two holy relics which he keeps in a pouch between his legs. All his students beg to kiss these holy stones – for that is what they are, the stones David used in his sling to kill Goliath – but none have yet to lay their lips upon them. Paulus, as we have all come to know, worries more about the education of womenfolk, he is so modern, and so has only offered his stones to the lips of the young ladies of the city, and their mothers, in the hope that the blessed relics will uplift them – and him.'

And the fool capered about the stage with one arm crooked over the other like a randy Priapus. Paulus laughed and clapped, and called back, 'Sir, you are lucky you do not possess the stones that I possess – for in a company of men such as yourselves, brothers of the stage, your stones would have been in other mens' hands long before now. Though such liberties, I fear, you would enjoy.'

And so it went on for a while, with well-known professors and staff and students trading wits with the actor on stage – who more than held his own, and reduced most to red-faced beaming mutes. As this backwards-and-forwards continued, the crowd laughed and roared harder, even though the jokes got no better nor more clever. It was the fun of participation with the actor which moved the crowd to mirth so much – they loved the Fool, he could have said anything: that all their mothers were whores or their fathers were sons of Sodom, and this would have only made them laugh the more.

At last, the Fool called the crowd to order, thanked them again, and introduced the first play – there were two to be performed – a comedy full of pranks and slaps and people falling over called *Theseus in the Maze*. The play began just as Theseus had cut the head from the Minotaur. Theseus slips in dripped blood before he leaves the maze and falls – and his head ends up inside the Minotaur's head – for it is that kind of stupid but amusing play – and Theseus, thus, is trapped within, appearing to all the world like the bull and the monster who everyone fears and hates. He makes his way out of the maze. Ariadne is horrified when she learns what creature it is – the Minotaur – that she has helped escape the labyrinth, and falls screaming off the stage to wails of laughter from the crowd. Freed, the Theseus-Minotaur terrorises the palace, though, of course, he does not want to do so. What made the crowd laugh the most was bull-headed Theseus being chased by palace guards – unable to see properly and so not fit to fight them off – running from them and declaiming like a Prince to his pursuers, 'My good sirs! I bid you understand that I am Theseus, son of Aegeus, who came to free you from the Cretan bull. I am no monster!'

The palace guards, though, could not understand his aristocratic Athenian accent – which was rendered in a moneyed High German –

through the head of the Minotaur and so thought he spoke the language of the bulls and was shouting at them the words, 'I am a monster!'

It ended rather weakly with Ariadne miraculously unravelling what had happened, and freeing Theseus from the bull's head – while the prisoners from the labyrinth distracted the guards – the princess then sailing off with Theseus, back to Athens, and their planned-for marriage.

Between plays Paulus said to me, 'I wonder what the next diversion will be? Usually something more serious.'

'Perhaps they will attempt the tragedy of Theseus,' I said.

Paulus cast me a worn glance, and said, 'That might be interesting, I suppose.'

'Yes, sir,' I said, as breezy and prompt as I could, 'it would be interesting to see how the troupe would reverse the mood of the audience and tell of Ariadne's abandonment and Aegeus' death.'

'I know the story, Willie,' he slurred a little with drink – though still not drunk.

'Catharsis, perhaps. Comedy followed by tragedy on the same theme. That would be quite exciting.'

'I know the theory too, Willie. Wear your learning more lightly,' he said, though he smiled half-mouthed, and I felt a little less foolish and cut as he meant no unkindness – for that was just his way of showing me I was a clumsy coltish dolt. He offered me another drink of wine and I took it, and drank as well.

Two of Paulus' younger students came to the foot of the platform where we sat and asked him how he was and if he enjoyed the play.

'The end was too Apollonian, I like the Dionysian,' he said. 'Isn't that right, Willie?'

I nodded. I would not deign to speak if I was being mocked.

The taller one – I think his name was Grabel – said, 'But is it art, sir?'

'It's entertainment, stupid boy,' Paulus said, and he turned to the Dean of Faculty beside him – to his left, I sat on his right, I recall – and said, 'Isn't that correct, your grace?'

The Dean, who was a bishop, smiled like he'd drunk vinegar, for he'd refused the actors' request to perform on university grounds until Paulus had his friends at court instruct him otherwise. I can not remember the Dean's name – though he was not a man of much charisma so it is little wonder all these years later.

The two students waited – meek and ambitious boys.

'And what do you think?' Paulus asked the other student – smaller, fatter, but more pleasant in his manner.

'Entertainment can be art? Sir?'

'Of course,' said Paulus. 'You can learn something of the world at a bear fight.'

Paulus offered his flask to the students.

'Good life to you, boys,' he said, and tipped his hand to his mouth, giving them permission to drink. They drank and handed back the flask. Paulus took a swallow and handed the flask to me. I wiped the lip, drank, and he took it back, offered it to the Dean and said, 'Sir?'

The Dean cast a vinegar smile again and turned his head to the stage.

'Goodbye, lads,' said Paulus. They walked away, chattering to each other, like girls in love with the local young lord who had just given them a posy of picked flowers. I grimaced.

The next play was *Abraham and Isaac on the Mountain*. It had such great power – I had never seen a play like this before: just two actors on stage, and the voice of God, coming from offstage, but only heard by Abraham, not his poor son. The spareness of the cast made the horror of the words more crisp and all the more affecting to me – and I could see that sitting beside me Paulus was moved too.

'This is very new and fresh,' he said to me, as the play began.

What baby does not know the story of the prophet Abraham and his covenant with God? But the play began at an interesting place. It did not begin with Abraham and the riches that God gave him, or Sarah being blessed by the three Angels of God with her only child Isaac – it began at the foot of the mountain, where God has told Abraham to lead his son Isaac, his only true heir, and sacrifice him on the summit. The pair have just bid their servants goodbye, and Isaac totes the wood for his father to the pyre they will build to sacrifice to God at the top of the mountain. Isaac is asking his father, who holds the knife, what they will offer to God as they have no goat with them. Abraham tells Isaac that God will provide a lamb for a burnt offering, and he sends his son off to search for a kid goat. The stage is silent and still. Then God speaks to Abraham, booming, while Isaac looks for a lamb on the slopes of the mountain, clicking and sucking his teeth, and clapping his hands, like a baby calls a pup – and deaf to the voice of God which only his father can hear.

The voice of God seemed to roar from below the stage, I thought. 'I have promised you descendants as numerous as the stars, Abraham. I have promised your children the land of Kenites, Kenizzites, Kadmonites, Hittites, Perizzites, Rephaims, Amorites, Canaanites, Girgashites, and Jebusites. I gave your wife Sarah a child when she was barren and beyond the age of bearing children. Now give me your son, Isaac – your only heir.'

The actor playing Abraham grovelled on the stage like a dog before its master and wept. 'Oh, Lord,' he called out, 'I love you Lord, but if I give you my son I will have no descendants and so there will be no line of mine to inherit the world.'

'You will have descendants,' the voice of God called out. 'Give me the life of Isaac.'

Paulus nudged me and leant to my ear, whispering, 'It is like the Devil – in the terror plays.'

Abraham begged God to spare his son, but God said, 'Think Abraham, and make your choice.'

Abraham was silent on the stage, kneeling. I could see in his face and eyes that he saw the world opening up to his descendants, like a river of slaves before a pharaoh, that he would be the king of a line which lasted until the end of time – that the life of one of these descendants, even though it was his one true son, was worth the founding of an empire that would never die.

Abraham called out to God that he would do it, and then God spoke the very words I had thought, 'You will give up your one true son's life for the glory of being the father of nations?' – for the quote from the Bible in German was exact, and it chilled me. Paulus gripped his knees.

Abraham looked so shamed he could die, but he nodded and picked up his knife and found his son, peeking over the far edge of the stage calling for lambs to come to him.

Abraham then walked with his son to the last slope of the mountain – the actors bent over and scrambled across the stage as if they might slip and fall to their deaths, lying flat now on the stage, and helping and pulling one another up steep gullies and sharp ridges. Abraham did not speak to Isaac who still kept asking where they might find a lamb this high up, and often said how he loved his father, and was proud to make this sacrifice with him, his first sacrifice as a boy.

They reached the summit, and Abraham who had still not spoken, grabbed his son and bound him feet and hand while the boy cried out,

'Father are you mad? It is I, Isaac, your one true heir. I am not a lamb.'

Abraham wept and shred his clothes and I was sure he would die of grief on the stage. The actors did not speak now, but screamed – on and on, and the audience was horrified but could not leave, or look away. Isaac screamed as he was lain on the ground, and Abraham screamed and struggled with himself, like he fought against his own body – he raised the knife above his boy – then, just as he brought the dagger down, God called out. 'Hold your hand, Abraham. You have shown that you fear the Lord your God, unbind your son.'

Isaac lay screaming on the stage and his cries rang out loud and long – for he could not hear God, he saw only his father above with a knife in the air, listening to the wind and nodding. Abraham moved to cut Isaac's bonds and the boy wept, 'I love you Father, do not kill me. I am not a lamb.'

Abraham was weeping too. He freed his son and embraced him and they wept together. The boy cried out, 'Why Father, why?' And Abraham said nothing for a long time. There came the sound of a goat bleating – some stage effect with a whistle, I imagine, from beneath the stage – and Abraham raised his head from his son's shoulder.

He said, 'A ram, my son, there – with its horns stuck in the thicket.'

Isaac turned to look and said, 'Where Father?'

Abraham rose and took his son by the hand.

'Where Father?' asked Isaac one more time.

They came to the foot of the stage and Abraham pointed out to the audience – to me, I felt – and said, 'There, my son.'

And Isaac said, 'I see, Father, now I see.'

It was a sensation of the stage. It had lasted no more than an hour – but the audience roared with love and approval – some were embracing, in relief that it was over and joy that they had lived through the experience. The two actors took their bow and the man who had been playing the voice of God appeared to take his bow too. I was crying myself now when God walked on – though I often cry at songs and plays and stories, especially poems – but so was Paulus, and most of the audience, standing in front of our platform, as was the Dean, though he shooed the tears away from his eyes and coughed very manly to gather himself together quite quickly.

The actors left the stage to cheers and waves.

'Art, my friend,' Paulus said to me, and pointed at the stage. The crowd was moving around now, some leaving, some staying to talk and drink.

'I don't know what to think of it as yet, sir,' I said. 'Part of me is horrified and part ecstatic.'

'Indeed,' said Paulus. 'Very Dionysian.'

This annoyed me – for he was being too clever and mocking again, when he should still have been full of feeling after the play as I was – so I said, with a little snap in my voice, 'Sir, what does that mean after a play such as this?'

'It is not a play in which order is restored – it a play that is trying to destroy the natural order.'

'How, sir?' I asked. I had simply been moved by the struggle and madness and then relieved at the end when no blood was shed. I could not see how order had not been restored, and family preserved, and history allowed to take its march through Abraham and Isaac to us sitting there that day watching a play in the university square.

Paulus leant towards me and said quietly, so no-one around could hear, 'God was the nemesis, the antagonist.'

'I do not understand,' I said. 'I felt relieved at the end.'

'Because God was a torturer, and he stopped.'

I looked around me, ghosted by the idea that someone might hear.

'God was bad,' Paulus said, and he was perhaps getting a little drunk, 'goodness lost. Evil won. Good was broken. What is that if not the destruction of order in one short little play built on old Aristotle's unities – which frankly I find overrated and over-admired. God was the evil one.'

'Be quiet, sir,' I said, patting down the air with my hands to hush him. I would not want to see Paulus put on trial even if I was bribed with love, family or gold – he could be overly cocksure when he felt his intellect was riding high behind him.

'I didn't write the play,' he said. 'I'm giving my critique. It is not my fault if the writer and the actors are heretics.'

'Sir, do not say that either, someone might hear and do them harm.'

'No-one will do them harm,' he said. 'I am taking these fine actors to my rooms for as much wine as they can drink, and you are coming with me, as I will need you to get me up in the morning at five so we can be on our way, and I will feel ill in the morning after drinking with actors all night.'

He got to his feet, and walked off the platform, heading to the little tents the actors had rigged up behind their stage. I followed him.

'Sir,' I said. 'I really think we'd better not.'

'Be quiet, you silly little mouse,' he said. 'We'll get up at five. I am having a night of entertainment before I leave for the backwoods of nowhere with a clan of narrow-minded priests and thick soldiers and you, you little mouse,' and he pushed me.

'Sir,' I said, put out by his roughness, for he was only cod-rough when he was drinking.

'What?' he said. 'I am playing. Come on, mouse.'

And he pushed me again. I tagged along behind. Up in his rooms, the actors and the writers drank and sang and talked, and Paulus held the floor in front of all these braggarts and show-offs as if he was their better. I think back and I had never been happier or more safe in myself and my future than that night. The evening swirled with voices and debate and more song and pieces performed for the room from plays new and plays that all of us could quote from start to finish. I drank and time became misty and when I woke on the floor, beside some actor with a beard like Satan's, Paulus was kicking me softly in the backside with the toe of his boot, saying, 'Get up, you drunken little devil – time to go to the back of beyond.'

Chapter Three

The party stops at the inn at Reissen, and the strangeness of first love is examined.

We rode from dawn. I kept Paulus company most of the first day, and he talked some about his life. That night we camped by a stream near woods, and Paulus got everyone drunk with the soldiers. In the morning, after the sight of the soldiers dropping their drawers, and shitting by the bank of a stream then washing their arses in the water – while I tried to cook breakfast with the priest's boy for everyone – we eventually saddled up again. Paulus had latched onto Karfreitag, the sergeant of the guard, and the pair of them rode ahead, laughing and shouting. Karfreitag was an old Landesknecht and wore his coloured sash from shoulder to hip like a swagger. I held back and rode with Fromme, our priest who was along with us – he was also a professor at the university with Paulus, and like him shared official duties for the state and court. I'd thought he would be a dull man. He had taught me a few theology classes, and his lecturers were uninspiring, but out on the road, he was a fellow of the world, and had plenty of stories about the parishes he had served in, and the scandals he'd had to deal with, as a confessor and guide. He brought religion into the conversation only a little – and I found him modern and likeable – but when he did speak of faith and his love of God he spoke with an iron tongue. Unlike Paulus and myself – in fact unlike all the rest of us on the road together – he was not of common stock. None of the rest of us, not even Fromme's clerk, who brought up the rear a forlorn young specimen missing his mother, none of us were born that far from the other's station. We'd all started from much the same place. It was only brains that separated us, and a little luck. Which was good. But Fromme did not behave as if he had been born high, or think himself greater or less than the rest of the party, or judge on status or manners. There were no airs and graces, among any of us – and though the soldiers could be passing common, still they made us laugh.

By late afternoon that second day, we came to the little village of Reissen, at the foot of the Steipplinger mountains, where we were to leave the carts and wagon, and load up our gear onto the pack team. I'd sent a rider ahead, who'd readied a place for us at the village inn and was under orders to look after the wagon and carts until our return.

I'd enjoyed the wine the night before when we camped by the woods, so when Paulus said we could all take one drink before unpacking and reloading for the next day, I walked into the inn before the rest of the party and ordered a beer. Now, the beer here, in this inn in Reissen, was something to be appreciated. The owner kept his beer bottled and hung in weaved baskets in a cold well at the rear of the inn. It was like drinking iced spring water – it sang in the mouth, and was light on the belly but took to your brain like a wick to wax. The rest of our party were in the inn now, and followed my lead when I told them about the icy beer. We all had two, and then Paulus called a halt, saying, 'Boys, two is good, three gets you so you want to get drunk. Let's get our work done and I will see you back here for our third and fourth and fifth in one hour – if you are fast. Be late and miss your next drink. Which I am paying for.'

We snapped to it like a well-trained platoon. I went to oversee the changeover of equipment from the carts and wagon so all would be ready for the pack team in the morning, and Karfreitag rostered his men to set up tents in the inn courtyard – the soldiers would be sleeping outside, there was only room in the inn for Paulus, Fromme, Fromme's boy – I was unable to remember his name, he was so quiet – and myself. The soldiers did not mind – this was a carnival for them compared to other duties. Fromme's boy prepared the rooms, and Paulus paid the innkeeper in advance and talked to him about Bideburg and what he knew of the events there – the man provided little. Fromme said he would help the innkeeper's son feed and water the horses – which he was well appreciated for, as a churchman could be expected to sit on his arse and do nothing, yet he put himself forward to a bit of hard work. Each of us did our job, and did it quick and well, and by dusk we were back in the inn, having that third drink, and deciding to get drunk as friends together. I sat by the bar and thought I too would try my hand at getting some information from the innkeeper, so I talked to him about Bideburg.

Folk from the village began to arrive in the inn now – a few more than usual said the owner. 'They are probably interested in seeing what the

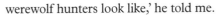

werewolf hunters look like,' he told me.

'Who is Stumpf anyway,' I asked. 'What do you know of him?'

'Stumpf? Nothing. I hear he is the werewolf.'

'So we have heard. Have you met him?'

'No,' he said. 'They are on the other side of the mountain – way off in the forest. All I know is – he owns land.'

I walked between the tables to Paulus, who sat by the fire with Fromme. A group of men from the village had made a circle and were tuning up their drum and whistle and fiddle. Fromme's boy was sitting in a far corner by himself. I opened my mouth to call him over, but as I did not know his name, I walked to him and said, 'Come and join us.' He came back to the little circle of players with me, and stood, awkward, by my side, as the men started up their music.

The drummer called out, 'This song is for you fine men.'

And they played a tune they called *The Werewolf Ballad*. I can not remember it all but it had this as a chorus, which stuck in my head for days:

The wolf he ran by moonlight
and he ate the virgins fair
he slipped them in his belly
and he licked their bottoms bare.

It was a ridiculous song, terribly composed, and sung and played woefully, still it had the room weeping tears of laughter. The singing went on and I drank some more, but the room became so hot I needed to go outside. Fromme's boy was as dull as a ditch. On the step, in the night air, I took a long breath, and walked to the inn gate, looking up and down the one short street of Reissen.

Two young girls, of around my age, were standing outside the gate, talking and laughing. They looked up as I checked their village from left to right.

'Hello,' I said, a little forward, as I was drunk and they were both very pretty.

They said hello back, and I asked if they were coming inside.

'We are having a party,' I said. 'It's a lot of fun.'

The darkest one said, 'Well, we have no-one to accompany us, and two young girls can not go into an inn all on their own.'

'Then I will accompany you,' I said, and I opened the gate for them and walked them inside.

One of the players – the fiddler, I recall – looked up and cast narrow eyes on the dark girl. I took him for her father straight away.

'Frey,' he shouted over the din, 'behave or go home.'

She smiled at her father and blew him a kiss. I chose to bow to him, by way of trying to show I was a gentleman, and his daughter laughed and pushed me. The fiddler smiled too and went back to his playing. The song was something about a stonemason's pillar and two pebbles, and what all he could do with them – put a crack in a wall, and such like, if memory serves me right – and the inn was roaring with laughter again.

I talked to the dark-haired girl, Frey, for the rest of the night. I do not recall what her friend was doing – she may have had to spend the evening with Fromme's boy, whom I still could not remember the name of, for love or faith or money.

Old men tell you all the time about the first girl they fell in love with – and usually it is a passionate wild affair, with thwarted love – her father hated them – or jealousy and rage – she was promised to another – or tragedy – she died. That night, I believe I simply felt a deep attraction to a woman, a girl, for the first time in my life. I hung on everything she said – and she was a country girl, with at best one year of schooling in her head – but she intrigued me, in her difference and strangeness. And she was pretty – or in my head she was pretty. Her face was the face I came to crave in the faces of all the women I have ever wanted or loved. She was the archetype. Dark, pale, flitting and funny, a bow-shaped face, with an exquisite pointed nose – believe me, this is strange to say, but I fall in love with a woman's nose before I fall in love with her, it is the nose which makes me love them – a Frey nose – and if I love the nose then I can love the woman.

And yet, I can not remember her surname. We spent three hours together. Frey told me her second name once, I am sure. When I kissed her goodnight – outside, quickly, in the dark, before her father left to take her home with him – I could not recall her surname – I was scared to ask it again – and yet I went to my bed in love.

The only remnant of our conversation that I remember to this day is her telling me that her father sometimes hit her – I had told her that I loved my parents and missed them – and then Frey spoke of how she wanted to run away sometimes to the city to be free of him. I know I told her that I would come back from Bideburg over the mountain in a few days. She looked at me waiting for me to say something more, but I said nothing, just smiled like a sheepish schoolboy, bashful and scared and stupid, and told her she was lovely.

'You are lovely,' I said. 'I can not wait to see you again.'

'You are lovely too,' she said.

After she left, I stayed up a while longer, but within an hour – it was well into the night – Paulus shooed everyone to bed, raising his voice when some of the soldiers were slow in getting to their feet and leaving when he told them so. The villagers had long since gone, and now it was just our party, drinking, with little talking.

Paulus and I shared a room. I lay in bed in the dark and stared at the ceiling.

'Goodnight, Willie,' said Paulus, from the other side of the room.

'Do you mean goodnight, or did I have a good night?'

Paulus laughed. 'Did you have a good night?'

'Yes, sir,' I said.

'Good,' he said.

'Did you?'

'Yes. It was a pleasant way to waste my life.'

'Good, sir,' I said.

'You know what, Willie?'

'What, sir?'

'If you want to, you should marry that girl. She was very pretty.'

'Sir,' I said, putting on a little indignance as he had embarrassed me. 'Please. That is silly, if you do not mind me saying so.'

'I don't mind,' he said, and I heard him turn over in bed. 'Do what the hell you want, is all I am saying.' He coughed. 'And you are the one being silly. Goodnight.'

'Goodnight, sir,' I said.

'Make sure we are up on time, Saint Valentine.'

I fell asleep telling myself I would dream of the dark girl but my dreams were grey and empty and then it was blue morning time and we were on the road and soon at the foot of the mountain, leading the horses and pack team, by sunup.

Chapter Four

The first part of the history of the priest Carolus Fromme, and his transformation from soldier to loving doctor.

It took all the daylight hours to make it up and over the Steipplinger mountains – and this was high summer so it was late, maybe ten at night, when we came down over the other side and into the foothills above the forest valley where Bideburg hid. I rode with Fromme and his boy Aesop Jodel – I had finally got his name studied in my head – as Paulus was either laughing and joking with Karfreitag about places they had both been to at one time or another, or else instructing him about what his men's duties would be once we reached the village.

Paulus had told me plenty about Fromme before I met him – and I knew much of his stern and heavy reputation already, as did all the young men at the university, whether they took the few classes he taught or not.

Fromme had been a classic dissipate, Paulus had told me before we left for Bideburg – fourth or fifth son of a very minor noble, from east in the Empire somewhere, near Moravia. His mother died when he was young and his father had little time for anyone in the family but his heir, Fromme's eldest brother. So the story has often gone for such men in such positions – as life repeats itself, that is one of the few truths. Fromme had gambled and whored and drank as a young man, and been thrown out of the family home before he reached the age of eighteen. He joined the army and had fought all across the Empire, and in the Italian campaigns and against the Turks. He had risen high and fast in the military and was recognised as a brutally effective commander in the field. The Turks, it is said, put their own dirt on arrow tips, and pike points, on sword blades, and the balls of lead for their guns – the filth poisoning any wound made. Fromme was shot in the hip while leading a scouting party in Dalmatia and evacuated back across the Adriatic to a little monastery town on the north Italian coast, where the monks were paid by the Emperor to care for the wounded soldiers, and bury the dead. It took four days to get him to safety, and by then he was dying of blood poisoning, his wound black and green, infected by Turkish shit.

He lay with death for a month, tended to by these brothers, but did not die. They cut the rotten flesh away, burned the hip to cartilage – bathed him, fed him even when he was unconscious, which must take great care and love and patience – and kept him hovering on the cusp of life. When he was safely free from death – the infection beaten – he lay barely speaking or opening his eyes for weeks on end, as his body healed. The monks spoke to him and read to him from the Bible on his request, and tended to his hip. Two months after arriving at the monastery, he was able to rise from his bed, and walk in the gardens for a few minutes at a time. His limp was slight, and the cure praised as a miracle – though a minor one, for he would always be a little weakened and would never fully recover in his body. Fromme ate his meals at a pine table by the window in his room, looking out at the hills full of thyme and laurel and rosemary, leading down to the sand and bay and sea – across the coast from Dalmatia. Each day one of the brothers would come to sit with him, and read the Bible and talk of God and the church. The brothers paid him special care – he was the highest ranking officer who had been placed in their hospital – and with fighting quiet now over the sea, there were only a few regular soldiers to tend to, and very few dead to bury, so they had time to make him a charge of high importance.

On the ninetieth day of his time in the monastery hospital, he was fit enough to take a circuit of the grounds on his own – the limp not easy to perceive now, unless you looked hard, and saw his leg swing a little at the hip – he was able to dress and wash himself too. He told the brothers in the morning though that he would like to have the evening meal with them in the refectory instead of in his room with whichever monk was scheduled to share his time with him over food.

When he came to the refectory, he listened to the sermon and said the prayers before the meal, and then ate with them, quietly, asking only for the bread or wine to be passed, exchanging the mildest of comments – the broth was just right, the butter so creamy – with the brothers sitting around him at the long wood communal table.

Once the meal was over and before the serving boys had cleared away – and the monks gone off to their evening duties and studies and meditation

– Fromme stood and asked if he might address the members of the order. The father of the monastery said, yes, he may, and Fromme spoke to them 'Brothers,' he said, 'I owe you my life – but I owe you much more as well. I owe you not just my life temporal, but my life spiritual. I have not read the Bible since I was a boy in grammar school. I had forgotten its lessons. You have awakened in me a love of God and his teachings that I do not think I ever knew. You have shown me the true hand of Christ in the way that you cared for me and rose me from the dead. I wonder if God had not intended me – as a sinner and killer – to be hit here in the hip,' and he laid his hand on the still tender wound, 'and brought to you, so you might clean my body and my soul. I am like a child now before you – and I wish to be taken by the hand and led into a new life. Will you please, brothers,' and he walked to the centre of the refectory floor now, amid the tables, and knelt, slowly and stiffly, 'will you please, brothers, accept me as one of your own, take me into your home here, and guide me so that I may become one such as all of you. I ask only to join your order and follow your instructions. If you refuse me, though, I will understand that a man as worldly, and as sinning as I, has no place in the bosom of your love and I will prepare myself to leave within the week, ensuring that all my valuables and money remain with you as payment for your kindness and care.'

All the monks were weeping now. The Father came to join Fromme at the centre of the room, and knelt by him, embracing his shoulders, saying over and over, 'Oh, my son, my son. The ninety-nine may be safe, but the missing one has come unto us.' The monks gathered round, and prayed over Fromme, their voices hoarse and brittle from tears.

He heard some of them say – to him, to their fellow brothers, to the Lord God, as well, maybe – 'we knew this would happen', 'he has come to us', 'a soul saved and dedicated to God'.

The Father raised Fromme up, and the monks took him to the little meditative garden and pool that hid behind the monastery in the woods. There they stripped him, and washed him with the water from the pool, and put on him the robe of a novice. His hair was shorn, and he was read the rules and strictures of the order, that were to command his life from now until the moment of his death and his ascension to Heaven to sit by God. And the commandments were: poverty, cleanliness of mind and body, chastity, obedience, learning, industry, courage and caritas – most of all, charity which is true love of God's divine creation, man and woman.

Fromme sent letters to his officers, with other letters of confirmation from the Father, that his wounds had rendered him incapable of full military service, and he had retired to the monastery to take Holy Orders. There was no complaint from his commanders, he had fought long and hard – at twenty-six, he had more than eight years' service behind him, and he was told that his new life was commendable and that the Emperor thanked him for his duty personally.

His life was one of calm and study and learning for some years – and he had long been made a full brother, and become a much loved member of the monastery household, when the troubles in Dalmatia across the Adriatic rose up again. Injured soldiers started arriving daily now at the monastery and in great numbers – some with wounds so horrific that the monks kept them drugged and without consciousness until they died, and sometimes the drugs speeded up that death, which none thought a wicked thing. The dead were being buried by the dozen each day.

The small town of Devbergrav across the sea had been changing hands as far back as Alexander. Greeks, Turks, Serbs, the Empire, Venice – back and forth like a ball played amongst children. It sat on a dour hill, facing the sea, walled to the land – commanding the way south by road, and the sea for forty straight miles along the coast, a vital little foothold in any army's campaign. Now the Emperor had it again, but the army was dealing with a determined Turk campaign, though it was low in its intensity – neither side having men or resources enough to mount full-scale war, as they were engaged in so many other places with much greater stakes at risk. None the less, Devbergrav was worth fighting for – at least for some while longer, until it changed hands again, and then peace would settle for a few years once more.

At Easter time, a senior commander was brought back to the monastery, injured in a fall from his horse – a broken leg. He'd live. By now Fromme was a competent man of medicine, and took it upon himself to treat the soldier – if Fromme had still been in uniform they would have ranked together.

He checked the splints each afternoon, and talked to the commander of the need for a hospital in the field, a nursing station at the dock side, and a medical ship.

'Here is my thinking,' said Fromme. 'Devbergrav is empty of citizens. There are just soldiers there. You have no civilian doctors in the town. You have one army surgeon to deal with all military death cases and casualties.

For the squads in the countryside, you need a small team of doctors with them, in the back lines. If a man is injured his life could be saved in the field, before he arrives dead back at town. Once you are evacuating the injured, they lie on the beach or at the quay for a day or more – I was there a full two days myself before being shipped back – in that time a man can die, easy. And on the boats back, there is no medic. Two men died on the journey back with me. You have no medical support – it is like having no cannon or wagons or spies. Use doctors, save men, win the war.'

Fromme was allowed to establish a team of medics and orderlies – from any of the monks who would volunteer, and a handful did, as well as from the walking wounded among the military at the monastery as soon as they were fit for duty. Twenty soldiers – suffering only minor injuries, the worst blinded in one eye, the least of them a limper or a lost finger – they were picked and trained up, to act as nurses to the sick, and as guards to the monks who would doctor. All were happy to take the job.

Across the sea, Fromme divided up his men, and took one of the brothers and five soldiers to the front to act as the field medical unit. He won glory on his first day – saving men on the ground amid blood and fire, and taking them back to the town on wagons for dispatch to the beach and then by his medical boat to the monastery.

I asked Fromme to tell me a story of this first day back in battle as we rode and took the top passes of the Steipplinger mountains, but he wouldn't, saying only, 'We all just did our best.' All that I knew of him came from others, though he and Paulus were of an age and knew each other so Paulus told me most.

Today, after the way the military has changed in my lifetime, I still find it astounding that there was no such thing back then as doctors on the battlefield – this being only, what, twenty years before Bideburg when Fromme returned to fighting – but it was true, they had no doctors with the troops. So, of course, the tale of Fromme and his doctors from the monastery made it back to court – and there to generals and ministers of state, and the Emperor, one imagines. Fromme was summoned – by the Emperor – and ordered to address all medical matters relating to the imperial army and navy.

Now, his life became one of logarithms and ledger books – logistics: numbers of men divided by numbers of medics, and this number adjusted for the risk posed to the battalion or regiment in question, set against the strength of the enemy, weather conditions, food supplies and water. He sat at his office in court and got fat. When peace came – though peace never came, there were only periods of less blood and conflict, less war and fighting – Fromme spoke to the states minister, whose ear he had because of his good work in the interest of the Empire.

'My Lord,' he said. 'I can no longer remain at court. I am not a man for desks. I must be either at my prayers and in quietude or out in the world doing God's work, which is saving the lives of my fellow men and women. I would ask that I be given duties which befit my talents so that I may serve you the better. Please send me where you like, that I may act in the world and be part of it, or let me return to my brothers and the monastery, so I may be free from the world.'

The states minister sent Fromme away – saying he would think of some duty for him, as he was not about to allow him to return to Italy and squander away his days amid the laurel bushes. A week later, he was summoned and told that he would be sent north to the Hansa league towns on the Baltic – there was plague and therefore disquiet, and he would lead the state's efforts in trying to relieve the suffering of the sick and dying. The level of illness was adding to anger in the towns and making them ungovernable. He would be accompanied by a group of court officials – they would be the government of the Hansa towns and represent the Empire and state. Local assemblies and all legislative chambers were to be disbanded until the illness was eradicated and the towns put back under rule and order. Once that was done, Fromme would return to court with the rest of the state officials and their military support.

★ ★ ★

Our party had cleared the crest of the Steipplinger mountains now, and were coming down through a glacial gully, where we dismounted and trod slow, slow, slow for fear of the horses slipping – we guided them like babies taking their first steps on ice, and they whinnied and steamed twin plumes from their black leather muzzles.

Paulus had called me up to him now, and we walked side by side, leading our horses down the snowy verge of the gully – away from the ice – snug against the mountain's long running spine. He was bored of the soldiers, I could tell. Fromme may have grown bored of me as well.

'I have details for you, Willie,' he said, and details could mean anything from getting his shirt laundered to passing on false gossip. He listed some chores for me to be about once we arrived in town – getting the pair of us lodgings together was chief among them – good lodgings – and getting him – and by extension myself – a warm meal and some decent drink.

'How has Fromme been?' he asked, keeping well away from the ice sheet that ran down through the heart of the gully, and instead tiptoeing as I did over the thin crispy line of snow that sat up close and narrow to the mountain wall, constantly watching over our shoulders so the horses kept to the snow too and away from the skittering ice.

'We talked a little. I tried to ask him of his past as I wanted to hear the stories but he told me hardly anything. I find his boy so dull. Does he never speak?'

'Jodel comes from a respectable family, and is, I am told, quite intelligent.'

'You'd think he was his catamite.'

'And I would think that you would think before you thought it wise to say such thoughts aloud. That would be a good way to make Brother Fromme very displeased with you. And he and I are old friends, so you should also think about who you are speaking to – you have been on this Earth sixteen years. Fromme and I, we have been here forty, and I've known him for ten of those.'

I looked ahead and felt myself colder than the snow. Paulus would not whip me. He had never whipped anyone in my sight, and never laid one hand upon me – but I felt I had placed myself in that position where only punishment can come, and was perhaps deserved.

'I am sorry,' I said. 'I spoke stupidly. I am tired, sir. Forgive me.'

We walked on, and after three hundred paces – I counted them all – he said, without looking at me, 'You can be an idiot, Willie. Keep your ears up, listen, and think. Think, Willie.'

'I am sorry, sir.'

'It is done,' he said, and we walked on for a while and then, in a quiet voice, he told me the story of how he came to know Brother Fromme – they had both been sent north to deal with the plague in the Hansa towns and restore order, one as a medic and one as a – 'You would have called me an officer of the law, I suppose,' said Paulus. 'A tribune, maybe. Gauleiter?'

Chapter Five

The second part of the history of the priest, Carolus Fromme, in which he, together with the state's official Paulus Melchior, fought the plague and rebellion in the Hansa towns of the north, but then faced witchcraft in its place.

'Beautiful old brown-brick Lubeck – with its black-piked towers – was suffering the worst,' Paulus told me, 'and as it was the chief of the Hansa cities we were ordered there first. Fromme and I did not go north together, though. I arrived two days behind him. He had already set up travelling hospitals to go from Lubeck to the smaller towns and villages nearby, and hired burial squads from among the population. He sent delegates of his to the other Hansa cities of Bremen, Luneberg, Hamburg – where they were to follow his lead. I thought his practice sound and copied its logic and pattern for my own purposes – establishing a military court in Lubeck, with justices under my command dispatched to surrounding towns and villages, ordered to bring back to my court any cases too complex for them to deal with summarily on the spot. Likewise, I sent officials to all the major Hansa towns where they were to mimic my practice – sitting as judge and jury in the city they occupied, while dispatching justices under military escort to mop up dissent and discontent in the hinterlands.

The task of quarantine, however, fell to both of us – with our combined medical and judicial expertise. We shut up areas where the infection rate ran at anything above ten percent of the population. I pressed locals into building enclosing walls, and stationed my guards at gate points, Fromme's staff of medics catered as well as they could for the sick inside, sometimes choosing to go within the walls and stay there to tend the ill until either the infection passed or they died. Many of Fromme's staff were men of God, so their selflessness, while brave, was not unsurprising – they had taken vows to tend and love the sick after all. Caritas even unto death.

We met many times across a desk as colleagues, but it was weeks before

Fromme and I talked as just two people – we were too busy for such niceties until it seemed we had a hold on a system that would make the plague burn itself out on the folk of the Hansa towns. After our regular morning conference, Fromme waited behind to speak to me. He said he had a maritime proposal. I had command of all shipping – given the importance of the league to trade. I pushed away papers and maps and asked him to take a seat by me. Although I was the governor of the city, I held Fromme in high regard, and wished to show him every courtesy. I could make him my friend, I thought, and we could be useful to each other. We ate a good lunch with wine and talked a little – of the weather, and of court, surprised that we had never met, but then unsurprised because the nature of court is to keep those who might be allies apart. We were similar in our dedication to our duty, and our knowledge of how the world worked and spun around the sun, for that is how it goes, as we both knew. Fromme was no good at this type of idle gossip, though, which I find my natural niche on Earth, so when the meat was finished he moved to his point quickly.

Quietly and reasonably, as we ate cake, he asked to be allowed the use of a boat to turn into a medical ship – there were brigs and barks by the dozen floating in the harbour, forbidden to dock and forbidden to leave, as the port was under total quarantine and ringed with gunboats. Men were dying on these ghost ships daily. Men from all across the Baltic and beyond – Scandinavians, Poles, Russians, Lats, English, French, Irish, Scots, Spaniards – far from home. If you stood at the quay you could see them throwing their dead into the green water, and at high tide the bodies washed to the dock wall with the marks of the plague on them. We fished them out and buried them with the rest. Guards were placed to shoot any swimmers, or any deserters from the ships trying to come ashore in their little boats.

"I would like one ship," said Fromme, "and a crew of competent sailors to take me to the sick and dying in the ghost ships in the harbour."

I agreed immediately. There was no reason to disagree. If the ships could be cleared of the infected and the cargoes retrieved, I could have the goods on the road and off to their respective destinations within days rather than months, and trade – which remains the sole point of the Hansa towns – would be served handsomely, and my job better done.

Fromme ordered that no other members of his medical staff would be allowed to volunteer to treat the sick on the ghost ships. By the next morning, I had a ship commandeered for him, and a crew of foreign sailors reduced to beggardom to sail it. I walked to his rooms a few streets away from my own quarters, in the centre of Lubeck, with two carters who were to load his medical supplies on board with food and water in case the sick on the ghost ships were short of sustenance – which they must surely have been, for they'd rocked there in the bay for weeks. When the wind was in the right direction, it seemed that voices could be heard coming from the ghost ships calling for bread and water – certainly figures waved to us constantly, at shore, and fluttered white flags of desperation from their masts.

Fromme's servant showed me up to his rooms, where he was dressing. In the centre of the room stood a mannequin. Fromme lifted the long wax-covered ankle-length overcoat from off the dummy, and buttoned it about him. He called it his Doctor's Ulster – for it seemed some Irish physician from the last century had developed this protective uniform while in Italy treating the plague, and the name had stuck. He put on his mask with glass eyeholes, and I helped him buckle his doctor's leather beak around his face – the cone was filled the ambergris, lemon balm, mint leaves, camphor, cloves, laudanum, myrrh, rose petals, storax, it was a parfumiere's store box, and once he lifted the beak from the leather case he kept it in the smell filled my head so I was dizzy and wondered how he could wear such a drugging thing all day and do his work as a doctor to the sick. His shoes were high-soled and high-heeled to keep them from infection on the ground, and with him he took a stick, patterned with a doctor's twining serpent, to beat any rats that came near, and to lift and move the clothes of those too sick to do it themselves in order that he might inspect them. He stood there a spectacle of bird-like horror – half-devil, half-man – and on top of his head he sat a wide brimmed white hat, with a red band.

"This is to identify me as a doctor," he said, his voice deep and strange behind his masked beak.

I laughed. "What else can you be? A parrot from hell?"

"It is tradition," he said. His voiced hummed but I could hear a smile on his lips as he spoke. "When first we wore such clothes to tend to the plague no-one had seen them before and to stop them running in fear we put on the traditional white and red hat of the hospital so that the public would know what we were. It has stuck with us who tend to the plague."

I walked with him to the docks – the people in the street moving aside for him as if Beelzebub trod smouldering and sulphurous toward the harbour. From the port wall, I watched all day as his little tug moved from one ghost ship to another. Each visit saw medicine and rations unloaded from Fromme's boat, and the dead swapped in return. He spent an hour or more aboard each vessel. Long after night fell, he was still working, and I went to bed. In the morning, he had left me a note saying that some ninety-five dead had been taken from the twenty ghost ships hard out to anchor in the furthest waters of the port, and that some two hundred and five men were still alive. There were signs of infection among fifty-one of this number. Fromme had taken the decision to turn one of the ghost ships into a quarantine hospital for those plainly ill. He transferred the well men from this ship to those floating nearby, and took all the sick to the floating quarantine once it was emptied. Logistical perfection. He is a master of organisation. Within a week, all were dead on the quarantine ship, and none of the other men in the rest of the ghost barks were showing signs of sickness. A day later, they were unloading their cargoes of fabrics and iron and delft and wool and amber and gunpowder and all else they carried at the port. Dockers took the goods to the gate and off they went onto the roads and the trade routes that vein the Empire.

In the city, the infection had reached its peak. Even the street I had my lodgings on – the best part of the city, near the civic chambers and the mansion house – had the dead piled two deep in the gutter and on the corner. In the slums, it was six deep. Of my entire staff, one sixth had died by now. I looked on each day as a straight game of chance – we had no idea what caused the illness, the air most said, or animals or coupling and touching or God. Everyone breathed the air, there were animals everywhere – especially now as many of their owners were dead and their creatures were running wild, another job for my guard to deal with – we all still made love, more than ever as many believed these were their last days, though none behaved as if the End Times had come, such a way of looking at the world was over now. Munster finished that. We still all touched, and God knew us all too. Maybe he was taking the sinners. If so, half my guard should have been dead, and me along with them also, rather than old ladies who lived their lives in charity and little babies newly born. It was chance that was killing people. But I have been lucky my entire life.

Fromme needed huge burial parties – many men to dig graves and cart the dead to the pits – and I dispatched my guards to round up work groups for him. I accompanied him to the burial pits outside the city gates as I thought to write a pamphlet on my time in Lubeck so the world would know my witness – and had gone more and more out into the streets to see with my own eyes what was happening. Fear – I felt it for sure, but I simply went masked through the city, with charcoal rubbed on gauze inside needle-pointed leather to let me breathe, and kept myself gloved, touching nothing or no-one. Fromme still wore his beak and heels and waxed coat. He no longer needed his hat as a beacon, unless it rained. The bird doctor was well known throughout Lubeck.

The funeral parades were hurried – the mass being said over the carts full of the dead on the walk to the pits in the plain outside Lubeck. If the party walked too fast the mass had to be read quicker by the priests as we came near the pits – the gravediggers would not wait around in the presence of so many bodies, and who could blame them – and this angered Fromme.

The dead were tipped off the end of the carts into long trenches, tumbling over each other, in sweeps of arms and legs and swinging heads, some clothed, some naked. The gravediggers flung their dirt. At the first pit burial I attended, when the grave was half-full of earth, one body moved – its arms raised up, and it cried out. Its mouth was like a skull's and I did not know whether it was a man or woman.

Fromme shouted, "Dear God, one lives." And he fell to his knees. One of the gravediggers leant forwards over the pit and hit the crying face hard with his shovel – it fell back dead in the dirt.

Fromme rose and threw himself at the gravedigger, beating him, biting, and clawing at his eyes. The gravedigger was screaming. The guards pulled Fromme away and he raged like a devil, demanding the gravedigger executed on the spot.

"Order his death, Paulus," he screamed at me. "Order his death."

The guards and the gravediggers babbled that this was the way they dealt with such things – that the dead often came back to life in the grave, or the living revived from the point of death. They were not of this world any longer, though – they could not live if they were plucked from the mud, they were plague skeletons with life just hiding in them, waiting to scream one last time when the dirt fell down on their faces. It was kinder to kill them.

Fromme gathered the priests around him, then, and ordered them that no funeral masses would be said until fifteen minutes after the earth had covered the last bodies in the pits. That way all would be dead – and none miss their rites and passage eased to Heaven.

"We are burying the sick alive," he said to us all. "You are not human. Sin has caused this curse, and your sin is adding to its claim upon us."

Fromme was sick himself now – at first we thought he had caught the plague, but his fever dropped after a day, and then he lay listless in his bed, awake but not there, if you understand – like he was dazed. He often cried and did not eat.

I visited him quite often and told him of the work I was doing on my pamphlet – though I liked to call it a treatise when with the educated. The plague was clearing from the city, I told him, but still quite rampant in the villages and smaller towns, and our men were out looking after the sick and keeping order.

One or two of my men were coming back to me with stories of small isolated villages where they had taken to witchcraft to protect them from the plague. Their houses hung with corn dollies, and pentagrams on their hearth floors. Animal bones laid out. These were the people of the hills, and they were working the old forest magic. They still prayed to God, but supplemented his seeming abandon with a worship of things I can not even dream about when I am drunk or have taken a pipe.

Fromme roused himself a little and asked me to tell him more. I fetched my papers and notes and read him the briefings I had taken from the squad commanders, and a few chapters I had written for my treatise. The gossip piqued his spirits. My company sergeant, I told him, had been to one backward village such as this and said the people were harmless – terrified and base – but docile and decent of soul if not behaviour. The sergeant was like Karfreitag – carved from the same loaf of bread. A swaggered-up Landesknecht who likes to roll when he walks. Twenty peasants notched on his sword.

Fromme was still darkened, but he started to recover, and the plague was being finally tamped out – the doctors and the soldiers and quarantine and restrictions and executions had driven it down like a foot drives down a daring flame. Soon Fromme was functioning again, up and about – the liveliness had returned to him like a spring flood. He was dispatching letters north, south, east and west to his officials and back to the minister of state he answered to at court for the health of the Hansa cities. I was preparing to leave. Order was back. Once the troubles were over, stability returned like a tide – like a sigh, a deep breath of peace. No-one wishes disorder and fear, and the people took to good governance again like hungry dogs to their dinner bowls.

My power had run its course and I handed it back to the Lubeck city government in a quiet understated ceremony inside their city hall. I would leave the next day. After the ceremony, as I left the wood hall, Fromme took a hold of my sleeve and pulled me to one side in the street. He was on fire, I felt.

He started to read from a letter but stifled by its bureaucratic babble, paraphrased it to me. "Put short, Paulus. I have new orders. Your witches that your men spoke of? I am to clear them from the countryside. And you must accompany me on the first excursion to report back as a court official. I will obviously report back to the church."

"You went behind my back to court?" I asked him.

"Not in the least. I had evidence which I addressed to the ecclesiastical authorities and they made a decision and gave orders, in conjunction with officials at your court, which I am now acting upon, and which you now must act upon as well. I do not wish to delay. Your function here in the town is over, and you have new commands to address."

I rode with him to the little hamlet I had first named when he was sick, with a party of ten soldiers, and two of Fromme's doctors who had now returned to their religious duties and were to act as inquisitors and judges – for that was the power they now operated under, and it was not to be played with or prodded or parlayed.

The people of the village may as well have been the cannibals of the West Indies for all they understood of the process they had now been caught inside. They all knelt and sang the Lord's Prayer and twenty-third psalm when they finally grasped that they were facing death for rejecting God and consorting with the Devil.

There were seven or eight families, in all, in this little village on the cusp of the woods and fields. They lived like newborns and knew nothing of the world. Fromme set their main hut aside for interrogations, and soon, one by one, they were taken in and then they were screaming.

Fromme came out often and told me how they weaved dunce's Caps from corn stems and called to the Devil in the fields at night, under the guise of the winged goat Baphomet, and were whipped up in a whirlwind where they rode through the night sky and mated with Satan. On their night flight, Satan would give them poison which they poured down onto the cities of the Hansa league and the towns and countryside, for Lucifer wished to kill the good world and offer it up to his loyal disciples – like these idiots in the woods, I said. I told Fromme this was ridiculous – the people were half-savage and had turned to old superstitions when they were afraid. "They still prayed to your God," I said.

"Your God too," said Fromme.

"And your village, Fromme. You are in charge. My job is to record what happens. I will do so, and report back to court. You should proceed and consider me only a witness and loyal servant of the court."

He burned them all. Every last person in that village – man, child, woman, grandmother, grandfather, a baby – for it had been born from a coupling with Satan, as the mother confessed.

When I rode out, back to Lubeck, to collect my possessions and return to the court, the sky was red and black behind me with fire, and the smell of the village cooked in my nose and mouth. Fromme rode ahead with his priests, and the guards rode with me – I was still their commander in their eyes, no matter what they had done in the village, or what I had said.

I left for court, but had my friends still living in the town send me reports of how Lubeck was progressing. More and more in my letters I heard of Fromme's witch hunts and how he had cleared sorcery from most of the north. Later I heard he was sent to the south and worked again in Italy – always as an inquisitorial justice, never as a doctor any more – and to the east and the west. He was everywhere, though I saw him very seldom, and when we did meet at court just the other day we were like old friends – for we are as brothers and I am fond of him, indeed.'

Chapter Six

The party approaches Bideburg, and Paulus relates his duties undertaken in the town of Keinweggstein in pursuit of vampires causing hysteria among the living.

We hit the meadows above Bideburg as we rode down off the foothills in the Steipplinger mountains. It was late and deep in the night – gone two now, for sure.

Paulus hollered over his shoulder to Karfreitag to take a point on the town once it came into view and shoot a flare overhead when we were within five miles of the outskirts. He wanted to be about his business as soon as we arrived and needed to rouse the town to our coming.

The night smelled cool and sweet with summer flowers blooming in the moon, after the chill blank air in the mountains. The wind barely breathed, though, and just a few weak clouds floated slow over the stars.

Paulus had been drumming into me, since we left, that we were to put a man on trial, not a werewolf – but, in truth, I would have preferred the trial of a monster.

'Would it not be more fun,' I asked, 'to preside over the trial of a real werewolf?'

'I'm saddle-sore, son,' he said. 'Don't make me answer your silly questions.'

I was saddle-sore too, but bored with the trudging of the horses and the scrape of their hoofs – our party rattled like pennies in a can with our clanking weapons and rides and crates – and I wanted to engage Paulus in talk, for if I didn't I felt I would fall asleep and slip to the dirt, and that would mean a mocking and a slapping, if Karfreitag got his hands on me before Paulus.

'Sir, I just want to know how you can be so sure – that is all. I apologise if I phrased my question childishly.'

We rode on a while and his horse crept in front of mine. 'Keep up,' he said, and when I drew level with him, he told me how he knew – or at least why he believed he knew.

'There is nothing supernatural in or on this Earth, Willie,' he said. 'Years ago, my first real political command came at the request of one of the lords of the south – in the Black Forest. He was a nothing in terms of power, but his family were related and sworn loyal to our Prince-Bishop and so I was sent off to deal with a complete breakdown of governance in his area. Bringing order – that is the job of the likes of you and I, Willie.'

The story – he told it broken-wise, jumping from one event in the past to another in the future, but I can tell it better, for that is one thing I excel at more than Paulus.

This lord was not really a lord, or in nothing but name only. His wife ruled his lands – which were minimal and mostly dense forest that he did not have the manpower or money to harvest for wood. He was young and feeble-minded – lantern-jawed and weak in his body like a baby, it was said. The family could count itself back to the pagan past and was called Keinwegg – their town Keinweggstein, for it was built around a stone pillar dedicated, before the time that Rome rose, to ancient gods.

This was the backwoods. The noble family's seat was a house no better than a village town hall. The people lived in a state of near blindness to civilisation – no-one read, there was no priest, close cousins had children with close cousins. They tilled and ate and slept and bred and died in moral darkness.

The only light of manners and learning thereabouts was the Scottus Monastery – filled with Irish and Scots monks, Gaels, who'd founded their mission when the Irish Church was still powerful, back in the days of Charlemagne, it's thought. They were tolerated by Rome – they did good and no harm and spread the word of God in a part of the world few priests wanted to go – and the monks tolerated Rome in return, swearing loyalty to its teachings, but teaching as they saw fit themselves, which often went against the style of Rome, if not the message. They kept their ringed Celtic crosses around their necks and on their altar and in their graveyards, shunning the crucifix of Rome.

Paulus and his party were to lodge at the monastery, some twenty miles from the town, before making the final leg of the journey into the forest to Keinweggstein. The monks were friendly and hospitable, and even put on a show of music and comedy for them – all written and performed by the brothers themselves. The food and wine was good. The beds good too. But when it came to talk of the town, the monks merely shrugged their shoulders and said such people were lost to them, they could not be saved as they were too savage, and the word of God was to be sung and praised here in the monastery – and to those in the countryside with ear and soul to hear it – not disgraced by the effrontery of the people of Keinweggstein.

'How often do you see them?' Paulus asked the father of the monastery.

'As little as we can – some trading, that's all,' and his German was thick and strange with his harsh foreign accent. The father twiddled his thumbs in his lap, and added, 'They are no good. That is all. Different to the people of the other towns hereabouts. I believe this is about witchcraft – and we want nothing to do with that. We will stay here and tend to priestcraft.'

The mission set to Paulus was this: the lands under the lord and lady were in ruins. People were reporting that the dead had risen from their graves. That the dead were killing the living – eating them, drinking their blood. That if you saw one of the risen dead, a vampire, you too would become one when next you slept. That the undead were breaking into homes and stealing children. That undead children were then seen walking the roads at night luring their parents to graveyards to have their blood drained. Those who had not fled the town and the surrounding villages were workless, and so pointless to the state – the people remaining, they hid in their homes and only came out to turn to theft to feed themselves. They did not till or sow or chop or carry or dig. There had been murders and rapes, no taxes were being raised and no taxes sent in turn to the Prince-Bishop in exchange for his protection – so now it fell to the Prince-Bishop to show his loyalty and assist his relative and subject, the lord, in his worst hour, in order that all may go back to how it once was before, and tithes be paid again.

Paulus slept well at the monastery and the next morning his party left for Keinweggstein. They arrived well before sundown. The town was empty – though town is too grand a word for this place. It was a street, with an inn, some shacks and the lord's family home – built high and narrow, but with no more rooms than to sleep ten in beds, and another ten on floors. There was a granary and stables and a graveyard. Other shacks were strung out across the land – sometimes in little hamlets, sometimes isolated and alone. In all, perhaps, the lord ruled over five hundred people. It was a place of poverty and cold, even for the highest risen in society.

Paulus pondered as he rode slow into the town why the Prince-Bishop would care a damn about the few pennies to be had from Keinweggstein. Principle, probably. Promises. And promises have to count to the small as well as the big if the big are to ever heed them. It was Paulus' first major command – but he could see that his duties here counted of little importance, though, in the schemes of state; and to him this was a reflection on his standing that made him squirm a little in shame in his saddle, and be glad to be down from his horse once the party drew up at the town crossroads.

Paulus sent his boy to the lord's family home by way of introduction and was invited in – inside, the lady, Irma her name was, she sat in the main hall, the back of her high chair hard against the far wall, with a company of ten armed men around her. She too was armed – a pistol in her lap and a sword by her side.

'What did you see in the countryside as you rode into town?' she asked.

Paulus walked towards her and bowed and introduced himself.

'I know why you are here,' she said. 'I sent for you.'

Paulus asked to see the lord, for it was the lord's signature attached to the letter of request which had been sent to the Prince-Bishop and which Paulus had here in his satchel of orders.

Lady Irma got up from her seat and took Paulus through a thin, high corridor to the lord's chambers. The lord was sat upon the floor playing catch-up-jack and petting and playing with a small toy of a dog beside him. The room was hot – a fire blazed in the hearth – and there was food on a table by the wall. A large soft bed stood in the middle of the room. Two kittens slept on it.

'My lord,' the lady said.

'My lord,' said Paulus.

'Frederick,' the lord said, and he stood up, dusting off the seat of his clothes – for the room was without rugs or even mats.

'My Lord Frederick,' said Paulus, and he bowed.

'So, you have come to help us?' Frederick said. He was not the child of nature that had been expected – true he was not quite a full man, but certainly not an infant in his mind or an idiot – though he had an air about him which was strange and awkward. He walked over to the bed, moved the two kittens, who mewled and scrabbed at him, and sat down, cross-legged. He lifted a pillow and placed it on his lap. 'Please sit by me and talk,' he said. The cats jumped back on the bed and he slapped them away.

Paulus took a chair from by the wall and sat before the lord. Lady Irma remained by the door and watched and listened.

The land, it seemed, had been slowly taken over by the dead. The young lord spoke well and fluently, though his voice was flat and his eyes wandered. More than three months ago the first case of a corpse returning from the grave had taken place: a farmer from the north of the town had died, along with some of his cows. The family prayed hard as they thought they were cursed with such losses, and buried the man. On the night of his burial, he was seen walking outside his house and crying. The next night he came into the house and tried to speak to his wife. His sons beat him out of the door, and he bit and clawed at them. In the morning one son was dead and the other in a fever. The wife gathered her cousins and kin and went to the graveyard where they dug up the body of the farmer. There in the box, he was livid – skin ruddy, lips drawn back, teeth sharp, blood in his mouth.

The family cut off the head and filled the mouth with herbs, and took the body to the crossroads where they staked it to the ground through the heart. A day later, another family who had lost a brother claimed they too had seen their loved one the night after his burial – and soon they were also haunted and attacked, and had staked their brother and son to the crossroads. Another and another and another – till over months there was barely a family untouched by the rising of the dead. Animals were drained of blood in the fields, babies were stolen in the night and found white in the forest come the morning.

Paulus took his party to the crossroads. The dead were piled across the dirt, headless, staked and mouldered – some were fresh and still pink, others were just bones and rags. Dogs and birds and cats ran and leapt barking and cawing and miaowing with their fur and feathers red. Rats and mice crept among the heap.

At the lord's home, Paulus asked if any family was currently plagued, and the lady sent a group of her men out to inquire.

Paulus told them – the lord and lady and their advisors – that under order of the court, disinterring of the dead and defilement of the dead would have to stop. Lady Irma said that it could only stop once it was proved to have no efficacy. Paulus said he would therefore send men to each family reporting their kin as dead and come to life, and action would be taken which was appropriate with the discoveries made.

He had no idea what he was dealing with – and did in truth believe at first that he was indeed in a nest of vampires. The young lord, though, claimed the people had just gone mad.

'We had a bad harvest,' the lord said. 'The worst in years. I keep notes.' And he showed Paulus a set of ledgers where the weighing of crops and measuring of taxes and trade was noted. Also noted were the deaths and births in the town – most of the folk thereabouts did not marry, conventionally, but jumped the broomstick.

'See,' said the lord, and he showed Paulus how bad crop years measured up to high deaths and few births, and good crop years gave high births and less death.

'I believe it is the weather,' the lord said. 'It affects the crops and cattle and it changes mood too – in man.'

The lord was not a fool, as Paulus had been told – though he was certainly strange, like a changeling creature. Although he did not look unusual, there was something odd about his manner and gait, and the way he cast his eyes. Nor was he a lunatic, but his mind ran at a different pace and in a different place to others – he seemed bored of all around him, and confused at how they acted, this made him melancholy and sad, and sometimes angry, but when angry he could be bullied and scolded into discipline like a child, which his wife meted out like a mother. He was not a natural child – those elfin folk with the high eyes and cheeks and fatter mouths than us – he was prepossessed like a normal man, yet he was not a normal man, and that could be seen to all who met him on the second they met him.

Paulus, and two of his guards, spent the night at the home of a woodsman and his family who said their son had died of fever after seeing a dead cousin walking in the trees. The people believed that looking in the eyes of the dead would transfer the curse to the living. The family moaned and prayed all night. In the latest hour, they ran to the window and said they saw the dead boy walking along the tree line in front of their home. Paulus saw nothing, and sent his men out to search. The youngest child, a girl of four, fell down on the floor of the hut and shook, white and wild, with foamed lips. Her shaking quit and she lay like death.

The mother held her and wailed, 'She is dead. My baby is dead.'

The father said, 'We must cut off her head. If the sight of her brother's corpse has killed her, then she'll rise and become like him – and then we will have to cut her head off regardless, or she will be the death of us.'

The family began to cry and wail that one of them had to cut the little girl's head off – and now before she rose. The child lay on the floor among the raving family. Paulus put his ear to her chest and reckoned a heartbeat. 'She is alive,' he said. 'Take the baby to her bed.'

The family stilled, and the mother picked up her child. She said, 'In the morning we must do what is right and set my son to peace. If we do, perhaps my girl will live.'

Before they slept again, the guards came back and said they had found nothing but some looters and criminals on the far side of the forest robbing the home of an old widower man. The thieves had killed the old man, and the guards had killed the thieves.

At dawn, Paulus oversaw the disinterring of the son's body himself – as the mother and father had asked. The diggers dug down and the plank box showed itself in the earth. The exhumation did not take long as there were so many bodies to bury each day that the holes had become more shallow one by one.

Paulus got into the grave and used a bill-hook to crank open the box. The lid of the coffin came off easily – iron nails were in short supply – and the boy lay inside, his hands up to his chest like claws, the mouth pulled wide, the tongue chewed to a stump. In the lid, embedded in its wood, were six ragged half-moons – nails from the boy's fingers.

'We have seen this before.' It was the lady of the land – come to watch and make sure that all accorded with her care for her people.

The people nudged forward and gasped and crossed themselves and said 'vampire'. The family of the dead boy wept by the graveside and crossed themselves too.

'It was alive and died in the box trying to get out and attack the people,' the lady said.

'No,' said Paulus. 'The boy was alive when he went into the box. I have seen this before. This is a burial alive. He tried to claw his way out of the box. He chewed his own tongue off in terror. This is a dead boy, not a monster.'

The boy's mother said, 'But his heart had stopped and he was dead when we buried him.'

Paulus looked up from the grave and said, 'And your doctors told you this?'

'This can not be true,' the boy's father said.

'There will be no more dragging the dead from their graves. No more mutilation,' Paulus said, loud and calm.

One of the villagers spat down into the grave onto Paulus and called him 'killer'. The lead guard took the man aside and broke his jaw on Paulus' order. It took five punches and Paulus watched.

When the punishment was over, Paulus asked who else had dead family haunting them – and three groups put up their hands. He opened the graves. In one there was the rotting body of an old woman, and the family crossed themselves happy that their grandmother was not walking the Earth.

'But,' Paulus said to them, 'you told me you saw her the other night and that she tried to kill you.' And he pointed at the oldest man there – the old woman's son.

'She did,' the man said. 'But that was the first time she has ever troubled us. She has been dead two years now – and until two nights ago we had not seen her.'

Paulus pointed at the grave, 'But she is dead and rotting.'

In the second grave, the corpse, a man it turned out of nearly thirty when he died, was turned face down – its back was purple, as if filled with a crown of blood. The crowd screamed – sure this showed the creature asleep, and gorged, and waiting to wake and come up from the ground and its grave at night to terrorise them.

Paulus screamed back at them – getting wild now. 'You have buried another living human being. This poor thing has rolled on its belly to die. Look,' he said, and he pointed to the coffin lid – again dotted with little half-moon rings of fingernail, 'it tried to get out and turned over to die.'

The wife of this creature said her husband had died after meeting his dead father in the field, and had come back to attack her the past three nights.

'He died in the box alive,' said Paulus. 'He did not walk the Earth. You have killed him.'

A few asked why the man's back was filled with blood.

'He is starting to rot,' said Paulus.

In the third, lay a parchment corpse – almost skeleton, but still clad in a tight dry cloth of skin. The hair remained thick on its head and its hands and feet were clawed and sharp. Its shroud had disappeared into dust around it.

Paulus looked to the family. 'This is in the ground five years or more.'

The family stood dumb.

'When did it trouble you?'

'Two nights ago,' said a girl of fourteen – it was the oldest daughter of the dead woman in the box.

'It has lain dead in the ground for years, lost to the world before you claim vampires came to your town, yet it only decides to rise from the ground on Tuesday? You believe this?'

The girl said, 'Look – it has been growing hair and nails.'

'Look,' said Paulus, and he grabbed the girl by the collar and dragged her to the mouth of the grave, 'hair and nails do not rot. They remain. The flesh rots. I should burn you for spreading heresy and fear against the rule of law.'

Paulus pushed the girl away – she fell and her family rushed around her, giving comfort. The lady, Irma, she touched Paulus softly on the arm, and asked him to come with her.

'Cover these graves,' she said – and she addressed herself to every person standing around her.

Paulus shook himself free from her.

'Every family,' he said to the crowd, 'with a claim of the dead haunting them will report to my guard. We will post a sentry with you for five nights. If there is no proof in five nights of your family being haunted, you will be indicted for working against the good of the state. Sedition. Execution. Prove that you are haunted and you will be rewarded by the state. In gold.'

In five days it was over, bar a few executions. People returned to the fields and taxes were gathered and the village continued in its own low way as before.

★ ★ ★

We were off the Steipplinger foothills now, down in the valley-head leading to Bideburg. Paulus called out to Karfreitag to ready up a flare there and shoot it high right over the town – he wanted to announce his arrival in style.

I asked him, then, what started the panic.

'Why did they believe the dead had risen in the first place?' I said. 'Why did they think the living were dead, and burying them alive?'

'Argot, maybe,' he said. 'I've heard stories of beer or bread being infected with a mushroom – like the dreaming mushrooms but worse –

which makes folk believe they are being eaten by the Devil, or are dead, or made of rock, or must slit their own throat in order to save their children's lives, or slit their children's throats so they save their own lives or the life of God – for that is how strange it can affect the mind.'

I had heard of that too. 'Do you believe that?' I asked.

'Not really,' he said. 'Maybe they just went mad like the young lord said. I do not know. But there were no vampires – and never have been – even if I can not explain what happened.'

I nodded, unsure, but not fit to argue with him – it was so late and I was so tired, and had no answers for him anyway. Karfreitag fired off his scarlet flare, which went up into the sky like a whistling devil and blew itself to pieces over the little red-bathed town of Bideburg down below us. We rode on into the town.

Chapter Seven

Bideburg is reached, with the strange topography of the area noted in order to map the unchartered lands around the town, and the Prince-Bishop's party is met by local officials.

Bideburg was a lordless town. During the uprising and war, nearly forty years ago now, the people had rid themselves of their lord and his family, as many people in many towns had done then across the western Empire. Like many towns, when the war was over and the uprising put down – the holy poor scattered – the people were allowed to keep to their new settlement, and govern their own town, under the protectorship of state lords and masters, instead of local ones, and Bideburg's council was answerable to the Prince-Bishop and so had sent letters of request to him, when they caught the wolf which had been frightening and killing around the town since before I was born.

It was still night, warm and black, when our horses left the valley mouth and crossed a plain, coming from the south towards Bideburg. We leant back in our saddles as ballast to balance our mounts, and travelled silently till we reached the dusty road for Bideburg. Paulus told me to note the topography and write a full description of the land and draw up a rough map once we were settled in the town – there was no accurate cartography of the area, beyond a dot with the name Bideburg by it. The path to Bideburg followed the flow of a mountain stream, and wound up and down. We passed a deep pool that the stream made. The pool let out into a faster running river that dipped down towards the town. Soon before us, on the road, stood a high black avenue of trees – like a natural entrance way into the town of Bideburg. The trees were tall and gathered together, from either side, over the road, their top branches meeting above and interlinking like the crossed fingers of old maids – they formed a steeple above our heads. The dark trees covered the road for a good five hundred paces, and we all rolled our heads back to look up as the horses walked slow through this tunnel of wood and leaf. The stars could not be seen above, so thick were the fingers of the trees locked together.

Fromme's boy, Jodel, spoke. 'This is a wonder, is it not?' I heard him say behind me.

All of us looked at him for he had spoken no more than half a dozen words since we left the university.

Fromme said, 'It would have been planted like this – for effect. Nature could not have laid this out without the hand of men.'

As we left the tunnel of trees, the road pointed down gently, following the river to the town of Bideburg, gathered around it on the right bank, the east bank. It was not a godforsaken town, but looked well laid out. A broad main street, cut in two at a crossroads by a road leading up from the river, through the town. Rolling off to the east of Bideburg were the fields beyond where farms stood. Many houses – the type of home a decent family would own, the butchers and shoemakers, tailors and such like – lined the streets around the crossroads. Even from here – a good twenty minute ride from the town – we could make out these larger buildings, and the inn and town hall, I guessed, and a large black keep or jail, a stout brick cylinder maybe four floors high, was set hard against another ridge of the Steipplinger mountains, heavy with woods, which loured over the town to the north. The river skirted Bideburg to the west – on its far shore, more mountains – and it drove through a high arch carved by time and water in the north wall of the Steipplingers. A path followed the flow of the river under the arch and through the mountains to the forest beyond. The mountains behind us closed the town off from the south. Bideburg filled a stub of river plain, and its land rolled out to the east, in fields and steadings, for some ten miles, until it staggered to a halt at the foot of the farthest eastern run of the forest mountains. It sat like a toy in the black stiff cupped hand of the Steipplinger giant.

There was a shanty of shacks – perhaps fifty rough-hewn cottages – clustered on the riverbank when we cleared the steeple of trees. Each cottage had a patch of kitchen garden, an allotment. We rode past and no-one stirred, or at least no-one showed they stirred.

Our soldiers were more jittery than the horses, they kept turning their heads from left to right, scanning the land. Paulus told Karfreitag to throw out the men in guard formation. The sergeant set four of them to ride at the sides of the road, while he took up point position and set the last man as the tail guard. Paulus told me and Fromme and his boy Jodel to ride with him between the soldiers. Each soldier led a pack horse. It felt imposing, crossing the land this way, with soldiers strung around us for protection. Though I wondered what made Paulus scared.

'I am not scared,' said Paulus. 'I am designing our arrival. If we straggled into town, we would look like a group of fools from the city. This way, we are a little army, in good formation, with its headmen displayed at the centre of the parade to show power – ringed by men under my command in armour with guns and swords – and a terrifying old Landesknecht at the head of us all, with his sash slung about him. It will excite them, and intimidate them. It will speed things along for us.'

Karfreitag assembled the Prince-Bishop's spear-banner – an eagle clutching keys – and held it above him. The man was like a grey bear, and sixty if he was a year old, but he hoisted the banner, the length of three men, in the air as if it were a taper. When the banner went up, the guard to our rear beat a little drum he had taken with him – he had pulled it from his pack while his ride rolled beneath him and set it between his thighs on the saddle. Our horses' hooves fell into time with the drum's one-two rhythm.

The darkened cottages were far behind now, and the road opened out again. Ahead, where the first good homes of Bideburg began, a clutch of torches bobbed in the night. The heads of the men holding the fires moved around in the orange light, but their bodies faded from the shoulders down, and their bellies and legs were lost in pitch blackness. I could distinguish five men, in all, among the shadows and flickering torch light.

Our party was soon on top of these men, and drew to a halt without a word, as Paulus had instructed. There was no sound, save the deep lusty panting of our horses' dripping mouths and the clank of the soldiers' armour and weapons as they rocked in their saddles.

I looked at Paulus, stock still beside me, on his horse. He did not move or speak.

'Are you the party from the Prince-Bishop?' said the man in the middle – a fat fellow in late life, sixty maybe, dressed well, with a chain of office around his neck.

Paulus heeled his horse and it moved forward. He directed it so it shunted Karfreitag's horse to the side, and Paulus made his way to the front.

'And who else would we be, with six soldiers, an inquisitorial priest, two scholars and a judge?' He reined his horse hard and the animal stopped sharp and breathed down upon the men. The men moved back a little.

'Stay still,' said Paulus. 'Who are you?' And he pointed directly at the old little fat man who had spoken. The horse switched its head to the side, and caught the man on the chin. He fell back on the ground.

'I am Joachim Kroll, Your Excellency. The mayor of the town of Bideburg,' he said, holding his hand up in front of him, to keep the horse away.

'Do I look like the Prince-Bishop, sir?' said Paulus. 'Do you think His Excellency would ride over those mountains to your spit in the ground because you say you have found a werewolf?'

'I'm sorry,' this man Kroll said from the ground.

'Get up, Kroll,' said Paulus, and he pulled on the reins of his horse so its head shied away.

Kroll struggled to his feet. The townsmen around him did not help him stand, but stood looking at the ground in front of them.

'Let me introduce you properly. My sergeant-at-arms, Bran Karfreitag. An old friend,' and he lent over in his saddle to pat Karfreitag's arm. 'His men,' Paulus waved his arm around at the soldiers to the sides and behind, 'under my command. All veterans.' He turned in his saddle to look behind him. 'Our religious advisor Brother Fromme, and his apprentice and secretary, Jodel. My assistant and court scribe Lessinger.' He pointed to each of us in turn.

The men mumbled greetings, and Kroll nodded his head, repeating, 'yes, sir, yes, sir' as Paulus addressed him.

'And your friends, Kroll? Who do we have the pleasure of attending to our arrival at this late hour? Are they as important as you in the town?'

Paulus looked down from his horse at the other four men and cast his eyes, lazily, over them.

Kroll straightened up like a little rooster and began his introductions. 'Yes, my sir, we have here the most prominent citizens in our town.'

Paulus cut him off. 'Talk as you walk, sir. I wish to see this werewolf of yours immediately, and then sleep. Walk by my horse's side. Tell these friends of yours to hurry on to town and arrange lodgings for the ten of us. Good lodgings – and food and wine. We are tired and have travelled a long way to come to this place you call your home.'

Kroll shooed his four friends away and they jogged smartly into town. Paulus rode his horse at a slow clopping pace, and Kroll walked at his side, looking up to speak. The rest of us followed behind.

'Do you wish to hear of the werewolf?' Kroll asked.

'No,' said Paulus. 'I wish, as I said, to know who it was who came to meet us with you.'

'As you please, sir – but if you wish me to relate what I know of the werewolf, I would be humbled to do so.'

'I have no interest, Kroll, in hearing anything from you but answers to the questions I ask.'

'Yes, sir.' And Kroll explained who it was who had accompanied him in the night to meet the Prince-Bishop's party from the city university.

★ ★ ★

Alongside Kroll in the greeting party there had been Jens, the town high constable and sheriff; Rodinan, the ranking member of Bideburg council, and a young landowner; Odil, also on the town council, but the owner of the village inn, and landlord to most of the major holdings in the town – the river wharf, the butchers, the tailors, and many of the smaller steadings which he leased to poorer farmers; and Pastor Barthelme, the village churchman. Barthelme, like his parishioners, was not a follower of Rome, but of Luther, though he was far from militant – and as the settlement among the people allowed them to follow the religion of their conscience, as long as they obeyed the state in all its orders, he was well disposed to follow instruction from our holy Catholic Prince-Bishop.

The farther one got from Rome, I have learned, the less the Catholic clergy love Rome. Like a magnet, the priests in the Holy City cling to Rome, without thoughts to trouble their minds – though they often flout the commandments of the church, and it is in Rome were most of the sinning by the clergy is sinned, this we know. The more distance, though, that a priest puts between himself and the Vatican, the weaker the hold becomes – things oscillate at the edges and hold firm in the centre, it is a natural rule of science – which may explain why the English and the Scots and the Danes slipped more easily away from the rule of the Pope, as did parts of our dear Empire. France had once held the Pope's court in Avignon, and so, the sway of Rome was hard and fast there, and in Spain the people are too sleepy in the heat to work out ways to think other than those thoughts imposed upon them from across the sea in Italy, through their King and Queen. Likewise, the Russians and the Serbs and other Slavs have found their own path to God – and that does not follow the map of Rome either.

With the Lutherans, the same can be said – but in reverse. The closer they come to a Catholic lord the more likely they are to get down on their knees and kiss the hem of his robe. It is also a rule of science that great objects drag other objects into their orbit. So, Barthelme, here in Bideburg, was free to pray to his Protestant God, but when his Catholic rulers asked him to jump for them, he was only too happy to ask, 'How high my most loving Catholic lord?'

Our party was at the head of the town's main street now – the dry well-swept road led straight to a black keep, the last building in Bideburg, its back set tight against the wall of the Steipplinger mountains, and its dark forest ridges, the river running by. I could see clearly now the natural arch that the river had cut in the mountain. A rough, hewn, grassy beaten path led along the right riverbank. The path and the river carried on under the natural arch of black rock – like a Cathedral roof, high, high overhead – and then moved off together into woodland, twinned, losing their form and definition as they crept into the wild forest beyond.

Bideburg, I noticed, smelt cleaner and more fresh than any town or village – and of course, city – that I had ever set my foot within. The midden had to be far off, I reasoned – Bideburg was not large, but it had enough space to set the town tip away from the places of population. I could smell wood smoke and cut grass that must have been mown just hours before, though at the back of it all, I was sure, there was the tang and taint of blood and meat. I looked about me and saw that we were passing the town butcher – the hooks hanging from the rafters at the front of the shop.

As we drew level with the inn, at the crossroads in the centre of Bideburg, Odil appeared from the shadow on the steps, with the pastor Barthelme. Jens and Rodinan stood behind. Kroll left Paulus' side and made his way to them – a whipped schoolboy seeking refuge from his master with his friends.

'Sir,' Odil called to Paulus. Our party drew to a halt. 'Sir,' he said. 'I have rooms available for you and your men.' Large stables were cobbled onto the side of the inn, and Odil motioned to them, 'My ostler can care for your horses and pack team.' Odil stretched out his hand behind him, into the shadow, and pulled a lanky youth forward.

Paulus dismounted, and the rest of us followed suit. He pointed to the keep and addressed Jens, 'You are the sheriff, I am right? Is the prisoner held there?'

Jens said, 'Yes, sir. Yes, sir.'

Paulus then fired off one of his flurries of commands. I thanked God I was not on the receiving end, for even in the university, after I'd had a good night's sleep and a full breakfast, when Paulus had a mind full of orders, he would rattle them off with such a speed, and with so many instructions buried within other instructions, that I often could not keep up, even with a pen and paper in my hand, but at this hour of the morning after a march of ten hours, I was not fit to think or speak, let alone take this list of commands and execute them for him. Instead, he addressed himself to the town representatives.

All the soldiers, save Karfreitag, were to rest immediately – and they were to be fed too. The ostler boy would clean and feed the horses. Karfreitag would accompany Paulus, Fromme and I to the keep to interrogate the prisoner immediately. Fromme's boy would find a bed for the night with the village pastor – and Fromme would join them after the interrogation. Paulus and I would lodge with the town sheriff, Jens, once the prisoner had been spoken to and initial notes taken.

'I take it you have room for me and my secretary?' Paulus asked Jens.

'Of course, sir. I would be honoured, divinely honoured,' Jens replied. 'Though my house is small, it has room aplenty for you both. And my wife will make you a breakfast that is the pride of Bideburg. Our hen's eggs are the most luxurious for miles around, and the ham, well, we just slaughtered a hog, two days ago, to celebrate the capture of the werewolf, and the meat is fine and sweet and tender.'

'And the wheat for your bread, I am sure, is milled by angels,' said Paulus. 'Thank you for your hospitality, Sheriff.'

Jens coughed and silenced himself.

Paulus stood, hands on his hips. 'Am I waiting for some divine intervention – or will you follow my commands before I have to repeat them?'

Odil pushed his ostler boy down the steps and the lad began leading the horses to the stables. Odil stepped forward and extended a hand towards the soldiers, 'Your beds are warmed and waiting and I will bring bread and meat and cheese and pickles and beer to you in your rooms.' The soldiers clanked one by one into the darkened inn, and Odil followed them inside, walking backwards and bidding everyone remaining in the street a good night.

'Sirs, you may leave for your homes,' Paulus said to Kroll, Rodinan and the pastor. 'But you boy,' he spoke to Jodel, Fromme's lad who once again had returned to his studied muteness, 'go with the pastor and then return to wait at the inn for good Brother Fromme. You will lead him to your lodgings when he is done at the keep.'

Kroll and Rodinan said goodnight – the pastor bowed but did not speak – and the three of them walked up the eastern path from the crossroads, toward the rich, rolling farm lands of Bideburg and the thick dark forests beyond that ringed the foothills of the Steipplinger mountains. Jodel scurried behind them.

That left five of us – Karfreitag, Jens, Fromme, Paulus and I – standing in the street alone.

Paulus put his arm around Jens and said, 'Now lead on, Sheriff, and take me to this monster of yours.' He gave Jens a light shove between the shoulder blades. Jens tottered forward, and turned to beckon us to follow him to the keep.

'This creature that we have, sir,' Jens said to Paulus. 'It is a wealthy man, if you can believe that. One of the richest men in all this land hereabouts.'

'Be quiet,' said Paulus, 'I am talking to my colleagues.' And we walked on, but Paulus said not a word to anyone.

We carried on behind Jens, the five hundred paces to the keep's iron door. Paulus threw his arm around my shoulder now, and I feared some mockery was coming my way as it had Jens. The arm around the shoulder was seldom a good sign from Paulus – it meant condescension. But this time, though, for a change, it was genuine – an arm thrown around me in fellowship.

'Willie,' he said, and he said it loud, so everyone could hear, not just I, 'life is about leadership and command – which means delegation. I want you to learn how to tell people what to do – that is as important as your Latin, law, rhetoric and languages.'

I nodded at him – and let his arm hang about my neck – even though I detested anyone to use me as a leaning post, with Paulus it felt fine and right. Without thinking, and before it could embarrass me, I had lifted my arm and put it around his neck. He patted my shoulder, and we walked, linked together – the rest of the party ahead of us – toward the keep, which hunkered before us, dark and fierce, as you got near its black, heavy height.

Under my hand, I felt that Paulus' neck was damp and cold with sweat. Not hot, thick sweat from heat or exhaustion, but slick, cool sweat. I looked up at him – he was half a head taller than me, but I had not stopped growing yet, and when I did, in a year, perhaps, I would match him in height, and be a good sized man. He saw a little question in my eyes – for I was thinking to myself: is he scared? And Paulus smiled such a crooked smile as I had never seen him cast before. It was the smile of a child when caught at mischief – shamed, worried, unsure of what to do.

'All is fine,' he said, but his voice sounded tight and clipped – awkward in his mouth, the way lying words sit wrong against the tongue. He slipped his arm from me and pushed me ahead of him through the door of the keep which Jens held open for us.

Chapter Eight

The great rebellion and siege of Munster is spoken of, and the interrogation of the prisoner and alleged werewolf Peter Stumpf begins in the keep at Bideburg.

I came to know Paulus' mind. By the time that we were finished with Bideburg and Bideburg was finished with us, Paulus and I were no longer a master and a student, we were friends and brothers – more, I know. I knew of his past, and of his soul.

I finish my life as an historian – for a job is what determines a person's value these days, their worth on Earth and in memory – but even as a green boy I had in my make-up a love of stories, stories of real people and of real events, mind you, stories which make sense of the past, not fairy tales concocted by rich poets who have the resources to spend all day lying on their couch dreaming up fantasies that the world does not need.

I had heard of Munster before I came to Bideburg, for sure. I was a clever young fellow, as I know I have told you, and would not have made it into Paulus' service if I had not a good grasp of the times in which I lived. Paulus, however, brought the history of that city of his to life for me, throughout our time in Bideburg. And he told me other things too – of his heart and of his mind.

For example, later – but not that much later, perhaps on the third day in Bideburg – he told me that as he walked through the entrance doors of the keep on that first night in the town he was repeating to himself these words, 'The man will not be a werewolf.'

Paulus was sure of that. He told himself, 'I will meet a man, not a werewolf.' But if it was a werewolf, against all the laws of reason that he knew – and if it broke out from its cell, for surely a werewolf transformed by Satan could break metal – if it was a werewolf and it attacked him, then he'd ask God for death. But that would be a foolish waste of pointless prayer – nothing that God is ever asked for is granted or listened to. God is deaf, Paulus told me, and I crossed myself and told him to watch his words. He shook his head like I was an infant to be pitied.

God – he had asked God many times for a little help; not for money or power, though he had plenty of both now, and for that his enemies could go hang themselves – but for the most simple of things that God could grant his creatures: a little pity, sympathy. It was for the want of pity and sympathy in the world that Paulus said he felt fear – for it was lonely to be without an intercessor to offer its hand and lift the weight of the world from the shoulders of the living.

'My face reddened up as we walked into the keep, Willie,' he said. 'I could feel it – though the keep was cooler than the night air outside. For I felt a little fear and I was ashamed of my cowardice – which is a habit that gets men killed – and I showed my shame with the sweat on my face, and that made me fearful all the more in case you or Fromme or Jens or Karfreitag saw my shame and intuited my fear.'

I walked close behind him through the keep's main corridor and saw Paulus glance ahead at Jens. He wiped his hand through his hair and across his neck, aware of the sweat crowning his head and running down his back, cold and thick – his body a swamp. Paulus pulled at his collar, sodden and chill, and wiped his cuff across his wet face.

Paulus later told me that he was thinking then of the cruelty of God. How if there was a wolf in the cell and it broke free that begging God would not help him or any one of us a jot in the course of fate. God would not help or listen. Only God, he said, could be cruel enough, distant enough, to make his children suffer even when they begged him to let them die – like Job.

★ ★ ★

Aged twelve, Paulus had knelt in the yard of his family home in the great grey city of Munster and cried to God to die. His mother raped by man after man – soldiers – in front of Paulus and his father and grandparents and his brothers and sisters, in the yard before the family's printing shop. Then stabbed by one soldier still on top of her. His father and four grandparents beheaded by men who took bets on how many blows it would take to sever a neck. Sisters raped and stabbed. Paulus and his three brothers were told to fight. The boys wept and hugged each other. They were told that the last one standing could live, but only if the winner killed the others. Paulus was the biggest, the oldest, and knew he would win. He lifted a sword one of the soldiers had thrown at his feet. And then it stopped – as officers and priests arrived and told their soldiers to disperse or risk grave penalties. One officer said, 'The killing is over. No more, or you risk grave penalties exacted in God's name.'

Paulus got on his knees – just twelve – and cried to God right there to kill him on the spot. The officers and priests thought he was asking them to kill him, and they would not do it, and God paid not a tinker's thought to Paulus and his wishes. An officer bundled him up in a coat and took him away, out to the field of flags and cannon and row upon row of men and horses and siege machines – out through the city gates and beyond the city walls.

Paulus told me he often had to shake his head – to clear it of these old thoughts. That night, I saw him stop in the keep's long, dark corridor, shake his head and then walk on, and I followed behind.

At the cell door, Jens glanced back at Paulus, who walked slow – and even stooped some now – up towards the locked room, and in his look Jens held a little disgust and pity that I saw. Paulus straightened himself, readied his shoulders hard, and wiped his sticky damp face again with the back of his green coat sleeve.

He said to Jens, 'What are you looking at? Open the damn door.'

'It's no shame,' said Jens, 'to have a little fear of the Devil.' Though, in his heart, I saw Jens did think it shameful for fear to show so clear on a man's face the way it did with this Paulus who just a moment ago was marching around proud and cocky like Alexander in Babylon.

'Get out of my way, Jens,' said Paulus – and he walked through the studded wood doorway into the hot thick glowing stone cell of Peter Stumpf.

I followed him in, and Fromme and Karfreitag came behind. The cool air of the corridor died on my body as I entered the room, and I began to sweat and pant now too.

★ ★ ★

Stumpf sat burned and cut and bloodied and beaten, dressed in a torn potato sack on an iron chair, inside a double cage – an inner one of wood, an outer one of steel. The heat was unbearable – a killing heat. A fire two foot high blazed in a hearth. Stumpf sweated and flicked his head back, tossing drips from his eyelashes and beard and hair – little wet diamonds in the dark, orange air. He wiped his brow on the sack, against his shoulder – his hands fixed in grey steel links between his thighs, his feet manacled to the floor. A chain round his waist fastened him to the iron chair.

As the cell door closed behind us creaking, it sent a skin-shiver of cool outer air through the room, and Stumpf seemed to bathe in it. He sighed as it washed over his body, and looked at us, running his eyes, soft and almost dreamy, until they fell on Jens. The prisoner held his eyes on the sheriff as if Jens was a slave, an urchin – a pig to be cut and flayed and eaten.

Paulus walked slow, toward the cage, and the prisoner studied him – the way one would a map. Stumpf looked to Paulus' boots, his belt, his green hunting clothes and black gloves, the short-brimmed riding hat Paulus held in his hand.

Jens shouted, 'Stumpf – the inquisition has arrived for you.'

'They can have you after me, Jens,' said Stumpf.

Jens cut in front of Paulus – like a dog anticipating its master – turned on the spot, looked around the room, and finding nothing he could use as a weapon on Stumpf – no spike or gaffe to poke hard through the cage slats – lifted a coal scuttle near the fire and scooped up a cup of hot embers from the hearth.

Paulus said, 'What do you think you are doing? Put that down and get out.'

Jens stood still, hesitating, and gawped. Karfreitag marched towards Jens, took the scuttle from him and led the sheriff out of the room. The door shut.

Paulus approached the cages and said, 'Paulus Melchior – I am the legal authority in your case and in this town. You answer to me now, alone.'

'Peter Stumpf.'

'So you are a man with a name?'

'I am a man.'

'Not a wolf?'

'Not a wolf.'

'Nor werewolf?'

'No.'

Paulus signalled to me, and I drew up a bench before the cages. Paulus sat, and I sat beside him. Fromme remained standing behind us. The prisoner lifted his chains as if to say, 'If I was a werewolf would I still be in these and not at your throat', and a waft of stink came from him, that made me cough and lower my head. Neither Paulus nor Fromme reacted.

Stumpf cast down his head, and said, 'I apologise for my condition.'

'They said you confessed – though not in writing – to being a werewolf,' Paulus continued.

'They beat me. I am not.'

'But you are a murderer?'

Stumpf waited a moment, not thinking of his answer I saw, but holding back for impact, theatricality, it seemed.

'Yes,' he said, and the word came out, snaked between his tongue and teeth.

'How many have you murdered?' asked Paulus.

'A great number.' Stumpf frowned and shook his head – weary, sagely – then smiled, his gumline red with blood, and teeth fresh broken like shaped flint razors.

Paulus nodded and said, 'Very good.' He turned to me and tapped the satchel, sitting unopened in my lap. I took out my notebook, pen, inkhorn and sand bottle – and with the pages balanced on my knees began to write. Paulus felt no fear now, I was sure. This was a man not a wolf – a boy like me could see that, so Paulus was calmed. He took off his green over-jacket, folded it and laid it on the floor by his feet. His shirt beneath was green too and sweated through.

'Go on,' Paulus said. 'Your confession is heartening because it is quick.'

'I've killed many, over many years and am caught now.'

Paulus cleared his throat. 'They say you had a magic girdle – in the indictment. That when they found you killing a child and pursued you, that you were in wolf form and as you fled, you threw off a green girdle and transformed back into a man.'

'I know what they say. Sir, if you were a wolf – and pursued by soldiers – would you throw off your girdle and change back to a man – to be caught and end up here?'

'Perhaps the Devil inspired your imprisonment for some wider plan,' Fromme said behind us.

'No, that is not the case,' said Stumpf, looking past me, over my shoulder to Fromme, 'I have confessed but I will not tell stories for this town. If I was a werewolf, would I look like this?' And Stumpf showed off his face to the firelight, tried to turn his bound arms and legs – his chains rattled as he moved – so we could see the poker burns and cuts, the welts and bruises, his new lost teeth, a black plug of blood in his nose, closed eye.

'You've been beaten. That is all. What if I torture you?' asked Paulus.

'Then I will say what I said when I was being beaten – that I am a werewolf – but it will not be true. Have you been tortured, sir?'

'I am the questioner, Master Stumpf, and I am no inquisitor, though my friend behind me follows such a calling. I can bring the rack in, however, if I please, on civil authority. It is within my power and I have no compunction using the powers granted to me by the state.'

'I do not wish to be tortured any more and that is why I am telling you the full truth now, sir,' Stumpf said – he beseeched but he was not cowed.

'There are some sixty-eight deaths, I believe, committed in the Bideburg municipality that you do not deny,' and Paulus clicked his fingers at me. I rooted in the satchel and took out a ream of paper rolls and folders and ledgers, making up the indictment and written notes I had made on the case before we left for Bideburg. Paulus spent five minutes in silence, reading, flicking quickly to and fro between the pages – counterchecking and clarifying his train of thought.

'Yes, sixty-eight – at least – it is written here,' said Paulus, 'including the child three days ago, are all admitted.'

'Yes, sir, they are.'

'Then perhaps I should hand you over to the church,' said Paulus, and he jabbed his thumb over his shoulder in the direction of Fromme. 'I fear as the civil authority your crimes may be outside my remit.'

'Why, sir?' asked Stumpf – and now he was afraid. Better be tried a murderer or rapist or thief, than taken by the church as a witch or devil or werewolf.

'As you must be part and parcel with the Devil. What man does this – kills nearly seventy souls, some babies I read here?' And he tapped the pages in front of him.

'The Devil?' Stumpf asked, a smile in his voice, though not on his face. 'No other man has ever killed so many people as I without being in league with the Devil?'

Paulus sat back in his chair and studied Stumpf – looking for some sign in his bearing, his face, that might explain his nature. Stumpf played soft, I could see, and let himself yield to the gaze. He could tolerate being a new-found beast on display for a little while.

'You are a man with voting rights, I see,' Paulus said.

'I am a wood-mill owner and a timber merchant.'

'Very good,' said Paulus, and he returned to reading his papers.

'May I ask?' said Stumpf.

'Ask what?'

'Will this be a long night?'

'I believe so – I am something of an owl in my working habits.'

'Then may I ask for some beer or wine and a little food. I have not eaten or drunk since yesterday night.'

Paulus frowned and said, 'Of course. A good idea. We are hungry too.' He called for Jens. Karfreitag opened the door and allowed the sheriff back into the cell. Paulus instructed him on the food and drink we all required. Jens returned with plates and jugs and cups – sniffing and put out – and was dismissed. Paulus passed food and drink to Stumpf through the bars – chicken, pickles, some black rye bread – careful, I could see, that his fingers did not cross the threshold of the grille where Stumpf's hands could touch or grab his own, and we all ate as Paulus continued his reading.

'So why do you care?' asked Paulus, without looking up from his papers. He sipped from his beer.

'Care for what?' asked Stumpf.

'Whether you die a man or a wolf. You will die anyway – probably the same death either way. In fact, the people here in Bideburg might feel more disposed to a werewolf than a madman who killed for pleasure – as the wolf can't help its nature. A madman's death might be worse.'

'I can answer,' said Stumpf, as he ate, politely, tidily, the chains clanking when he lowered his head to the plate in his lap. 'If you are a man, would you like to die as a werewolf, when that is not what you are?'

'But let us say that I torture you to make you say you are a werewolf – why not just admit the lie and die easier?'

'I had been told,' said Stumpf, 'that the proper legal authorities were to try my case. That I would be listened to, and judged fairly. So I have told the truth.'

'Have you indeed? Why would a killer ever tell the truth – your nature is lies and wrongdoing. Whether you are in league with the Devil or not, your soul is destined for Hell for you have behaved on Earth like a creature that is not human.'

Stumpf sagged in his chains. 'I tell the truth, sir. I will not have the people of this town say wolf blood runs in my veins, or the veins of my children.'

'You have family?' asked Paulus. He sheafed through his papers. 'That is not written here.'

'I have family, sir. A wife, two daughters, two sons – though my sons are married and do not live in Bideburg any longer. Thank God.'

'Are you wealthy?'

'I am wealthy, sir.'

'How wealthy?'

'I have more money than any other citizen in town – many times over. And they do not like it. They envy my land.'

'This is not a case of tort, sir,' said Paulus, and put down his plate. He drank a swallow of beer and sighed happily.

Fromme spoke. 'So, a rich man and a werewolf,' he said.

'Not a werewolf, brother. I have sinned, but only as a man.' Stumpf drank awkwardly, hunching over to lift the cup to his mouth – his hands were chained to his waist-link, and bound too tight to rise higher than his breast.

'Perhaps it is being rich, which makes you lie,' said Fromme, wiping a dab of grease from his chin, clean-shaven and cool. 'An executed rich man will still be rich in death. An executed creature, which has consorted with the Devil, though – why, the church will have your holdings, sir, and all you have. And we will have your family too – for what family would not know that the head of their household was a sorcerer, a werewolf. They would be as full of guilt and blasphemy and sorcery and heresy as you. Your wife a whore that mated with wolves, your children – half-breeds, half-human, half-wolf or devil.'

We all jumped, all except Karfreitag, as Paulus clapped his hands – palms crisp and woody now, despite the heat, the sweat and fear long dried on him, his green shirt cooled, its damped stains disappeared. 'I see. Very well then, we will play a game for the sake of your children and your wife, Stumpf. A religious game, a legal game,' Paulus said, and he stood and, taking Fromme by the arm, walked to the far wall with a quick step, out of hearing.

Stumpf sweated on, the heat eating him, his heart at a gallop, I could see, his breath fast and shallow. Paulus could be speaking to Fromme about the bringing in of the instruments of torture so that they may be shown – then accepted if there was no confession forthcoming, and then used. I did not know what they discussed. Stumpf waited, giving himself to waiting as the only act he had power left to carry out – and then I saw his eyes freeze in his face, his heart and soul dying, and I knew that he was thinking that life now for him was just one act of fearful waiting – and then blackness. If not blackness, then God or the Devil.

Paulus took something from Fromme and walked back across the cell, at a clipping pace, his green shirt billowing, making for the cages. 'Sit straight,' he shouted, advancing, and he threw something at Stumpf. Vitriol, I thought, for I saw a glass bottle glint, Stumpf must have feared the same for he flinched hard, but the chains stopped him covering his face. Only water splashed on him, though – tepid and dull.

'Drink this,' said Paulus, and he thrust a small brown glass bottle up to the bars of the cages. Stumpf took it and drank – it was the same bottle that splashed him.

'Holy water does not burn him,' Paulus said to me. 'Note it.'

Paulus put his right hand slowly through the double cage grille of metal and wood – all the way in – and offered Stumpf a consecrated wafer.

'Eat,' said Paulus.

Stumpf took it, careful not to touch Paulus, and put the wafer in his mouth. It stuck to his palette and he pushed it down his throat with his tongue. He opened his mouth wide to show it was gone and swallowed, gulping.

'Recite the Lord's Prayer,' said Paulus, hot now, and sweating again, his green shirt darkening to black almost, stuck to him, his voice sharp and excited, frightening.

Stumpf prayed – not bowing his head, or closing his eyes, but watching Paulus.

Paulus clapped his hands again when Stumpf said, 'thy will be done', and pointed at me – almost throwing his finger – ordering, 'Write that he prays to Jesus.'

'Now denounce Satan,' said Paulus.

'I denounce Satan,' said Stumpf.

'Kiss this.' Stumpf kissed the crucifix Paulus passed him.

Paulus swept back his wet hair and took his seat close to the cages again.

'I will try you as a man,' he said. 'But I will have to make your death hard.'

'I am a man,' said Stumpf. 'I take your judgement.'

Fromme stood behind again, quiet. I could not see him, but I could feel his anger, his resentment, throb from him, the way you feel your wife's displeasure without her needing to cast a look or open her mouth. His anger filled the room more than the heat from the fire.

Paulus shook his head from side to side, like a dog jumped from a lake, sweat flying from him now. Though this time from excitement not fear. He had forgotten Fromme and did not look to him or speak to him.

'Get ready to write, Willie. And use your quickest shorthand. I want no words missed.'

His wildness was making me sweat now, and my heart raced. The water dripped from my nose onto the paper. I wiped my face with my cuff, and readied myself to write. The room stifled with the fire. The notebook – black leatherbound, and set with a gold buckle – on my knee. The uncorked small white ivory inkhorn – no bigger than a little finger – on the bench beside me. I dipped in my pen. The sand bottle to dust off and dry my pages as I turned them was between my feet on the floor. I leant over the page, and my pen danced in the air, in anticipation of what I would hear.

Paulus leant far over, so his face was near the cages, and said, 'So Stumpf, tell me about the first.'

Chapter Nine

A history of the Dummy tradition of Bideburg, and a full report on the first murders committed by Peter Stumpf, accused as the werewolf of Bideburg.

'We called them dummies,' Stumpf said. 'Do you know of our dummy tradition? Back when the war started, and the rebellion, the country was full of the wandering poor. Are you old enough to remember? I must have nearly ten years on you, Master Melchior. Whatever – there were many more wandering poor when I was a boy than there are today. God give thanks to insurrection and uprising. A few of these travelling paupers even arrived in Bideburg, seeking work or charity. We are a hard town to stumble across – forest and lake and river and mountains, one road in, one road out – but some unlucky folk made it here. A number chose to live in the woods for a while; others arrived lost, looking for somewhere else – none planned to come to Bideburg. We had no work we could give them. We were a hard-working little town, with nothing to go around, and already did all our jobs ourselves. So, to justify our charity – for we had some sort of duty to feed and shelter these people, not wanting to look at them dead in the street in front of us – we told them to keep the birds from the fields. Scarecrows are no good – birds soon realise they are not human beings – but a real person stationed all day in a field can run up and down frightening away the birds. And these people – they looked like scarecrows anyway. There were soon so many poor that each farmer – even a smallholder like my father, for my family was poor when I was a boy – each farmer had one dummy for each field. My father had one dummy – we had one field – a woman called Berta, and her daughter.

I was fourteen and at nights me and some of the other boys – like Jens, who is my age – we'd go and play with the dummies. We even played with the ones who had menfolk with them. Most were alone or with children, but if there were men there – then what would they do? It was the fields or the road again, and if they did fight back there were six or more boys to one of them.

Some nights, when we went to play with the dummies, we'd find our fathers there before us, and held back watching, and they played just as hard as we did, and if truth be told – for that is what I am here to do – they knew we played with the dummies too, though that was never acknowledged, and we never acknowledged their games either. I guess – though I do not know – that our women, our mothers and wives, knew as well. Again, I guess, that they also kept their mouths shut. You should ask them. Women of my age or older.

My family's dummy, this Berta, was from Munster – though this was before the siege – or rather some village near Munster, I think she said. I listened to her only for what I needed to hear. It was during the war, when the land was in chaos and she'd fled with her children. I know nothing of her husband, nor why she came here – whether it was by accident or design.

Berta was still young – maybe twenty-five at most – and her daughter eight or nine, perhaps. I'd accompanied my father to the town hall on the day this latest batch of beggars – Berta's batch – were assigned to the smallest landowners, the last in the queue for dummies – which had caused no little agitation among such hardworking folk as my father. They asked, "Does it not say 'the last shall be first'?" And a promise had been made – back then, in the first days of the war and rebellion, we still had a lord – that if more beggars came they would go to the smallholders of Bideburg. The day my father and I went to the town hall was the day the poorest farmers were collecting on the promise from amongst the new arrivals.

On the walk back to our farm, Berta was wild with thanks, and crying. I say a farm, but we grew crops to feed ourselves – and sold no more than a tenth of our yield in a good year. Berta, though, even danced and hugged her child.

At the door of the farmhouse, my mother appeared – a whirlwind with a broom, sweeping dust and droppings before her, mad-haired – and she called a halt to us all in the yard. My mother walked towards Berta, and placed the tip of the broom against the young woman's breast. She said, "You must work to justify your keep here. There are six people in this house – myself, my husband, my three sons and one daughter. There are two of you, with your child in tow. The yield and profit from this farm must rise by thirty per cent, therefore, or you do not justify our charity. Everything has a price, and I am not to blame for your circumstances."

Berta smiled – a real honest smile – and curtsied, very genteel, and thanked my mother with genuine words. "God love you for your kindness, madam," she said. She knelt then in the dusty yard and kissed my mother's hand. Berta told her daughter to kneel too, and the girl obeyed, and in turn my brothers and sister and I, and my father, we all stood before them so they could kiss our hands as well.

Berta was beautiful as she knelt, with her head bowed and her eyes down, and she kissed my fingers. I allowed one finger to trail across her lips, opening her mouth, as I walked away – and my sister took my place.

It was exactly this time of year – high July when children go frogging. Have you seen our children frogging? Watch it while you are here. I chose not to go frogging that day – despite being the Master Frogger of Bideburg, for that's what my friends called me, I may add. Instead, I stayed with my father to show Berta the shed that she and her daughter would be sleeping in – for we had no barn, and had to use the half dozen communal ones – and then I led Berta to the field she'd be watching over.

Berta was safe in our shed. The shed was built up against the farmhouse and no-one could have interfered with her without my mother, or some other else, hearing. The dummies most at risk of being played with belonged to the bigger farms, and slept in outhouses and private barns – from where they could be taken to the woods, or played with quietly on the spot.

I decided to make Berta my friend. She worked hard on the family farm. I'd greet her at dawn with milk and bread, and at noon bring her and her child stir-about and buttermilk in their field. I did not talk much, but if the time allowed I'd sit with Berta while her child paced the field, instead of her, scaring the birds away with claps and hooshes and whoops.

On most farms, the dummies were soon doing more chores, during the day, besides dealing with crows. They were digging latrines, wall building, sharpening, weaving, clearing stony land so it could be cultivated. Most farmers and their wives soon found there were many jobs dummies could do – apart from scarecrowing – so they could have a rest and put their feet up, smoke a pipe, cook a good meal, talk, pray, whatever the owner wanted and could fashion out of their dummy's time and work. Our holding was so small, though, that aside from mending and washing the few clothes we had, and feeding and cleaning the pigs, and such like, there was little for Berta to do. Dummying was her main and most task. My mother would not let her cook, so she spent the vastness of her time in the field. Still, it was my mother who made most use of her, when she was not a scarecrow. My father liked his tasks and wanted no help at all with hefting and lifting and man's work. He stayed away from Berta.

Berta offended no-one. She was humble, polite, and so, unlike most dummies, never beaten. She seemed intelligent too – not lumpen like the rest. She might have been a lady once, for all I know. The people on the road were of all kinds – there were some wealthy and disowned, for the armies of the holy poor were starting to reclaim the lands of the rich and of the church now; but mostly on the road the roaming, landless people were peasant-bred, either fleeing from the Landesknecht killing the poor wherever they could be found – believing all poor must be rebels and intent on terror – or fleeing from their own kind for fear of being forced to fight in the army of the holy poor. Berta told me nothing of her past, though, and for a while I was happy just to sit with her. Still, being accustomed to anyone too long makes them as common as the forest floor – my love runs hot and cold – and Berta made no sign of wanting to be the friend to me that I was to her. I still stayed by her, though – some – but the hours with her became less and less. Times came when I sat by her a while and felt I was a ghost, and my stomach turned.

A good year passed, and then it was announced that a troop of yet more beggars, maybe twenty, was a day's walk from Bideburg. The farmers and their wives wanted indeed, they said, to take them in – and they meant this, truly. But they had done the arithmetic and there was no room in barns and sheds and outhouses, or enough scrimped food to go around – despite the extra hours to be had in bed or at the stove sipping wine and beer. We needed no more dummies, it was decided, or we would have nothing to do in the town but eat and sleep – and honest people like at least some hard work, they say.

That afternoon I brought stir-about and buttermilk as usual to Berta and her child – who looked on me now as something regular in their life and reassuring like a daily cock crow, or the stars coming out, or sleep arriving. I took Berta aside and told her that my mother and sister were going away to see our aunt, dying of scrouf or plague or miasma or something – I do not know exactly what I said. I scared her – I told her my father and brothers planned to have some games with her and her daughter that night – for dummies talked to each other when they could, and knew what went on.

"I have taken my family horse," I told Berta, "and tethered it in the woods." If she came with me now – her and her little girl – they could ride wherever they wanted, get away, sell the horse somewhere and live, perhaps. She agreed, and thanked me, crying. She did not ask what trouble

I might find myself in for helping her and stealing my family's horse. Or beg me to run away with her either.

I took them to the woods, deep inside, where the horse was tethered, and I drew out a knife. I tied the child to a tree and gagged the girl, and on the forest floor I had all manner of games with the dummy Berta. I ate some of her, if truth be told. I've said it now, and it is true. She tasted sweet and gamey, and her blood on my tongue – it had the tang of licking new iron.

When I was finished, I did the same again to the little girl – who tasted better. Young flesh does taste better – like lamb does, or veal calves or piglets. This time, though – with the little girl – I was much slower. I had learned so quickly with Berta the risk of rushing ahead too fast.

I cut a lock of hair for memory's sake from Berta and her daughter, and buried them where I killed them – and I can take you there now. No-one knows of this, and there was no need to confess it to you, except to prove I speak only the truth to you.

I took the horse back home. My family presumed the dummy simply ran away with her daughter – they often did that. It didn't matter. The next day the new band of beggars arrived, and my family took the oldest female child from a family of man, wife, baby and this girl we now owned aged twelve. I was fifteen by then. I don't remember what happened to the rest. They moved on, I guess, as no other Bideburg families or farmers needed any more dummies.

I did not get to know this girl. I left Bideburg for the army life.'

★ ★ ★

The sky was growing lilac when we left the keep: ahead, stars were dying, the sun hiding, waiting to rise, just under the rim of the Earth, the moon's smile disappearing with the night. Jens padded behind – half spaniel, half slave.

Paulus told Karfreitag to go to the inn, wake his best man from among the troop and ride to the Stumpf house.

Jens said, 'I already have two men posted there, sir.'

Paulus ignored the sheriff, and said to the sergeant, 'Treat the family decently. They are accused of no crime. Tell them I will visit them after I have slept.'

Karfreitag walked to the inn with Fromme, the priest, to find his boy and then set off to his own quarters at Pastor Barthelme's home.

'I need to sleep now,' Paulus said to Jens, 'so take us to your house.'

'Sir, I have been ruminating,' said Jens. 'I would like you and your young scholar here to take my chambers – and my wife's chambers – it would be an honour of great magnitude.'

'I don't want your room, Jens. Just make us up somewhere quiet to sleep – a bed on a floor would even be fine.'

'Sir, I could not broach such an inhospitable act – it would offend me, to my very soul.'

'Jens – I have no desire to listen to your wife roar when you drag her from her sleep. A bed, that's all I need, for a few hours' rest. And I have orders for you to carry out before you sleep yourself, so you may not want to waste your worry on where I put my head down.'

We walked to the town crossroads, and took the east road that cut through miles of fields and homesteads and farms till it came to the foot of the wide mountain ridge. With the night paling, the mountains loured up fiercer than before. The Steipplingers swept a semi-circle round the town, hugging it hard and forested from north, through east, and to the south. The Bideburg river slit the town off on the west. Bideburg lived on its sliver of cultivated land between hard old rock, forest, and fresh running water – unknown to the outside world, and knowing nothing but what happened in this shut-off space ringed by stone and water and wood.

A few middling-sized farms dotted the side road to the Jens' house. Paulus counted out his orders to the sheriff as we walked. The Jens' house was a few miles' trudge from town – it sat at the foot of the black towering south-east range of the Steipplingers – a looming wall, pitted with the broken fingers of trees clinging to the black earth among the dark rock.

'Order one, Sheriff Jens,' said Paulus, 'is this: Stumpf has confessed to two more crimes – of a woman and her child, a girl aged around eight or nine, killed thirty-five years ago, more maybe, when Stumpf was still a boy. He buried them in the woods. These are his first murders. Go back to him, do not harm him, get precise directions and send a party of your men to exhume the bodies. Immediately. Two…'

Jens stopped and said, 'Without question this beast is lying to you, sir, and wasting your precious time. There was no werewolf in town back then.'

'That is my point, Sheriff. I need to know if these victims exist – so do as I tell you. Get the bodies dug up.'

'Very well, sir. Though, if we do find bodies, how you tell if they are a woman and a little girl, as he says, is beyond the knowledge of man. Could it not be a man and a boy, or woman and a dwarf. Whatever they are, if they are there at all, they will be nothing but dry bone.'

'Jens, I can, from a skeleton, ascertain sex and approximate age.'

'Sir – really – it can not be done. There will be no flesh left, no private parts, if they are thirty-five years dead, to see if they are man or woman or what – except dead.'

'The pelvis, Jens – the hips and their structure. A female skeleton has a different pelvis to a male.'

'Is this true, sir?'

'Yes. Women bear children, Jens. They are different.'

'What about telling a child from a midget?'

'Jens – male, female, child or dwarf – there would still be two bodies in a grave in your district that Stumpf has confessed to killing. Do you understand the duty of bringing a case to law by fact?'

'Sir,' said Jens.

'And to finish our lesson, the joints and bones of a child are different in shape and structure – density and wear – to that of an adult, whether full-sized or dwarfen. For pity's sake, Jens. Do you read? Can you read?'

'Of course, sir, I read the Bible often in church for the congregation.'

'Well, stretch yourself and read more – more than just the Bible. God gave you a brain to use, not for it to sit and turn to grey soup in your skull.'

Jens dogged his eyes down, and Paulus paused. 'Secondly – I want to speak to the family of the accused. Not at the keep, but at their home. Take me to them when I wake – and tell no-one about this visit I am planning, especially the Stumpf family. Thirdly, wake me no later than noon. What time is it now?'

'Gone four, I would reckon, sir.'

'God, I am tired. Fourth, once Stumpf has given you directions to the graves, I want you to unchain him – at least his waist, free him from the chair – so he can sleep lying down. And give him a blanket if he wants one, and water.'

Jens looked at Paulus as if he had defrocked God. 'Sir – what? He should be strung up by his toenails and flayed alive – not allowed to sleep in comfort like a pet dog.'

'Jens, just do what I ask of you. Things will be quicker that way, we won't have to spend so much time in each other's company and neither of us will die of old age before the task in hand is complete. I want Stumpf fit to talk. He has confession in his heart, and I am taking it. The Prince-Bishop will want to hear every last detail of what Stumpf has to say, every syllable. I would not be the man to let him down, Jens.'

'As you say, sir,' said Jens, trotting to keep up with Paulus, who marched on ahead, even though he did not know where he was going and had to be pointed in the right direction by Jens at the appearance of every fork in the path. Jens, with studied timing, kept himself always just two paces behind Paulus.

'Fifth, and lastly, arrange a meeting of the town council at dusk – after I have met with the Stumpf family – so I can brief all the relevant individuals.'

We were at the door of the Jens house now. The sun was almost risen and the sky was dawn-blue and blush. The Jens house was big and tall, and well-made of blonde wood, its shutters painted red and yellow, a blue door dead-centre, flowers hung from the cornices, and green summer seats were set in front of a rustling kitchen garden. Pretty was the word – like a handsome housewife – though the black Stiepplinger Mountains, sat aloom, and towered deadening and dark over the house.

'Now just a bed, or a quiet spot with a blanket on the floor somewhere, Jens. I want to be – I will be – asleep in five minutes.'

'We have an empty servants' room, sir.'

Jens opened the door, and said, 'May I ask, sir, the details of the werewolf's confession? The circumstances of these two new murders?'

Jens was put out that he had been excluded from the cell and missed the werewolf's story. But he had been a good spaniel on the walk from town. Jens led us inside, bowing and ushering. The house still slept. Paulus whispered, 'It was some beggar servant girl.'

'Pardon, sir?' said Jens.

'Some beggar girl his family had as a servant – and her child. Dummies he called them. They are the new victims he told me of – the ones in the grave.'

Jens asked no more questions. He took us to the empty room, at the back of the house.

'Goodnight, sir,' said Jens. 'Goodnight, young master,' he said to me.

'God bless,' said Paulus, and he was asleep within five minutes, just as he had predicted. I had no troubled dreams – though I hoped Jens did – no memories on the cusp of sleep that kept me stirred up and frightened, wakeful with worry and the past – for I was not guilty of any long-forgotten crimes.

Chapter Ten

The home of the werewolf Stumpf is attacked while the Prince-Bishop's party sleeps through the night.

Divara and her mother Madame Stumpf. And the little mouse in the wainscoting, Rosa. I had not met them yet, though I would in a few hours, but if I had known then, as I lay my head down to sleep, what was happening to them at that moment, I would have picked up a sword and pistol and ran through the dawn to their home. Instead, I slept, and later was told, by Divara – and Karfreitag who arrived as instructed to stand guard over the women – of the events at the Stumpf house on the night of our arrival.

As Paulus finished the first of the interrogations with Stumpf, his wife and daughters were cowering in their home – sat north-east of the town, in the forest which the family owned – and their dog pack howled in the kennels behind the house. If they set their mind to it, a troop of killers from Bideburg would take no more than an hour's steady walk to reach the Stumpf home. East at the crossroads, then north along a dirt path leading through fields to the fringe of the forest, and then, on through a winding woodland track to the Stumpf home sat amidst the trees. Now rich, the Stumpf family owned the long-dead long-deposed local lord's hunting lodge. It was big and as grand as many a manor house – though the lord's manor, which had sat some miles further east, had been burned to the ground during the war, and was now communal land. Of the lord's properties which remained standing after the rebellion, such as the lodge, they had been bought and sold among the more wealthy townsfolk over the decades. Stumpf had bought this home nearly twenty years back when he knew he would never be poor again and could afford the property of a rich man. His sons were already walking by then. Divara was born within a year of the Stumpfs taking possession of the lord's old lodge. Rosa was a long time coming.

As I slept – blanketed on the floor by the bed which Paulus lay in –
Divara and her mother were in Madame Stumpf's room, huddled together
at the foot of her oak bed – draped in heavy green covers and white sheets.
They held hands. There was a bang – then another – like a foot kicking a
door. A thin scream came from the wall by them. Madame Stumpf ran to
the wall and said to the wood, 'Be quiet, darling.'

Then another bang – the noise came from outside, from downstairs,
at their door, the great white door that led into their clean, wealthy home.
And the dogs in the kennels behind the house took up their barking and
yowling.

Madame Stumpf gasped and touched her daughter's face. Her
daughter held her hand – and another cry came from within the wall.

Divara rose now, slowly, and walked to the wall; she pushed at it, and a
man-sized panel in the wall swung open; inside was a hiding hole, the size of
a standing coffin. The little girl, Rosa, sat hunched, her hands to her head.

Divara knelt down and said, 'You must shush. You are safe in here, but
only if you make no noise. Yes?'

'Yes,' said the child, and she gripped Divara by the shoulders and
pulled her sister to her.

Rosa's mother appeared over her sister's shoulder, and said, 'You must
be brave. You can not cry out any more or I will punish you.'

Divara petted her sister, and Madame Stumpf said, 'Divara', and Divara
kissed Rosa and shut the wall panel. The child looked at them, but said
nothing, as she was closed into darkness. Madame Stumpf put her mouth
to the wall and said, 'I love you, Rosa. Be quiet and all will be well. Cry out
and you will have us killed.'

Men shouted then – Jens' guards – and the women recognised the
voices. Madame Stumpf and Divara had thanked the men for keeping
watch over them, before the house was closed up for the night, though the
men had only shrugged and nodded. Then, though, there came the voices
of other men, more men – there were only two guards, and there sounded
at least four or more men opposed – and these voices were louder, angrier
and were shouting down Jens' men.

'Blow out the candles,' said Divara – for the light flickered at the
window in the lilac night. 'It won't be long till dawn.'

The women got up and hooshed over each flame. They returned to the
foot of the bed, sitting on the floor, not touching any longer. They both

looked to the wall. The small fire, though, burning in the grate, cast orange wisps and curls around the ceiling – its light sure to be seen in the night, from outside. The women stared at the fire now, and the shadows and dancing light. Divara pulled her linen night-gown hard across her knees, put her head down, and held her feet. Her mother sat alert, ear cocked, eyes wide.

Another bang – a kick, for sure, at the front door. The dogs outside barked louder. The wall was silent.

'If the guards run away we are dead,' Divara said.

'Have they gone?' her mother whispered, hard.

'I do not know. I will go and let out the dogs from their kennels.'

'No,' her mother said. 'They may be behind the house as well and take you.'

'We have guns,' said Divara.

'We have, Divara,' said Madame Stumpf. 'Get them – and we will keep ourselves safe in this room.'

Divara crawled across the floor to the chest by the far wall, and opened it.

'They are loaded already,' her mother said. 'Just light them.' Divara took out two fine silver inlaid hunting pistols – big-barrelled and hefty. She put a taper to the orange coals in the hearth and then held it to pistol cord so the guns were lit and ready to fire.

The shouting was up close by the main door of the house now, it rose up the staircase towards them, came into the bedroom – the rolling noise turning to words. Whores. Witches. Murderesses. Cannibals.

Then there was calm – silence – the dogs had stopped barking as well – then there was talking again – for a long time. Low and murmured. On and on it went – a quiet churning drone, the words could not be made out, but fast and blurred too – like a cattle auction. The women sat beside each other, touching hands again. They looked only at the wall. There was silence. The sky came undone from the last hold of darkness. It blued, and reddened with the rising sun. The women dozed for a moment. Then the shouts started again – this time screams and demands to have the household taken outside – for burning, for execution, for harbouring a wolf.

Divara and her mother rose and sat with their backs to the wall, now – with little Rosa behind them, hidden by the panel. Their pistols on their skirts. They talked to Rosa, through the wall, as the men shouted. Divara told her that they would play tomorrow in the garden with a puppy, and

Madame Stumpf said that she would have the men at the door whipped and hanged and their property taken from them. Rosa was good to her word and said nothing. She waited in the dark and counted her toes and fingers over and over again until the number ten, the word ten, meant nothing to her but a noise as cruel as the men screaming outside.

'We will kill the whores,' a voice shouted. The dogs in their kennels took up their howling again.

One of Jens' guards ordered, 'Stand back. We know you. You must go.'

A shot was fired. Hard and brutal in the weak morning light. But a sign of worse to come, for sure. The faintest little squeak came from the wall. Divara and her mother scuttled across the floor on their knees, saying 'shush, shush', and knelt on the thick Turk rug before the door. They held their guns in front of them.

'Step back or I will fire again and this time aim to kill,' Jens' guard shouted from outside the great door.

Then another shot sounded from further away – down somewhere on the road to the house.

'Jesus, more are coming with guns,' said the mother.

The women crawled to the window, and chanced a look. Down below, six men – they were masked, but they were townsfolk no question – the men were walking backwards, slowly, away from the house. Jens' two guards followed them, advancing, also slowly, guns up. They were telling them to leave – that much was clear.

Another two men appeared on the path to the house, on horseback, guns also raised. The dogs were barking in a steady rhythm now – one dog leading, the others following, a chorus of howls behind the barking beat.

'Soldiers,' said Madame Stumpf.

'What does that mean?'

Her mother said nothing.

The two riders were dressed in breast-plates and steel gauntlets, greaves on their legs, rimmed helmets. The soldier in charge, it seemed – for he had the coloured sash of an old Landesknecht across his breast, and the other younger man did not – dismounted, and walked up to the nearest townsman. The old soldier took the butt of his gun and stove in the face of the townsman. His teeth came through his mask and the villager went down like a poleaxed heffer. The soldier stuck his gun to the head of the next masked man nearest to him. The other younger soldier, still mounted, moved his gun from one townsman to the next, smoke wisping from the firing cord set in the barrel. The townsmen put down their weapons now – knives and hoes and shovels and scythes only, no guns – and moved away from the soldiers and Jens' guards then, dragging their bloody half-dead friend with them, and made for the road to town. The soldiers laughed and aimed kicks at them. The dogs barked. As the men ran, they pulled off their masks, and one turned back and looked up to the window where the two women watched. Madame Stumpf saw his face. It caught the sun, fully up now. It was Odil. He drew his finger across his throat, smiling, and ran onto the shadowy path to town. The two soldiers shook hands with Jens' guards and patted them on the shoulders, then they pointed to the head of the road leading to town. Jens' two guards took up position there – placed pawns. Karfreitag told his junior to tie up their horses, and then our two soldiers stood square in front of the house – sentinel, until we arrived, much later than we expected. By then, though, even the hulk that was Karfreitag was swinging on his heels, faint from lack of sleep. We relieved them, and ordered them to rest, after taking full report of the events of the night and morning.

The little girl Rosa was taken from her hiding hole. The panel in the wall was an affectation of the lord's when he owned the Stumpf house as a hunting lodge. It was a lover's nook – where he could play with his mistresses. It smelled dark and deep. Rosa cried when her mother and sister opened the wood panel, and said she wanted to stay inside the wall – and eat and sleep there, take her lessons there – for it felt safe now and she was not scared of the dark any longer. Her mother told her to shush, and her sister lifted her out, but was soft with the little girl and kissed and petted her. Rosa smiled, but her smile was flat.

★ ★ ★

Divara told me days later – when we had become closer than blood – that her mother Madame Stumpf thought to go outside then and thank Karfreitag and his man, but feared to do so in case they had come to kill them as well – but, as soldiers of the state, were ordered to act more honourably than the men of the village, who would have raped them and slit their throats. Perhaps these guards from the city planned to wait until the allotted time and order them outside for hanging on a tree. Maybe they had only saved their lives from Odil and his type so the state could exact its punishment on them formally and judicially. Still, the mother took the two hunting pistols, and snubbed out the firing cords, unloaded them, and put the guns back in the chest. She knelt on the floor in front of the chest, and slumped. Her shoulders heaved.

'We are dead women,' she said.

'Bed,' said Divara, and she took her sister Rosa from the room. The child cried, and said, 'Let me stay and be with you.'

But Divara took Rosa's twig of an arm and walked her down the hallway. She kissed her sister, and raised her finger and pursed her mouth – a warning to Rosa not to speak and make Divara cry too. She pointed to Rosa's bed and the child slunk under the covers, and lay, turned to the wall away from her sister.

Divara returned to her mother's room. Madame Stumpf still sat, head on her chest of guns.

'We have done nothing wrong,' said Divara.

'Who will believe that?'

'Who will believe any of this? It is nonsense.'

'It is not nonsense. Your father is what they say.'

'They say fairy tales and slander.'

'He has confessed to sixty-eight murders, they say.' Her mother's voice rose. 'Sixty-eight. He was found with a child, for God's sake, Divara.'

The mother shuddered – like a current of cold water had run through her – and put her hand to her mouth. 'A child, Divara. Oh my God.'

She got up and walked the room. 'Murder and ruin and shame and death, Divara. We are finished. We are dead. As dead as him.'

'Mother,' said Divara, 'we are safe – there are men outside guarding us. Would they be here if we were to die?'

'Keeping us prisoner for whatever they will do to us, maybe. They stopped Odil and those other animals from coming in here to us, that's all – but they may want to deal with us their own way.'

'What have you and I done to be dealt with?'

'We lived with him,' her mother said.

They sat again on the floor, in front of the fire, and were quiet.

'You must look at this,' her mother said, after a while.

Madame Stumpf went to the chest and took out a deep dark long wooden box. She brought it to Divara, sat down beside her on the floor and opened the lid. Inside, there was a green felt base, padded. On the felt there were dozens – it seemed – dozens of little locks of hair. The forget-me-nots that mothers take from their babies or lovers take from lovers. The locks were tied in black velvet ribbons and pinned with golden tacks to the felt base.

'What is this?' asked Divara.

'I do not know,' her mother said. 'I found it in your father's room.'

Divara ran her fingers over the locks of hair. There was soft hair, like the hair of newborns; wiry twisted hair, kinked like an African or Jew; grey, brown, blonde, dark, red. There were short tight bundles – the hair of men – and longer locks, of women and children. The hair of the children was easy to identify, still so silky though cut long ago. All these little tied bundles of human hair, pinned and placed on the green felt cushion.

'Have you counted?' asked Divara.

'Sixty-seven.'

'Then that's not sixty-eight.'

'There was the child he was found with. If he had not been caught, and had taken the child's hair, you would have sixty-eight locks in this box.'

Divara shrugged and said, 'I have no idea what this is I am looking at.'

'What else is this, Divara? Tell me now?' Her mother's voice came hard at her, scolding, demeaning.

'It could be anything.'

'Go take this to the soldiers outside and tell them you think this could be anything.'

'Mother, be quiet,' Divara said.

Her mother threw the box of hair across the room and stood. 'Take it,' she shouted. 'Take it or talk to me as the woman you now are, and not as some simple spoiled child.'

Madame Stumpf reached down to her daughter and grabbed her hard by the arm, dragging her half-way to standing. 'Get up.'

'Mother,' shouted Divara, trying to sit back down – the women tussling, awkward and clumsy.

'Get up and do as I tell you or sit and listen to me and do as you are told.'

She pushed Divara away from her and the girl fell heavily back onto the ground.

'What do you want then?' Divara asked.

'Burn this with me,' her mother said.

'Fine and well,' Divara said. 'Burn it.'

The women went to the little fire in the grate and unpinned each lock of hair. They threw in the red and the blonde, the black and the brown, the young baby hair and the old foreign hair. It lit and frazzled on the logs, bitter-smelling like burned bone, shrivelling like slugs under salt, and it vanished in the fire – all the locks of hair, gone – moth-dust between fingertips.

'We have to be compliant,' her mother said, as they burned the last lock.

Madame Stumpf walked towards the bed and lay down.

'Get out, Divara,' she said. 'And take that box back to your father's room. Get it away from me.'

Her mother fell asleep. Immediately lost to the world.

Divara picked up the box and walked into the hallway, bright white and burned with dawn light. She opened the door to her sister Rosa's room. The child lay on her side, towards the door, and looked long at Divara.

Divara smiled and Rosa smiled back. The child shut her eyes.

Divara shut the door and walked down the great staircase to her father's study.

★ ★ ★

While killers ringed his home, and while Paulus and I dreamed like babies in the servants' room at the house, Stumpf did as he did every night as prisoner – for he came to tell me of his routines and thoughts, and he was a man of routine and much thinking, I learned.

In his double cage, inside the cell, within the keep, Stumpf tried to sleep, curled on the ground, still chained by his foot to the iron chair, riveted to the brick floor. The fire was dead now in the black mouth of the hearth, and the air gone from hell to winter. Jens had given Stumpf a rotten horse blanket when he returned to take directions, as instructed, to the dummies' grave site. He did not want the prisoner falling ill now in case it angered Paulus. Stumpf pulled the blanket, thick with a horsey stink of sweat, around his back and belly. He shivered but willed himself to rest – to be gone from the world for a while and lost in a dream, for his dreams could be sweet, and sometimes took the shape of the myths of old times, in the state of nature, when men and women lived without work or war or shame or suffering or wealth or guilt.

He felt himself dropping low and almost gone, and saw himself in this first Eden – a community of naked men and women living and loving in a glade, with fruit dropping from the trees, no need for clothes as the sun always shined, and it never rained, and the body was not a source of filth. No blood was ever spilt among these people of the lord.

Stumpf was not with these people, though, or their lord – he was in the trees of the glade, watching them. The few animals they kept were hoofed – and these were for milk, no blood was ever spilt – the rest roamed free like the men and women, undisturbed.

But Stumpf decided to capture an animal and eat its flesh. And he brought death into the world. Then from his watching place in the woods, Stumpf saw that men began to take wives, and claim land, and make other men their slaves. And God – did nothing. The lord did not walk in the Garden. He did not play the hide and seek of death with men and women to chastise them, as was told. He did not call, pretending he could not see them, 'Adam, where art thou? Eve, where art thou?' He was not there.

The glade became a town and a city and soon spread over the world – and it was a ruin, of smoke and beggars and whores and kings and canker and despair. Yet Stumpf remained hidden behind his tree, considering this world of God as it played out for him, watching and still unseen. Stumpf slid back into the wood – after months and years of watching – far into the forest, away from the towns and cities and world, to the deep trees where men and women only came to play now when they left their war and work and death and starvation – drawn to what they once had but had now forgotten – and he watched them there in the forest, where they were soft and weak, when they were soft and weak, in the place that had once been theirs as a paradise but which they had long since abandoned and left for the towns and cities, corrupted into a sink of loss.

And then Stumpf – he sneaked out of his watching-spot and he came upon a family of these creatures – violent, cruel, ugly, forked, ruinous – and he killed them. He butchered them and bludgeoned them, he stamped on their faces and broke their backs, he opened them and let himself go over the purple string of their deep insides, and he ate them. Ate them so he could retreat to the woods and his watching-spot and pass them out from him – consumed and destroyed, though tainting him through their touch and taste as he exorcised them from the world, and his body.

And he rose imposing above their land, he dreamt, from his forest hiding place.

Chapter Eleven

Morning on the first day in Bideburg, and Brother Fromme and Pastor Barthelme become acquainted despite their differences.

Brother Fromme was called bleary at eight in the morning by Pastor Barthelme's housekeeper. The two men had said little more than 'hello' and 'sleep well' to each other the night before, after Jodel, Fromme's boy, led him to the church house on Far Hill – on the south road of town, close by the Dark Hedges, as the townspeople called the high steeple of trees that led, by way of a natural tunnel, into Bideburg.

Fromme had promised Barthelme he would relate everything that needed relating come the morning – and thanked him for his hospitality, one man of God to another, although they sat on different sides of the great dividing question which asked how man and woman communicate and worship their creator: one of Rome, one back turned to Rome. Still they wished to be affectionate despite the gulf between them – for they saw themselves forward-looking men of their times. Barthelme had seemed friendly – sleep-bedraggled but friendly – and genuinely solicitous the previous night. Now it was the morning and Fromme made his way, coughing his announcement, to the dining room were Barthelme sat at the head of a dark wood table. Jodel had been sent to the kitchen to eat with Barthelme's servants. The dining room was decorated with painted tiles – blue and white illustrations from Delft, maybe, of Bible scenes, of Job, and Jonah, of the Fall, and Christ's resurrection – hundreds of these pictures lined the walls. Fromme took a seat at the opposite end of the table to Barthelme. Sitting to the side would be a little too submissive. The housekeep served honeyed porridge and warm, spiced wine. The men ate and talked quietly, with Fromme explaining to a nodding Barthelme the legal situation now in place in the town, the official stamp of court business on the process in hand, and the role the clergy must play in supporting the officials of the state in their duties.

Barthelme asked, 'And how does this affect my position in town, sir?'

'Cuius regio, eius religio,' said Fromme. 'It is your town and your religion. As long as you hold loyalty to the Prince-Bishop as the ruler of the realm, then it matters not what your religion is or mine, or indeed the Prince-Bishop. He recognises your rights, you recognise his. It is the fit of the times. Render unto Caesar and so forth.'

Barthelme nodded, dipping his head to his plate for the last spoonful of porridge.

'Indeed,' Fromme talked on, more to himself it seemed than Barthelme. 'The settlement at Augsburg was for everyone, not just the Emperor and the church of Rome and the likes of me, but for you Lutherans too – you can worship as you please, as can I. You just happen to have a different route to God than me – and I will not burn you for it, as we all worship Jesus Christ. I do not have to agree with you, however – and you do not have to agree with me, as the treaty of peace said, but we are no longer heretics in one another's eyes. Too much Christian suffering has been caused by turning disagreement into action rather than debate. We need to be united against the Devil, not divided over schisms which the Lord in Heaven would surely find a waste of time in the universal fight against Satan.'

'Putting the past to rest has been a long time coming,' said Barthelme, bringing his hands together as if he were praying. Though clearly Barthelme was not praying – for he was smiling, wide, at Fromme. 'Though still the followers of Rome ascend more quickly to power and money than those who seek a different way.'

'Sir, as proof of friendship,' said Fromme, 'and as proof that I value you and your hospitality – and as a sign that the future can be ecumenical – may I ask that you accept my offer to become my aide and advisor on all matters – including religious ones – while I am here in Bideburg? I hope you do not find this presumptuous or patronising.'

Barthelme was flattered – relieved, even excited that this Catholic inquisitor from court would offer friendship to an unvarnished Protestant preacher from a backwoods town, for that is how he thought of himself – and with his country clothes and simple peasant face, that is how he looked to all the world as well.

'Sir, presumptuous, no, sir. And, of course, yes I would be glad to assist, if you think I would be of any aid to you at all,' Barthelme nodded. 'I doubt in matters of state and law I can help you, though, but I know the people of this town well having grown up among them during the revolution and the war and now in the peace.'

'Local knowledge is a most precious thing,' said Fromme. 'For any inquiry.' He took a purse from the hip pocket of his brown coat and opened it. When not at his work – in the interrogation room, or courthouse, or the corridors of court – Fromme wore the clothes of a petty merchant, not a brother of the monastery. Barthelme, though, was got up as if he was about to address his congregation. Fromme counted out twenty gold coins, put the money back in the purse and said, 'Please, take this. All of it. I wish I had more. It is for your hospitality.'

'Exceptionally kind, sir,' said Barthelme, rising from his chair and walking to Fromme's side to take the money. 'I will use the funds for church charity.'

'As you wish, sir,' said Fromme, and he pushed his empty plate away. 'Now, may we talk a little business for a moment now that breakfast is over?'

'Certainly, sir. I am at your command.' Barthelme drew a seat up close to Fromme's right elbow and sat down. He smiled wide.

Religious differences – even ones which had spilt the blood of one hundred thousand people for decade after decade – such differences could easily be resolved if two believers in the one true spirit of Christ sat at a table together, talked just as men, and ate and drank – of course, it helped if one had absolute but quiet power over the other, and sweetened the power with friendly words and money.

'This Stumpf,' said Fromme. 'What is he?'

'Sir, I am in no doubt that Stumpf has consorted with the Devil. I have lived here the forty years of my life and known Stumpf all that time. He is an ungodly man and brings ungodliness wherever he goes. A werewolf has terrorised this town since Stumpf returned from the war – fighting first for the Protestant armies against your Catholic Princes, but later fighting against the revolutionaries at Munster when your Catholic Princes and our Lutherans joined together to wipe them off the Earth as heretics, lunatics. God be praised.'

'God be praised, indeed,' said Fromme. 'A blessed union that fruited the peace of Augsburg. But why a werewolf? How do we know this? Did he become a werewolf while in the Protestant armies?'

'I do not know, brother, but the bodies that were found were ripped to pieces and eaten in parts. I have seen these bodies over the years and said prayers for them. Even if he wanted to, the strongest, most cruel man on Earth could not with his bare hands, or even with knives and axes, do what I saw done to the bodies of the werewolf's victims.'

'And how did this happen – that a man can be a wolf?' asked Fromme.

Barthelme had not been to university, but he had read the biographies of learned men and their recollections of student days, and felt that here he was being taken through his paces like a scholar by his logic professor. He liked this challenge – and it sparked his mind – for he knew he had the answers, and the wit, though it was left unused in Bideburg.

'The constables who came upon him eating the boy some days ago claimed at first it was a giant wolf that was feeding on the child,' Barthelme said. 'It fled – as they approached, firing. Then as it bounded off, it seemed to tear a green belt or girdle from its hips, and change into a man – into Stumpf. The soldiers saw the transformation, and emboldened now that their quarry was just a man not a giant wolf, chased harder, closed on him, and beat him to the ground with staves and clubs. The girdle is lost somewhere in the woods.'

'Indeed, I have read the reports. Is that all we have?'

'Sir, these are the reports of men with their own eyes – and Christian men. I have given much study over the years to demonology and witchcraft. If this were just a case of demon possession it would be bad enough. But a werewolf, sir, a werewolf breeds werewolves. This is known. I have books on it,' and he rose to fetch a book from a nearby dresser.

'I was reading this morning before you rose about other werewolf cases,' he leafed through the book in his hand till he found the page he was searching for and showed it to Fromme – there was a woodcut engraving of a werewolf, holding a child and eating its head, men fired at it from a distance. 'See,' Barthelme said. 'It wears a girdle, given it by the Devil to aid its transformation.' Fromme nodded. 'And here, this chapter tells how,' Barthelme continued, running his finger along the lines, 'the families of these creatures are contaminated and so cursed themselves – either, to one day become wolves too, or to pass on this wolf blood to others through mating. The spouse of a wolf is contaminated through intercourse, and the children – why, they are in the worst of all cases, for they are not fully human, but part conjured wolf. Where the curse first started, it is hard to say, but some say it was handed down by Cain after the fall of Adam, others that it is a price Satan puts on a pact. If I were to offer myself to Satan for money or power, then he could, it is written, say, "Very well, Barthelme, but you will put on the wolf's form for me at night and kill good Christians – that is my price. And here's your girdle." Of course, this is not the price of every pact, just some. And think on this – if you do not know it already – Stumpf left this town a penniless boy and returned from the army a wealthy man. Within a matter of years, he wasn't just wealthy, he was the richest man in town and owned half of Bideburg – even most of the old lands of the old lord. He rubs the people's faces in his wealth.'

'I have read the same books as you,' said Fromme, 'and I see that you and I, we think not just similarly, but hand in hand. So together we must look more deeply into the arguments for trying this case not as subject to state law, with the accused arraigned a man, but under church law as a werewolf.'

'My library – what there is of it – is at your disposal, sir,' said Barthelme.

'Thank you, sir,' said Fromme. He cast a glance at the handful of tatty old books on the dresser under the dining room window, and rose from the breakfast table. 'Again, I thank you, but now duty bids me go.'

'Do you need me to accompany you, sir?' asked Barthelme, eager to follow.

'Not just now, sir. I have closed business with colleagues which I would not be permitted to bring you to – for now, at least – but in future we shall work close together in tandem, if you would do me the honour of giving me your assistance.'

'Of course, sir. It is my honour to help you destroy the werewolf Stumpf and his family.'

And yet, despite this new friendship, the matter of 'sir' still hung between them. They could not be fellow brothers, or 'father', or 'reverend', to one another – their division separated them forever, in this life and the next, although they both loved their God with a ferocity which could have summoned storms and torn Bideburg from its moorings.

Chapter Twelve

Paulus is forced to run, much against his will, to the town of Bideburg, where he finds the werewolf under interrogation without his authority, and we learn what Paulus saw as a boy during the rebellion of the Elect in Munster.

I stirred slow and softly – coming awake over minutes, stretching, turning, eyes flickering open and closing again. A seam of light registered in my mind, but I turned again, sighing and smiling, eyes still shut, the blankets warm like a womb – deep and safe. My eyes opened, hazy, again. Bleared. They closed. Opened. Things were clearer now. I was in an unfamiliar room. Curled up on the floor. There was a window. Curtains – drawn. Strong yellow light outside. A dresser. Chair. A door. A bed beside me. Paulus sleeping in it. Jens' cosy house. A woman singing somewhere down the hall. Smell of bread. Paulus sat up in bed and rubbed his face. It felt later than noon – but it couldn't be. Jens hadn't called us.

We rose with few words. Paulus opened the curtains and window and, while I dressed, he splashed his face and rinsed his mouth at the washstand on the dresser. The day was warm and blue. Children were laughing at play in the fields outside. Paulus dressed while I washed. He put on his green hunting clothes and brown boots. He left his black coat and gloves behind on the bed, and walked from the room – telling me to hurry along – with his black brimmed hat in his hand. I was hungry now. We walked as loudly as we could, hard-heeled, down the corridor towards the sound of the singing voice. We didn't want to frighten anyone or be subjected to women's hysterics once surprised – and manners prevented us hollering our approach down the hall. Paulus coughed as he came to what I guessed was the kitchen door. A woman called out, 'Is that Master Paulus, I can hear? And his laddie?'

I looked at Paulus and silently mouthed 'laddie' at him, wrinkling up my face at how peasant this wife of the town sheriff sounded. He shrugged his shoulders.

Paulus entered, and I walked in behind. He offered his deepest courtly bow to a frumpish farmer's wife, with blotched face and hands. I followed suit. 'Madame Jens,' he said. 'A pleasure to meet you, and thank you for your hospitality.'

'My pleasure, sir. An honour. My husband has been and gone, sir,' she said, standing by the griddle cooking hot cakes. She tipped her head to us and whispered, 'Setting about the task you instructed him, sir. The bodies.'

'Your husband is a sheriff like no other, Madame,' said Paulus. She smiled. Paulus pointed to a kitchen table, tippling with vegetables and cuts of pork and beef for tonight's stew. 'May we, Madame?'

'Of course, sir. Sit and I will bring you both some cakes. Would you like some beer or mixed wine?'

'Milk, Madame, please. And thank you,' he said.

'And for me also, please, madam,' I said, pushing some cabbages and onions to the side to make a little room at the table. We sat in well-made wooden seats with carved backs.

'I admire your table and chairs, Madame Jens,' I said. 'They are fine and strong.'

'Made by the Stumpf family mill – from their wood, by their men,' she said – and shook her head as if the furniture was confirmation of devil worship and lycanthropy.

Two cakes sat on a side plate, Madame Jens flipped two more fresh from the griddle on top and set it before us. She sploshed thick, yellow-tinged milk from an earthen jug into a pair of earthen cups and handed them to Paulus and I with a sweet fat smile and a dip of the waist – her best attempt at a heavy curtsey.

Paulus slathered on some soft butter, took a bite and tossed the hot cake around inside his mouth to take the heat from it. He swallowed and took a long draught of milk. 'Madame, can I inquire the time? How near to noon are we?'

'Noon? Oh sir, you've slept till gone two after noon. You were so tired it seemed, I did not want to wake you.'

Paulus grabbed his head with both hands. I stood and looked around in panic, like a frightened chicken. 'Two? Did your husband not tell you or your servants to wake me by noon at the latest?'

'No, sir.'

'Take those cakes with us, Willie,' he said to me. I placed them in my side pocket and ran back to our room for my satchel. He was through the far kitchen door, leading out to the courtyard and stables, when I returned. 'Madame, I am very late now,' he was saying. 'I had many things to do before two after noon. May we borrow a horse, a cart? Ours are still at the stables in town.'

'I would, of course, lend you a horse, sir, but they have all been taken by my husband and his men for the task you set him.' She leaned forward again, and whispered, 'The bodies, sir.'

'Oh hell damn and shit on you all, woman,' said Paulus. Madame Jens gasped and covered her ears.

'Sir,' she said.

'Sorry, Madame, sorry,' I said. He patted his pockets for his glass. It was there. He slapped his hip. His knife was safe on his belt.

'Do you have money on you, Willie?' I patted my own pockets and heard the chink of gold.

'Some. Enough,' I said.

'Goodbye then, Madame,' he said, 'and thank you. I apologise for my profanity.'

Paulus ran out of the gate, heading for the Bideburg crossroads, with me at his heels – Madame Jens shouting 'sir', 'wait', and 'what' behind him. We had five miles at least to go till town. I was a slim youth back then – and although not a great sportsman, I was fit and strong and fast. Paulus, though, since his army days ended, had done little but drink and read and argue. He was near the age of forty, maybe older – he played lies with his age sometimes – and while tall and broad and still imposing, was heavy like a family horse.

'Running is detestable, Willie,' he said to me, as I padded beside him at an easy trot. His feet hit the ground, hard and flat, the thud jolting up from his soles to his jaw and skull with every beat.

'Running. Not just detestable, but draining,' he said. 'Dull and empty. It blanks the mind – draws it toward death. Running makes thought dead. Boredom, that's all running is – boredom is its soul. And boredom is death. Running. Boredom and panting, and sweat, and a heaving heart and chest. Pounding. Jolted.'

'It is easier if you do not talk, sir,' I said, keeping up a good clip at his side, edging forward to try to spur him on. 'Try thinking of something to occupy your mind.'

'I am unable to think of anything when I run,' he said. 'Nothing from all my books – religion, law, rhetoric, medicine, astrology, poetry – nothing turns to thought except the beating of my own feet on the hard dry mud, pounding in my brain, on this damnable long road to Bideburg crossroads.'

His stopped to pant, hands on knees, and drew a breath like a dying dog.

★ ★ ★

Running. Running. Paulus had told me of his running in Munster. Everything was at a run in Munster when he was young. Life ran. Time ran. He ran. Running to see his father when he came back through the city gate from his deliveries of paper and pamphlets to the towns and villages nearby, in the days before the rebellion. Then, when the great takeover of the city took place, running behind his father and cheering the salvation of Munster – that it would be the city of God and all its inhabitants children of the Elect, free and equal, without lords or priests. Then in the first days of the Kingdom of the Elect in Munster, running to bring food, water, gunpowder to the men on the walls, his father among them, to repel the heathen godless armies of the Catholic Princes and their Protestant allies – and winning that first great battle as God's hand moved upon their pistols and arquebus, swords and cannon. Then later running to see his father crowned one of the Elect – as the End of Days approached – Paulus' feet pounding through the streets of Munster as a young boy to the market square before the Kirk where the high stage had been laid out for daily assemblies, and for his father now. All of Munster, in his memory, seemed a place of running and breathlessness.

'Your father is being crowned,' a neighbour had called to him, while he and his brothers loaded pamphlets and free-sheets and post-bills onto a cart outside their family's print-works. Word had whipped from town centre to their street, and Paulus and his brothers left their work and sprinted for the market square. Heart beating and feet thumping, but elated and riding the air with ease, delighted to throw out their legs and swing back their arms and take the streets in bounds till they ran gasping and joyed into the square before the great Kirk where the high stage had been set up.

They ran to the stage as their father mounted its wooden steps. Jan van Leyden himself stood on the platform – dressed like the Lord of Days – arms open to greet Bernard Melchior, as if Paulus' own father were the long lost child of van Leyden, though van Leyden was barely twenty-five and Bernard nearer fifty. A crowd of five hundred or more cheered, and the air rocked and shook afraid with their fervour and Christian love.

Knipperdolling, van Leyden's minister, hushed the crowd. 'Listen, you holy of Munster, we have another of your ranks made Elect here today. Chosen on the instant – on the moment – for that is how it happens when God speaks to his prophet Jan. Bernard Melchior – printer, champion of the cross in the legion of the poor – will be raised by King Jan of Munster, prophet and God's spokesman, here to led you to Heaven and forge this city as a new Jerusalem, which will be a beacon to the downtrodden, low and Christian of the world, and a flaming brand and sword to the sinners, liars and anti-Christs of Rome and Luther at our gates.'

Knipperdolling retreated a few paces, giving way, and van Leyden stepped forward, taking the stage like a galleon taking the wind in its sails and conquering the sea before it. Actorly. He clutched some paper to his breast. 'Brother Melchior – God has told me, you are of the Elect.' The people cheered for Jesus – as if Jesus himself had spoken in the market square. 'And your good works have shown it. This pamphlet of yours that I read just one hour ago,' and he waved the paper in the air, 'it is God's good work you are doing. Praising the host and damning the heretics. And you have fought the fight on the city walls of Munster as a soldier of Christ too.' The people roared their love again. 'So God,' van Leyden continued, 'God has said to me you are Elect, Bernard Melchior. That you are destined for Heaven, and that your family will follow there with you. That you will be here a good counsellor to me in my kingship over our freed city. Are you Elect, Brother Melchior? Do you accept my election of you to the realm of saints on Earth and angels to come in Heaven ever after?'

Paulus and his brothers stood before the stage, heads tilted back, mouths open. Their father did not see them, so fixed was he on his king. 'I do, your holy majesty,' said Melchior, falling to his knees, and crying. Their father had never cried before.

'Rise up, Brother, for you kneel to no man on Earth, only God, and be baptised as one of the Elect.'

Knipperdolling called out, 'Bring up one of the traitors and heretics.'

Two guards in the clothes of ordinary citizens – but with the red armbands of the rebel poor on their sleeves – dragged a woman of perhaps sixty up the wooden stairs and onto the stage.

Knipperdolling called out, 'She was overheard saying that the city could not hold on, that if we had priests to pray for us we would fare better, and that she wished the Prince-Bishop would send his troops in now before we are defeated.' He spat the word. 'This is what she said – and words worse which I will not repeat here.'

The crowd gasped and screamed at her as a whore and witch and anti-Christ. The woman tried to tear herself from the guards' grasp, and shouted, 'Your majesty, I said nothing. I swear by Christ and my life.'

'Are there witnesses against her?' asked van Leyden.

'Her daughters-in-law. They are all married to members of the Elect,' said Knipperdolling.

'Her sons are of the Elect? Who are they?'

'No, your majesty, her sons fled, and her daughters-in-law were given as wives to members of the Elect after their desertion. One is married to my brother minister, Hoffman.'

'Kill her,' said van Leyden, and he slid his sword from its scabbard and offered it to Bernard Melchior.

Paulus turned to his brothers. The two younger boys dropped their eyes to the ground. Paulus looked up at his father on the stage, the Kirk's spire rose behind him like an iron spike stuck in the sky.

The guards pushed the woman to her knees. One put his boot in the small of her back, and grabbed her arms, holding them straight behind her, the other stepped in front of her and held her head out and down by the hair. Melchior took the sword, and swung without word or sound. The blade struck the woman across the shoulders, opening her, and she wailed, terrible and low. The guard holding her hair said, 'Watch out, brother. I have fingers.'

Melchior swung again, hitting her on the back of the head. A deep rent opened and the woman toppled forward. She gurgled. The guards dropped her. Knipperdolling said, 'Finish her off.' Melchior put his foot on the woman's back to still her, for she squirmed on the ground like a worm split in two, and took off her head with three more blows. It rolled from the stage and onto the ground before Paulus and his brothers. Her body gushed. The crowd whooped.

'Give me the head, boy, quick,' said van Leyden from the lip of the stage.

Melchior looked and grinned wide and said, 'My sons, my sons – you are here to see my glory.' He bowed to them, proud that his boys had witnessed this great moment in his life.

Paulus picked up the head, with both hands, by its ears, and offered it to van Leyden – the neck ran with blood. The King of Munster bent low on the stage to reach. Van Leyden rose, with the head in one hand, held by the hair. The crowd cheered for Jesus. Paulus wiped his sticky red hands on his thighs. There was vomit in his throat and his mouth ran with water. He spat on the ground, in the blood, and breathed soft and shallow to hold himself down. Van Leyden put one arm around Melchior, pulling him close, and lifting the old woman's head, addressed his people.

'You have all been baptised with blessed water,' said van Leyden, 'not just once as an unaware child, but a second time, by my hands, as grown men and women – as witness to your consent and dedication to the gospel of Jesus Christ and the battle for the poor as revealed through our martyrs and prophets. You would not be here in the city of God without taking that second baptism. But those among you who are Elect – now welcomed and admitted to Heaven while still in this life – take one more baptism. This third. The mark of a soldier of Christ, washed in the blood of sinners and heretics. For the flesh of a saint can clear the taint from any blood. And that is what we practice in the name of God and Jesus Christ ever after. Amen.'

The crowd responded in hushed church voice, 'In the name of God and Jesus Christ ever after. Amen'

Van Leyden lifted the woman's head over Melchior, but it had nearly bled out, a few drips and clots fell on the printer only. Van Leyden shook the head, trying to force the last spatters onto his new minister of the Elect. A final spit of pink freckled Melchior's face.

Van Leyden rubbed the neck across Melchior's forehead, marking a bloody cross on his brow, and threw the old woman's head from him into the crowd, and shouted, 'Elect! Elect! A new minister of the Elect!'

Melchior smiled, wide and wild, and trembled, throwing back his head, and held up his hands to Heaven praising God and eternal Jesus and the holy saviour King Jan of Munster, champion of the common people.

Paulus watched as other boys in the market square kicked the woman's head between them – his brothers too – running with it between their feet, down a side street, whooping and shouting. Cheering. His father was taken by van Leyden and Knipperdolling, and a group of guards into the old city council house – now the Palace of the Kingdom of God and the Holy Poor. Van Leyden's wives, led by his queen, were at the great door of the Palace, welcoming all inside.

Paulus ran then – exhausted. Ran back shaking and sweated weak to his street, his brothers still playing in the square, to his mother and her skirts, and the quietness of their shop's back printing room when the press is quiet and stopped, but still warm from its work. It was a blessing to end his running then. And he wanted his father never to return.

★ ★ ★

Paulus drew up, breathless at the crossroads in Bideburg. I trotted to a halt beside him. Two of Jens' town constables were dawdling in the street outside the inn – nothing to do now that we had charge of Bideburg – laughing and pushing one another.

Paulus tried to shout, hands on knees, panting, 'You two, come here at once.' But his chest rasped and his voice dried in his throat. He walked to the men, holding his hips – like a woman, I thought. He straightened up, and dropped his hands, and the two constables drew to attention.

'Where's Jens and where is my colleague Fromme?' he said, gathering himself.

The taller, seemingly more intelligent one, said, 'The sheriff has led a party of townsmen to the woods to search for these bodies as ordered, sir. That is what you told him to do, I am told.'

'Yes.'

'And my colleague the priest?'

'He is with the werewolf, sir.'

'No,' said Paulus. The men looked at each other. 'Willie, run ahead.'

It was two or three hundred paces from the inn at the crossroads to the keep, backed up against the wall of black mountain, and its forests. I ran. Paulus walked slowly behind me.

At the keep, two of our soldiers, now on guard, waved me through the dark double doors and I strode the corridor, to the holding cell. I walked in, fast, without knocking. The cell was bathed in orange again – the fire relit in the big black mouth of the hearth – and flickered yellow from the torches and candles placed around the walls and on the floor and table. The air smelt sick, like fright, and musky, sweated out. Fromme stood by a tall wooden board in the centre of the room – the board seemed to tremble and shake and vibrate. Our last two soldiers held the board upright in place. All three turned to look at me as I walked towards them.

'Tip him up,' said Fromme.

The wooden board was set on a pivot, like a see-saw, and the men pushed down on its upper most tip. The men pushed and the board swung one hundred and eighty degrees – as it turned, the far side came toward me and the near side vanished, and Stumpf appeared, dripping and gasping, struggling, strapped to the plank. Now straight up again, vertical once more, Stumpf faced me. A deep bucket of water sat behind the board, puddles on the sodden uneven floor.

'What are you doing, Brother Fromme?' I asked.

'This creature is talking. Go tell Paulus. It can not take the ducking stool. It seems to fear water above all else. Look,' he said, and waved to one of our soldiers, the youngest of the pair in the room. 'Fetch that poker.'

The young soldier drew a poker from the fire – an orange spear. He brought it to Stumpf's face and Stumpf cowered from the heat and threat, but kept silent.

'Now look,' said Fromme. 'Dunk him,' he said to the other soldier.

Stumpf screamed as he was tipped upside down once more, 'No, no, please, I will tell you…' And his screaming turned to gargle and bubbles as his head went under the water. His body shook and writhed, and the board bucked and sprang.

'Get him up,' it was Paulus, standing in the doorway to the cell. He stepped forward into the room, walked to the board and pushed down on the top of the plank, lifting Stumpf from the water.

'No, no,' said Stumpf, as he was brought straight again. 'I am a werewolf. I can find the green girdle.' And he slumped in his bindings and would have slipped to the floor half-dead had he not been tied.

'Why are you acting without consulting me?' Paulus asked Fromme. 'We are here to work in accordance with the lawful governance of this town.'

'My dear friend, I am certain this creature is a werewolf and is tricking you. You were not here to consult with – I did not know where you were, but I believed I had to take action in order to preserve the lawful governance of this town. I fear the Devil is at work and I must act against him with all the talents I have.'

'Consult me at all times, and do not act without my say-so. I thought we had that understood,' said Paulus. Fromme stood with his hands behind his back and nodded. He kept his head lowered. Paulus told the two soldiers to cut Stumpf down and return him to his double cage. Before they took a knife to the ropes tying him, they hooked an iron collar attached to a dogcatching pole around his neck – the kind used to keep captive rabid dogs at arm's length. They cut Stumpf down and he collapsed. The soldiers shunted him forward like a cumbersome parcel for rough delivery – pushing him with the collar and pole, and kicking him when he fell forward, too faint and weak to move.

'Stop it,' Paulus said to them. 'Unless you want me to kick you like that. This interrogation is over.'

The soldiers prodded and pushed Stumpf into his cell as gently as possible now.

'Bring him some food and drink,' Paulus told them. 'Any more injury happens to this man and I will replicate it on your bodies threefold. I need the prisoner alive and well.'

Paulus led Fromme from the room by the arm. 'No more, brother,' he said to Fromme. 'The trial is under my command. Do not threaten your position as religious advisor to my court, or our friendship. You do not need to torture this man to make him speak the truth.'

'As you believe, Paulus,' said Fromme. 'We will see if he speaks honestly, soon enough, I imagine.'

'I am happy for you to begin checking him for signs of compact with the Devil and such like, as law agrees – but later. Not now. I fear this is a man we have before us not a devil or a wolf or a sorcerer, and so it is a matter of state not church.'

'Why fear a man?'

'What man would kill like this?'

Chapter Thirteen

An understanding is gained of the Bideburg custom of frogging, Madame Stumpf and her daughter Divara are met, and we are Greeted full well.

The Stumpf house lay deep in the Bideburg woods, but it was not difficult to reach. Stumpf had ordered his hired men to swathe a two-mile connecting path, linking his home to the mid-section of the East Road leading from the town crossroads. That was nearly twenty years ago, and Stumpf's men had kept the path clear, with cutting back and rolling twice a year – for not many walked this path, unless they were invited and had personal matters with the Stumpfs at home, and so the way could get overgrown without tending. If anyone wanted Stumpf on business – which many did – then all they had to do was walk to the very end of the South Road, just before the Dark Hedges, to where his timbermill and merchant yard sat. He was often there. More often there than at home. Stumpf liked to keep his home and work well separated with lots of wild running woodland between house and mill.

Paulus and I turned off the East Road onto Stumpf's Path, as the locals called it. He'd brought the more intelligent of the two local constables he'd found loitering outside the inn with him – for direction, he said, and to act as introduction. Raben was a fine young man. With a decent set of city clothes, he could have passed for a green student – if lifted from the backwoods to a university, and taught to drop his accent.

'Can you read and write?' Paulus asked, as the three of us walked the narrow stone path, that cowered from the close woods on either side.

'I can, sir, and it is a pleasure for me.'

'Good – what do you read then?'

'I read the Bible of course sir, but I like the pamphlets that come from the big towns once a month or so. I like the stories of events happening around the world. There was one, maybe six months ago, which I still read – about the savage people in the New World. That they go naked, eat human flesh, that they have hundreds of gods they believe live in trees and rivers. I would love to see such places.'

'As would I. What else?'

'Well sir, there is a regular pamphlet written by a Cologne trader – in Welsh wool, I think – a very rich merchant, now moved to London in England on business, who writes of the court there, and their customs and whatnot. It comes irregularly by letters he writes to his brother back home who then prints these reports up as pamphlet stories.'

'I've read it. And what do you make of the heresies there, as some call it?'

'Sir, we are a recognised free town here, and have been since the war and treaty. Our loyalty is to the Prince-Bishop as the ruler of the land in the name of the Emperor, not the church to which either belong – though some here still believe in Rome, and that is fine – we leave them to it.'

'I asked you about your thoughts on the English court, son, not a disposition on the status of your town – interesting though it may be for you to relate.'

The lad Raben looked mortified.

'Still,' I said, to help Raben out, 'the English can hardly be classed in the same rank as Luther, can they? Their old King seemed to change his God every time he changed his wife. Now he is dead and the country is ruled by women and doesn't know what it is – Catholic, Protestant, a friend of the Empire, a friend of Spain. Weak and vain – and propped up because it is ringed with water and no-one can bring it to heel.'

The lad smiled and nodded his head.

'It is just talk to pass the time, son,' said Paulus. 'Speak as you please.'

'Well,' said Raben. 'To pick a fight with the church over simony and corruption, of elevating wealth before the poor, all that is right and fine and any man should have the power to choose how he worships Jesus Christ. But, from what I understand, if the pamphlets are correct, making war on God over who sleeps in your bed, can not be supported theologically as it seems not to come from a holy place. As a Lutheran then I can not condone what goes on in England.'

'How old are you, Raben?' asked Paulus.

'I'm nineteen, sir.'

'You are bright. What does your father do?'

'Thank you, sir. He owns a stretch of woodland sir, and a decent farm.'

'Your family must have dealt with Stumpf then?' asked Paulus.

'Yes. My father trades nearly all his wood to Stumpf,' Raben replied. 'We have had to sell off parts of our property to the Stumpfs over the years when debts were tight. There are two older brothers of mine working our remaining land, so my father bought me this commission to the constabulary, as I will have to make a lot of my fortune myself. Another brother has enlisted in the army, and my eldest brother has been bought a position as a steward in one of the great houses in Cologne – it is he who first sent me the pamphlets of England. Two sisters are married, but we have a very ugly sister who will never find a husband, I believe, and as such she has some claim to the profits of our land.'

'Have you thought of getting yourself educated?'

'My family could not afford that, sir, and I wouldn't know what to do with an education – where it would take me in life?'

'It could take you to the Americas where you could study the Indians, then you could write books about them, not read fanciful pamphlets full of cannibals and dragons by men who have not been there.'

Raben laughed, a little boy bashful laugh, and Paulus, I knew, had set himself to speaking to the young man's father at some point before he left. Paulus prided himself on being a great student-catcher and lifter-up of young men. There was plenty of money from bequests to the college set aside for scholarships for the poor, and Paulus had already put nine young men from the lowest orders through university so far. I would be the tenth. And this boy, Raben, looked like he would follow on my heels. Raben's class was not so low, in fact – his station was probably no better than mine or Paulus as a boy – but what went against him was his age. I would be graduated long before my nineteenth birthday. Poor Raben here would be twenty-five by the time he was through with his studies. Still, Paulus could spot them – and when he did think he had a young lad from a meagre background ready to be raised up, he would lend them books for entrance exams, put them forward for scholarship, and even let them stay in his quarters while they settled at the college if they passed and matriculated. This young Raben would make a great Paulus Boy.

Halfway along the Stumpf Path, the wood cleared back some from the road. It was hilly here, and the road wound upwards. A glade opened up on the left, a little way further, and beyond the glade a small waterfall plunged off a black cliff. A din of squeaking could be heard. The squeaking was loud even above the rush of the waterfall. Squeaking and crying – like dozens of new born babies were being pinched and bitten. The squeaking came from down below the cliffs – where the waterfall must find a stream.

'What is that, Raben?' asked Paulus.

'I think it may be children frogging, sir,' said Raben.

'Ah, frogging, let me see. I have heard of this.'

Paulus hopped and skipped – jumped a few times – eager over the little drumlins of the glade. He clambered up a slippy ridge and looked down into a small gully – the waterfall at its head, and a white-foamed stream leading out into the woods between two gentle sloping green banks, thick with dark brown reeds and golden bulrushes nodding in the water's edge where it slowed its flow from the falls. Children were playing on the closest bank. Four of them – two boys aged ten, perhaps, and two girls, slightly older. The children didn't see us as we drew up behind them on the hill.

The children had three weaved baskets with them – with weaved lids. Two of the children were rooting about in the reeds by the bank of the stream, while the other pair popped their hands in and out of the baskets. Every few moments something would flash – like a mirror in the sun, I thought at first, wondering if the children were experimenting and trying to start a fire – but then a squeak would rise up, cruel and sharp.

'They have knives,' Paulus said.

'Shears, sir. For frogging, sir,' said Raben.

Paulus and I watched on, and worked out what was happening in this pantomime – for it felt as if the children were performing, despite being unaware of their audience. Maybe, children perform like actors for each other at that age, I wonder now, though I have no memory of doing such a thing or having such a desire when I was as young as them, many, many years ago. And I was never a father. I had no children of my own that I could study.

The children had set up a production line by relay, a workshop, like a group of artisans. Two children would catch frogs in the reeds, with nets and staves using bits of meat as bait – or so it seemed from the ridge above – though it could have been old carrots or turnip; they placed the frogs in one of the baskets as a holding pen, and then the other two children picked frogs from the basket at their whim and snipped off the creatures' arms and legs – with squeaks and bloody spray. The legs and arms they put in a second basket, and the limbless frogs in the third. The children laughed and shouted and swapped jobs every six frogs, changing places – so the catcher became the snipper, and the snipper became catcher. They carried on like this till the last basket with the limbless frogs quivered from the numbers inside, and the children gave up their jobs of catching, storing and snipping. The children opened the last basket and sorted for the dead frogs, tossing them into the stream one by one. The rest of the limbless frogs in the basket – the still living – they took out and set to various races. Some were raced on the ground – the children picking two or three frogs a piece as their own. The frog to get furthest by the count of one hundred was declared the winner. The tallest girl, red-haired, won this race. The children jumped on the losing frogs – squeaking and burping under their feet – and threw the winner into the gush of the waterfall. Some were raced in the stream. Each child again picked their limbless frogs, and they threw them on the count of three into the water. The frog which lived longest – writhing its ruined body to keep above the water, and bobbing to the surface for the final time before it sunk away – was declared the winner. The tallest boy, fair-haired, won this race. All frogs dead, the children turned to the basket filled with frog legs, and the winner of each race – the tall boy and the tall girl – divided up the meat between them, and used the weaved baskets to take the food home to their parents.

Raben said, 'Of course, if there is just one winner – say, a child wins both races – then they take all the legs. It's a custom – and good summer food, if the legs are cooked with onions and mushrooms, and some herbs and cream. On toast, it is delicious.'

The two winners picked up their baskets and walked from the bank of the stream, up the gully. The losing children followed behind. They spotted us on the ridge, watching them.

The boy who lost – the smallest of the children, and loitering at the rear of the group – shouted, 'Ho! The werewolf man.' And set off at a pelt up the gully to Paulus.

The three other children ran behind him, shouting and crowing.

'Are you the werewolf man?' the boy said – fat in the face, but with a strong little body and a fighter's look.

'Do you mean am I here to find out if you have a werewolf in your town?' said Paulus.

'Yes,' the children all cried.

'Is there one?' the smaller, darker girl asked, the one who had lost.

'Of course there is,' said the stocky little boy.

'Old Timber Stumpf is the werewolf,' said the boy who had won the frogs.

'And who are you?' Paulus asked the loud boy – the youngest, the loser – the bold one who had led the march up to him.

'Willy Jens, sir. My father told me about you this morning – and I even looked in to check you were still sleeping to see if you wanted some breakfast as my mother asked.'

'You should have woken me, young man.'

'Yes sir – this is my sister,' he pointed to the tall blonde winning girl. 'Jenny, Champion Frogger of Bideburg. Are you off to the werewolf's house?'

'Jenny Jens. Well, indeed. And who is this lad?' Paulus asked, pointing at the winning boy.

'Filus Rodinan, sir,' the winning boy said. 'And my sister Flora.' The girl was dark and sallow and lowered her eyes to the ground.

'I have met your father also, children,' said Paulus, and he bowed to them all.

Raben said, 'Right – sket – get on, you lot, and leave the gentleman alone. Get yourselves home.'

'Why? There's no werewolves any more,' said the little Jens boy, Willy.

'We don't need to go home,' said his older sister, Jenny.

'Yes, we can do what we want now,' said Filus, the Rodinan boy.

'And you have the werewolf's house surrounded – we looked,' said his sister, Flora, with sugared slyness.

'Get home – that is an order from the Prince-Bishop,' said Paulus.

The children drew up quiet, gathered in a tight group, threw glances at each other, took their baskets and left, running when they got a few feet beyond Paulus, and taking Stumpf's Path down to the East Road.

'Goodbye, sir,' shouted Willy Jens over his shoulder.

We returned to the path and continued to the Stumpf house – now just a few hundred paces away – an arrow shot.

'What a horrible tradition,' said Paulus. 'Did you do that when you were a child?'

'No, sir,' said Raben. 'Well, I tried it once or twice, but did not like the cries or the game itself to be truthful. But I do love the taste of a good frog.'

We took a dark, leafy bend in the road, and once turned were at the foot of a small hill leading up to a gleaming whitewashed manor house. A whitewashed stone wall slung around it. Dogs were barking somewhere – many of them. Two town constables manned the head of the path in front of us. Two of our men – Karfreitag, his sash tied perfectly across him, and his lad – stood by the doorway, one on each side of the step.

★ ★ ★

Greet told me that she was with the Stumpf women when Karfreitag gave one hard bang to the door of the house when we approached. They jumped like beaten cats, she said. The mother shooed young Greet from the family room to answer the door. Werewolf or not, Greet had decided she needed to work as she needed to eat, so she'd chosen to stay with the Stumpfs – loyal as a good maid could be for the time being, though time was passing fast, she felt. Loyalty ticking down like a clock. Greet walked into the hallway – a wide whitewashed staircase behind her leading up to the bedrooms and storerooms above. There were rooms leading off from the square hall she stood in downstairs: library, dining room, family room, and a passageway by the staircase to the kitchen, pantry and servant quarters and cellar. An open and airy home – all walls washed white. Only a few dim hangings of rural scenes – hunts and hay-making – and heavy brown furniture to save the eye from endless white. Even the floor's dark wood, throughout the house, had been given a wash of white. But the deep brown grain still rose through the paint, and tainted it, like plague on skin. The doors were painted white too. Dogs barked constant from kennels at the rear.

The maid unlatched the door and pulled it open. Raben stood in the doorway. Paulus shifted on his feet uncomfortably – a little too heavy, unworked from a life of sitting it seemed, though Greet said that when she saw him she thought him still good-looking, and very well dressed in his green hunting clothes, with his black hat held in his hands. The two soldiers hovered, listening. The dogs yalloped and whined behind the house. Greet says she did not even see me there – which makes me sad.

'We're here to see the family, Greet,' said Raben. 'Could you introduce Master Paulus Melchior, head of the legal delegation from the Prince-Bishop? Please?'

The girl escorted Paulus, Raben and I to the family room, where a long-legged woman of maybe fifty stood and then curtsied to Paulus as he was introduced. The barking of the dogs was louder now. The woman was striking on the eye – tall, grey hair swept back, still handsome despite her age, slavic at the eyes and nose and chin. Tired though, maybe scared, but composed. Fake aristocracy, I could see. Two girls, obviously her daughters from their looks, also rose – a young woman of coming twenty, perhaps; a cold beauty, tall and dark, cat-mouthed, her mother's likeness cast as reproduction in her face – tired too, and more likely scared, but arrogantly poised, like her mother also – and a girl of ten, at most, too babyish still to be called a beauty, but pretty like a dark doll. She was most definitely scared and meek, and held her mother's hand.

The mother said to the maid, 'Take Rosa, Greet, and entertain her.' She pushed the child forward.

The little girl shuffled towards the maid, and took her hand. Greet and the child left the room – also whitewashed, and laid out with deep comfortable chairs of pale wood and pink cushions, a thick rug of the lightest yellow on the sanded planks of the whitewashed floor. The floor was new. There was a fresh pine smell from the wood. The curtains were drawn back, and hard sunlight stabbed the air.

'My assistant, William Lessinger, Madame Stumpf,' Paulus said, waving his hand at me.

Madame Stumpf turned her head to her daughter, and said, 'This is Divara. Our eldest daughter.'

We bowed to each other, and agreed that we were all delighted to meet.

'Master Paulus,' Madame Stumpf said, pointing to a high-backed chair.

'Sir,' she said, pointing me towards a lower couch.

Raben received no such invitation and stood awkward near the door as we took our seats, Paulus thanking her and offering his warmest respects to both Madame Stumpf and her daughter. Paulus turned his head a little to Raben and said, 'Son, would you be kind enough to go find your captain, Jens, and return. You can take me to him when I have finished my conversation with the Stumpf ladies.'

Raben said, 'Yes, sir,' and clumsily about-turned – he was a poor constable – and marched in bad time from the room.

Madame Stumpf paid Raben no more attention than a departing dog, nodded to Paulus and, pointing to her elder daughter, said, 'I am concerned for my daughter Divara.'

'Divara,' said Paulus. 'I have not heard that name in quite some time. I thought few people would use it any more.'

'My husband fought at Munster against the rebels, in the Protestant armies aligned on the side of the Prince-Bishop and the Emperor. You should be aware of this as he is loyal. The name of van Leyden's queen caught his ear. He thought it beautiful, he said, and brought it back home with him. I warned against it, but it has not brought her any woe, so far.'

'You and your children have nothing to fear,' said Paulus. 'This matter, at the moment – and if you satisfy my questions – attends only to your husband. And his fate is assured, as you well know.'

The daughter, Divara, spoke, 'Would you like something to drink, sir? Wine, brandy? And Melchior is a well-heard Munster name too, no?'

Paulus smiled at her – a broad genuine smile that I rarely saw him give – and he accepted a small glass of wine, as did I. Paulus, as we all knew at the university, had an eye for young ladies with money – and sometimes their mothers, if they were still beautiful.

The wine was from a vineyard owned by her father several dozen miles away, Divara said to Paulus, as if I was not there. I tasted it and it was very good – soft and thick, full of fruit, but not heavy.

'Thank you, ladies,' said Paulus, clapping his hands to his knees. 'Now, forgive me for getting to the meat with little grace or build-up, but time is at my heels, and I must ask you both to tell me all you know of these crimes.'

'We know nothing,' the mother said.

'Nothing,' said Divara.

'They are not alleged, ladies, they are confessed to. He admits to nearly seventy killings – sixty-eight in all – going back to his years when still a boy.'

'And that means what, sir?'

'That he has killed many people, Madame.'

'As a man, though, yes? There is mad talk from everyone, even my household staff, sir – I know that, though they would not dare say such a thing to me. You think he is a werewolf. For God's sake, that is the stuff of grandma tales. Is it not, Divara?'

Madame Stumpf looked to her daughter, and Divara said, 'It is madness, sir.'

'No, ladies – I did not say Stumpf is a werewolf. He is a killer. A lust murderer. This is something I have studied. A man who has killed women, children, old and young men, babies even I believe. Has he not, Willie?'

'He has,' I said, and put my eyes hard onto the two women, who looked ill in their bodies.

'Tell them what we know of babies, Willie,' Paulus said.

'Why?' Madame Stumpf asked loud and sharp – to kill the word 'babies' still hanging in the air, and she twinned her hands in her lap. Her daughter sat unmoving. Their faces were careful – no tears mixing up their minds.

'I do not know why,' said Paulus. 'That is why I am here to speak to you. I would urge full co-operation – these are crimes of magnitude.'

'Are we accused?' the mother asked.

'No,' said Paulus.

The two women were silent in their seats. The dogs carried on barking, barking, barking outside in their kennels – filling up the room with their circus of noise.

The mother turned to Divara and said, 'I want rid of those dogs.'

'Is this all the Stumpf family?' asked Paulus. 'The three of you?'

'No,' Madame Stumpf said. 'Our two sons are also on their way back to town. My daughter made it here a day ago. My boys have further to travel. My youngest child, you saw, still lives with us – with me. I am worried for our safety.'

'It might have been best to keep your family from the town,' Paulus said, and a grey flash of fear ran across the women's faces. 'I do not mean to frighten you, but this kind of case can rile up the uneducated. Thus the men I set at your door to keep anyone from your home.'

'There were people here last night – till dawn – shouting,' said Divara. 'Your guards though sent them on their way. Thank you.'

She tried to smile at Paulus, then turned to her mother, 'That's why we need the dogs, mother.'

'Ladies, I am the man who must try your husband – your father, miss. I would ask that you show me his rooms – where he kept items precious to him, where he may have his journal, notebooks and such like. I would also ask that you get a man you trust from among your workforce and dispatch him to meet your sons on the road where they are coming from and tell them to about-turn and head back to where they came.'

'They should not come?' Divara asked.

'No, and I think you should not have come either, miss. Madame Stumpf, I can spare those other two town constables outside to accompany your daughter if you wish – if you have the horses – and have her leave the town.'

'That will be Divara's choice,' Madame Stumpf replied.

Divara drew herself up straight – proud and like an officer – and said, 'I will stay, mother.' The barking of the dogs ceased for a moment and then began again.

Her mother said, 'Then go take Master Paulus and his assistant to the rooms he needs to inspect. I will arrange a letter and a messenger to halt your brothers before they reach town.'

'This would be best,' said Paulus. 'The fewer men the better.'

Madame Stumpf went to the dark wood dresser – a black spot within the wide, pale room – and took out writing material. She stood to write, leaning on the dresser top. Divara rose and said to Paulus, 'This way, gentlemen.'

She led us to a study and library across the hall. It was dark inside. A reverse of the white light of the rest of the Stumpf home. Deep brown wood on the walls and floor – dark furniture and shelves, heavy dark green curtains almost closed across the window. An unlit cave within the whitewashed house.

'If there is anything of my father's to find in this house, it will be here,' Divara said, opening the curtains to let light in.

Paulus walked around the room, looking at the books Stumpf had on his shelves. The werewolf was well-read it seemed – a lot of history, books on science and geography, many more books on husbandry, forestry, trade and business. Tracts on war and conflict, soldiering, citizenry. Pamphlets, mostly of a serious nature, few with illustrations, about government and politics, were piled up in all four corners.

'How did your mother and father meet?' asked Paulus as he leafed through one text on increasing profit and managing workers in a modern agricultural business.

Divara pulled open the heavy curtains, and hoisted herself up onto a table, under the main window. She sat, the sun behind her. 'After Munster,' she said. The barking of the dogs grew louder still.

* * *

'My father was poor as a child, and left Bideburg to join the army – maybe a year before the Peasant War ended. He remained in the army for ten more years at least, till his mid-twenties, pacifying towns – that is the term

– when later rebellions broke out, or counter-rebellions with the change of order; campaigning in Italy for a while, even, he told me. Munster was his last main posting. He was a platoon commander – mid-ranking sergeant – and with his share of valuables and money after the siege – loot or booty or whatever it is called by you soldiers – he went looking for a wife in the towns and villages between Munster and here, as he made his way back home to Bideburg – planning to buy land and build up a business and raise a family on the soil that had grown him. A family was his greatest wish, he always said. He spent a few years, travelling and trading – and this is where he built up his skill as a businessman – but all the time looking for a woman, he said, that made him love her. A wife.

My mother was a widow in the town of Freiburg. Her father was the local tax collector, and invested in town businesses. Her husband – a school teacher killed in the war. He'd also fought at Munster, a Protestant with the Catholic battalions too, but died early in the siege – when the Children's Army rode out to meet the Prince-Bishop. A teacher killed by children. What a day for the world.

She was a few years my father's senior, but had no children from this first marriage. She had run the town school as teacher since her husband left to fight – for there was no-one else to take the classes – and he had been gone many years, and was now long dead. My father says he loved my mother from first sight, asked her father for the right to marry her, begged no dowry – my father is a modern man in many of his customs – and promised to make her a rich woman; laying out his plans for this timbermill we have to her father, and showing him the money, gold and jewellery he'd earned and taken on campaign. He gave my grandfather enough money to hire a good replacement teacher – for the school is one of the best within a hundred miles – and promised to pay the salary in perpetuity so the school would always be open and successful, and named ever after in memory of his dead son. *The Walter Brau Academy of Frieburg*. All my father asked in return was one tenth of the profit. A fair deal. My mother says she liked my father's calm ways – he was dark and handsome too back then – and wanted a family as well. A life with him would take her somewhere.

They married and came to Bideburg. My father bought up woodland near his own family's one-field farm. All his family had died and he now owned the land. He leant money to struggling farmers and landowners

114

who could not pay their bills, and called in their debts for their land when they defaulted on repayments. The lord who'd once governed here was long gone by then, thanks to the war, and my father bought up some of the noble estate too. Like this house. It is not the manor house. That is far away, and burned now. But this was the lord's hunting lodge when he came to pay Bideburg a visit, way back in the old days. So my father took over. My family runs the town – and the world is better for it. Land and property grow land and property and soon – well, certainly by the time of my birth – we were the largest landowners here, and giving people jobs – unlike the lord when he was here, sitting on his lands and doing nothing with it but hunting with his royal friends and braggarding around. We made businesses prosper on the back of our business. A mill needs a carter, and a carter needs a wheelwright and wheelwrights need drink and a bed and God and so it goes. That's what my mother taught me – though, she did buy up the carters and wheelwrights, when she could, so we had that share of profit also – but we employed the carters and the wheelwrights to run those parts of the business once they were in debt and working for us too. All was fair. For the most part, they'd say they all got richer under a Stumpf than when they were in charge of their own affairs. Riches grow riches. If there's a lord in this town now, though, my father is it. And we have come to like to kill all lords in this country – which is why I would ask you, sir, to look hard at this case.

My father worked day and night – so it can not be said that all he did was seize up land. Businesses fail and he bought them to save the failing businessman from starvation. And we made our businesses work. This timbermill supplies wood as far away as Bohemia and Flanders, and every city in between. My mother worked too – even more than my father. She is the banker, if you like, of this family – the papers, money, investments, deeds, contracts, wages – all this falls to her. My father runs the labour, the mill, oversees the work, the deliveries, maintains machinery, trains our apprentices. My parents do not love Bideburg, however – even though they keep it half alive. My mother hates these backward people, and on her decision each one of us children has left the town at ten years old for Freiburg, where we attended our grandfather's school, both girls and boys. I have started teaching the younger children at the school myself, and had stayed on with my grandparents until now – when this happened, which I can not believe. But here I must make sense of it to you – for my life, I fear. My brothers are older – one an officer-cadet in the army, and one at your university, a doctor in the making. Both engaged to be married. I have not yet chosen a husband, and my mother and father are not of the mind to make a match without my consent – they have a modern way, and make it plain that I should choose the man I want when I wish to marry and not before.

We children, we did not know our father well growing up. For many years now, all we have had is summer and Easter and Christmas here, when we returned from school away. He was a man always at his work. The same with my mother.

To explain his character. What a question. I would say, acts of open love were not of him, though he was not an unkind man – save to his dogs. Quiet. That is my father. Though he could often lose his temper. Over what – it was rarely clear, but a rage would come on him – red and hot at times, and he would rise, fast, as if he wished to get away from my mother or us children, and he would leave the house for the kennels, and there he'd go about beating a dog to death. That's what he did. I shall hide nothing from you. But those dogs would drive anyone to vengeance – their yelps so regular they were like our nursery rhymes at night. He bought up dogs from tinkers and the like, gypsies, weekly sometimes. Never less than twenty in the pound. He kept them to select the best for hunting. The rest, those that were not of use, had to go, one way or another. And so some were there to take his wrath, which was rare, I repeat – but all men, even women, need to let out rage sometimes. Not once did I see him hurt another human soul. Never did he beat my mother or me or my brothers or sister. He is not a man of violence. If anything, he was a man of mildness mostly. Some animals were unfortunate, that is true, apart from the ones that made it to become good hunting dogs. Those he kept – and he cared for them like his children, kissed them and loved and pampered them. He used that stick – see, the one with the heavy head by the fireplace – he used that on the dogs that had to go. It is flat on one side now, where it used to be round. But he was a loving father and a sincere man. I do not know what has happened.'

* * *

I sat at Stumpf's desk, my pen in hand, writing, with my ear cocked. This was a courtroom interrogation, though conducted as polite conversation on a summer's afternoon, and the young lady Divara was aware of that, I believe. I blew on my notebook to dry the ink, sprinkled a little sand on it from my sand bottle, blew that off too, and covered my pen with its enamel lid.

The interrogation seemed to have found its natural hiatus.

'Thank you, my lady,' said Paulus. She nodded her head, the sun poking fingers of light through her hair as it shone down through the window behind her.

I put my pen, inkhorn, and sand bottle back into my little hand-made black-bound and buckled writing carry-kit – a gift from Paulus on matriculation – and put the carry-kit in my satchel, along with the notebook. I tapped the side of the satchel – the pistol was safe in the flap, with the powder, plugs, wicks and bullets.

'Invaluable, my lady,' Paulus said. 'Invaluable.'

'Just family stories, as you asked me.' The dogs were quiet now. Being fed.

Paulus moved a works ledger in front of him. It sat on a sheaf of pamphlets. The first pamphlet bore the woodcut head of a nobleman as illustration on its cover. Hard, iron nose, cruel full mouth, raven wing brows, a Slavic crown. Inside, more woodcuts showed the prince killing his mistress, throwing his counsellors from the palace windows, nailing the turban of a Turkish emissary to his head. Babies boiled in kettles. Boyar bodies piled in boyar piles. 'The full and detailed account of the terrible reign and…'

'You read this material too?' asked Paulus, showing her the pamphlet before I could read the full title. He picked up the next, lying beneath – A History of the Wolf Trials of France. Paulus pushed both pamphlets towards Divara.

'Sometimes, I read them,' she said. 'Pamphlets like this are everywhere.'

A third pamphlet reported on sorcery trials from the British Isles and the Low Countries to the Russian Steppe. A fourth, a series of revenant cases in Bohemia and Moravia, where the dead rose from their graves and terrorised the towns of Czechs and Germans and Slovaks.

'May I borrow some? I have nothing to read but law books on this trip, and I often like a little light distraction,' he said, and smiled. Divara laughed, though I could not see why, as the sallied joke was weak.

'Yes,' said Divara. 'Of course. Take what you like.'

On the cover of the last pamphlet, there was a woodcut of a creature I had never seen before. Some man made from stone, it seemed. Block-like – with no face, save seven holes for ears, eyes, nose and mouth – vacant and huge and implacable. On its forehead was Hebrew script. Hebrew has always taken me a brief moment to decode – the monolithic letters best transposed to Latin, I find, for Greek would then require another quick hieroglyphic decode, even though Greek should be a good scholar's natural default from Hebrew. *Life*, the letters on the creature's forehead read. Above the stone-man-monster ran the title of the pamphlet: *A true and extraordinary recounting of the legend of the Jewish Golem and his master a Rabbi.* This pamphlet was older than the others, yellow and dry.

'This must have been printed twenty years at least,' Paulus said. He could still tell from the touch and smell of paper, the feint of the ink, and colouring, just how long ago a printer had pulled a page off the press. He put the Golem pamphlet to his nose and smelled deeply. Vinegar. The smell of good paper when first printed remains. Paulus flicked around the pages, looking for a date, or a hint of a date. Beneath the preamble on the frontispiece, it read, *Printed in the year 1545, by the grace of God, though the events here told took place many years before.*

'Not bad,' said Paulus. 'I was off by just a few years.' Paulus bent his lips in a downward smile. He felt pleased with himself that his old skills learned in boyhood still stayed with him, when it came to books and their mechanics.

'Jews,' he said, showing Divara the pamphlet. 'I never quite understand them – though I know a few of these fellows.'

'Yes,' she said.

'I'll take this one, if I may. I have not read it.'

She nodded.

Paulus put the pamphlet inside his hunting coat, and walked over to the dresser. 'And what is this?' he asked. He pointed to a wooden box – a kind of cabinet, the size of a cathedral Bible.

'I do not know,' said Divara.

Paulus opened it. Little gold tacks sat pinned on a green base cushion.

'How strange,' said Paulus, leaning close to inspect the box.

Divara stood and walked to his side. She leant over his shoulder, and her heavy tight blue and yellow dress rustled. Her hand leant on the dresser close to his. Paulus smiled at her. She looked long at him, then spoke.

'Perhaps a box for flies – for fishing? My father liked fishing,' she said.

'I don't think so, miss,' said Paulus. 'Look.'

He clicked his fingers at me, and said, 'My glass, Willie.'

'It is in your pocket,' I said.

He rummaged in his huntsman's pockets and found the small black ebony case, shaped like a little drum, unscrewed it and took out a little jeweller's spy glass.

'The tiny knife, Willie,' he said.

I rummaged in the satchel flaps and gave him the short blunt knife, that he'd filed to shape himself. He took it, put the glass in his eye, bent low over the box, and pointed with the tip of the knife.

'See here,' he said, and he handed her the glass.

She put it to her eye, hesitant, and leant down. Paulus pointed to the third from last pin with the tip of the knife. 'Look here,' he said, 'just above the pin.'

Her back, in her summer coloured dress, was flat and slim – a perfect isosceles from shoulders to waist. Her legs dainty. Feet small. Her black hair fell over the green baize, and her arms were slim and strong.

'What am I looking at?' she asked.

'Blood,' he said. And pointed to a spot of rust above the golden pin.

'How is that blood?'

'It is blood, miss. I have attended many vivisections and know blood when I see it – and its deterioration to this rust state. Blood contains iron. We turn to rust when we bleed.'

'Sir.'

He took the little blunt knife and scraped at the rust spot. He scraped the rust flecks onto the palm of his hand, set down the knife, dabbed a finger to his mouth, moistening it – nodding to Divara, by way of apology for doing something so coarse – and rubbed the rust. It turned pink in his palm.

'Blood,' he said.

'I see, sir,' said Divara. 'The blood of a fish, maybe?'

'And look here too,' he said, pointing to the first row of golden tacks. 'And here,' he said, pointing to the end of the second row. 'And here,' the tip of the knife went to the middle of the third and final row. 'Hair. A few strands of hair. I know of no fish with hair.'

'I do not know what you are asking me to see, sir,' Divara said.

'There are sixty-seven pins.'

'And…'

'And your father confessed to sixty-eight murders.'

'Then there should be sixty-eight pins?'

'The boy he was caught – eating – in the woods,' Paulus said. 'Add him and a pin with his lock of hair to your box and you have sixty-eight.' He held her gaze, and her pale, pretty face turned ghost on him.

'It is not my box,' she said.

'Of course,' Paulus said. 'I know.'

Divara leant back against the dresser, her fingers touched the hair-cabinet, and she pulled them back as if they had lain against scorpions. She pushed the hair-cabinet to the floor.

'My family is finished. Do you mean to kill me?'

'Miss, please do not be afraid,' said Paulus, and he ran his hand down her arm, for comfort I thought, then drew it back fast, shocked at what he'd done. He placed his hand behind his back, like a steady soldier. Divara stood, calmed some, and took hold of his other hand.

'Thank you,' she said.

'You have nothing to fear as long as you co-operate with me,' he said. 'Your father will be sent to trial, he will be convicted, and he will die. I am sorry for your family, but this is my duty and this is justice and it has to be done. Your father has done so much wrong I can not calculate it. But you must settle yourself to this, and so must your mother. I promise you will be safe. I represent the law.'

'I will be compliant,' said Divara. She let go of his hand.

'You do not need to be compliant. Just help me, like a person after truth, do what is right.'

'We will, of course.'

'Have you or your mother done any wrong?'

'No.'

'Then all is well. Take that as my word. Unless you lie to me.'

'You have been told no lies,' she said.

Divara led Paulus from her father's study. In the hallway, Madame Stumpf stood waiting, she curtsied to Paulus and led us back to the family room.

'I want to know one thing,' Madame Stumpf said on the threshold. 'Why did they let that child go into the woods?'

'I do not understand, Madame,' said Paulus.

'That poor little boy,' said Madame Stumpf, and her voiced closed on itself and her face collapsed. Paulus looked hard at her, he even leant his head forward a little to see deep into her face – to assure himself that there were real tears there. This was no fake show.

'What happened, Madame? I do not follow what you are saying.'

'They saved the little boy and then come the evening he was found killed in the woods. Who let him go? Why did he go back to the woods?'

'Willie,' Paulus said to me. 'What is the full story we have from the indictment papers?'

'That a werewolf was caught having killed a man, a woman and their child, a boy thought to be aged between ten and eleven.'

'The boy was not killed with his parents,' Divara said.

'No?' asked Paulus.

'No. The boy was saved on a Friday,' Madame Stumpf said. 'Our maid was among the women who saved him. His parents had been earlier killed that day. That evening he is found – with Peter, in the woods.'

She cried now, hard. Paulus looked to Divara, and she walked to her mother and held her.

'I have heard nothing of this, ladies,' said Paulus. He left the family room, loitered in the great hall a moment, and then went to the main door, opened it and called for Raben. I followed him and heard the sergeant's voice.

'Not back yet, sir,' said Karfreitag. 'Still looking for Jens as ordered.'

Greet, the maid, poked her head from one of the sculleries or pantries behind the great staircase – and gawped at this man walking around the Stumpf house as if he owned it, then cut me a look of anger and went back to her work.

'Go and relieve this town's entire constabulary of their duties,' Paulus said to Karfreitag. 'Stand them down. Tell them that I order it on the Prince-Bishop's word. And you, my old comrade, and the rest of our boys, are now the only legal state force in Bideburg – under my direct command.'

Paulus shut the door. He looked weak and light and his hands were shaky. Hunger and excitement made him feeble like a child sometimes, and he had his hunger-sickness on him now, I could see. The hunger made him feel like a bag of lead falling from a church roof, on the sudden – that is how he described it – and unless he ate as soon as it came on him he'd be faint and fit for nothing. He turned to make for the family room and wobbled on the spot. I went to him and held him up by the arm. Greet's head dipped around a corner wall again like a bobbing blonde flower.

'You, young lady,' I said.

'Me?' asked Greet.

'Yes, you – would you be kind enough to fix my master a little food.'

Greet, I saw, felt this the most grievous insult since the Israelites danced with the Golden Calf behind the back of Moses, but winced a smile and said, 'Yes, sir. A moment and I will call you.' She vanished back behind her wall, beneath the staircase, to her kitchen or pantry or wherever.

Paulus walked unsteady into the Stumpf family room. The women had parted, but still held hands. He dipped a halting bow. 'Ladies,' he said, 'could I trouble you to allow me to eat in your kitchen? I have eaten one cake since I woke, and ran most of the way to your house – for fear of your safety.'

'Master Paulus sometimes feels faint with lack of food,' I said.

'Shut up, Willie,' he said to me, and straightened himself up, though he was pale grey and sweating to look at.

'You work too hard, sir, and do not take enough time in the day to eat properly. I will look after him if you allow me, Madame,' I said.

'Of course,' said Madame Stumpf. She spun around on her toes, facing to where the kitchen must have been located and hollered, 'Greet.'

'Don't trouble yourself, Madame,' I said. 'We will make our way to your kitchen, and leave you and your daughter in peace. And many thanks for your hospitality.'

'Once I have eaten,' Paulus said, 'I will bid you goodbye and arrange our next meeting. You will be kept fully informed of developments.'

We turned and he walked slow and leaden from the room. He paused in the great hall – took some deep breaths – and then we followed the direction in which Greet's head had recently vanished.

Greet was plating cold chicken, bread, cheese and pickle, and mixing a hot cup of ale with milk and nutmeg. Paulus fell into a chair before the kitchen table and dipped his head. He lifted the food to his mouth and ate with a long slow determination to fill himself and feel right once more. The dogs took up their barking again, and I ate too for I was hungry as well, though not faint like a dying infant the way Paulus could become without food.

I watched Greet clean the kitchen as we ate, and she turned to look at me, just once. She stared a moment and then flicked her head away, as if she were shooing a fly.

Chapter Fourteen

The true and the false tale of Rabbi Lev Solomon, the Golem-Maker of Terenstadt.

Paulus pushed his plate aside, feeling square and whole once more. Greet brought some thick honey cake, layered with cream, and a warm cup of buttermilk. He ate on and took out the old Golem pamphlet to read. I sat alongside and read with him. The first paragraph said that this was the story of Rabbi Lev Solomon – the Golem-maker of Terenstadt.

It began with the tale of the Jew's son, some hundred years ago. This boy, Solomon Solomon, had fallen in love – smitten to his heart, read the rather fervid first page, I considered – with a Christian girl, the daughter of a goldsmith, and she loved the rabbi's son in return. Behind their fathers' backs, they met at night in the fields outside Terenstadt, and swore they would marry and raise a family regardless of religion. Neither cared what God they worshipped as long as they had each other. The author of the pamphlet – unnamed – found this to be a mortal sin against the girl, for a Jew can abandon their faith and turn to Christ and find a place in Heaven, safe from the Hell they are destined for, but the other way round, and it is guaranteed damnation for a Christian. Satan, the author said, reserves his worst punishments for a Christian turned Christ-killer. Bad theology on behalf of the author, I thought. Surely God, not Satan, should be written as the architect of punishment – that would be more theologically correct, if the concept of God's great omniscience is not to be breached. An inquisitor could have many days of fun twisting this writer's mind to prove he was a heretic and have him burned for the good of the world – for within his writing, although he did not know it, this writer had confessed that he believed Satan to be more powerful than God.

The affair between the Jew and the girl was discovered – as I knew it soon would be, for so these stories go – and the brothers of the goldsmith's daughter killed Solomon Solomon. They found the pair in the fields and beat and hanged the boy – the daughter fled, and being a girl of no friends or knowledge, she made her way to the synagogue of her lover's father, the old Jew, Rabbi Lev Solomon. She told him what had happened – that his son was dead – and added, on bended knee in front of the old man, that she was pregnant with his grandchild. The old man raised her up, brought her to his study, whereafter he gave her a strong glass of wine, and the girl fell drugged to the floor, dying. The rabbi then cut his son's unformed baby out from the girl's belly – it had been inside her maybe twelve weeks – and once he'd chopped her up into fourteen bits – two feet, two calves, two thighs, two hands, two forearms, two upper arms, one body, one head – he burned the girl in the furnace of the synagogue.

The rabbi consulted his Hebrew spells – which spells these were the pamphleteer failed to explain, and I wished the writer had braved his imagination a little more to create a few. The rabbi read the incantations aloud as he ground up the foetus into mincemeat. He gathered earth from the Jewish cemetery, whatever bitter herbs Jews use in their ceremonies, and – dressed as a Christian, his headlocks hidden beneath a hat – he stole holy water from the baptismal font of Terenstadt High Church.

The baby, the earth, the herbs, the holy water – he mixed and cooked on a stove in his synagogue. The mixture was then removed and bottled, placed on a shelf before a Hebrew candlestick in his study and prayed to at dusk and dawn. The foreign ancient low songs of the Jews lulled over it night and day. The bottle was shown the Torah and the clay was asked to come alive after each prayer was sung. At last, a life took hold inside the bottle and the liquid shaped into a floating lump that resembled, almost, a human, but brick-like – as if profane man, unable and too ungodly to fashion life as flesh, could only put the spark of existence into clay blocks.

The rabbi broke the bottle on the floor and the thing lay there, writhing, and stretching its face – not breathing, for it didn't breathe. It was alive but not alive – animated by spells, not a soul. Lev Solomon took it to a crib, by the stove, and laid it down. Blood that had been drawn – in the way Jews draw all blood from the throats of butchered cows and chickens – he fed to the Golem. After it fed, the rabbi pricked his thumb and dropped a bulb of his own blood into the Golem's mouth. Then it would sleep. And day and night, he sang to it, and told it stories of the suffering of the Jews – from Babylon to the Flagellants to now – and how his only son had been killed for the sake of a Christian whore, but his blood – the rabbi's blood and the blood of his son, Solomon Solomon, and of his people back to the House of David and on then to Moses and Abraham – this blood has made you, little thing, little Golem, he sang.

Soon, the Golem grew big – within a week it was the size of a five-year old child. In a month, it was built like a lad of thirteen. When it reached this size – the size of a boy come to manhood – the rabbi took a holy knife – the knife used during the Jew circumcision rituals – heated it in a flame and then carved the Hebrew word for Life into the flat, brown forehead of the Golem. The heavy dolmen letters of the magic word like the Golem's heavy dolmen body. It gave a cry then – the first and last of its existence – when the knife went in, as understanding entered it. Now, the Golem was the rabbi's creature for ever more – he had created it, raised it, given it the name that binds it to its creator – Life – and now it would do his bidding until flame or rendering it in a thousand parts destroyed it.

With the Golem fully formed – the height of two men – the rabbi sent his creature forth at night to kidnap Christian babies – freshly baptised. These, the rabbi slit their throats in his synagogue and mixed the blood with flour to make the bread for the festivals of Purim and Passover.

The pamphlet recounted at length the ten or more abductions the Golem carried out, and all were merely a variation on a theme of baby snatched from cot – though one featured the Golem accidentally stealing a Jewish child and the spectacle of the rabbi whipping the Golem's brick back for its error, though the Golem felt nothing and stood still, almost laughing at its master, it seemed, while the rabbi spent his wrath on it. Paulus flicked forward through the pages, though I would have been content to read on more slowly. There was some speculation by the author that Satan lent certain rabbis the knowledge of raising Golems in order to destroy them and show to the Christian world the canker that the Hebrews are in society. Again, this was a theologically sloppy devolving of power to Satan, I thought – when God is the one in control of the world and all things in it. Or so Paulus would have had it in discussion – and I agreed with him, for he was a good teacher.

Then – at last, I thought, for I wanted to see how the author who dreamt this story up could come to a fitting ending – then, the Golem is spotted one night and chased by a group of artisans – printers, goldsmiths and the like – through the streets of Terenstadt. The Golem kills many of these men – who had miraculously been blind during months of kidnap and murder yet then suddenly one night were able to see this monstrosity walking in their midst – but the monster is outnumbered. Pikes and staves beat and pulverise its brick body. Its fingers are beaten off, legs splintered like flint. If a Golem can die, this one risks death.

A Golem has life, though, of sorts, and it has understanding, so even though it lacks a soul, it still has fear, like a dog or cat can feel fear without having the breath of God in them. Scared, it makes for the Jewish quarter – its home. But the superior Jews have been busy building their wall higher, the pamphlet says, keeping Christians away, sealing off entry ways to their ghetto – so there are only two gates, one in, one out – and the Golem is trapped at the ghetto wall, his old familiar route closed off. A hundred men are on it now, and in panic and madness, the Golem beats down the ghetto wall and flees towards its father, the rabbi, and his synagogue. The brave Christians, the writer says, race in through the breach in the wall, after the Golem, cutting down any Jews, whether they are men or women or babies, that get in their path.

They see the Golem disappear inside the blue and white painted synagogue, with its golden dome – and there and then decide to burn the ghetto to the ground, starting with the synagogue. And that is what happens in the pamphlet. These people – at least in this story – they burn the Jewish ghetto to the ground. The Golem destroyed and the rabbi with it. Those Jews who won't leave the city immediately, the townsfolk kill them on the spot – with hammers and hoes, table legs and knives – others are killed trying to escape the town. By morning, only a few bricks of the ghetto wall remain – and those are soon taken by afternoon, to add to garden walls and outhouses in the homes of artisans across Terenstadt.

The pamphlet ends with a warning to Jews not to return to the town of Terenstadt, the way they did many years ago. At the bottom of the last page, it reads, *Printed by Pieter Morgan and Sons. Printers, Terenstadt.*

* * *

We left the Stumpf house once Paulus was full and we had bid our leave. Raben had come back. He had found Jens, and Jens had found the graves of the dummy girl and her daughter in the wood. Paulus told the guards to accompany us to the site.

'I knew Pieter Morgan,' Paulus said to me – while Karfreitag and the rest of the uniforms hefted on in front.

'Who?' I asked.

'The printer of that pamphlet. I knew him.'

Terenstadt. Paulus jolted, he said, with a breath-halting leap in his chest, when he read the name of the town on the first page of the pamphlet – as if something unseen had taken its finger and flicked hard at his heart. Then he read the name Lev Solomon. Paulus was not a superstitious man any longer, but coincidence, repetition in numbers and signs, frightened him – he felt such things as an omen.

The trial of a Doctor Lev Solomon of Terenstadt had been the first legal case that Paulus had taken part in after he graduated in law and was articled to the magistrate of Terenstadt, Frederick Frengle. He was almost eighteen – the best performing student of his class, by many marks, as we all know – and on academic furlough from his military training. The trial of Lev Solomon had taken place just a few years before these printers published their pamphlet telling of a Golem being raised and bringing terror to the town, those were the words the author chose.

The Jewish doctor, at the trial Paulus had attended, had been arraigned as an abortionist. He had been well known for this practice inside his ghetto, Paulus said. Outside its walls two Christians, a midwife and a metal-worker, took on the business themselves for women of their own faith. The Jew Solomon, though, had come to the attention of the authorities when the Christian daughter of a goldsmith procured his services and died from loss of blood – not down to the doctor's lack of skill, but her own poor constitution, as it turned out.

The Golem pamphlet had these same principal characters as the trial – the Christian girl with the goldsmith father, the Jew Levi Solomon, though in the pages of the story, however, he was a rabbi not a doctor. The writer had taken the fabric of the real story and turned it into something spun upon a different loom.

So Paulus told me of the truth of the story. Magistrate Frengle was a stickler for full scrutiny of the cases he was called on to administer – a habit retained by Paulus to this day. After the arrest of Dr Solomon on charges of infanticide, Paulus accompanied Frengle to the Jewish quarter to inspect the doctor's home and surgery, together with a contingent of ten or more soldiers – there, primarily, to keep townsfolk from mobbing the ghetto, rather than to make sure no Jews got up to mischief. It was hard to remember the exact order of events, Paulus said, now so many years had gone by, but in the old doctor's study they discovered a number of foetuses preserved in brine and vinegar – that Paulus did not forget.

One of the soldiers – it was the thick-set sergeant, Paulus was sure, but his name he could not recall – the sergeant picked up a jar and asked Frengle, 'Is this a homunculus, your honour?'

The sergeant shook the glass jar and the unborn baby inside wobbled in its preserving agent. Its flesh like clay, and features and limbs stunted, only part formed, more toad than human. Built in blocks of flesh.

'That is a child, sergeant,' the magistrate said. The sergeant replaced the jar and baby, carefully, with two hands, and stood back a little.

The soldiers watched as Paulus and Frengle leafed through notebooks and texts. One young soldier, about Paulus' age, asked if the books were witchcraft manuals, grimoires, when he saw Frengle open the pages of a Hebrew text on geometry full of squat, strange script, and equations and intricate diagrams – circles, stars, triangles, multihedrons.

'Mathematics, boy,' said Frengle.

There had been talk – as there always was when it came to Jews – of the doctor using the blood of the Christian babies he had aborted to make Passover bread for rituals in the synagogue, and Frengle, although he did not believe such things went on, felt duty-bound to make a search of the doctor's quarters that would satisfy any of the more political members of the town council who would want a full account at the trial, questions raised – and most likely demand seats during the proceedings.

During the trial, at which Paulus was chief clerk and first assistant to Frengle, Dr Lev Solomon was shown the instruments of torture but made a full confession without their use. He offered a high blood payment to the goldsmith and the family of the Christian girl, and accepted conversion to Christianity. Frengle dealt fairly with him – allowing the Jew's family to retain all property and possessions once the blood payment was made, and ordered the old man beheaded.

Throughout the trial, a young printer, Pieter Morgan, befriended Paulus – who was a little lonely in the strange town he'd been ordered to – buying him drinks after the day's work was done, letting Paulus borrow new books sent from Munster and other big cities which the Morgan family shop was producing and that no-one else in Terenstadt had yet seen or read. Pieter knew every adventurous back alley in Terenstadt – and it was a big town even back then of twenty thousand or more. And on the last day of the trial – after the verdict and sentence were in – he took Paulus to the Red House where the whores danced like gypsies – where one payment, though pricey, on the door guaranteed as many drinks as you could drink, the woman of your choice, and a bed for the night. The next morning, Pieter took Paulus to his home, where the family of printers treated him to breakfast – and welcomed him like a long lost son, when Pieter explained Paulus was the son of a printer himself, but now a great lawyer in the making, and had just sent the Jew Lev Solomon to the chopping block.

Years of dormitory breakfasts in monasteries, school and university had made him miss, like a lover, a family in full flight and chatter at the table in the morning, and Paulus treated them to the story of the Jewish doctor and the babies he had seen in jars, in return for the joy they were giving him.

'Jews should be killed,' the father, Master Morgan, said, as they finished their eggs and ham and bread, and hot spiced honey milk.

'Everyone – everyone – among the artisan class wants them out of this town,' said Pieter. 'Anyone who believes in progress.'

'We have been killing them for hundreds of years but still they come back like rats that can't be exterminated,' the mother said. She was blowsy and red-haired. 'We killed them – all of them – in this town for their witchcraft when my great-great-grandfather was a boy, but still, look, there are hundreds of them now. They sneaked back. And they are given protection behind their wall – given their own area – given special trading rights. Their ghetto. As if they are better than us.'

Paulus nodded and even smiled, for he seldom heard this kind of talk behind the grey walls of church or college. Of course, he'd heard the criticism of the Jews, and even calls for their exile or forced assimilation, but it had been a long, long time since he'd heard ordinary working folk like these – folk he loved and missed – speak in their direct and honest and unfettered way. He didn't care what the subject was, he was just happy to be amongst this straightforward style of talk. This was how these people felt – not how the Bible and law allowed them to construct their feelings from the phrases of others and the notes of long-gone scholars. As for the Jews, he was unmoved. They confused him – he could not understand why they wished to live the way they lived, separate and shunned – but they could do as they pleased as long as they, like everyone else, obeyed the law. They meant nothing to him. No law, though, said that the people – however good the people are – could just stand up one day and slaughter who they pleased. No-one should believe such a thing. But he did not say so as the talk at the table wound on about the Jews and their perfidy. This passionate talk at breakfast was just the printer family letting loose their anger, the way all folk do. Soon, the Jews were forgotten, however, and all the talk at the table was of the latest books and the latest ideas they brought with them – like one the printers were just now setting to stone which attacked the concept of astrology. This to Paulus was revolutionary. Timely, he told the family. And they nodded – for he was a lawyer in the making, and knew of books, like them. How, this text asked, could the thousands of people born on one day across the known world be of the same character. A cannibal and a king. It said the planets were not for prophecy, but for study – that the word astrology should be removed from university curricula, with only astronomy remaining in its place. Paulus fully agreed with the author and clapped his hand on the breakfast table when he heard what had been written – he had often taken professors to task for peddling what he saw as unacademic superstitions – although only in the last few months or so, now he'd graduated and been made a semi-fellow and felt the right to fence with his brains a little against men he'd learned were less clever than himself. In addition, his astrological sign was Aquarius, and he thought this the most burdensome of the zodiac. It must, he reckoned, have come down as some sort of symbol from the poor slaves who in ancient times had to drag water to the cities of the men who styled themselves bulls and archers, and their women goddesses.

Breakfast over, Pieter and his father walked Paulus back to the centre of town. There was a council meeting at three where the issue of the Jewish doctor would be discussed, and Paulus was needed to assist Frengle. The printer Morgan had leather and colours to buy, and Pieter intended to watch the council proceedings as well. 'I've seen the trial, and now I want to know what happens after a trial,' he said. 'Once the old Jew's head is off, that will be the show over for me. Story told.'

As they walked up the street from the printer's home and shop, Pieter and his father called out to friends and neighbours that this was Master Paulus Melchior, one of the youngest lawyers in the Empire and that he'd helped convict the Jew Solomon. Folk smiled and waved, some came over and slapped his back and shook his hands. All said straight and clear and loud that the Jews should be driven out of town, or burned in their ghetto if they didn't go. It had been a long time since Paulus had heard such relentless talk of the Jews – not since his boyhood and Munster. Certainly, at court or in the university, it was spoken of and a matter for talk, but on and on went the folk in smaller towns like this, it seemed, as if they had nothing else to think of but the Jews. Paulus was a little bored of the Jews now, if truth be told. He had never seen Jews do much harm in the world, though they complicated it a little.

'Well the old Jew has given us the excuse to march there tonight and kill every last fucking one of them where they stand, sit or sleep,' said the printer Morgan. The little crowd around them cheered. Paulus picked up his step and hurried on – the printer and his son caught him up and walked him to the council chambers.

Before the council meeting, Paulus mentioned to Frengle the talk he'd heard about the Jews, stirred up by the old doctor and his practices.

'I'm aware of this,' said Frengle. 'I will be raising it with the good aldermen and baillies.'

At the conclusion of the council meeting, a vote was taken – on the recommendation of Magistrate Frengle – to provide some financial assistance to the Jews of Terenstadt so that the ghetto wall could be built higher in order to protect the Hebrews in case of an outbreak of anger among the population of the town. Four of the ghetto gates would be bricked up – allowing only two entrances into and out of the Jewish quarter – making it easier to guard.

With impressive speed, Jew workers and hired Christian labourers – the Christians on five times the hourly wage than usual – reinforced and raised the ghetto wall. It took just two days for the work to complete, and no assault was made on the Jewish people of Terenstadt. Paulus left the town one week later – his training done with Frengle, though he still kept close to his old master magistrate, now a dean of law, to the day he told me this story – and returned to his university under the instructions of the Prince-Bishop's advisor on legal affairs, ordered to complete new studies in rhetoric, languages and anatomy. His training – both academic and military – was far from finished, he had been informed by official letter, and he owed a great debt of gratitude to his eminence the Prince-Bishop which would only be repaid by the good service expected of the most qualified of advisors. The court was pleased, however, with his progress in the law, so far. On the journey back to college, Paulus decided he would take on further studies, at his own expense now, in poetics, the classics and philosophy. Languages, he would find interesting. But rhetoric and anatomy – the pointless dissection of argument and cadavers – did not appeal, though, of course, he would complete those studies too and pass perfectly, leaving his classmates in his wake. And all these new studies added a few more months to the precious time he had left before his military furlough ran out, and a full-time life in the army took him away from his beloved classroom.

Chapter Fifteen

The disinterment of the bodies of the Dummy and her daughter, and the arrival in Bideburg of the Stumpf family sons.

We stood in a verge of trees and watched without them knowing. Paulus had raised a hand and told us hush when we came down through the woods above the glade where Jens and his men were digging. Jens swayed like a reed. His men dug. The oak tree above the hole was the biggest in the forest. Its canopy shadowed the ground below like a pair of great arms thrown wide to shield the bodies in the earth from the hot sun that hung in a bare sky.

The men hollered when they found rags, and Jens stepped forward, unsteady, his feet sprawling. He looked down into the brown dirt. The men bent to their work again, and dragged on the rags. The rags shifted and the earth gave way around the old cloth.

A skull rose up. Dirt rolled over the bone, plugged with mud and gravel. The men tugged more on the other side of the old piece of rag and a hand and shoulder appeared. 'It's waving,' Jens said. He laughed and stepped back and sat down, clumsy and heavy and reached for the bottle of the rare old mushroom beer he'd brought, corked with a straw stopper. He took a sip, then a long swallow, and lay back on the grass, dreamy.

'Get them up,' he said to the men, his eyes shut. The sun above sparking lights and shapes behind his lids.

He wake-slept – all a-lull with the tugging and grunting and digging of his men. The breeze was soft now and warm, and seemed to come in time with his breathing. The world grew distant and quiet and pale.

Paulus nodded to Karfreitag and sent him forward. We followed behind. Jens roused a little when he heard his name shouted. 'Jens.'

'Just get them up,' Jens tried to say, with his eyes still shut, but he must have heard himself slur and mumble – far away inside his head.

His name was shouted again – this time like the tolling of Heaven's bells above – and he opened his eyes and looked up. A man – red-bearded and huge – was throwing his hands down towards him.

'Who are you? I know you,' Jens said, his mouth drooping, to Karfreitag.

Jens was lifted, his chest felt like it had been ripped apart; his left breast torn off as the Amazon women did so they could shoot arrows like men. He rolled through the air and his breath left his body. He was on the ground now and a fist was coming at him. It knocked him flat and then a boot followed and he was gone into blackness and far away from himself.

His men had thrown up their arms in full surrender as the red-haired sergeant, with the coloured sash across his breast – the one who'd been with Paulus and the monk, they realised – walked fast from the line of trees, his sword swinging on his hip, calling Jens by name. The sergeant cast down a look at the grave and the bones, and leapt over the pit. He stood above Jens and shouted down into the sheriff's face as he slept off his rare old mushroom beer. Jens lifted his head and muttered something and lay back again.

The sergeant picked Jens up by the front of his shirt and threw him at the great oak. The sheriff spun through the air like a sycamore twist in the wind and his back cracked against the oak's trunk. The men were sure Jens had broken his spine, and so was the sergeant it seemed – for Jens lay stiff at the foot of the tree and the sergeant stood still. But then Jens rose on an elbow and looked around him – to find, it appeared, what force had taken hold of him. The sergeant stepped forward quickly and punched Jens to the face – above the eye, opening up his brow line like a glutted red leech.

'You broke command,' the sergeant shouted, and he kicked Jens on the jaw. The sheriff's head rocked and he fell back as gone as a man could be and still not be dead.

'Sergeant,' a voice came from the tree line. The diggers looked up. Paulus walked towards the men, his eyes on the grave.

'That's fine now, sergeant,' he said. 'Tend to your sheriff,' Paulus told the diggers, without looking at them.

In the grave, there were two strange articulated skeletons – bones in some sort of joke geometry, thought Paulus. There was the skeleton of a child – that was obvious – and that of an adult too, a woman, the wide pelvis was bare from the earth. The diggers had pulled them partly from the ground, and they lay in tumbled ruins: an arm where a leg should be

– a child's hand in the place of the mother's head; the girl's skull on the mother's hip. Fingerbones mixed with toebones. A jaw for a crown. Ribs heaped like a dinner thrown into a midden. Dressed in ribbon rags. The earth had not let them fully go, though. Their backbones were still beneath the soil; a knee here or elbow there, sunk under mud, unfree; bone faces turned towards the earth as if they missed its cold damp shelter and could not look on the world with its sun and trees and men.

'Good enough,' said Paulus. He told the men to take the bones – with all the reverence that mothers and sisters and daughters deserve – and carry them to the pastor, or priest or whatever they had in this town. Prepare them for a decent burial.

'Once you have done that – if Jens is still incapable, take him back to his stupid wife,' said Paulus. 'Though do not say I called her stupid or be insulting.'

Paulus nodded to me and to Karfreitag and we walked back towards the tree line, and four black mares tethered in the woods. We had brought the horses from the Stumpf house, and Raben was standing, holding the bridles, and patting their heads and shushing the animals. They nickered and stamped, and flared their leather muzzles.

★ ★ ★

Folk had already spotted us and started moving down the road towards us, when we drew the four black mares up sharp at the Bideburg crossroads and the town square. Paulus and Karfreitag dismounted. The sergeant checked a look to Paulus, who nodded, and the sergeant unbuckled one of the pistols, with cord smoking, from across his chest, cocked it and fired in the air. The folk jumped like gypsy dancers.

Paulus shouted, 'I am not even waiting for you to gather – either hear this or don't. But it will be law when it is said.'

Folk came from the inn, Odil trailing behind his customers and staff, and families poked their heads out of the nearby homes, men and women appeared from the meeting hall – the town hall – the tailors, the bakers, the butchers and leather-makers; the buildings emptied. Some children came behind. Paulus began, and those who made it late, they had their neighbours whisper to them and explain what had been said, and then of course the neighbour lost pace with Paulus and his declaration which was in such a grand language few could have made head nor tail of it, if they'd had it said to them personally in a quiet room with a drink and a warm fire. Fromme and his boy Jodel walked from the inn, last out, and made their way through the crowd to Paulus – standing behind him. Kroll pushed his way to the front of the crowd, as his authority as mayor privileged him.

'Under executive powers,' Paulus shouted, walking around, back and forth across a few short yards, 'the evidence I have accumulated does not on balance of all probabilities indicate that the accused is in any way subject to the authority of the inquisition – there is no substantive or even circumstantial proof of demonism or lycanthropy. All logical supposition leads to no other conclusion than the accused is a man – in biology, and metaphysically – and under no influence of anyone other than himself, certainly not of powers beyond the natural order of things, namely Satan or an infernal spirit or supernatural creature. And so, I will move towards civil trial under state law and statute. I will allow the representatives of the church, as canonical authorities, to stand as official observers of the trial due to its unique circumstances and interest. The trial will thus be two days hence. That is now spoken and that is now law – only the word of the Prince-Bishop can reverse my decision.'

Kroll raised his voice just slightly, and said, 'May we ask a question?'

'No,' said Paulus. 'Your town needs some law and I am giving it. And I have further inquiries to make which will mean me speaking to you.' He pointed at Kroll. 'And,' Paulus looked around the crowd. 'You,' he said, pointing to Odil. 'All your town leaders. Jens, when he is fit for public appearance, will also need to speak to me about one outstanding matter which worries me regarding the conduct of this town and the handling of these crimes prior to my arrival. Have you any more questions now?'

Odil shook his head. Kroll stood as if the Gorgon had looked him in the eyes.

Our sergeant waved his gun at the crowd – he had lit his other pistol with the smoking cord of the first he'd fired – and shouted, 'Get out of here.' The folk flinched and moved off, in little groups, talking and looking back at Paulus and us, his company. Odil took Kroll by the arm and led him away – his face still frozen.

Fromme walked to the gate of the inn, a good number of paces away, stopped and said loudly, 'This is not the done thing, my old friend.' And for the first time, I heard aristocracy in his voice.

'Don't be ridiculous,' said Paulus. 'The man is a man. Stop it with your nonsense. This town is corrupt.'

'It needs full inquiry,' said Fromme, 'and the church its say. We are friends.'

'It does need full inquiry, and you are my friend,' said Paulus. 'So listen then – do you know that they set the child out into the woods – after it was saved? The last one.'

Fromme shrugged. 'You must need to explain.'

'The child was saved. It wasn't killed with its parents.'

'No-one said it was.'

'No-one said it wasn't.'

'And?'

'And the child was saved – I have this from the girl who saved him. The boy was taken to the keep, and then next he is found being murdered by Stumpf in the woods.'

'This is the Stumpf servant you talk of – as witness?'

A rolling deep noise came from the Dark Hedges – up far from the crossroads so we could not see. Paulus turned his head.

'Yes,' said Paulus. 'A well-admired girl in the community. She saved the boy. He was then killed by Stumpf in the woods.'

'So?' said Fromme.

'So, what child saved from a monster in the woods runs from a keep back into the woods and the monster?'

'I don't know but perhaps the child did.'

'Jesus Christ,' said Paulus. Fromme walked towards us and stood by us – his ear cocked to the noise as well.

The noise shaped into the beat of horses hooves – coming at a hard tilt towards us, still hidden by the drumlin mound that crested into Bideburg.

'Bait,' said Paulus, and he turned to Fromme and jabbed his finger hard into the monk's chest. 'Bait. They let the child go. Took him to the woods. This little group of town leaders. They let him be killed.'

The oncoming horses took the hill into town now – all dappled, all mares, four of them, sweating and mouths flung wide. Two Bideburg constables rode in front, bridle-stringing two unmounted horses behind them. The constables were shouting as they rode.

The folk who remained in the street had stopped and looked towards the noise. Our sergeant held up his hand, though the horses were still a fair gallop or more away. The riders dragged hard on bit, and the mares slowed, their eyes rolling, taking the last one hundred paces to the crossroads at a canter. The two mares at the rear, however, where not unmounted. Two bodies were tied to their backs – strung on the saddles, lashed with thongs of leather.

Paulus shouted, 'What has happened?'

The horses were trotting now, and their hooves made a sweet rhythm on the ground. There were short crossbow bolts feathering the backs of the two bodies tied to the horses. Three in one, four in another.

The youngest guard pulled up his horse and said, 'The Stumpf sons, sir.' He gestured to the mares behind him. 'We went to meet them on the road as ordered and send them home. This is what we found.'

Chapter Sixteen

The Committee of Public Inquiry is convened, and I begin my dialogues with the werewolf, and learn of his practices in the woods and by night.

Paulus convened a Committee of Public Inquiry – on the spot, standing in the dust of the town square. He dragged me aside – truly dragged me, by hand, and quite fierce – and screamed for Karfreitag like he was screaming for a medicine to quell pain. The sergeant ran up to us at a trot.

'You,' Paulus said, pushing me in the chest, 'are to get Rodinan – he is the one headman I have not seen. Take the boy Raben. Get to his house and bring him here.'

Paulus said he intended to prepare indictments for murder against anyone knowingly involved in releasing the child into the woods, if it could be proved they did so with the intention of the boy being used as bait to catch the werewolf. Indictments were also laid against those who killed the Stumpf sons. Paulus said full power of deputy was invested in me and I should use it. If I failed to use it, I would be judged unfit for service. Paulus had never spoken to me in such a way before, and it scared me as I was not well-trained in interrogation, despite having watched Paulus at his work. I stood a little dumb as I listened to him.

Paulus pushed me again. 'Go,' he shouted. I ran to Raben, and heard Paulus tell Karfreitag, 'Get that bastard Jens here on the double. And tell your soldiers to keep near Kroll and Odil – I do not want them talking to each other without our ears close by.'

The councillor Rodinan lived far out by the forest. The house sat in a cleared woodland patch and was built big, strong and square – two stories high, whitewashed and with a long porch running around all four sides, the door set below a Greek style Doric arch. Very artistic in its design. A wooden love seat was coddled in a thicket of red and yellow rose bushes.

Raben said to me that he thought it best if he waited away from the house and did not come with me to the door when we made the head of the path to the Rodinan home. 'It would offend him and make your job more difficult,' he said. I agreed and walked on to the house.

'Hello,' I called, for the house seemed abandoned and cold. 'Is anyone home?'

I heard laughter from the back of the house, and walked around the white panelled side wall. There was a sharp bark, the bark of a little dog, and more laughter – light and crackling, the laugh of a child.

Behind the house, there was a small kitchen garden, and a run of lawn framed by hedges. A boy of maybe ten sat upon a barrel by the back wall and watched a little girl – she could have been no more than six – kneeling on all fours on the grass. A dog – a badger hound – was clambering on her back. The girl's dress was rucked up on her hips, and she was bare beneath. The girl laughed and the dog thrust at her – pink and pointed and wet – and barked. The boy did not move or speak or take his eyes off the girl and the dog.

I stood for a moment, confounded. The boy, I realised, I had seen before – it was Rodinan's son, one of the children I had watched frogging. Filus. The girl I had not seen – the child in front of me was young, and the sister I had met was older than the boy Filus.

'Stop,' I shouted, and the boy sprang up like a jangling puppet. The little girl laughed and rolled onto her back, the dog licked her belly. She scratched its head and laughed more and wrestled in play with the dog on the grass. It sat on her crosswise, still hard and hammering its hips. The dog looked back at me.

I crossed the yard and kicked the dog in the ribs. It rode across the grass like a kickball, and lay there in a hedgerow yampering and crying out. It could not stand or take a breath. I walked to it and I brought my foot down on its head. The children were screaming and a woman came out of the house, through a back kitchen door, along with a girl – the older sister I had met before at frogging. The woman screamed, 'Martin.'

I shouted at her, 'What is going on here? Are these your children?'

She ran back into the house, crying, 'Martin, Martin. Come quick.'

A man emerged – it was Rodinan, and he hefted a short sword in his hand. I raised my palms in peace and said, 'Sir.'

He recognised me, and looked to the dog and his children and said, 'What have you done?' He pushed his oldest daughter back into the house behind him. She squealed and ran into the dark corridor.

'I came upon your children, sir,' I said. 'The dog was attacking the young girl in a way I can not think to speak of and your son was doing nothing. I killed the animal.'

The little girl was wrapped around her mother's skirts and screamed – like a Devil, 'Bjorn was playing with me. You hurt him. You are bad.'

'Sir,' I said, and looked at Rodinan's wife for shame and then looked down, 'the dog was on your daughter's back. It was trying to couple with her.'

Rodinan looked at his son and said, 'Filus?'

'Bjorn was getting rough just as this gentleman appeared, father. Eloise was not scared though. I did not think anything was wrong. They were playing rough and tumble.'

'Son,' I said, 'that dog was going to hurt your sister.'

I spoke to the mother and father now, 'Please, I am sorry if I have upset your family, but I feared for what was going to happen. Your children, it seemed, did not understand what they were seeing.'

'They are innocent,' said the mother, fierce at me. 'Did you have to kill it?'

'I am sorry,' I said.

The little girl ran to the dog in the corner of the garden and lay over it. 'Bjorn, Bjorn,' she said and she cried.

'I am sorry,' I said.

Her mother went to fetch her, the girl's dress and hands were thick with mud and covered in blood now. The boy began to cry and walked to his mother. She held him, and the girl let her mother go and walked past me to her father, casting me a tear-stained scowl.

Rodinan told the girl, 'Get out of those filthy clothes, Eloise, and go to the pump and wash. You are dirty.'

The child stopped still and stripped naked on the grass, standing between me and her father. She slipped off her dress like a snake shucking skin, then stepped lightly, with high-pointing toes, as if she half-danced, to her father's side.

'But father,' she said. 'It will be cold.' She curled her leg around his leg and slid her arm between his thighs – ivy on a tree.

He knelt and kissed her on the mouth and said, 'Once you have the worst of this filth off you, I will pour a hot bath in the kitchen for you, and wash you. Does that make you happy?'

'Yes, father,' she said, and she ran skipping to the pump. The pump was down near where the dog lay, and she did not cast the animal a second glance as she stepped over it, took the pump handle and put her head beneath the gush. She squealed and laughed and stamped as the cold water fell over her.

Rodinan threw his sword at the ground and it stuck in the grass, juddering. 'What was it you came to see me about, young man?' he asked. 'Or did you just come to kill my daughter's dog?'

'Bjorn was my dog too, father,' said the boy, Filus.

'Get in the house,' Rodinan said, and his face fell cold with anger. He took the boy by the neck and pulled him from his mother's waist.

'You are a failure. You should protect your sister,' he said, and he threw the boy into the house through the back kitchen door into the dark corridor. 'Get out of my sight.'

His wife, picked up her skirts and walked quickly through the door behind her son.

'Please bring us some wine,' Rodinan said, as she passed him. 'It is a pleasant day and we can take our talk outside.'

His wife nodded.

'I have some seats at the front of our house. Sit with me there and tell me what your master wants. I take it you come on his orders?'

'Yes, sir,' I said. 'I come with his full authority, which means the authority of the state and the Prince-Bishop. I will not need wine, but you may take some if you wish.'

He turned his head on his neck to look at me, as if it would break.

I gestured before me, and said, 'The seats you spoke of, sir. Shall we go there?'

He walked stiff around the side of his house and I followed him. His back and shoulders were tensed and hard, and scared, I knew. After we talked, he drank no wine, and I took him with me. Raben and I escorted him to the town.

★ ★ ★

When we returned, Paulus was on the steps of the town meeting hall. He had commandeered the long, low, dark building for the Committee of Public Inquiry, and instructed Fromme's boy to draw up a list of witnesses for the first round of interviews with townsfolk. There would be a running order to decide who would be called to give solemn evidence before criminal law in the case of the child who had vanished from the keep.

'I could have done this job, sir,' I said.

'No,' said Paulus, and he grabbed me by my collar and dragged me behind him up the street. 'I have need of you.'

He shouted over his shoulder at Raben, 'Keep councillor Rodinan by you, please, Constable.'

'Am I to stay here?' Rodinan shouted back.

'You are.' And Paulus pulled me on like a puppy on a string.

I was tired of this manhandling and wrested myself out of his grasp. 'Let me go, god damn you, sir,' I said. 'I am not a dog – and you have not treated me as such, so do not treat me now.'

He stopped, and a look of outrage passed over his face – it vanished, like a wind blew it away – and he nodded. And then he bowed, which took me off me guard. 'Of course,' he said. 'I am busy, and things are urgent. I need you, and was unthinking. Apologies.'

'Of course,' I said, and I bowed back, but he was already off on his way again and missed my graciousness. I ran behind him. He made for the keep.

'Hurry up,' he shouted.

When we arrived at the black iron and wood door of the keep he told me, 'Say nothing to him about the death of his sons.'

The keep was a windowless four-tier cake. During our days to come in Bideburg, Paulus examined it well, many times, for he felt it was his property, and I tagged along behind once or twice as I was interested in the construction of buildings and how they were made for purpose: why a kitchen is better there, say, than a storeroom here or quarters. We had studied such issues in a mathematics class on architecture and it was one of the few topics under examination in that subject which I took to with an interest, and performed well at when tested. The first layer of the keep was below ground. The cells and the armoury – and it made sense to me to station these important parts of the building subterranean. Two rooms were set aside for holding prisoners. One large and big enough to hold a single prisoner and to conduct an interrogation. It also held the instruments of interrogations – this was where Stumpf was kept. The second room was of the same proportions – just a fraction smaller, perhaps – with a long cage inside to hold a group of prisoners. A fair way to divide and organise the custodial side of the keep's work, I reckoned. Between the cells and the armoury there were many passages, with bricked up or empty rooms on every side. This was an unholy waste of space, I thought. The rooms could have been employed for storage of some sort, I imagined. The armoury was small – a room split in two, with weapons lined on the walls, and barrel upon barrel of gunpowder and explosives locked inside a cage, which ran from floor to ceiling at the rear. In the floor of the corridor outside the armoury there was a hatch down to an old bolt-run that led under the walls of the keep, ten feet or more below the earth, and came out in the ground behind the walls, hard up against the mountain – a tunnel and route to escape if enemy came in through the iron-bound front door. Sensible and not unexpected, in my opinion – all defensive quarters need a method of retreat, otherwise siege is the only recourse when outnumbered or outgunned. Above, on the first floor, there was the congregation room, the washrooms, the kitchens, offices for Jens and the quartermaster, and a messhall. This seemed ergonomic and wise in its partitioning and design. Next, on the second storey, were the quarters. I would have placed quarters here as well – again, it was ergonomic. Though, perhaps, the armoury might have been best-placed on this level too – near to the sleeping guards. On the third floor, the provisions were kept – wine, beer, dried fruit, pickled vegetables, flour, salted meat. Enough for months. I thought this positioning a mistake – and would have hived off part of the ground floor for provision, to keep food nearer the kitchens and mess-hall, and prevent the expending of unnecessary energy by the guards up and down the stairs. The fourth floor was the crenelated open roof – crested with battlements shoulder high. A stairway and hatch led up and the men often practised their combat up there in the clear air, we were told. I liked this feature, it added a dash of theatre to an otherwise municipal and unoriginal building – despite its black and lour air. In all, I would have given the keep's architect a mark of six out of ten.

Paulus and I walked in through the heavy wood and iron-bound front door – four men wide, two men high, as thick as a human body, of excellent defensive design. We made our way down to the cells in the orange torchlight.

Down there, Stumpf said he knew nothing of the boy – until he found him in the woods at night. He did not know the child was even the son of the man and woman he had killed that afternoon. He knew a child had fled, but he had not seen its face.

Paulus talked to our wolf, Peter, but the wolf did not answer beyond a yes or a no. The wolf was respectful but the wolf did not like Paulus – though he looked at me, while the three of us sat there – him in his double cage, us without.

'Willie?' Paulus said to me.

'Sir?'

'I do not think Master Stumpf wishes to speak to me.'

Time stopped for a handful of seconds and I thought to myself – this is the moment, Willie, when you can make your name. I was not afraid, and I did not doubt myself. Unlock this man Stumpf before you, I thought, and you will unlock a world of fortune and fame for yourself.

'I am happy to take over if you wish a rest, sir,' I said.

Stumpf – burned and bloody and a little broken – looked pleased with himself. Paulus seemed shamed that he had not made his prisoner talk, but he was not a man for the whip at the first bad turn of events. He wanted Stumpf's story, and did not mind how we got it – so he left the cell.

'I need to inspect the keep,' Paulus said as he shut the door behind him.

I poured us both beer from a clay jug, and passed Stumpf his cup through the double cages. I raised my cup to him. We drank, and I waited a little while.

'What was it like to kill that boy?' I asked.

'Easy,' said Stumpf.

'I would like to hear about it,' I said.

'Why?' Stumpf asked.

'Because it fascinates me,' I replied.

Stumpf giggled to himself, a chirruping laugh, like a wicked bird – a strange note in the throat of a man so big and worldly and bright.

'Of course I knew the boy in the woods that night. I saw him that afternoon with his parents, and I saw him run,' he said, 'but I was dealing with his father, while his mother still lived, and could not get to him. He was gone. Later, once all was done, I looked for him. But from far – in the trees – I saw he was with the women at their washing. Greet was there, by hell. Our own Greet. Come the night, I was in the woods, and there he was. I ate him.

The boy, and the sixty some others that I killed – that you talk to me about – I was not in uniform when I killed them. And this I want you to know – I killed many more back when I was wearing a military badge.

Have you ever felt the need to put your hand in fire – so great that you did it? Or to jump from a cliff? Steal something you did not need? I can recount all of them for you if you want – give you enough to fill up your little notebook twice over with detail. However, they were all the same, but they were all different as well.

I skinned a man once – back when I was in uniform. On the orders of my commander. And that does not count as a crime in the eyes of your masters. It was a year before the siege of Munster, perhaps. I removed the pink skin gloves from his hands, shaved off his sleeves, the skin from his legs, stripped his back and belly like I was removing the coat from a gentleman. He was so red and quivering – just bare, by a fraction, to the world. I peeled off his face – slit from hairline to ear, round the jaw, slashes at the eyes, nose and mouth – and if you pull the face, it slides away. I unmanned him as well. My skinning skills were not fit to do that bit better and leave him there, between his legs, still intact but peeled and dangling raw.

Naked man. It was the wrong man, though. It was his brother we wanted. We never caught the brother. I was decorated – given another war ribbon for my good service.

But the ones that I killed in my woodsman's clothes – the ones you say are crimes – I can recount them if you want – all for you, as I said. Though it would be better if you just let me tell you about my best.

In each act, I sought certain elements. Moments, sensations, reactions – roles that I could play and which they could play. I have always loved plays, drama – especially the old miracle plays. Modern plays – of princes that reign over us and the like – or history plays with Caesar and Alexander – I can read about those people and events in books, so on the stage they do not interest me. I like make-believe. It's been a long time, however, since I have seen actors perform upon the stage. So, I will tell you the story about my best one.

Most often, I would scout the roads around Bideburg – to see travellers coming to town. Everything has its rhythm, so if it was a lone traveller – and that is always a man – and I knew they could not reach the town by nightfall, then I'd shadow them through the woods and come the time they made camp – far out before the Dark Hedges – I'd wait for them to sleep and then it was done. A good event, though, would be a couple or a family passing through town – going out the other side, past the keep, and under the Steipplinger arch, on into the woods. They'd draw up at the inn, water their horses, check their cart, eat, drink, wash – and by then I would be far out in front of them – off past the keep, under the arch, along the road and into the forest. Waiting. A prime arrival would be a party of noontime visitors. They'd pass the afternoon away in town, then head off again just before dusk – the man driving while the family slept. I'd tie my horse in the woods and wait, three hours trek in front of them – so it was night when we met.

I find it comical that the chase which ended my run – that brought me here – that it was the first time I broke my pattern, my plan. I saw that family last Friday, and it was daylight, and it was not in the order that it should have been, the rhythm was wrong, but they were like fire, or jumping off a cliff, or stealing and I thought I could do it – maybe in a new way, for the first time in a long time. In daylight. But I was wrong, and the boy got away, and so now I am your guest and interlocutor – is that the correct word for what I am?

Back to this best time, though – this perfect event, Willie – it was a mother, baby and father. I had a routine, which I am sure you would like to know. Wolves don't talk, you see, and I do. I'd stand in the road – always at a different point, for luck and not for any other reason – and as they approached, I would wave to them – hands flapping and friendly, high above my head. Dressed in my best peasant clothes – not ostentatious, not wretched either. The clothes of a good working man. I'd ask, "Could you let me ride with you a little way up the road to my house?"

And this family – they said, yes, as nearly every family riding a cart did, because it is unfriendly and suspicious to do otherwise.

As we rode, I talked to them at first – for a good long time. Questions of their health, and their destination, and their family and what brought them on the road. Most folk, they love to talk only of themselves, but after a while, once they have told all their little tales and watched you listen – for that is what makes them happy – they will feel the need to ask you a little of yourself too, for they have nothing else to talk of, and then I would talk of God, my wife and children, my hard work and humble farm, and my happiness.

We'd ride along, content and safe and close with each other now, and there would often be a little silence, while we all thought of what we had said to each other. Such moments could be warm and dear.

Then I told my story. I always told my story – and it always worked. "Sir," I would say to the man, "sir, this may sound like the wildest of claims, but there is something I must tell you."

The man would turn around to look at me – where I sat propped up on their baggage and sacks in the wagon bed – and say, "Oh, yes?"

"Sir," I'd say, "many years ago, I was in this wood on my thirteenth birthday and a fairy – now please wait and listen, believe me – a fairy told me that I would find my fortune here. That a good woodsman, and a good boy, who had served God his whole life would be rewarded with treasure – that was hidden somewhere amongst all these trees."

The woman would usually turn too now, and say, "Indeed? Are you playing with us or is this true?"

I would swear to Jesus that I spoke the truth. "The fairy," I told them, "the fairy said to me that if I could find one true Christian spirit on the road, then that would guarantee that I would find the treasure. Just one honest person who loved God and had done no wrong. If I could find this pure soul, and they agreed to search with me, then I would be sure to find the treasure, and was honour-bound – on my life and by God – to share what I discovered with them. But I have been travelling this stretch of road for years and searched with hundreds of folk hundreds of times, and still found nothing because I have not found an honest soul."

This family – like most – would say, "Then let's dig. We are good God-fearing folk."

I would always say, "I can see that. Tonight will be the night."

And I would tell them that the fairy said whatever treasure was waiting was one hundred paces from the road. And off we would go into the woods. Sometimes the man would say that he'd bring a shovel with him, to dig the treasure up, but I would tell him it was not necessary as the treasure was just waiting there – perhaps a chest of diamonds or a great bag of gold – sitting on the ground, not hidden beneath the earth.

Often, once we were one hundred paces into the forest, and it started, the events went out of my immediate control. I liked this though – the running and chasing and fighting in the woods, that had no plan or rhythm to it, just action. This one, though – the best one, that I am talking of – this one was like a dance perfected over years, patterned perfectly in every way.

We took a torch – the husband, the father, carried it; the mother with the baby at her side – and we walked one hundred paces into the wood.

By a great tree, I stopped and said, "Pass me the light, sir." I knelt. I said I saw something among the ferns and brambles. I dropped to my knees, rooted on the forest floor. I said, "My God. It is true, look here. You must be good Christians."

I stood and cast the torch down a little, the man dipped to look. I grabbed him by the hair and thrust the torch up into his face, and kicked his legs from under him. His hair took fire. He fell, screaming, beating his head, his cuffs now catching fire. I pulled my knife and turned on the wife, holding her baby. She screamed and ran, into the forest, not toward the road. That was fine and well – and what I wanted. They never ran towards the road – for it is in the forest that people think they can hide. On the road, you are bare to my eyes.

The flames were out now, on the man's head. I kicked him in the face and he went out and down, and I stamped on his ribs, to be safe. They cracked a little like dry twigs under my foot. I took his shoes off and slit the tendons at his ankles. He woke, crying in pain, and I beat his head off the great tree till he was out again. I tied his hands behind him with some bailing twine I carried in my pocket. The cinch cut him at the wrists.

I turned to the forest and shouted, "I am coming for you and your baby." When you run in fear – and you'll know this just as well as I – when you run in fear all you can hear is your own breath, your own footsteps, and your heart and blood. You think your pursuer can hear you swallow. And fear makes you clumsy and loud. I could hear the woman – the girl, eighteen, I guess – stumbling through the trees, maybe another hundred paces further into the wood.

I took up the torch and walked after her – waving it before me, so she could see its flame coming for her. Then there was silence. She'd stopped running and was hidden somewhere. I walked, and every minute or so I shouted, "I can smell you." I could see where she'd ran through the trees and bushes – stamping the ground flat and breaking stalks and thin branches. Then her baby cried. And then there was silence. She'd covered the baby's mouth, I knew. I listened hard and could hear the softest mewling – a wail behind a hand. I followed the noise. It took me to a run of deep bushes – she was inside and still. I could see flits of her white dress through the black-green mesh of leaves. She lay on her side, and was drawn back hard inside her hiding hole, her baby cupped to her belly. The baby sobbing behind her hand was almost too soft to hear now, but it was still there, to my ear.

I stood and panted hard. "Where is that bitch?" I said. "I will find her." The baby still sobbed – so quiet though. The sound smothered then, like a pillow on a face. I waited by the bushes, scratching myself, growling. A quarter hour went by, maybe. The smothered sobbing grew fainter and quieter and at last it ended in the softest of sighs ever heard by two people – me and her. I waited another minute. The bush quivered and then shook like it had come to life, and the bush screamed, "My baby, my baby."

I leant down and pulled the mother out by the hair – her baby, suffocated-blue and dead, in her arms. I took her baby from her and held it by the leg. I dragged her back to her husband, the child swinging at my side. The man was dying. I sat the woman down before him, and said, "If you love him you can kill him." She looked at me, mad, a ghost – not a woman any more, though her figure was fine and her face, if fear had not been on it, would have been appealing.

"Or you can watch me kill him," I said. And then I lifted her child to my mouth and I tasted it, sir – the sweet calf meat from the fat of its back. She screamed, and I swung the child by its arm – the whoosh of it, a white circle in the black air. "Be quiet," I said, "or I will throw your baby into the dark." She was quiet and I gave her the baby. She cradled it.

Should I carry on? I worry that my confession is too much. But if you wish, then I will.'

Stumpf waited. I nodded. Stumpf nodded back to me, and continued.

'Her husband nodded too, like us – he nodded to me and asked his wife to kill him then, and I sat down to watch. She held her child, still, and crooned over her husband, as he kissed and touched her, though he was very weak. She didn't look at me but she said she would kill her husband, and he brushed her face.

"Good," I said, "well if you wish to do that then enjoy each other one more time."

Neither understood at first, but they followed when I took my knife and told her to undress and to undress her husband too. And then they did what I told them to do on the floor of the forest. A dying man can not perform, though, it seemed, so I set their baby between them and said, "Be a family, then."

Shall I go on? If that is what you want then I am happy to do so.'

I said, 'Go on, Stumpf.' And I held his eye for he wanted me to break away, and look down from his face, or ask him to stop.

'I watched them on the ground – eye to eye – and let them be a while, quiet and untroubled together. The wife told the husband, "It will all be well."

I told her, "You should not have said that. Kill him. Now." She went back on her word then, and would not kill him. But when I took their baby and threw it in the air, playing catch in the torchlight, they both agreed to get it done. It took her ten minutes or more to choke the life out of him – for I'd told her to use her hands on him and look her husband in the eye, kiss him when he said goodbye to her.

Afterwards, she was not a woman any more – so I played animal games with her. I made her play a snuffling pig, a mule for riding, a breeding mare, a clucking chicken and then a breeding mare again. I stood and let her kiss me where I pleased, and then I watered her – telling her I rebaptised her as a good Christian woman now she had found the treasure.

I could have played with her all night. She sang and danced for me. She sang songs she'd sung to her baby in its crib, as it lay on the forest floor, and she held her dead husband on the ground beside the child.

Later, after much of this exploration, I asked her what her name was, and she could not say. She asked to die instead. Asked me to kill her. I told her she could hang herself if she wished, for I had to go home to my wife and children. She lifted her torn dress from the ground and made a knotted loop in it for her neck. She climbed one of the great old trees to the first branch – higher than a man she went. And she tied one end of her dress to a bough, looped the choke around her neck and slipped from the tree like a silk unrolled.

I watched her, and she turned back into a woman – a person. She took a little while to die. I felt sorry for her.

Do you see what had happened? I had killed no-one. She had killed them all – her baby, her husband, herself. This was the best, Willie.' Stumpf nodded and said, 'Do you want me to go on? With more?'

I said, 'No. I do not want you to go on. I know enough. You should be dead, and I will help kill you.'

Stumpf made a sound – a laugh, a sigh, a moan – and said, 'Yes.'

Paulus had returned to the cell, and stood in the shadows, quiet for a long while. I had forgotten he was there, but now he coughed – with such feigned respect – and the thread between Stumpf and I seemed to dissolve in the air like spider silk.

'May I ask a question, please?' asked Paulus, and he stepped into the light.

'If Willie says yes,' said Stumpf, 'then yes, sir, ask a question.'

'Willie?' Paulus said.

'Please, sir,' I said, ashamed.

Paulus said to Stumpf, 'Do you not see others as people?'

'What is a person? What are people?' asked Stumpf.

'Me. You, surely, Stumpf. You say you are not a wolf, so what are you?'

'I am one of you,' he said.

And I would have killed Stumpf – there and then, in his cage – if I had not believed in the full process of the law, and that blind justice should stand above me. That justice should be better than any man or woman.

Chapter Seventeen

The Committee of Public Inquiry hears the testimony of Greet Werren regarding the rescue of the child, known as the Red-Ripped Boy, which began the series of events leading to the capture of the werewolf Stumpf.

Paulus called the Stumpf's maid Greet, whose family name was Werren, to give first testimony before the Committee of Public Inquiry, which he had established. I was admitted as secretary and notetaker. There were no other officials. Fromme had no role, beyond church observer.

The inquiry was held in the town meeting hall – low, dark, airless – and the public were admitted – though not those townsfolk who were also to be called to give evidence. Greet arrived – fair, straight-backed and strong – and took her seat before the table where Paulus and I sat. She looked a little like the girl Frey, back at the inn in Reissen, but clearer of face and more intelligent in her eye. Paulus had put on his black robe and cap, as had I.

He asked Greet of Madame Stumpf. 'She and her daughters are grieving very badly for the two boys,' she said. 'And they send word to you,' and she offered up a sealed letter, 'that they ask justice to be done for the murders.'

'You can tell the family that they are assured I will pursue justice for these murders. Whoever killed these boys will suffer retribution just as Stumpf will suffer retribution. A murder is a murder.'

He looked around him, wanting to see a face in disagreement, but not a head raised, all eyes kept to the ground – for many there held Greet dear to them, I could tell by how they had cast fond eyes at her when she entered the room, and so she could say what they did not wish to hear; their affection for her would silence what she said, in their minds, for now. She was only a maid being loyal to the family who paid her, after all. Her words did not matter if the people looked away and shut their ears, and did not see or hear her become the Greet they did not wish her to be.

I swore Greet in, and she began her testimony relating to the rescue of the boy.

Today, as an old man, I remember that afternoon back then, as Greet gave her evidence, and I realise now that ancient Bideburg had already changed such a lot by the time we arrived and these events took the town over. We are foolish if we think that a town or village or city has always been the same as the moment we step into it. The places we live change too, like the Ship of Theseus – but wash-day on a Friday had stayed the same since Jesus was a boy for these Bideburg people. Whether there was plague, a lord, a dead lord (which meant no lord), a war or peace – washing clothes on a Friday was as constant as star fall. This day – the day the women rescued the boy – was as always and as ever and as good and as warm as any summer day should be.

'We were laughing by the town river when it happened,' Greet said.

Skirts and shirts were dunked and rose, and the water plashed and frothed. The summer sky was grey and lilac after rain, and the sun burned hard behind the last large clouds. The women screeched about their dirty husbands – pushed and shoved for play – belched in turn, like music scales. One pulled a pair of dirty blotched drawers up from the river and said, 'The old Pope's pants after a night with the nuns.' The rest roared and flicked wet clothes at each other's faces.

'Our fun was such,' Greet said, 'that we did not see this ripped and bloodied child take the crest of the hill behind us.'

The red-ripped child, though, he just walked on half-step by half-step down the dusty path worn into the Bideburg hill to the washing spot by the river, out beyond the Dark Hedges. The women unaware. His stocking soles left scarlet lines on the sand and stones, and blood tripped and dropped from his white fingers. The boy turned off the path and crossed a wet field of thin green grass towards the laughing women – too rowdy and alive to hear the blank child draw up behind them.

The women washed and joked on. In turn their whorish neighbours, lying preachers, greedy mayors and measurers, crooked traders and landlords, ungrateful children and again their filthy husbands all took a turn on their roasting-spit tongues. The boy stood still and unseen behind them. A skein of geese dropped low from the lilac sky and glided to land on the river. The women stopped their washing and their play and gossip. They looked at the geese, all graceful.

'How pretty,' said one – the oldest, Erma, Greet's sister.

'Indeed' and 'Yes' said the women on either side of her.

Greet – who was the youngest and the last in line of washerwomen, as status was ranked by age and years spent at the river – said, 'Dinner', and slipped a little catapult from her apron pocket.

The red-ripped boy spoke then. 'Help me' – his voice wailed, too loud for his ears for he clapped his hands to his head. The women jumped and turned, panting, clutching hearts and breasts and foreheads – gasped at the sight of the torn child, maybe eight years old at most. 'Is this place safe?' he asked. 'Am I dead?'

Now, of course, there came an hysteria of leaping up, and running around from here to there and back again in less than the length of an eyelash, some screaming, till Erma slapped the loudest one of the crowd – a cousin, Efer.

Young Greet shouted, 'Shut your mouths.'

And the women fell all silent, though Efer sobbed and held her face.

Greet said, 'Be calm, for Christ's sake. We need to deal with this boy.'

The boy's clothes were shredded like claws had scourged him. Greet's sister, Erma, moved to touch the boy – turn him – hesitated for fear of hurting him more, then ran her hands over his hair and face and body. She turned him. There seemed no wounds on the child except for shallow scratches that laced his face and arms.

Erma lifted the boy's bloodied hands, pointed to his red feet. 'Is this your blood, son?'

The boy looked at his hands and feet and said, 'No, my parents' blood.'

'It's the wolf. It's the wolf,' wailed Efer, and Greet, who stood beside her, turned and delivered such a slap to her cousin's cheek – the one that hadn't already tasted her sister Erma's hand – that she knocked her flat on her back.

'It may well be the damned wolf,' said Greet, 'so let's take the child and go. Stop your noise or God knows what will hear us and follow the sound.'

The women started moaning and sobbing – three, wild-eyed and hair truly stood on end, Greet swore, took to their heels and ran for town.

'Wait,' shouted Greet – who, if she'd wished, could have led women into war. 'Stay together.'

'Don't go off on your own,' said her sister Erma.

The three runners drew stiff to a halt, and looked about them. Town was two hills and one mile away. The road before them was grown over, from the woods on either side. The black road of beech trees joined above any traveller's head, twinned like twisted hands.

'We Bideburg folk call the stretch of road the Dark Hedges,' Greet said. 'No sane man or woman would take that walk without a little foreboding – but to run it when a wolf or werewolf or madman was circling the town? Not these three – not on their own – they about-turned and came back to the safe circle of me and Erma.'

The women debated what best to do. Greet let the talk run for a moment and then stood forward and said, 'Erma, you and I take the child – the rest of you can take the washing. Carry mine and Erma's load between you.' She turned to Erma. 'Yes?'

'Yes,' said Erma. She was her older sister, but knew in her heart she was not Greet's better. 'We will mind the child here until you gather our washing in. Be quick.'

The women rung the half-clean clothes half-dry with twists of fast wrists, dumped the still soapy washing in baskets, gathered up their beer bottles, food and kneeling blankets.

'You're not hurt?' Greet asked the boy.

'No,' he said.

'What happened to your clothes?'

'I hid in brambles and tore myself.'

'Fast, fast,' Efer said to the women, whipping their belongings together. 'The Devil might be behind us. Ask the boy what happened,' she said to Greet and Erma.

Greet said to the boy, 'Where are your parents?'

'Dead,' the boy said. And he pointed behind him, the way he'd come. 'About one mile over that hill.'

'A mile?' said Erma.

'That's close,' Efer shouted from the river bank.

'Hurry up,' said Greet to the women. 'Now, let's go. Leave what we haven't got already.'

The woods sighed and the women set off at marching pace – soldiers in skirts, stomping the stony white path to town. Erma and Greet walked in lead, each holding the boy by a hand.

Efer ran up beside her cousins, lugging a sopping washing basket under her arm. 'I'm sorry,' she said. 'I was scared.'

'Quick enough about it then and all will be fine,' said Greet.

'What happened to you, son?' Efer asked the boy as they walked.

'None of us want to hear,' said Erma.

'The constable and mayor and such can sort this out at home,' said Greet.

Efer said, 'I want to know.' She asked the boy again, 'What happened to you, son?'

'A man who said he was a wolf came out of the trees,' the boy said. Then, as they all stepped under the linked black hull of the Dark Hedges, the red-ripped boy stopped and screamed. He lifted his hands and punched his face and screamed and screamed.

Greet picked him up under one arm – for he was little and as light as a sack of wool. She closed her hand over his mouth. 'Quiet,' she said. The boy stiffened like a planed plank, ready to be slotted into place, but his screaming carried on behind her hard hand. Greet ran, then, and called behind her, 'Run.' And the women ran through the Dark Hedges, the wind on their tail, and they could hear sounds in the woods, breaking and groaning and crying out for help – yelping and laughing, the pad of feet and crack of branches. Then a bark, but a bark like a man playing at being a dog for a day. And they ran hard and fast for town.

The First of the Werewolf's Meditations
A discussion on the nature of sickness and God

Greet's evidence took up most of the morning as she needed to be questioned and requestioned to bring out the full detail of her story. At break for lunch, Paulus sent me, without my asking, back to the keep to sit and eat with Stumpf.

'He likes you,' said Paulus. 'Or likes something in you or about you. Such men do not like anyone, truly – but he must get something from you, or you give him something. So, go, talk to him – share food with him. Find out what you can, but search yourself to see what it is he sees in you too.'

I walked to the keep, waved my way through the guards and in Stumpf's cell I drew up a chair by the double cage. I called for food to be brought to us, and while we ate, we talked. I told him of the death of his sons. He put down his plate and cried. He seemed deformed and disjointed as he wept – like his body had lost its shape and cohesion, and come undone from itself. I watched him. He wept, jagged and broken, for five minutes or more. He stopped of a sudden. He dried his tears on his sleeve and drew a breath into himself. His body composed itself back into proper shape and form, and he was as a man again.

'Paulus will pursue the murderers for justice,' I said.

'Well and good,' he said, and nodded, and picked up his plate again.

'Do you wish to talk of your sons?' I asked.

'No,' he said. He cut some meat and took it to his mouth, in his chained hands.

I asked him if he was a Christian. He chewed and looked at me and smiled.

'I am not an educated man,' he said, and he picked daintily now, as he talked, at the meat and bread in front of him, 'though I have read deep and long over my many years – but my conclusion to the great question of life is this: God is not a good god. Thus I must ask myself: wherefore did God create Peter Stumpf?

God may be all powerful and all-knowing and in all places – but he is not all-loving. To say otherwise defies, surely, the basic tenets of philosophy, of which you must know, as you are educated. Either that, or God is indeed all-loving but he is not all-powerful – for why would a good god not destroy disease? Do not start with talk of man's free will. For canker has nothing to do with my free will. Canker, like man, was created by God. And do not either talk of the fall of man and woman – for an all-loving God would forgive the bite of an apple. God then is wicked, or weak – and we are not worshipping our God as we should.'

'Shall we burn you as a heretic as well?' I asked.

'It does not matter what I say any more, so I say what I believe to be the truth. Light the fire and burn me now if you do not wish to hear me speak.'

He ate on, and I said that we worshipped our creator as best we can, and as best we know how, with our limited means and minds. Stumpf finished his food, and wiped his hands on the sack he wore around him. He looked at me and grimaced – not at my question, but at the act of wiping his hands on his clothes, as if it shamed him.

'I once met with a caravan of cripples on the road to Bremen,' Stumpf said, 'many years ago, now, and after I left the army. It was coming on to Christmastide, and I saw their wagon tracks in the snow before I saw them. I rode on – the plain was flat and white but the sun shone hard and the earth smelt of smoke and the air had that crisp bite in the nose I like so much of wintertime – and I caught up with them at the town of Achim, where they had been given permission to set up their tents in the grounds of Saint Lawrence Church, in a field set aside for new graves yet to be dug. The church is red-capped and red-spired, though its walls are brindled with bricks of red mixed with others of white and black. The door is most striking as it is painted blue and stands out, too loud, and does not seem part of the solid, strong church.

The caravan was to put on a show for the people of the town. I had business in Bremen, regarding some shipping in trade down the Weser that I was part of – but I could rest the night in Achim and see what performance this band of cripples had to offer.

I ate at the better inn in town, and stabled my horse and went to the new graveyard of Saint Lawrence's Church to their camp. I could see no properly formed man or woman among them. They did not have a master or mistress who employed them and travelled with them – but seemed to be autonomous, in charge of their own affairs and business.

Of course, there was the usual run of creatures that we see in all such caravans – dwarfs and giants and fat men and women, girls with beards, and so forth – and they did their usual acts of balancing and juggling and fire-eating, or simply sat there to be gawped at by the crowd. This caravan, though, had many more stricken souls, than one would usually see. I spoke to the two cripples who ushered the crowd around, took the money, and introduced the acts and the rare creatures lying within various striped tents. These two were a dwarf – as of course, folk can deal more easily with dwarves as they are not rare and seem like us – and a young girl, of perhaps fifteen, who was like a skeleton. She told me she was known as "The Girl Who Does Not Eat", and she had not taken food for more than a month now. She would eat again at Christmas but after that, it would be Easter before she touched meat or bread once more. She could have been beautiful, I believe, but her face was drawn over her skull, and her eyes set deep in the bone. Her limbs were twigs and her body, no fatter than my right thigh.

The pair told me that they would let no well-shaped, healthy person work or travel with them, as full-grown and proportioned folk used the crippled and deformed like cattle or slaves.

This made sense to me, and I asked them for a showing. I wished to see the more stricken creatures, not the dwarfs and those born with shrunken legs.

"The cost is high to see our special friends," the Skeleton girl said.

"I have plenty of money," I said.

Natural children – the high-eyed, fat-faced simple ones – they tended to the cripples unable to look after themselves, and walked those customers who paid toward the striped tents, and then stood chattering to one another at the entrance ways.

In the first tent, there was a woman made of jelly it seemed. She was boneless. Her arms and legs were like fish's fins, but even then, to touch them, it felt like the cartilage in your nose – loose and wriggling and soft, not hard like the bone of a finger or toe or arm or leg. She did nothing but let me touch her.

"She is not an imbecile," the Dwarf said. "She has just been touched and looked at so many times that your presence to her now is no more than air."

I asked to see the second tent. Each tent cost more to enter than the one before. The dwarfs and giants and fat folk milled around outside the striped tents and entertained the crowd, but extra pennies had to be passed to see the stricken souls within and talk to them.

In the second tent there were two things I could not fathom, and you will not believe me to talk of it. The first was a Frenchman, naked to the waist, and from him hung another man – his brother, but this twin was a shrivelled, wretched worm – no bigger than a baby, with a gaping mouth, that panted and slobbered. Its arms and legs hung about it – for its hindquarters were inside its grown brother's belly. You could feed it scraps of food and it would mewl and roll its eyes and move its mouth.

The Frenchman showed me how he washed his twin and cared for it, talked to him. While he talked, I looked at his belly where his brother grew from him – and there was no join. It was not a trick.

Beside the Frenchman, sat another twinning thing – an Englishman, and from the top of his head there grew a smaller head. No arms or legs or body, but just a face emerging from his crown, with eyes, nose, mouth, ears, even a chin – flattened though like a weight pressed on it. It rose from his hair and it had hair too, on its own head and thick on its face and about its lips, like a little monkey. Its teeth were tiny razors and its breath had the stink of a grave.

The Englishman told me he was noble-born, but had been locked away – and to live a life he had escaped and come on the road with many caravans and crossed half the world until he met this party he travelled with today.

"They are the best in the world," he said. "We are an army."

This face that grew from the top of his head did not move or speak. I asked to touch it. The Englishman gave permission, and I stroked its cheek with the back of my hand. It sighed.

"Listen," said the Englishman.

The face began to mutter. It seemed as if it was talking in its sleep, for it was not awake, that I could see.

"What does it say?" I asked.

"I do not know," the Englishman said. "But, sometimes, it talks and talks and talks and I do not like it. It could be casting a spell upon me. Often I think that is what it is doing."

And he lifted his hand, and slapped the face that sat upon his head. Its mouth opened, like an angry baby, and it fell to silence.

The natural ones – the grown elfin children – that took me from one cripple to the other, told me in their jabber that I could not go into the next tent, which was small and green-striped with a scarlet pennant flying from it. Whatever creature was inside was not ready to be seen yet. So they led me on to the main wonder they had. Outside this last tent – the fourth tent – one of the natural ones, more clever than the rest, who was able to talk, she said to me that in the next tent I would see Man.

The Dwarf and his skeleton wife – for I learned as I talked to them that they were married – they told me that it was not any man I would see within, but Man itself. Life ungarnished. If I dared to look. And so, I paid the heavy price, *many many pennies, to go within.*

Within, there was a mass upon a long, low bed. A large white sack, it seemed, with limbs. The natural ones walked me closer and jabbered to me that this was Man.

"This is called Man," the girl one, the clever one, said.

If a baby took clay and squeezed it with its fingers trying to form the shape of its mother or father – this is what it would have made. The creature lay upon the bed, for it could never sit or stand. Its body was like molten flesh, and its head emerged as a cowled stump from its shoulders. The face was perfect though, handsome, and smiled. It had two thick long arms that ended in hands like cauliflower, but its legs were well-formed, though thin as sticks.

"I am Man," it said. And I fell to my knees. Its voice was deep and commanding, but thick like it was drunk.

"Get off your knees, friend," it said. "I am your friend."

The natural ones pulled me up to my feet and patted me all over, dusting down my clothes, and pushed me forward.

"Talk to your friend," the Skeleton Girl said.

The Dwarf husband placed a seat behind me, and sat me down before the creature.

"Thank you for wishing to see me," the creature said.

I reached forward and touched the end of its arm, where its hand would have been, were it normal.

"You are brave," I said.

"You know me well already," it said.

"Are you a human?" and I turned to look at the Dwarf and the Skeleton, but they simply stared ahead at their friend.

"I am," it said.

"How can you bear it?" I asked.

"I can not," it said.

"Why don't you die?" I asked. And the natural ones started hissing and pushing me, but the creature shifted itself, like a command, hard – arching its back – and the elf-eyed grown children calmed, and left me be.

"I wish to die," it said. "But I can not. To kill myself is a sin. I am a man and to kill myself would strike me from Heaven – and I very much want to go to Heaven. I have asked God many many times to take my life and let me die, but he does not, and so I must believe that he has reason for me here on Earth, in this way I am, and so I speak to good folk like you."

I felt my heart leave my body for this creature. Never had my soul played such tricks on me, that I could feel the suffering of another living thing. I cried for it. But the Dwarf shouted from the tent doorway, "And he speaks to you, good sir, for good shilling. And that is the way of the world, suffering or not. But your paying makes his suffering less."

The natural ones started to dance flat-footed and the creature smiled. The Skeleton Girl came to me and said that I had seen all there was to be seen now, but as a guest who had paid so much I could join them all for drinking later, if I wished to walk up and down among the tents for a while and watch the acts, for free, until then. They had to cater to other paying customers for a few hours still, but I should remember I was valued highly.

I left the tent, but the clever girl among the natural ones, she grabbed my arm and waved my hand toward the creature. Her tongue lolled when she smiled at me.

"Say goodbye to Man," she said.

I said goodbye and he wished me good travels.

The clever girl among the natural ones held onto my hand and walked with me along the rows of tents, and the people of the town who had come to gaze. They stopped and stared and pointed and laughed at all the different sights they saw, and after a while I stopped and stared and pointed and laughed at the town's people.

The clever girl looked at me confused. "Why are you laughing at the visitors?" she asked me, and I said, "They are the fools and the malformed. Look at the world in which they live, and they think you and your friends are the strange and unfortunate."

When the town's folk left, I sat around the bonfire the cripples had built and drank some wine with them.

The Dwarf said to me, "Do you wait to see what was in the green-striped tent, with the scarlet pennant? Is that why you stay?"

I had forgotten that I had not visited this tent.

"No," I said.

"You have not heard who is inside?" the Dwarf asked.

"No," I said.

"Well, come then," he said, and he took me, with his skeleton wife, to the green-striped tent, with the scarlet pennant.

Inside, it was dim – a fire burned in a brazier – and well-furnished with rugs on the tent floor and a large bed, draped in dappled fur. On the bed sat the most beautiful girl I have ever seen, with the face of a goddess and she was naked – breasts round and full, long dark hair, running thick to her waist, covering her lap. But she had no arms or legs. She sat propped upon pillows and cushions and smiled at me as we entered.

"This is Woman," the Skeleton said to me.

The limbless girl spoke and said, "Sit upon my bed."

I sat by her, and the Dwarf said, "If you wish to be alone with her, you must pay double, and we will go."

The limbless girl said, "You may touch me if you pay."

I paid the double price, but told the Dwarf and his Skeleton to stay.

I kissed the limbless girl on her mouth and told her she was beautiful, and then got up and walked from the tent.

The Dwarf and Skeleton followed me. He said to me, "What is wrong? You may stay with her. This is her choice. Not ours. She would not have asked you otherwise."

The Skeleton said, "Are you afraid of her?"

"No," I said. "And I do not want to pay for such a beautiful woman. She is like a goddess."

I stayed with the caravan until late into the night, talking in front of the fire with the cripples who came to drink and meet with one another now that the town's folk were gone and the show ended. Seldom have I sat and drank and told stories with strangers, but with these cripples my talk flowed free and easy from my mouth.

"You are a good man," the Skeleton said to me. She sat beside me on a bench before the fire and sipped water from a wood cup. "What a shame you are not crippled."

I rose to leave then. I wished to stay with them and travel on the road with them, but I could not tell them so. Nor could I tell them the reason why it was just and right that I should stay with them and live with them – that the people of the towns and the cities and across the Empire were to me the strange and stricken ones, and life here among cripples would be a place I could find a home.

"Those people," I said to the cripples around the fire – and I gestured over my shoulder with my thumb to the town, "those people, they wear a mask. If you could slit off their skin and see what hides behind their faces you would see ugliness and disease and malformation."

The cripples smiled and nodded and bid me a safe journey.

"I would you were a cripple," the Skeleton told me once more as I left.

I walked from the gates of Saint Lawrence's Church to the inn. In my room, I lay on my bed and I wept for the goodness and honesty which had been beaten out of me by walking among the well-formed people of the Earth, who have nothing in their hearts but despair and hate, and nothing coming in their reckoning but blood and fear and pain and death, from their God.'

Chapter Eighteen

The evidence, given by the many unremembered people of Bideburg regarding the Red-Ripped Boy, unfolds before the Committee of Public Inquiry.

The Committee of Public Inquiry resumed in the late afternoon, and was to carry on into the night until all evidence was given. Paulus was thorough – every man, woman or child who had seen the red-ripped boy brought into Bideburg, all torn, after the washerwomen and Greet had found him, was called before the panel.

Some historians have a knack for building up a picture of an event from every perspective. Say, if they were trying to tell the story of the siege of Munster – one chapter may be the tale of van Leyden, another of the Prince-Bishop, another of Knipperdolling and Hoffman, another of how the rebellion could not have happened without the Peasant Wars, the last maybe on the execution of the rebels and the restoration of the city under imperial rule. Paulus was so detailed and meticulous in getting the chronology and context of what happened once the boy was rescued that I thought I would go mad in the court, after a while, writing down over and over the same evidence from different mouths. I could see the events in my mind by the time the sitting was done and closed.

I came to know Bideburg intimately through the evidence of its folk – even the logistics of its town management, which as a subject of study should have been one to bore me enough to take my own life. However, Bideburg was built around fear and protection, and it fascinated me as I listened to the fathers of the town explain the safeguards they had built against the werewolf that terrorised their families.

Bideburg was rigged with alarms – bells strung on poles, each a square acre apart; chiming warnings dotted on a chessboard of green fields, town streets and farmsteads. Fifty-two Bideburg alarms in all. The bells would peal for one event only – not the arrival of a prince or a bishop, or Nativity or Palm Sunday – but a wolf kill. These bells had been tolling their warnings for near to twenty years now, I would learn. But on that day when they last tolled, it was the life of the little boy, the one all torn and bloody and brought by the Bideburg women, which would catch the wolf and make the bells turn silent.

The men in Bideburg's main square heard the first bell peal – Efer pulled it as the women ran bearing the child – it rang from up where the road left the Dark Hedges, it seemed, where the woods cleared and the town started proper. The pealing rolled through the town as each man or woman, if they were near a bell, tolled it hard once they heard the sound – and the pealing was taken up at the town head, and went on ringing out in the farmsteads and grand houses of the richer folks – hands pulling ropes as ears caught the sound of warning bells – clanging on into the far fields where farmers were tilling and gathering and tending; the alarms rang in the poor allotment homes on Bideburg's outskirts – where many of the washerwomen lived – and went on ringing into the square, and on to the black stone keep and armoury at the foot of the Steipplinger mountains, crashing up at last against the long ring of the black peaks circling the town.

The high street was full of men – because it was the time of the men of the town, Friday gone noon, when the women were washing or cooking and the children at play, and men free to drink and talk low as you please. Once the chimes rang out, there came that flinching among men at a time of danger. But the men came out of the inn, anyway. A squad of four Bideburg constables and the high sheriff, Jens, ran from the keep at the foot of the town – where Bideburg ends and the mountains and woods begin again. The ordinary men picked up what came to hand: knives and shovels – a tankard can be a weapon, so can a stool. The constables and the sheriff had fat pistols with cords already smoking, staves and swords.

The sheriff Jens called, 'What is it?'

Odil, the innkeeper, stood in the road and said, 'It's Jesus Risen. Yes, Jens, the Second Coming amongst us sinners.'

'Shut up. We don't need your stupid jokes,' the sheriff, Jens, said.

'Perhaps the dummies have forgot to scare the crows,' Odil said. And his mates and hangers-on laughed, though those who did not like Odil – such as young Rodinan, the new town councillor and a fast-rising farmer – they shook their heads and looked at the high sheriff, though they drank with Odil too at night, made business with him, money with him, and feared him all a little for he was cruel and sharp and clever.

'The first bell tolled from the south,' Rodinan said.

The sheriff nodded at his constables, and set out forward, up the road towards the Dark Hedges, the river at their side. Rodinan padded behind. The rest of the men stood where they where. Odil swung on his heels. The town mayor, Kroll, neither spoke nor moved.

The squad had not gone one hundred paces when the women came into sight, over the brow of the little drumlin mound leading down into Bideburg. There was terror among the women. None of the men had spotted the child as yet.

The men said what all folk say when a sight shocks their hearts – Jesus, and Sweet God, and Mary Protect Us, and Fuck, and Hell, and Damnation. Murder. And then they all started towards their distressed women – as each of us, even the worst of men, would do. The two groups – the men, and the women – came together like dry clapping hands, on the road from the allotment homes, where the town's poor lived and fended for themselves. One by one, and then as all, the men stopped their questions and shouts – and they saw the boy, now quiet again, but still red-ripped and white-faced, in Greet's arms, cradled like a baby. And there and then the high sheriff got the story, of the washing and the boy and the wolf and the chase, straight from the mouth of Greet, with additions from her sister Erma.

'You were chased?' said Jens. 'So the wolf is where?'

'Behind us,' said Greet. 'Right there. We could hear it in the trees.' And she pointed to the Dark Hedges. The men brindled like dogs before a fight, their shoulders up and hair tight.

With cries of 'right, no more', and 'I'll not risk my family' – the men who had women among the group of panting pale washers took them home. Efer was marched away by her brother – for her father and husband were off hunting. She shook his grip from her arm, and pushed him as he muttered, 'Get yourselves home and to safety.' And on Efer marched ahead of her brother, picking up pace each time he drew to her heels – for she would not be seen walking with such a cretin and bully.

Erma left with her young husband, but Greet said she would stay, and remain alone among the men with the red-ripped boy clinging to her hip – she felt it fell to her to care for the child. The guards dispersed the remaining townsmen – who sloped some few paces down the road back to Bideburg but then idled to listen.

Jens asked her, 'What do you believe?'

'The boy was attacked by the werewolf,' Greet said. And she laughed. 'Or so he says.' She cried, her face folded ugly, and she said, 'I don't know.'

Jens nodded to his constables and they shooed the dawdling townsmen away. The men moved a little down the road and stopped again. Greet and Jens stood the boy up straight. He swayed. The child was blank as paper, but he held his feet.

'Let's go back to town,' Jens said. And the constables hefted their hands on the swords on their hips and took that march forward which tells all those not in uniform or authority to move and move fast or else be marched over. The townsmen strode briskly home ahead of them.

Greet and Jens walked, the child between them, and Jens asked the boy, 'Son, what has happened here?'

Jens took out his loaded smoking pistol, turned and walked backwards, heavy and sweating, watching the Dark Hedges and the woods. The boy didn't speak.

Greet spoke. 'He says the wolf did it.'

'Is that right, son?' asked Jens.

The child stayed silent, but he raised his head and looked at Bideburg in front of him – the houses and crossroads, the round black keep with the mountain wall behind, the river, town-hall, butchers, inn, the men watching them approach, some women that he'd seen – the woman who'd been slapped, walking away, a man behind her – and dogs snuffling in the street, and he lifted his head high then to the lilac sky and the coming sun through the breaking clouds and down he fell to the road, in the blackest of black sleeps a child could ever gather about itself.

Jens lifted the boy, and Greet walked beside them as they made their way to the town's keep – backed hard against the mountain – where the constables barracked, and decisions could be made amongst the voting men of Bideburg.

* * *

Paulus finished with the eyewitnesses and folk of secondary testimony. He then called the men who had been with the boy in the keep after his rescue: two town constables, Kroll, Rodinan, Odil and Jens.

He ordered Kroll in first. Kroll was a very mole-ish kind of man. Small and dark and fat and pinched. He wore a velveteen and the dirty nap on his clothes was like a mole's pelt.

The boy, Kroll said, had been taken to a cell in the keep, lain down and given medicine to make him sleep. The men had voted there and then on the spot – as the majority on the council and largest landowners – to recruit a party to hunt the wolf.

'Where was the cell?' Paulus asked.

'In the keep, sir,' said Kroll.

'Where in the keep?'

'The basement, where the cells are,' said Kroll.

'And the medicine?'

'We gave it to him.'

'Where was it from? Where did you get it?'

'Medicines are at the keep.'

'What is the medicine?'

'I do not know. It brings on sleep.'

'And did he sleep?'

'Yes.'

'And once the party was raised – to hunt Stumpf, you call him a wolf – who remained with the boy?'

'No-one.'

Paulus sucked at his teeth in a way I found almost shockingly voluptuous, and said, 'You can go.'

Kroll stood, and Paulus spoke. 'A moment, please. I have forgotten something.'

Kroll hovered over his seat.

'Did you speak to the boy?'

'Speak to him?'

'Yes. Did you converse with him? Ask him questions.'

'A little. Not much.'

'What did he tell you?'

'That he had been attacked.'

'And?'

'And it was by a wolf.'

'The boy said wolf?'

'Yes.'

'Thank you, please go.'

Kroll left and Odil was called. He walked to the witness table – slowly, like a little rooster – and pulled the chair out far, before he sat, dragging it under him, with a great scrape, as he took his seat.

'Why were you at the keep?' asked Paulus.

'What do you mean, sir?' Odil said.

'Well, why were you there? What was the point of an innkeeper being present at an event of such importance?'

Odil drew his shoulders back, and pushed out his chest. 'I have voting rights in this town, sir.'

'Why would voting rights come into an issue like this?'

'What?'

'Why would any of you think that the issue of voting rights was of importance when a child had survived a werewolf attack, as you believe, and was in need of protection and medical treatment?'

'We didn't.'

'So why were you there?'

'To watch, I suppose.'

'So why bring up your voting rights?'

'I do not know, sir,' said Odil.

'Who grows beets in this town?'

'What, sir?' said Odil.

'Who grows the beets?'

'A family called Westren.'

'Why was Master Westren not at the keep?'

'I do not know, sir.'

'Why was the coffin maker not there? Or the priest? Would it not have made more sense to have the priest there? Anyone but you – an innkeeper?'

'I do not know why the priest was not there, sir,' said Odil.

'I do not know why you were there, innkeeper,' said Paulus, 'and I would like an explanation.'

'I have told you, sir, I was there just to look as I am friends with the others – the mayor and sheriff.'

'And your fellow town councillor – that farmer, Rodinan. Why was he there?'

'For the same reason, I suppose. We were nosey,' and Odil turned to look at the spectators in the hall. He pinched his nose and laughed – a giggle like a boy of five.

Paulus banged his hand on the bench, and roared at Odil. 'Get out. Out of my inquiry.'

Odil sat motionless, staring at Paulus – but Paulus roared again, 'Get up and get out of my sight.'

Odil leapt to his feet.

'Wait, you,' Paulus screamed, and his voice was hoarse now.

Odil became a statue before my eyes.

'Who cared for the boy?' said Paulus, quiet now, with threat.

'We all did, sir,' said Odil.

'What did you do for him?'

'We bathed his head and dressed his wounds and gave him water and food – though he did not want food.'

'Is that all?'

'Yes.'

'Where did this happen – where in the keep?'

'In the front hall where we put him.'

'Is that where he remained?'

'Yes, sir.'

'Very good. Get out.'

And Odil scurried from that room the way I've seen mice run from my feet when I kick at them.

Rodinan was next – lanky like a heron, sloping into the hall feet first. He sat. Paulus wrote in the ledger before him, and sheafed through papers. He leant over and whispered in my ear, 'I am going to keep him waiting and make him sweat. Nod to me.'

He sat back, and I nodded to him. I looked at Rodinan, then looked back at Paulus, and picked up my pen. I began to write in the ledger in front of me. I wrote my name over and over again, and drew a laughing face.

Time had turned to sludge for Rodinan. He sweated and smiled, and flicked at his wet hair and eyebrows. Drips fell from neck to collar.

'What did you vote on at the keep?' Paulus said at last.

Rodinan flexed in his chair – like a horse when you pull the reins as it grazes.

'We voted on how to hunt for the wolf, sir,' Rodinan said.

'Nothing else?'

'No, sir.'

'And how did the vote go?'

'We sent our two constables away to raise a party to hunt the land to the south of the town, and we would lead a party through the forests.'

'And who is we? Who was in your party?'

'Jens, Kroll, Odil. Me. And we called on Odil's two sons as well, who are also town constables.'

'And how many were in the other party? Searching the south of the land?'

'Ten or fifteen.'

'And in yours there was six?'

'Yes.'

'Why?'

'The wolf had last been seen by the Dark Hedges to the south.'

Paulus cocked his head to the side, so his cheek was almost on his shoulder, and looked at Rodinan.

'And how did the boy get out?'

'I have no idea, sir.'

'Imagine it,' Paulus said.

'I can't,' said Rodinan.

'Have you no imagination?'

'No, sir.'

'Then you can't be a very good town councillor.'

'I am sorry.'

'Try,' said Paulus.

Rodinan opened his mouth and looked about him.

'Try to imagine, or you will not leave here,' said Paulus.

The spectators in the hall shuffled a little now, nervous.

'I can not, sir.'

'I can wait, and if you have not answered by the time I close this panel tonight, I will reconvene tomorrow after you spend a night in the keep for contempt of state authority.'

Paulus sat back in his chair, tapped me on the arm and said, 'Willie, take a note of my order.' I scribbled in my ledger, in my own scrubby shorthand: 'Rodinan for jail if no answer forthcoming on how he imagines child might have left keep.'

Rodinan was quick with his answer then. He sat up straight and wiped his forehead on his cuff, and said, 'Sir, if I have to imagine, I would guess that when we were all gone that he somehow got free from the keep.'

'How would he do that?'

'The keys to the keep are in the main room where he was kept and he could have found them and escaped.'

'Were the keys missing?'

174

'There are a number of sets.'

'Had they been counted?'

'I do not believe so. I do not know.'

'And the boy was awake and active? He could have physically escaped?'

'Yes, sir.'

Paulus said, 'You see, Rodinan, you do have an imagination, and so are fit to be a town councillor.'

Rodinan was persuading himself that Paulus was about to dismiss him.

'And so, it could not be, therefore, that there was someone in the keep who released the boy and took him to the woods?'

'No, sir.'

'You are sure, sir?' said Paulus, mocking.

Paulus leant over and whispered to me again. 'They did this,' his breath came in my ear, and as he sat back again, he said the word 'bait', loud enough to be heard – then he looked at Rodinan.

I longed for Rodinan to say, 'what', or, 'pardon, sir'. He said nothing. He sat like a trained dog.

'You can go then,' said Paulus. Rodinan got up and walked like he had been beaten, to the door of the hall.

I got to call Jens in – I think Paulus felt that a whelp like me summoning the sheriff before the panel would heap humiliation on him before the examination even began.

'Tell me about the last time you saw the boy?' Paulus asked before Jens so much as had his arse in the seat. His face still bloody, and bruising up now like a fallen apple, from his beating.

'We left him sleeping in the keep, sir,' he said, eyes down.

The townsfolk in the crowd muttered to one another a little, and Paulus had to do no more than raise a finger and say, 'Silence', for them to still at his command.

'Where in the keep?'

'The main room.'

'What had happened before you left him?'

'Nothing.'

'Nothing happened? You took the boy to the keep, placed him there, and left? Is that your answer?'

'No, sir – sorry, sir,' said Jens. 'We put the boy to bed.'

'Is that all?'

'Yes.'

'You didn't wash him, or feed him, give him any medicine, or ask him any questions?'

'He was not fit to talk. We cleaned him off, gave him water and let him sleep.'

'And he slept well?'

'The poor lad was asleep almost as soon as we put him to bed.'

'And where was that?'

'It was down in the cells by the armoury, sir, I believe.'

'Did you not just now say the main room?'

Jens ghosted.

'Sorry, sir, I got confused, sir. Yes, the main room, sir.'

'And then?'

'We left to hunt the wolf.'

★ ★ ★

Paulus dragged Jens over every detail of the wolf hunt like a Roman would drag a Christian over stones.

'It was coming on for dark when we left the keep,' the sheriff said, 'and we tracked through the north forest and up to the east woods, as well, for hours. It was a slow search and we went snail pace, quiet. Most of my men have seen at least a little service in the military, so we are trained to scout and surveil. The other party were sweeping the south and then crossing the river to the west to skirt the mountain ridge there. Once we'd hit the farthest point we could search, we turned around and headed back for the town, but again, sweeping the land at a slow, deliberate, scouting pace.

Not two miles from Bideburg, we heard screaming – the way a lamb screams when its throat is cut – and we took to a quick march. Five hundred paces on, down by the woodsman's store hut in the heart of the forest, we saw a wolf – huge and black, though with something of man about it in its size and stance – eating the boy. The child was dead. The wolf had not seen us. He was on top of the boy, tearing at his clothes and body. I fanned the men out around the glade – then I lit my wick, and filled my gun and took aim and fired, and I nipped that bastard's shoulder, you can still see the wound on Stumpf. It reared up and roared and ran.

The wolf got through our ring of men, and galloped – for it did bound more like a horse than a wolf, it seemed to me. But we were on it tight behind, though it was fast. It tore at its own body, I thought, as we chased it through the woods. The young boys were far ahead of me and Kroll, as we are the oldest. Odil was fast and kept up with his sons and Rodinan. The wolf pulled something from its body – like a belt or a sash – and a green flash shot through the forest. When we could see again, there was a man – naked – running ahead of us through the trees. We were on him though, close now, and he was wounded in the shoulder where I shot him, so was slowed. The man ran and dodged through the trees – but Odil seemed to follow him like an archer on a target, ducking and weaving in the wake of the man as if he were his shadow.

Odil drew up behind the running man and with the stave in his hand hit him square across the back of the head – he went down like the hangman's drop. When Kroll and I caught up with the rest of the men, they had turned the body over, and there was Stumpf. He had torn his wolf girdle off during the chase and tried to return to human form, but we had seen him at his magic, and this is the solemn truth, I swear.'

★ ★ ★

Paulus dismissed Jens and recalled Kroll, Odil and Rodinan – one by one. He asked them to recount the pursuit and capture of the wolf. The story each gave was identical to the one Jens told and identical to each other's tale. They had told it many times before to their friends in the inn, and their wives in bed.

Before each one left the court, he asked them, 'Why did no-one stay with the boy in the keep when you went to hunt the wolf?'

All said they had not thought it necessary.

'Do you regret your ignorance?' Paulus asked them.

They all said, 'Yes, sir,' and Paulus told each one of them to get out of his court. With Paulus' eyes on them, the people in the meeting hall were stony to the men as they walked to the door.

Next he called the two constables, Odil's sons. I saw they were the lads who had found the Stumpf sons and rode their bodies into town. It should have been a roasting they suffered from Paulus, but they were such mouth-gaping imbeciles that they were impossible to interrogate. Idiocy can defeat genius, this I have learned over my long life. The two Odil boys, they stared at the ground, and nodded, and said yes or no, or looked blankly at Paulus. The way they held themselves drove Paulus to a fury, and he growled at them to sit straight, as each slouched at the witness table, one after the other

– though in my memory they are so indivisible in their doglike dumbness, that they may as well have taken the stand at the same time together.

Paulus said to each one as they took their seat, 'You smell of horse.'

They sat dumb. He started his questioning. Both said they had stood guard at the keep door, while the town's headmen were with the red-ripped boy, and knew nothing of what had gone on inside, until they were called into the hunting party for the wolf.

'Why did one of you not stay with the boy?'

Both replied they had not been ordered to do so.

'Were the Stumpf sons dead when you found them?' Paulus asked – taking his track on a different path.

'Yes, sir.'

'Were you armed?'

'Yes, sir.'

'With what?'

'Sword, sir.'

'No crossbow?'

'No, sir.'

'Who killed the boys?'

'I could not imagine, sir.'

'Do you own a crossbow?'

'Yes, sir.'

'Do you carry it while on duty?'

'Yes, sir.'

'But not today?'

'No, sir.'

'Why not?'

'Forgot it, sir.'

'Even though you were sent out under orders to meet two boys who might have been under threat?'

'We did not think, sir. No-one told us.'

'What were you told?'

'Nothing, sir.'

Even the spectators in the hall were sickened by them as witnesses – and examples of humanity – and booed them when they mumbled their senseless answers.

Paulus finished each of their testimonies with the same words. 'Out,' he shouted. 'Out of my sight. You are not fit to call yourself human. Ape. Out.'

Then he dismissed the court, and I took my dinner with the werewolf – on the suggestion of Paulus.

'Sometimes the mechanics of justice produce only nonsense,' he said, as I left. 'And lies.'

The Second of the Werewolf's Meditations
A discussion on War and Munster

'*My war at Munster was a strange one,*' *Peter Wolf told me – for that is what I had taken to calling him, and he liked the joke as well as I did, it seemed. 'When the rebels in Munster took the city, they captured cannon and mortars as good as ours – so we could not set up a line close enough to the city to take down the walls without the rebels inside destroying our firing positions. We were both within each other's range – and that makes for a bad war. I was a good scout, and a good artilleryman as well, so I was sent with a four-party, led by an officer, into the bluffs and hills around Munster, to see if we could find a higher position within range, where we could place cannon and mortars to fire down onto the city walls. Some positions were perfect for placing cannon, though impossible to transport cannon to; others, we could get the cannon to, but we'd still be either within range of the firing positions inside Munster, or out of range all together. Our officer was the numbers man, and worked out the trajectories and distances and velocities and parabolas with his book of equations and instruments. Me and the two other soldiers climbed the bluffs and hills to recce emplacement locations.*

Above the city, I would often eat my rations alone – for me and the two other scouts split up to recce the land – and watch the scene below. I could see the little people move around inside the city walls, and from here they seemed harmless. The troops and tents of the army outside the city were like paintings on a map. The river and canals and waterways around Munster throbbed with light, and smoke from campfires without and chimneys within dotted the air like dirty smuts on glass. All should have died and left me to peace on the hillside.

On one of my first sorties in the hills, the Children and Grandparents Charge took place. I heard horns and drums from inside Munster and watched as the gates opened and hundreds of children – all little children, none older than ten – came running onto the plain before the city to meet the army. The army raised its hackles when the horns sounded, and a line of cavalry were rallied, with troops behind – pikemen, arquebus men, grenadiers, regular infantry.

The children – armed with swords and axes – ran screaming in rage towards our lines, some were singing hymns, but there were so many voices singing so many different hymns that I could not work out the music or the words. Behind the children came old men and women, and they sang hymns and screamed too. None had armour.

The cavalry had been slow to start its charge, and just as the horses took forward, the children were almost on our lines. They crashed around the cavalry, swarming on them, and although they dragged many riders from their horses and cut them to pieces, the Landesknecht swathed through the children like a great scythe. The horsemen rode on to kill the old people, while the infantry moved forward to mop up the remaining children. Rebels on the city walls fired down on the cavalry, killing more riders and infantry men who were now amongst the old as well. Our marksmen fired back and kept the snipers on the walls pinned down, while every child and their grandmother and grandfather was killed on the plain outside Munster.

It was over by the time I finished my rations of dried beef, bread, wine and an apple. From where I sat, I saw the rebels fill the city's main square, and kneel, hands raised to Heaven. A few men stood upon a raised stage in front of the kneeling city folk. The men on the stage walked backwards and forwards and must have addressed the people.

When the cavalry and infantry retreated, leaving every soul from the city who had taken part in the charge dead on the ground, the people in the square cheered and a great singing went up. It was a hymn I had not heard before – but later learned to be the Crucifigat Omnes. The ancient Crusader banner song declares, "Let this be the crucifixion of us all". They were happy, the people in the city. Their little ones, and their fathers and mothers, had all gone to Heaven now, as holy warriors, and soon they would rise again when the rebels turned Munster into the new Jerusalem, and Christ came to walk the Earth with them and enact the Last Judgement.

The singing angered the young Prince-Bishop and he set up the army drummers and pipemen to play as long and as loud as they could. The rebels inside took no notice, and some on the walls danced arm in arm so the army below could see them.

When I was not scouting the hills for firing positions – which we never found, for the high land was too unfriendly for artillery, and we had to keep to our *measured stalemate on the ground – I was sent with my squadron to hunt out spies travelling to and from the city, and anyone trying to break the blockade by smuggling food into Munster. Our Jäger squads were ringed around the city, and divided into two-man teams, each team was given an allotted square of land, drawn on the map, to dominate and keep free of spies and smugglers. The land each of our teams had to control was large – perhaps the size of a middling village, and on that land there could be woods and rivers and hills. It was a constant routine of patrolling – first one man took an eight-hour shift from dawn, then he would rest while the second took an eight-hour shift after noon. Then both would patrol at night for eight hours – the cover of dark, evidently, better suited to spies and smugglers. In the morning, whoever had taken the previous day's dawn patrol would rest, while his comrade began the morning rounds. And so it went on for months and months. Exhausting, repetitive.*

In all, my two-man team captured no more than half a dozen spies during the first three months of the siege. Most of these were coming from the city, trying to get to the towns and villages of the Empire to preach and spread rebellion. The square of land which my comrade and I patrolled was not suited to smuggling. We only had a few streams and gullies on our patch. Smugglers used the larger rivers and waterways and canals and tried to gain access to the city through its sewers. We were meant to take captives alive, but they ran or fought and I found it easier to kill them on the spot than drag them back kicking and screaming to camp – that way, I could pick them clean too. Spies usually have plenty of gold about their bodies. My comrade was of the same mind, and we buried whoever we caught in a run of woods near the centre of our patch.

War is often tedious because it is a form of work devised by man and all work thought up by man for other men is dull. But if you do not care about war – which side you fight on, the cause your officers are asking you to die for – then it can make you very rich. No-one cares about the equipment that an army possesses. It belongs to no-one – not the rank privates or the highest officer. So if it goes missing no-one bothers much, save a little bit of huffing and puffing that goes nowhere. Pots, pans, kettles, firewood, iron ingots, horses, carts, swords, guns, food, wine, blankets, tents. The camp followers – the whores and petty traders – make good intermediaries. They pay for what I give them and sell on in the towns and villages that circle Munster. We all take our piece, and get rich, and the army never gets poor because the state and court keeping paying and buying and giving – because if they do not, then they will not win the war. And so war kills the fools who believe in it, and makes those who could not give a damn who wins or loses wealthy men and women.

I was a soldier for years, and in between campaigns I learned how to bank. For I could not travel the country with a locker-chest full of barter, stolen goods and coins. Banking makes a man rich too – and a man getting rich makes his bank rich. And so the banks know it is good to fund a war, and the two go hand in hand like death and the maiden.

At the fall of Munster, I did not take part in the raid on the city. My squad had been held back, in reserve, in case the first rush went bad for us. I did not care. I did not want to kill the rebels any more than I wished to kill my own officer, or the Prince-Bishop, or the laziest camp whore. Though I would have happily slit everyone's throat as well – every occupant in the city, every man in uniform, every camp hanger-on, every lackey and statesman who thought up the entire venture, the Prince-Bishop himself. Killing, not killing. When it came to the siege and the rebels in Munster, I did not care. I had no reason to care. Killing wouldn't make me rich at Munster. And why should I kill at the behest of another man to please him?

After the fall of the city, I had to count the prisoners. There were a lot of youngsters – boys and girls aged between ten and sixteen. The younger ones had all been sent out to die in the Charge, for they were deemed the most innocent and likely to rise straight to Heaven. Most of the older rebels had been killed in the final attack on the city or the mopping-up operation after Munster was breached. Our prison camp seemed more like a school – no little ones, no old ones, just the generation about to flower left alive. I may have seen Paulus among their ranks, who knows.

And then the great united army – with its soldiers who supported Rome, and its soldiers who believed in the words of Luther – it splintered and broke up. The Catholic troops followed the Prince-Bishop into the city to re-establish order, and the rest of us, the Protestant troops, we went back to our principal role: acting as stacks of soldiers in the towns and cities and villages which were free from Rome, and waiting for the Catholic princes to turn their sights on us – should that day ever come again. And, of course, while these Protestant cities and towns and villages were free indeed from Rome, they were not free. The Protestant nobles who ruled these areas were only too glad of the threat from their Catholic cousins, for that allowed them to pile us like the tin soldiers we were in their towns and cities and villages – that way these city folk and villagers and townspeople would not get to thinking of freedom anywhere beyond the pulpit and the caps of their knees when they got down to pray at night.

I neither cared nor did not care that I was in the Protestant army. I would have been as happy with the Catholics. It does not matter to me what badge is on my shoulder or what flag I fly under when a man is trying to kill me. It just so happened that being from Bideburg, and being a young man when I was a young man, the only army I could join was the Protestant one. Our town had rid itself of our Catholic lord and sought protection from nobles who sided with Luther, who we now followed, so I could not very well expect soldiers who lived and breathed by the word of God in Rome to welcome me into their ranks and fight with me side by side.

Let me say, though, I did not choose to follow Luther, any more than I would have chosen to follow Rome. That decision was made by the adults of Bideburg when I was a boy. They could have chosen to pray to the sun for all I cared. Still, I think the moon may be wise, and if there should be any god worshipped, then the old grey moon would make a fine deity – for it is quiet and safe; beauty without passion.'

Chapter Nineteen

A recounting of the history of the Empire – with close reference to the Peasant War, and the rebellion of the Baptists in Munster and ensuing siege.

Paulus and I moved into the inn that night. Our room was fit for purpose – clean, warm, two beds, two chairs, a table – and we talked over spirit liquor. We were tired – but of that tiredness where sleep is impossible because the mind still spins, still works and will not stop, like a freed running clock cog. So drink and talk bring peace. I told him about the werewolf's story of Munster.

Munster, Paulus said, was the whirlwind at the centre of the world; the emanation of Europe's madness when the people were mad and the land mad. Luther had heaved the continent awake, a giant gulping its way to consciousness, and allowed men and women to stand directly in the light of God – no priests in their way. And with the path to God clear, some thought – the poor and the mad, the saints – the path in life had to be cleared too: of lords and kings. Even of property and laws. And the poor waged war against the rich. A just and righteous war, if you follow the Franciscan as I do.

'My father,' Paulus said, drinking and filling our glasses again, 'he could have kept his shop, stayed quiet, and sold his goods during the first uprising – when the peasant armies took to the fields and towns. He was not raised in a rebel family. But my father chose to fight for the peasants, although he was an artisan and a printer, and his class allowed him to see out the war on neither side if he wished – but he proved himself and joined the ranks of the Godly Poor.'

His father, Melchior, was young and just married when Luther began the rise against Rome. His words washed out over Europe from his hiding places, and in their path, priests took up his teachings and broke with Rome, or dug in hard against the tide that bore Luther's name. Princes did the same. The land was in glorious upheaval and division. Melchior's family were one of millions, once happy to be quiet and peaceful, who came to wed their new theology to politics and daily life. If they could speak direct to God themselves now, if priests had become just wiser elders not divine intercessors, then why should a titled man, a lord or king, have any sway over them in this realm of flesh? Equal community with God was preached, so therefore there must be equal community between men, based on the teachings of Christ. The church had sinned by not following God's word, and so had kings and princes and lords and ladies. Jesus preached of poverty and togetherness, not wealth and control. Kings and lords had wronged against God just as much as the priests – and so for the new Jerusalem to arise from the work of the poor and believers in equal commune with the Lord together, well, the rich had to die. Priests could turn coat and become ministers turned away from Rome. A rich man would always be rich unless you killed him and took his land and money for the people.

This was not the giant Luther wished to wake, though. Luther did not mind the poor being poor, or a lord treating his peasants like cattle. Luther wanted revolution in his church, not in the streets and fields.

'If men like my own father,' Paulus told me, 'had been able to look back as students of history on the mind of Luther, they would have judged him a sinner and killed him too, for he was not of the poor or for the poor. Instead, fools held his name as a banner above them.'

Melchior joined a peasants' battalion and travelled the land along the Rhine, burning the great houses and the monasteries and nunneries. These troops of men sprung up across the land like scarlet fever breaking out on a body – at once and spontaneous, with no collusion or planning. They emerged in this town to the north, that town to the south, those towns to the east and west over a matter of days. None knew the other, but some grouped together and formed armies, the rest stayed small and took the lord's sword and pennant and fire no further than the next valley or town. They were like children loose behind their parents' backs, and the Princes and Bishops quickly raised their own armies – not as large as the peasant forces, for hundreds of thousands of the poor were on the road and altering the face of power in the land, but the armies of the rich were organised and professional, and armed like Pharaoh's troops. It ceased to matter if a Prince or a Bishop were of the old church or the new, their religious disputes could be settled through treaties and in courts and academies. The poor – the unwashed, uneducated, landless mob – was cause for unity among the powerful, whether for Rome or against, and they battened on their armour together. Protestant and Catholic. Melchior told his son Paulus that the war against the holy peasants by the armies of the rich was a harvesting of souls on Earth by the Devil. First the sickle came down on the field – knights and cannon laid thousands before them. In some battles, the peasants took the lives of less than ten of the state soldiers, while whole fields lay littered with their corpses. Then, the flail was taken to the threshing floor – and those who'd fled the field or done no more than offer support or a place of hiding were whipped and stamped to oblivion, their bones and bodies thrown in ditches they'd dug themselves, and used to fertilise the earth they had once tilled. When the war was over there was nothing but seed dust and husk in the air. Power had not changed. All that had changed was that in some churches, a priest was called a minister and he took no confession and offered no sacrament. The poor were still animals – though now they were beaten animals and as such in merit of even harsher treatment. A few of those seeds remained hanging in the air after harvest and the threshing, though. Melchior among them. They floated through the valleys and along the riverbanks, they made their way to farmsteads and villages and some took root and survived – though it took many years, ten years till the seeds were strong enough to latch onto the land and grow again. They bore spores and one of those spores landed in Munster, and it found fertile soil, nurtured with martyrs' blood. Munster had sat at the heart of the land where the harvesting and threshing of the peasants was done. It had lain barren for a long while, but that meant the earth had taken the time to renew and was now rich enough again for planting. When the seed fell in Munster, the earth was so rich that the seed became a plant in a day and a tree in a week, within the month its branches reached up to Heaven, and touched the gates of Peter.

'And this was the city of the rebels Jan van Leyden and Knipperdolling and Hoffman,' said Paulus, near to drunk now, but cogent and excited – speaking more to himself for the thrill of memory than to me. He poured me another glass and I took it gladly to keep him drinking and hear his story finish. 'Munster was the tip of history – and history yearned for Apocalypse. Today, history tells us Apocalypse is upon us, but van Leyden and Knipperdolling and Hoffman brought apocalypse into history. The people of the city declared themselves the warrior poor of Christ, and those who did not join them – the clergy, many of the wealthy, the town council – they were turned from the city, out through the gates and into the countryside beyond. If they did not leave quickly enough they were killed, and their blood enriched the land on which the city stood and the government of the Divine Poor grew.'

And so it was decided that this was the city of God – the new Jerusalem. That the people of the city existed to do God's bidding as it had been done in the time of the prophets. All goods were to be in common – all property forbidden. Women were also to be in common, for hadn't the prophets taken many wives? All heresy was punishable by death. When a man was declared Elect, he was beyond earthly bounds and destined for Heaven by God's infallible will. He could kill a roomful of children and still not tarnish his bright path to God's golden throne once he was Elect. The Elect were beyond right and wrong. Their will was God's will. And the mark of the holy people of Munster was the second baptism. How can a baby offer itself to God, with no knowledge of God? Only men and women of majority age could take the water as offered by the Baptist John in full understanding. To the world, this was heresy – for it defied the right of the church to name a man or woman a Christian devoted to God, and granted that right only to man or woman. But to the Elect of Munster, the world was there to be stood upon its head.

Van Leyden took the crown of Jesus, as King of Munster, and printed coins – his head on one side, the Baptist on the other. The world, he told the people of Munster, was to burn to ash beyond the city walls, and the city and all who lived in it would rise shining on the mound, elevated to Heaven as the host took to the reaping and harrowing of evil souls on Earth. The city would be added as an extra circle to the circles of Heaven. This was van Leyden's vision. The end would come and the Elect live forever alongside the Lord and Jesus his son and our Saviour.

But all cities and all communities give way to power, and Munster became the playground of the mind of van Leyden, Paulus said, weary now – a city where van Leyden's will could run free as it chose with laws and decrees and the shaping of people and government. By holy decree, each citizen had to wash at least once a day, though water was scarce, as the Prince-Bishop cut off the surrounding countryside and dammed the rivers and streams as they approached the city of Jesus on Earth. Those who did not wash were killed. Van Leyden revoked the washing decree when riots broke out in the city bath houses. One new rule had it that children were the closest to God and so would walk amongst the people as Watchers, calling out to the Elect and the guards any adults deemed working against the grace of God – and that could be cursing the act of stepping in a puddle or having once slapped a child for being spiteful.

And then the gates of the city were closed, and the siege began – the people left within. Again, the Princes and the Bishops from both sides put their squabbles over God aside, as they did during the Peasant War, and united once more against the poor and the devout – to cut the final canker out, for that is how they saw the rebels of Munster, the last tumour in the body of the Empire. Luther himself counselled princes and lords who followed him to put their men under the control of the Catholic powers and the Prince-Bishop for the duration of the siege to ensure the annihilation of the rebels. The city held out a long time – a year and a half. It could have held out much longer had goods truly been held in community. For while van Leyden and Knipperdolling and the Elect ate fresh meat and newly baked bread, the people – those followers not yet lifted up, women taken as concubines by the Elect, men not yet assured of the straight path to God through election – these people ate mice and rats and dogs. Soon a dog cost as much as a woman. Paulus' guess is that perhaps one in ten were Elect – and so many starved. Those that lost faith and were caught fleeing were executed without trial as the judges were Elect and so could do no wrong as whatever choice they made was the will of God. The families of the condemned were executed with them, unless they were of the Elect, and their property given over to the community of goods as distributed by van Leyden and Knipperdolling and the rest of the Elect. Children were made Elect too, and they denounced their parents as heretics. Parents killed their children as heretics. Each then assured a position as part of the Elect for casting down sinners among the brethren. The Elect took the wives of their friends from the old times as concubines, and women left their husbands to be shared among the men of the Elect. Many families killed themselves together. The armies of the rich tied up the city tight and waited. There is no point in letting soldiers die at the foot of a wall when the people behind the wall can be starved into submission by their own leaders. It is a cheaper strategy in the long run. Hunger set well in, and the Prince-Bishop was assured of Munster's starvation by reports from the handful of men who managed to escape the city. These men, nearly all guards who fled while on watch, spoke of people eating people now; the dead being dug up for food.

The Prince-Bishop ordered a barrage to begin – to test the city's guns and range. Hoffman said this was his moment of calling – the battlements of angels were crying out for a champion of the Elect who could walk into the fire of lead and smoke and make the unbelievers lie down before him. Out he rode, Hoffman, with just three tin-clad knights of the Elect beside him – his own son, a carpenter who was now a prophet among the Elect, and a boy of thirteen who had led the work of the Watchers. His son's breastplate was cut and worked from the plate in the town council kitchens. Hoffmann carried a banner bearing the cross and the head of van Leyden. The four rode through the gates. The government army held fire, and watched them ride across the green stretch of open plain between the city and their ranks. Hoffman cried, 'Bow down before God and his band of the Elect'. A soldier called out the get-ready – and the fusillade of shot left the four smattered in the air like red mist. Van Leyden told his city that Hoffman was their martyr, whose role it had been to test the power of the Devil's forces.

'The rich are weak,' van Leyden said. 'Four men of the Elect held them spellbound till Satan roused their senses, so the army of the city of the poor could stun them to their knees and take the field for Jesus.'

Soon, though, the end came, with Munster and the dreams of the poor of Europe washed away across a field of blood – out through the breached gates, under the feet of soldiers and horses, lapping at the skirts of the Princes and Bishops who had brought the city to its knees and filled the sky with the spirits of the Elect and their followers rising to God.

A burning city surrounded by the dead, filled by the dead – watched by a thousand orphans, the captive Munster children, for no adult over the age of sixteen was left alive. And Paulus was among the children. He talked often of it, for it meant to him an understanding of himself – and was better spoken of aloud, he said, than kept within and dangerous.

'I saw the Apocalypse,' said Paulus, 'and it passed over me. And it will come again and again, but it is not God's doing, it is man's whirlwind, man's dream, man's madness. God has no thought to destroy us, he just created us and so has left us to our own path, our own will. We seek to destroy ourselves, and by doing that we have killed God here on Earth and within us. We will only know God in the afterlife and even then he will be the light of love, not a power that we have to bow down to and grovel before.'

* * *

Munster. It is strange to me that I have never set foot in the city, though I know it so well. I have only ever seen it in pictures. All the pictures I have seen date from before the rebellion, but still the drawings can not be looked at without thinking of the rebellion: the rebellion that sneaked its way to the city along the tiny side roads leading towards the canal that rings Munster, then crossing the water like a miasma by the little red bridges that are drawn on the maps, and walking bold as burnished brass into Munster through the city gate. The countryside around Munster was cut and looped with roads and waterways – marks on the land proving the city's great trading power. But these roads and rivers and canals let the sickness of the Baptist rebellion into the city. The world had poured into Munster in the years before the siege. After the Peasant War, the world poured in grain sacks, fabrics, dyes, silver ingots; and then following the goods, there came books and pamphlets and travelling preachers; actors, thieves and whores. With all this money and commerce and new ideas and people, came dangerous thoughts too. Just as a human being will more likely grow sick in a crowd if too many noxious vapours are drawn into the body through the nose and mouth, so a country or town or city can grow sick if the people who transit the land carry with them their own noxious vapour – beliefs and ideas.

When a city is the greatest on Earth, it will have many saints and many madmen, and it is those who live above the common herd of people who shape the way a town or nation will travel. Those who are of the greatest good and the greatest evil – or perhaps, as Munster shows us, people fashioned from both – they are the arrow of the times.

Munster was a spired city – many, many spires of many, many churches piercing up into the sky. The best hunting-traps that I have ever seen laid for poachers are made here in Scotland where I live – a piece of flat iron, the size of a man's hand, fitted with spikes of varying length and thickness, some high and thin, some short and squat, each with its own purpose: to pierce right through the sole, to break the bone beneath the ankle, to cut off toes and rip tendons. Munster, in the illustrations, looks like these traps, its spires spiking the illuminated clouds. In the drawings, those spires seem abandoned though, and lost without the revolutionaries gathered around them – declaring the New Jerusalem beneath the Uberwasserkirche; gathering the one thousand Elect beneath St Paul's to shed their clothes and prepare for the coming of Christ in the last days of the rebellion, as naked as unsinned Adam and Eve on the morning of creation; or the good young people chained and captured at the fight's end, watching their leaders van Leyden and Knipperdolling, broken and tongues cut out, hoist high in cages above the Ludgerikirche to die of thirst and hunger and the elements – their rotted death and ragged bodies testament ever more to their crimes against state, sovereign and God.

'Their bodies still hang there to this very day,' said Paulus. 'And now the city is quiet, as is the land – ideas are quelled and the people work. When they do not work they sleep, and all rolls on just as the lords and rulers like.'

Chapter Twenty

Written in praise of Greet – my Eve, the mistress of Stumpf's wolf cave.

In the morning after breakfast, Paulus reconvened the Committee of Public Inquiry. It was one of those sittings where it takes longer for the body of the court to assemble than it does for the judgement to be read.

Paulus was brief: there was discrepancy in evidence given as to the last hours of the child who had been killed in the woods – his name was never known, and fashion had come to refer to him as the red-ripped boy. An investigation into a conspiracy in the death of the red-ripped boy would be established at a date yet to be fixed. A simultaneous investigation would be established into the death of the Stumpf boys, on the grounds of murder. The state would also now proceed with a trial under criminal law of the convict Peter Stumpf, with no further involvement of church officials – although Fromme would be given official observer status for the purposes of reporting back to the ecclesiastical authorities. Paulus finished speaking, and I dismissed the committee and the members of the public.

Jens, Rodinan, Kroll, and Odil stood to leave, and five or six of the townsmen clapped them on the back as they walked from the hall. Paulus beckoned to Karfreitag and told our sergeant to get their names. He took a little purse from his pocket and handed it to me.

'Give this to the girl, Greet,' he said. 'It is a reward from the Prince-Bishop for her good service to the law and the state.'

I nodded.

'Speak to the Stumpf women too and make sure they are well. If they need anything – oblige them. Take the day to yourself.'

'Won't you need me?'

'No. I plan to sleep,' said Paulus.

'For the rest of the day?' It was not even noon.

'Yes. Or at least until I wake up hungry. You can vanish until tomorrow morning for all I care.'

Paulus was a man who loved to sleep – because he was a man who exhausted himself with day upon day of little sleep, and too much drink, and reading and talking. When he found a pocket of time that he did not need to fill with work – he slept like a hog in mud, and could stay in bed a full day or more if he had the chance.

The meeting hall was empty now, apart from Fromme and his boy, Jodel, who both stood by the door, watching.

'You want to see me, friend?' cried Paulus.

Fromme pushed his boy away – the lad scuttling out the door with a piece of paper in his hand – and walked to Paulus.

Paulus leant to me and whispered, 'Apologies for what I am about to do.'

Then he pushed me – harder than Fromme had pushed his boy – and sent me tumbling forward, almost losing my footing.

'Off you go,' he shouted at me. 'I have work to do.'

I scowled – though feigning – and walked past Fromme and out the door of the hall.

The day was fine and warm – and to be away from the law and the meeting house and the keep felt like a stone had been taken from my shoulders. I would have liked to have dawdled the walk to the Stumpf home as the day was so good, but I found myself walking faster than I usually do – for my habit is to stroll, I do not pace.

I walked to the rear of the Stumpf house, to the kitchen entrance and knocked the door. There was no answer. I tried the door. It was locked. I sat on the step and waited, leaning back against the wood panels and letting the sun shine on my face and the breeze flutter in my hair and on my eyelashes – I felt it rustle on the wisps of young boy beard that grew on my chin and lip.

I must have slept. It seemed like I had just closed my eyes, but when I opened them Greet was standing over me, saying, 'Hey, you. Master Lessinger lad. Wake up.'

I jumped and slipped down the steps and surely reddened up like a nit. Greet laughed. She was cocky, with her feet planted and her hand on her hip. I looked up at her and the sun crowned through her hair in pale flames. She offered me her hand and I took it and stood.

'Mistress Werren,' I said. 'I have come to speak to you.'

'You do not need to call me that,' she said, 'call me Greet.'

I bowed and said, 'Please call me Willie, Mistress Werren. Greet.'

She laughed – and I knew then that I was doing well and fell into the rhythm of it straight away, though this was the first time I had tried to impress a woman or a girl. Stupid boy that I was, I did not count my cooing and fawning over the pretty girl back at the inn at Reissen as real courtship – that was nothing but an overeager beginner falling off his horse – though I hold the memory sweet now.

I gave Greet the money and explained it was a reward from the Prince-Bishop. She opened the purse, counted it, and sat on the step, fanning her face.

'Is this real?' she asked me.

'It is, Greet,' I said. 'Paulus was impressed.'

'I will take this with pride,' she said, and she tucked the money into the pocket of her apron.

I offered her my hand now, to stand, and she took it, and I pulled just a little too hard so she almost bumped into me as she rose. She patted herself down and I smiled at her and asked, 'Would I be able to see Madame Stumpf and her daughter?'

No, she told me. The women were asleep. They had cried all night. The sons' bodies were in the cold store – with the pig sides and beef, and that had made the mother near go mad, with the thought that her boys were lying dead beside animals.

The little daughter Rosa had screamed at one point in the middle of the night and not stopped for many minutes.

'It is a house of madness now,' Greet said to me. 'Though Divara is strong.'

We had walked down into the little glade near the Stumpf home as we talked. Before I knew what I was saying, I was telling Greet of what plans Paulus had in store for the town – that he intended to try Jens, Odil, Kroll and Rodinan for conspiracy to murder the red-ripped boy.

'He believes they took the boy into the woods and left him there as bait for Stumpf,' I told her.

'The men of this town are not good men,' Greet said, 'and few of the women are good for that matter, either.'

'Then, he'll put Odil's sons on trial for the murder of the Stumpf boys. He'll toy with them all first, though. There will be no charges brought against anyone and no arrests made until Stumpf has been dealt with.

Paulus can be cruel when he pleases against those he dislikes – and he wants to make your townsmen suffer a little and sweat. Have them dangle.'

'All well in my eyes,' Greet said.

Gossip is a great sport – perhaps the greatest if you have a mouth that likes to run, and a mind to woo others. You can tell you have a friend for life if the pair of you are fond of putting each other's heads together and chattering about the world and the people you know in it.

'I must tell you,' Greet said. 'Stumpf was a strange and frightening man. Though at times, he could be kind and even gentle, when the will was on him. He never hurt me, but it scared me to be in his presence. It was like he throbbed – the way your thumb throbs if you hit it with a hammer. He pulsed an anger and a hate that I could feel. And I did not like to be around his sons either. Though they never touched me or were cruel to me, either. But I do not wish those boys dead, that is for sure. Madame Stumpf is a good mistress. Her daughter Divara is like a friend, almost, but she is spoiled and that makes her haughty though she can not see it – still I trust her and even like her. The child – well, Rosa is still an innocent doll.'

'We will kill Stumpf,' I said – and we were holding hands now, though I do not know who touched the other first. I hope it was Greet. 'It will have to be cruel. But better under the orders of Paulus, than of the church – for that would be something hellish.'

'Good,' she said. 'He needs to die. I do not care how they kill him.'

Young men get overcome – a face, a wisp of hair, a turn of waist, can make the brain fall from a young man's head. And Greet was striking and young and clever, it seemed, and witty, and strong – in her mind and body. She undid me a little on the spot – for she was also bashful; bashful because, I think, she knew of her own intelligence, but knew also that she was spoiled too, ruined a little, for such a good mind being born so poor.

Throughout my life, when I have fallen in love – and it has been many many times – I fall at the beginning, on a second, fast, it is there – and I am diving to the bottom of the sea, wishing to drown myself in the woman I am with. It is her to the exclusion of all else – friends, food, wine, sleep, even books, though these women have also made me write poetry to them and their bodies and their thoughts and the pair of us as two indivisible souls. Then I read the real poets and see my writing so weak that the flame dies down and the heat comes out and the love fades away, and mostly dies, though some stay longer and few stay forever.

Unlike most men I know, I like the talk of women, and their company. Most men are fools, and women are not. And when I talk to a woman I love, my craze for them deepens – they let the thoughts and ideas I have inside me come out and be free, when I did not know I even had these thoughts and ideas in the first place. And when they talk – and it is only women who talk well that I fall in love with – and they let me see inside them also, this to me is the story of loving, knowing the contents of the mind of the woman in my bed.

So Greet and I talked and talked – and we talked on through the glade, and as we talked we started to kiss and soon we had lain down on the ground, on soft grassy earth beneath us, the sun low enough to warm us, a slow dying fire on our bodies. And this is how things go – and God, whatever God may be, let you be praised for such moments as this on the Earth that we have to call home.

There is something deadening about perfection, though. It is to be looked at but not touched. A truly beautiful woman is a cold sculpture, there is no life behind the looks under your fingers. I do not want a goddess, I have only ever wanted a woman. Greet wasn't beautiful. She was pretty, though – and I am a slave to prettiness. When we undressed each other her breasts hung heavy on her, but they were pink and cream and smooth and warm. She handled me as if I was a horse being bought at market – ran her hands over me, stroked and measured me, and slapped the parts of my body that pleased her. Men say they want slim-hipped, flat-bellied girls, and I have said the same at times, but the roundness of Greet, the fleshiness of her body, how she moved, entangled my soul in her. I felt her as a woman. She smelt and tasted a woman. And she delighted in the body of a man – for I was a man now, at sixteen I was no longer a boy, my brain and body were as developed as they would ever be, I had hair on my chin – she delighted in my body like ancient Venus. My goddesses are pretty, not beautiful, with maybe one tooth crooked, their nose too pointy – and I love those noses – lips much fuller or more thin than they should be, bodies that roll like white hills, with women's souls.

Since time began, young lovers have lain naked in each other's arms after losing themselves in another human soul and muttered secret things. Men lay their heads on the bellies of their lovers and – whether they know they think it or not – deep in their minds they wonder on the baby that might be there. Women kiss their men's bodies and listen to their heart beat.

After a while, we found we were hungry – ravenous. And thirsty like a desert. We dressed, and she asked if I had to leave.

I said no, and she replied, 'Well, good. I have a place to show you. We can eat there. There's some wine. Be alone. If you wish.'

'Yes,' I said. 'Where is it?'

'Ah, shush, and you shall see,' she said, and wagged her finger at me. I moved to bite it – but she pulled it away.

This was her free day as well, Greet told me, and she could do as she pleased, for no-one was the master or mistress of her when her time was her own.

She took me deeper into the woods, in the direction of town. As we walked, I told her I loved her. I redden a little even now at my clumsiness back then – a clodhopper when it came to love and women. I had been with her, and wanted to be with her for the rest of my life – and my head was singing. So this was love, I thought. Her back was to me, as I spoke – garbled babble, but love was at the root of it, and she understood what I was saying – and she led me on by the hand through the forest.

'That is good,' she said, after a little while, without turning. 'I may love you too, perhaps.' And the earth rose up beneath me, thrusting me into the air, so I stood on a platform of land, looming over Bideburg and the Steipplinger mountains like a gold Apollo shouting down on the little people below, 'I have my woman now – see.' And my goddess strode ahead, leading me by her hand.

★ ★ ★

'Listen,' said Greet, as she pulled me through the woods behind her – pushing ferns and branches back, which slapped into my face and eyes, and made me holler and her laugh. 'Listen. Many years ago, when I was a girl of eight, my mother, God rest her soul, she was nurse to the Stumpf children – my father was their woodsman. God rest his soul too. The Stumpfs were good to my family, and my family was loyal and good to them. On my birthday, Stumpf gave me a dog he had found and named Bryn. I took it to the Stumpf house every day when I went with my mother, and Stumpf loved the dog. We all loved it. He gave it to me as he said every girl needed a dog to take care of her in the woods and at night – from the werewolf. These were his words. Bryn was big and half wolf, or so

Stumpf said. One day, my mother and I were walking in the woods near the Stumpf house, with Divara, down by the river where the children go frogging, and a group of youngsters threw stones at us from the bushes. Bryn leaped into the bushes and came back with two little fingers in his mouth, and screams behind him. They were the fingers of Odil's daughter. She is dead now – of scarlet fever – five years back or more. And I wish I had danced on her grave.

Odil wanted to have me and my mother put on trial for the injury to his daughter, but Kroll and the town councillors and my father and Stumpf would not have it as my family is well-liked – though my father and Stumpf had to relent when a compromise was suggested that the dog Bryn be put on trial before the town.'

Greet laughed a dead laugh and looked back at me through the trees. 'You are in the land of the mad here,' she said. 'This I promise you, on my heart.' And she touched her breast.

'My mother and father were compelled to hand the dog over. The trial was to be held on a Saturday – that I remember as Divara had no studies, and her father took us walking in the woods to occupy our minds – for I loved Bryn, as much as Stumpf loved him, and I had raised him from a pup. Divara was fond of the dog too, I am sure, but she is a distant creature with her love. I knew she was sorry for me though, and wished to make me feel well. She held my hand as we walked through the dells and picked flowers. Stumpf talked of the different types of tree hereabouts but the noise from the town grew loud as the people gathered in the square to put my dog on trial – and our quietness in the woods was spoiled.

Stumpf never swore in front of me or my mother – not because we were servants, but because he thought swearing coarse and low-bred, and he did not stand himself high over servants, either – but he said "bastards" now, and took me and Divara by the hand. We walked towards town, through the woods – the way I am leading you, Willie – and came out near the foot of the hills, at the back of the keep. No-one had seen us, as the way is overgrown and dark. Stumpf knelt beside me and Divara and pointed at the wooded steep hill at the foot of the mountain, rising behind the keep. He walked us through the trees at the base, and we came hard up against rock. The trees were thick and grown close, but Stumpf edged between them, telling us to hold hands – he holding Divara and Divara holding me by the hand. The rock face turned to the right and so did Stumpf still winding through the thick wood – then I noticed that we seemed to be climbing a slow rise. We came to another wall of rock. Stumpf stopped, picked Divara up, and she clambered onto a shelf of stone above. Then Stumpf lifted me and I stretched up my hands – Divara leant down and helped drag me up. Her father climbed after me. The woods were still so thick a man could hardly walk through them unscratched, but on we went along a narrow ridge on the lip of the rock, wide enough for one person and no more – to the left the cliff rose sharp and high, to the right the world dropped off, but the little ridge could not be seen from Bideburg below as the trees rose so high as to hide it from the eyes of everyone, save God, if he chose to look down. We climbed higher and higher along the rising shelf of rock. We were on the mountain now, and off the low hills.

"This is like a secret passage way in the living forest," Stumpf said – for he knew Divara loved stories of castles and knights and hidden doors.

The shelf of rock came to an abrupt stop – ended by yet another wall of stone. The trees grew tight in around the little narrow walkway and dead end.

Stumpf let go of Divara's hand and she let go of mine, and he walked into the trees, as if he were walking off the rock and into thin air. He vanished in the branches.

"Don't cry out," we heard his voice say – sounding just paces away. His hand appeared from the leaves and beckoned to us. Divara followed first. Then his hand appeared again and I took it and he pulled me to him through the trees. It felt as if I was falling for a moment – instead I had simply dropped a few inches onto a new rocky path hidden by the woods. The trees – they grew so thick and close that they hid a natural turn in the rock, which wound around the cliff. Divara and I followed behind Stumpf – the trees so near upon us that I found it hard to breathe. Divara strode on.

Soon though, the rocky path turned upwards, became clearer, and some light fell down on us. We walked up out of the hidden path onto a little rise of land – sheltered on three sides by trees and high cliffs – before us lay the town of Bideburg.

"Be careful here," Stumpf said. "This is the one place that you can be seen, so keep low and run to that cave." He pointed ahead of him to a black mouth in the face of the cliff.

We ran, and skittered into the cave entrance. He followed behind and sat beside us. I looked to Divara, but she looked out through the cave mouth – curved up and out from the inside, like the pouting bottom lip of a tired and hungry baby. Above, another curl of jutting rock hid the entrance in shadow. We sat in the mouth, unseen by the world, and looked directly down from the mountain onto the town below us – we could see the square, the keep, the inn, the meeting hall, the allotment homes – I could see my own family home there – and all the way to the Dark Hedges. The keep lay, perhaps, five hundred paces below us, and two hundred paces ahead of us. If we listened very intently, we could hear the people below if they shouted – though making out their words was almost impossible – that is how close we were to our neighbours, and unseen. Stumpf told us to stay watching, and went back into the belly of the cave. There were many people in the town square now. A platform had been erected and Bryn was tied to a pole to one side – a gallows and a noose was placed in the centre. It was a gallows without a drop – the kind where to hang a man the executioner must drag him off his feet by the rope around his neck and then fasten the rope to a hitching place until the condemned has strangled.

Kroll was reading something aloud, and Odil was standing at the front of the crowd, with his three-fingered daughter. There was drinking and singing and dancing and foolery. Stumpf returned. He held out a flask of wine and said "drink". Divara drank first and then I drank. There was meat that had been drying to cure but I did not want it and thanked him no. Divara ate steadily. Stumpf lay on his belly between us, as we sat in the cave mouth, and moved something up by his face – it was a crossbow. Divara placed her hand across her father's back, and kept it there, very still. He slid a bolt home and placed his eye to the length of the shaft, looking out and down onto the town and square.

"Say nothing of this ever," he said. "This place is my secret. Not even Madame Stumpf can know."

I looked to Divara and she nodded at me. I nodded back, and said, "Yes."

"You can rely on me, father," said Divara.'

Greet stopped her tale, and turned to wink at me. 'I have kept my word all these years until now,' she said, 'as I owe Stumpf no more favours, but you are the only soul I have told, Willie. So now it is your secret to keep with me.'

She turned her head away and swished on through the trees and ferns. I followed. She pulled me behind her, hand in hand.

'Down below in the town square,' Greet went on, 'Kroll finished whatever it was he was saying – and then he walked down from the platform. Odil took his place on the platform. Bryn was muzzled.

Stumpf turned to me and said, "I do not want to hear any crying or noise."

I shook my head. Divara watched calmly, as if she was in the high seats at a city theatre.

Odil untied the dog, took it to the centre of the stage and put the noose over Bryn's head. Bryn was as placid as a lamb. Odil took the other end of the rope and pulled slowly on it, so the dog rose up on his back legs a little, and his feet started to dance, his body leap, and he must have whined behind his muzzle though I could not hear him – and I had to keep silent and not cry or speak out. The crowd was shouting, "Hang him, hang him". We could hear that clear, as they were so loud.

Odil raised a hand in the air to them, and readied himself to lift the dog from the ground and tie off the end to the hitching post, so Bryn would swing and strangle there in the afternoon air. Stumpf was breathing in a deep, slow way, as if he was sleeping. Divara watched him, then turned her face back to the crowd below. Her hand still steady on his back. Odil pulled and Bryn began to rise. Stumpf let out a long deep breath and there was a little click as the trigger released and the bolt was slipped free. It rode through the air, curved its arc and just as Bryn was pulled off the ground, it found its mark, right in the dog's chest. Poor Bryn yelped and kicked, but was dead, thank God, before the last sound from him finished echoing off the rocks around us. Odil dropped the rope and ducked, fearing another arrow was coming his way. The people shouted and looked around, up and down the street – to the roofs of the buildings about them.

"It was better we kill him, than let them make him suffer," Stumpf said. "And give them their entertainment."

I nodded – for he was right – and I was grateful to Stumpf for ending Bryn's life quick, like the snap of his fingers. Divara sat silent, watching the folk in the town below scurry and talk and act like ants. She patted her father's back and took her hand from him. Stumpf moved away from the mouth of the cave, further in, and ran his hands over his crossbow – testing its trigger and sight and string. I turned my back to the town and watched him. This may have been how he shaped his kindness, but Stumpf frightened me more than before – because even his kindness was dark and silent and deep. Secret.

We waited an hour. Divara still watching the people in the town stumble around like fools, gossiping and speculating, then disappearing as supper hour approached. She turned to us and said the town was grown quieter. Then, we climbed back down from our invisible hiding place. We returned to the main woods and wended our way back to the Stumpf house. My mother would be finished with her chores by the time I arrived at the door, and she and I would make our way home, then, to the allotments and my father, if he was back from Stumpf's saw yard.

"Tell no-one of the place," Stumpf said, as we walked through the glade below his house. He patted his girl on the head, and then pushed us both on in front of him to run for home.

The people hated the Stumpfs after that, Greet said, as we came out of the woods at the back of the keep – the Steipplingers towering over us – hid from the eyes of the town. 'They said they knew it was Stumpf or one of their boys, but had no proof. Madame Stumpf was enraged when she heard this gossip and felt her family defamed with lies. After that, Madame Stumpf hurt any of them any time she could. A raised rent. A forfeiture of pay. A forced sale of land on a bad debt. She tried to break the town.'

We did not speak of the Stumpfs again. Greet led me to the hidden path, then, through the forest and up the mountain – it was a long frightening climb but I knew at the cave she'd become the mistress of all my secrets, and I would learn everything of her.

* * *

After a long time, we sat at the lip of the cave and watched Bideburg dissolve in the night, and the lights of the town come on like marsh wisps calling us down off the mountain. There was wine up there, as she said, and some dried stripped meat, apples, cheese, nuts, honey. Stumpf kept his hide stocked. The cave was deep inside, she said, and went far back into the mountain. But I had no wish to explore, and she said 'good'. We curled into each other. The air was cool, and smelled of the pine trees and firs. We were naked, but warm. I felt – languid, is the word, but it does not do my feeling justice. Loose, alive, safe, happy – sleepy too – but excited as well, and wishing to spill my heart in Greet's ear, and have her spill her own heart into mine. I was drunk a little as well, and Greet had drank more than me.

'Greet,' I said to her. 'Leave with me, when it's over.'

She laughed and I felt a little dagger of embarrassment take its course through my veins. The first of many times when the thoughts in my head have caused the scorn or the disbelief or disappointment of the woman in my bed – and it always cuts me.

'How can I do that?' she said, and lay back hard as if my question had killed all the kisses on her lips. Her change frightened me a little – as if I had wronged her by meaning good.

'You can,' I said.

'It would not be allowed,' she said.

'Your family would allow it, surely. I have great prospects. I am a gentleman. Almost.'

'I have no family now. Just me and my sister, and some far relatives. I will take care of myself and do as best pleases me.'

'I am sorry,' I said – it is a hard life to be a child without parents, especially a girl.

'Do not be sorry. I have no father or brothers to tell me what to do. I miss my parents but I am fine.'

She laughed again – but there was no humour in the sound this time. 'But would your family allow it? Master Lessinger?'

'I am making my way in the world myself and if I want to take a wife then I will take a wife. My father would allow it.'

'You are sixteen,' she said. 'I am seventeen. And I did not say I wanted to marry you.'

She had shoved a little blade into me again. Love always comes with an armoury of weapons – no matter who it is that lies beside you. And you carry the same weapons too and use them also, though you do not know it or admit it.

'Don't you though?' I asked. 'Wouldn't you wish to marry me now?'

I rolled on my side to her and put my hand on her bare belly. She let me stroke her, and she stroked my arm as my fingers played in the plain of her hips. I kissed her shoulder, and she turned her head and kissed my temple.

'Even if I did, it can not happen.'

'It can. Paulus is like a father to me and he will make it right. He would not see me broken-hearted. He would talk to whoever needs to be talked to. He can arrange a special licence of marriage. We could be married in the first town we came to once we leave Bideburg, by the first priest or minister Paulus can lay his hands on. In Reissen even. I am not having Fromme marry me here.'

'Well, you have lots of plans already, my husband,' she said, cruel with mockery. 'Tell me: what would I do as a lawyer's wife? The world is not solely about you.'

If a man had spoken to me with the sneer in his voice that her voice carried I would have put my fist in his face, no matter what his size or rank – but with her I felt as though I had failed her by not being poor and lowly; that she might have found me easier to love if I had not got myself an education and tried to make a life beyond the station I was born into in this world. I have hated money and what it does, and social class and what it stands for, since before I came to Paulus – but this talk with Greet, over the nonsense of breeding and status and wealth – for that is what we were talking about, I thought, regardless of it being bound up in other terms – it made me wish that all the gold in the world would melt into the air like dissolving water and leave the Earth.

Instead of saying this, I said, 'I may not become a lawyer. I might teach at the university, offer my services to the court. I have a gift for languages. Paulus is likely to be made an ambassador within a few years, and has his eye on Paris, though that is maybe too high a goal – still, I can do anything I want.'

'And what would I do? I ask again, Willie.'

'Raise our children. Be loved by me.'

'Then I'll remain a maid,' she said. 'A servant.'

'No,' I said. 'Do not choose to stay a maid. You could do what you wished as long as we loved each other.'

She shook her head and sat up and took another mouthful of wine from the flask we'd found up in the cave. She handed it to me when she finished and I drank also.

'Very well. I am a maid and a servant who raises children and tends a house.'

I did not understand her then, though I do now. So sitting beside her I did not speak, only looked dumb at the ground.

'And maids and servants,' she said, 'do not marry young lawyers or professors or whatever you imagine yourself becoming one day, to tend their houses and raise their children. I can be a maid and servant here.'

'A maid or a servant means nothing.'

'Oh it does, Willie.'

'My parents are not rich. If it wasn't for Paulus, I would be a printer's boy. Who would marry me if I was a printer's boy today?'

'Maybe a maid.'

I made an 'och' and an 'ach' at her, and threw myself back hard on the ground beneath us – for she beat me at every turn.

'Do not be a baby,' she said.

'I am not,' I said.

And she turned to me now, on her side, and stroked my belly – just along my line of hair and my eyes felt like they were turning to mercury in my head. I kissed her.

'I love you,' I said. 'Marry me. Come, Greet. Let's do it.'

'Would I be free?' she said.

'Free?'

'Yes, free. What kind of husband would you make? I would broach no cruelty or limits set on how I think and feel and talk.'

'Greet, I love you for those reasons. I want a wife, not a slave.'

'How do you love me? You do not know me.'

'Then how have we found each other like this,' and I pointed at us naked, and at the cave around us, and the moon in the sky outside above Bideburg, 'if I did not love you? Or you love me.'

'People can not fall in love in a day,' she said. 'They can be full of lust though.'

'Maybe they can do both,' I said – and then I built the next words very carefully in my head. I believed in them, and meant what I said, but I wanted the words to hit her. 'I have fallen in love with you. I know that. And I lust after you too – and that feeling will last in me till I die. But I love you more than lust – and that is time-enduring, is it not? And lasts forever. All I would ask is – have you fallen in love with me? If so, then we know the answer to our questions. We should marry.'

'You are a mad person,' she said, and she laughed – loud, almost frightening – and slapped me, hard on the belly.

'Are you happy or angry?' I asked.

'I am happy,' she said, and she kissed me, and I grabbed her hard around the waist and pulled her on top of me. She kissed me and then bit my lip, and I slapped the round softness of her thigh. Her face changed, a ripple of fear and anger.

208

'How can I believe you?' she said, moving off me. We sat beside each other, cross-legged – and I was too dumb back then to understand the changes in her. 'Men say they love a woman then they treat her like a dog and go off whoring. Is that not true?'

'Some men, Greet. Not the ones who are good. Why would I have said these things to you if I did not mean them? You did not raise it. I did. I could have got up and left, and never spoke of damn marriage. You asked nothing of me before we lay down. I have said what I did because I meant it.'

'Do not give me "some men", Willie. Are you a good man?' she asked sharply, for a sharp tone had come to my voice also – and the wine was playing with us. 'Or do you just want this?' And she took my hand and put it between her legs. She rubbed her hand over mine so I caressed her. I left my fingers there and curled them around her hair, still damp.

'I want this. I want you. I am good. I will be good to you.'

'Prove it, then,' she said. 'I am not going to give up the safe life I have here, walk to the next town with you and then be left for some other girl – or turned into nothing but a maid who carries your name.'

'Tell me how to prove it.'

She stood up, naked and white, the straw bedding from the floor of the cave stuck to her thighs, wrapped and snaked round her ankles and calves. 'I will ask you to prove it to me by showing me that you are more than just a man. Men can not lower themselves before women the way that women often lower themselves to men because of love. So if you love me and wish me to be your wife, show me that you believe I am better than you – that my happiness counts more than yours. For that is what men ask of women. If you do that then I will trust you.'

'I will do that,' I said. 'Happily.' Her body towered over me – her legs, her belly, her breasts, her face, her hair. I sat up, and ran my hand down her leg. I asked, 'Say how?'

'Let me dress,' she said.

She pulled on her underclothes and dress, without a word, rolled on her stockings and pushed her feet into her slippers. I lay back on the floor of the cave, the packed earth warm from our bodies, and watched her – it made my mouth water to be naked in front of her while she was fully dressed.

'Kneel,' she said.

I looked at her.

'Kneel,' she said. 'In front of me. Kiss my feet and tell me that you are mine.'

I felt no compunction not to do as she asked. It is shocking now to look back and think that I did such a thing, but I loved her, and if this was all it took to prove that then I was happy to comply, and kneel. And the wine helped.

The ground smelt of rich dark dirty living earth as I kissed her feet. Again, I relished my nakedness in front of her, for I could feel her eyes pouring over where her hands had pawed minutes before.

'I am your servant, Greet. You're my lady, and it will always be so.' I felt like laughing as I said the words, for I was acting – but the words were true too, and what I was doing was meant and honest. It should have shamed me also, though it did not.

She knelt down, and took me by the hair and raised my face to her. I was as long and as hard as I have ever been – in all these years no woman ever aroused me more than at this moment. But she was crying, a little, and I felt I had wronged her and said sorry.

'I can make you my husband,' she said, and she put her arms around me, but when she held me she clung too tight, like I was a tree trunk floating in the Baltic Sea and she a drowning girl.

It takes a long time to make a woman stop crying – especially when they cry from that place of mixed-up happiness and sorrow. We sat cross-legged again – and that is how I think of us to this day – Greet hooked into my arm, head against me, and we hunched over, like naked savages in old Europe. We patted each other, and she said she wanted me to speak to Paulus in the morning.

I said, 'Yes, of course.' And then she asked if I believed she was worthy of me. I told her to shush. We took one last drink of wine, and lay down. We slept together until the sun came up and woke us. We played, drowsy, with the morning air on us, and after a while when our mouths were dry and our bodies panting, we dressed and left the cave and the mountain and the forest.

Chapter Twenty-One

The trial of Peter Stumpf, known to history as the Werewolf of Bideburg, but judged here a common lust murderer and mortal man.

'Let me show you how to prepare to rule a courtroom,' Paulus said.

There were just the two of us in the long dark Bideburg meeting house. Paulus was in a bold mood – laughing, performing – as was his way in the times when his spirits seemed to lift his mind too high for him to hold onto its path and flow.

When I returned from Greet and said good morning to him in the meeting house, he had grabbed me round the shoulder and rubbed his knuckles on my head – like a brute uncle. I hate such pranking and manhandling.

'You stink of fucking, Willie,' he said, dragging me around by the neck, and slapping my back. He pushed me in front of him.

'What a trial this will be, Willie,' he said. 'What trials, rather. Bideburg will be the making of your career. Forget your fucking, this trial will be the greatest memory of your life.'

I was horrified at his talk – as if he had never risen further than the back street he was born in, and said, 'Sir, this is most uncalled for – I have no idea,' but he cut me off, saying, 'Shut up. Do you know anything about acting, Willie?'

I said, 'No.'

'Well, more fool you. Learn to act. You are most unconvincing in your lies for a young lawyer.' He set off to the platform and judge's bench at the head of the hall, leaving me standing and blushed to the bone. 'People,' he said, as he walked around the raised stage, 'think of acting as the work of whores and dwarves and such – not a bit of it. There are plenty of whores and dwarves – they are not all actors. Actors command space – people fill space – so actors command people. Simple logic. What is my courtroom

– or the palace court, for that matter – or the general assembly: but space with people watching you. Get up on my seat there, Willie.'

He pointed to the best seat that Bideburg had – a seat from Kroll's house – that had been hefted into the hall and placed behind the long oak table, that acted as the judge's bench, on the raised platform at the head of the hall.

'Get on up here,' he said. 'Sit.'

I felt that look of foolishness – of coltish dumbness – take up position on my face, the way it takes up position on all young faces when told to act older than their age.

I sat on his chair. He jumped off the platform and sat on one of the pews from the church that had been placed in the hall for the townsfolk to watch the trial.

'Bring the court to order,' he said.

I laughed. 'Sir,' I said, 'there is no court.'

'This is a court, boy – I am in it – I represent the state, so this place is now a court of law. Bring it to order.'

'But it is quiet, sir.'

Paulus stood up, bent at the hips, placed his hands on his knees and roared, 'Bring your court to order, boy.'

I hesitated. He was about to shout again. I banged my hand on the table and bellowed out, 'Sit down, sir. This is a court of the Empire. Come to order.'

Paulus laughed. 'I'll stand if I want.'

I sat like one of the field dummies we'd heard tales about.

'Bring your court to order,' he screamed at me, and it looked as if there was hate in his eyes.

'Sit down or I will have you removed,' I shouted back at him.

'Do it then – remove me.'

'Silence. Now,' I shouted.

'No.'

'Sit down or I will have you executed. Guards,' I called.

Paulus sat down and clapped. 'With the best will in the world, young Master Willie – and I say this as an official of the court and your friend – you can not have an irritant such as me executed. You could have me flogged if you wish for contempt, but no, not execution, Willie. Keep things in perspective. Still, your voice was good and you projected at the end. You can act.'

He walked up to the bench and sat beside me. 'You'll sit here, at my right, and note the trial, Willie. I did this at your age too.'

I had my own system of short-hand – I found the taught method much slower than the one I had devised, but still it was not fast enough to take down every word I heard. Paulus said fifty percent accuracy was good enough, if the spirit of the rest of the notation was true to the evidence. I should also note tone of voice, in the margin – the way a witness reacted physically to questioning, the position of their eyes.

'If they stare at the ceiling while talking, they are lying,' he said. 'Their eyes have gone into their minds to help them make up a story. This is crucial.'

I asked if we should run through the order of witnesses – if he wished me to help him search for points of written law that existed to clarify issues in the case which may arise.

'Do not fuss, Willie. This case depends on one question alone: is Stumpf a man? The murders do not have to be proved – they are readily admitted. If he is a man, then this is a trial of simple law. So many counts of murder result in such and such a punishment. If he is not a human being, then we quit the bench and hand over to our friends from the church. Stumpf, however, is a human. Do you agree?'

'I have no doubt at all, sir. He is a man and that is what is so horrible to me about…'

'Exactly, a man. And I am not here to prosecute the folly of the church. I do not want a fight over God in my court, or what constitutes a human being. I will exhibit powerful conclusive proof that Stumpf is nothing more than a villain and a killer. And I will do so quickly. Then we can move to a recounting of the crimes, and a properly weighted judgement for those crimes – that is our job.'

Like the Elect of God – Paulus had made up his mind and so his judgement would be as he decided whatever the evidence. He believed it. It was true, therefore. Justice had been decided before justice had been done in a court of law.

Urchin that I was, I thought his daring to rule before he had taken the trial to conclusion an affront to everything I had been taught – mostly by Paulus himself. Now, I see it as the wrong way to a right path – but back then I took my needle to him as much as I dared.

'Should we not hear all the evidence before coming to judgement?' I asked.

'We will hear what needs to be heard, Willie,' he said. 'But if a man wished to prosecute the sun for running away at night and making the world black would you be much interested in his argument?'

'How do we prove a creature that people believe to be a wolf is in fact a man?' I asked.

'By making these idiots lift their eyes above their feet and see reason. One of my first cases as presiding magistrate was when I was just twenty-three – twenty-three, Willie, one of the youngest magistrates in the Empire. So, if you are following my trajectory, as you seem to be doing with unerring accuracy, then you will be weighing life and liberty in just seven years. Seven years, Willie. Will you be ready to judge a human being's life by the time you finish your doctor of law?'

I shrugged.

'Don't shrink into yourself like a baby, Willie. Say what you feel. I was terrified when I sat in judgement of my first case.'

He told me the case was heard in a town called Waffentru – a nowhere place in the forest. A creature had been found in the woods around the town – it had stolen clothes and food, killed some chickens, scared folk.

'Just as now,' Paulus said, 'I was sent to the town, with a religious colleague – and just one guard, mind, no contingent – to bring some order to the people, for they believed they had an imp or a wildman in their custody. The town was much like this too – old, bred in on itself, dumb. Guess what I found, Willie?'

'A beggar?'

'No, not a beggar, for this creature was something that none of the townsfolk had ever seen before – and they'd kicked plenty of wandering beggars out of their town.'

There was no point in a guessing game with Paulus, he wanted me to give up, so I did.

'Have you ever seen a black?' he said.

'A black?'

'A man or woman with black skin.'

'No,' I said.

'Well, this was a black.'

'Did you know when you saw it that it was a black?'

214

'Of course, I knew.'

'Had you seen one before?'

'No, but I do not need to go to Africa either to know it exists. You know of Africa, I assume, Willie?'

'Of course, sir, and of blacks.'

'But yet you have never seen one – or been to Africa.'

'No, but I would know a black if I saw one. They are like us but black.'

'Indeed. These townsfolk had never heard of Africa or of blacks, unlike you, Willie. A black was like a charred devil to them. The fact he spoke a strange broken version of our own language confirmed to them even more that he was infernal.'

'And what were the charges?'

'That he was a demon and should be put to the stake. What is comic about such cases is that the people think a demon from hell, or a werewolf, would wait quietly in custody – in their keep or jail or dungeon – for a state magistrate to travel fifty miles and three days to prosecute them. My first point made when I assembled the court – even before explaining that a place called Africa existed – was that if our black friend was really a demon then would he not have laid waste to the town and brought death to them all the moment they laid hands upon him? They did not seem so Godly to me that the Lord would intervene or slow the hand of the Devil against them. This was a case of theft – some clothes, some eggs, a chicken. You know why I break your back carrying all those books with you?'

'Argument from authority?' He had told me more times than I have eaten breakfast that if I wanted to win a debate then all I needed was a well-flung quotation.

'Yes, and put more simply – to shut people up. Point to a book, and they will button their mouths. Even if the book is nonsense, which so many are. Back then, though, I did not drag such a library around with me as I do now, nor half as many experts on this or that law – or as many soldiers, for that matter, to watch my back. Years ago, I just had my law books, my books on natural sciences, books on history and geography, customs and beliefs – and a few helpers. I didn't even have an assistant like you.'

He gave my arm a playful push with his shoulder as he sat beside me in the empty meeting hall.

'When I convened the court, I had all the village burghers come up to my bench and I showed them an atlas I had with notations about each part of the world. I showed them Africa and the illustrations of the black man and woman in the margins. I tapped the picture and pointed to our friend, the demon from Hell who had sat quietly in his cage for almost a week awaiting execution and not calling upon his father Satan to destroy Waffentru. They looked and jerked their heads like chickens studying feed, and asked me what it meant.

I told them it meant the devil in front of them was some lost African. He'd stolen their food to feed himself and their clothes to keep warm. Africa is hot, I explained. We are a cold country – the devil must miss the heat of hell.

And then I took them before the court as defendants – as I like to do with litigants I do not care for. "You people," I said, "you people have dragged a representative of the Prince-Bishop half-way across country to try a chicken-thief as a devil. Your ignorance has cost more gold than this town will make in a year. Here is my judgement: who is the richest man in the town?"

A mill owner lifted his hand – once his friends and neighbours pushed and prodded him so I could plainly see. "Then I want as monetary fine this man's yearly earnings – you will pay it collectively, and decide among you how you divide up the burden as you see fit. The money will be with me by tomorrow or I will begin confiscating property as I see fit. I, on behalf of the state, will give one twentieth of this sum to the African – to recompense the time you have held him prisoner, and to remind you that charity is the first act of the Christian, and ignorance about the world the chief sin of Satan. From the African's share, I will deduct the cost of the chickens, eggs, clothes and other material he stole and return it to the injured parties – I will also levy a fine on him, payable to the state and equivalent to the value of the goods he took. I believe the African will still have enough money left over to secure his passage back to his home in safety and comfort.'"

Paulus paused and wiped at his beard, which needed trimmed. He had not made it to the barbers, I remembered, as I arranged for him the day before we left for Bideburg. He was too busy trying to make time to see the plays in the courtyard. 'I never fully understood how the African came to the Empire,' he said. 'From what I could make out – mostly thanks to drawings he made on paper for me – he was on a ship and journeyed to many countries then was left at a port by accident, I think, and wandered.

He got lost in the Empire. I believe he tried to tell me he had been walking for six months – six moons I reckoned he was saying. My mistake was to pass my judgement then leave. A good judge stays until the effect of his judgement is over, and settling into history. As we will be doing here in Bideburg once our work is done. But that is a hard thing to do – the new callings of work often demand a lack of attention once the main task is complete.

So, the money was gathered from the townsfolk, and the divisions made. I made sure the villagers traded fairly with the African so he had some food for the road, and then I quit the town. My party was on horseback and we rode slowly for a few hours, the African walking at our side. I wanted to find out about his land and customs but we did not have enough shared language between us to communicate well enough. This was the first time the idea came to me of writing pamphlets – treatises – on the cases I came across. He may have been with the English or French or Spanish, though, I figured. His tongue was so jumbled, and strange from his own way of speaking. We came to the hill that would lead my party back home. I bid the African goodbye, pointing to the south, saying Africa lay in that direction though he would have a sea to cross to get there. He bowed, like a gentleman and said the word "thanks". We rode on, but he followed us and did not turn south. He fell behind as we kicked the horses to a run – I waved apologetically to the black, as I had to go and could not dawdle – and we lost sight of him. There were no towns within riding distance and night was coming on so we camped a few hours later. After we ate, our party sat around a fire and drank. It was a cold autumn night – no moon or stars. I'd taken my last draw on the bottle when a line of fire shot up from the earth, maybe two hills away from our camp. Two of us rode over, a ride of half an hour maybe. It was the African, strapped to a tree trunk and burned like a lantern. The next morning I rode back to Waffentru and I brought the whole town into their meeting hall and I told them that unless the killers were identified then I would hang the mayor. Remember, I was young and in a party of just three – with one soldier and one priest and me – not a gang like we are now. No-one spoke up, so I did hang the mayor, with my own hands, from the lintel of the village inn. Not one of them moved a hand against me. I know I killed the wrong man – but what was I to do? Burn the village to the ground in retribution and have no justice at all? He was their leader. He must have known.'

'I would have done the same,' I said.

'Well and good.'

'Surely, though,' I said to Paulus, 'if you are going to prove to them that Stumpf is a man, then you have to explain to them why he killed? Otherwise his crimes are so monstrous to them, so out of the ordinary, that they will never disbelieve that he is a wolf.'

'How are his crimes so monstrous? Look at these people for a start. When my lord this, or my lord that, puts a city to the sword – is that monstrous? Or do you believe that is just the state at its good work, destroying those who'd bring terror to us – as we are told? And among those who bring terror there are babies, I find, when I look at the dead. I am not scared of babies. So, why have we killed them? There is blood and murder everywhere, Willie. It is not being fashioned day and daily by devils and werewolves. It is men who do it, and we know that. A man can not kill and eat some sixty or more people – is that what I am told? But the Lord your God can turn two cities on the plain to ash and kill thousands – for what? How they found their lovers in the night? The Lord can flood the Earth and kill off all mankind because we have displeased him by drinking and fucking? If the Lord can be a monster then so can the man. We are in his image after all. Ergo Stumpf is a man. Case closed.'

I did not upbraid him in my mind for his coarse words.

★ ★ ★

Who knows why a human being kills. A trial does not exist to explain why someone murders, but simply to prove who did the murder. I think I know why Stumpf killed, but I can never be sure. Our time – this period of history in which we live – is one of dislocation, of religion falling away and altering, of the power of kings waning, of change in the fields and cities and towns, the university is replacing the church, new inventions turn the world on its head – making some poor and forgotten, others rich and powerful. The world grows smaller and bigger at the same time. It is hard and lonely to be in the world, even for the best of us. Stumpf, I feel, was not a child of this world – that does not mean he was a devil, or a changeling, or one possessed or in service to Satan. Whatever passed for his soul was not only lonely here on Earth, but repelled by the world it found itself within. Some say there are creatures walking on the moon – living things –

shaped like rats or spiders or maybe forked and bare-skinned like humans here on Earth. Stumpf would have found as much comfort, more, among the people of the moon as among the people of the Earth. You can not love what you can not become, and if you can not love then hate or contempt are all that will fill the spaces in your heart – and so Stumpf killed.

None of this mattered for the trial, however – which began on the third day of our time in Bideburg. The meeting hall was packed by early morning, and the remainder of the town, those who couldn't get in – mostly the women and children – stood outside the doors, which had been left open, listening in the street in the warm summer morning, peeking over each other's heads for a glimpse of what was going on inside.

Paulus and I had put on our black cloaks and black court hats, our white collar ruffs. He addressed the crowd – though he treated the spectators as an audience more than a public gallery. He told them Stumpf was to be prosecuted under state law as a low criminal. A lust murderer. He said that there was no proof of any supernatural or infernal allegiances or acts – that the trial was itself a trial against superstition, and an indictment of the innate wickedness which lies inside humankind and needs no devil or imp to be awakened.

'Stumpf is a common murderer,' he said, pacing across the raised platform, in front of the judicial bench, at the head of the meeting hall. 'Common in that murder is not an unusual crime – though uncommon in his assiduousness as a killer, in the rate and speed and number of his crimes. Uncommon also in his skill at remaining undetected for so many years, and his brazen gall in living at the very heart of where he killed throughout his entire time as a murderer of men, women and children. Stumpf will be tried and executed as a man – a base human being.'

Paulus paused and stood still, his hands on his hips. He nodded to me, and then called to Karfreitag, 'Sergeant, bring the prisoner into the court.' Karfreitag set off to the keep – as Paulus had arranged to enhance his own theatrics.

'This is a court of extraction – we are not here to fight over differing versions of the truth, until what passes for truth at the end of the trial is unclear and uncertain – we are here to establish a definitive truth: what happened. We are here to extract the truth, not debate it. When the prisoner arrives…'

The crowd inside the meeting hall muttered to each other, and the muttering spread out to the people listening and watching in the street. Paulus looked at me.

'Silence,' I called out. My voice sounded hoarse and foolish. The muttering continued. 'Silence.' And this time I nearly screamed. The folk turned to look at me, and some were confused that a boy of sixteen could sound like an angry and dangerous father.

'When the prisoner arrives,' Paulus continued, 'he will be read the charges facing him and allowed to make a public confession. If he makes a public confession with full admission of guilt, I will sentence him accordingly and the case will be closed. I know these crimes have hung over your town for many years now, but if all goes well then this can be over in two days. Tonight we will finish the trial, and you will know the man guilty of the crimes he has confessed. Tomorrow he will be sentenced, and given the night to pray. The next day we will conclude with the execution which will allow Bideburg to return to a state of peace and prosperity.'

He paused. 'Pending, of course, the outcome of other investigations into the matter of the disappearance of the boy, and the murders of Stumpf's sons.'

I thought the crowd would hiss and whisper to itself, but it did not. The crowd was still and scared.

Paulus continued: 'Stumpf has already made a full confession to me and my assistant.' Paulus gestured in my direction, and the people cast their eyes at the boy who shouted, looking a little more respectfully on me now. 'I have no doubt that he will repeat the account here before his peers and God.'

The people outside the court began to move as one, away from the door, and there was jabbering and shouting among them. The guards brought Stumpf, chained and manacled, into the meeting house. Each guard handled a dogcatcher pole attached to the leather collar around Stumpf's neck, so that they led him like a brute beast to market. They manoeuvred Stumpf through the doorway and into the room. The crowd inside moved back as one, as if Stumpf had some polar or magnetic power streaming invisibly from his body, which pushed the people away from him. The folk drew in their breath. I could feel the panic and the fear in the room. Stumpf kept his head up and cast his eyes around the assembly – he was not fearful or cowed, nor stoic or proud, he simply moved in accordance with the demands made on him, as if his life was already over and the last days and hours belonged to others, as if he had already left his body, his mind elsewhere while his physical frame carried on, like an Italian automaton, without him.

'Unbind the prisoner,' called Paulus.

The crowd outside peered inside – a few boys my age jumped in the air to look over their elders' shoulders into the court. Those inside the meeting hall, however, moved about and lowed like cattle in the butcher's pen – some men nearest the door pushed their way out, dragging their wives with them, and the rest circled around in groups, gathering themselves as far from the werewolf as they could get within the walls of the wooden room.

'Be quiet and bring yourselves to order immediately or quit the court,' I called in my loudest voice.

Paulus followed on the last beat of my words, 'This is a man. Count the guards and constables in the room. We could cut him down in moments. And look,' he said, and drew back the hem of his black robe at the waist, showing a pistol on his hip – though it was for show as the wick was not lit. 'And here,' he added, showing a pistol on the other hip also. 'Both are loaded. You are safe under our command.'

As Paulus had told me to do, I took a short sword from inside my own robes and laid it on the bench in front of me.

The guards unbound Stumpf from his chains and manacles, and removed the dogcatcher poles from his collar. Karfreitag stood behind Stumpf with a cocked pistol, cord smoking, a span from the back of his head.

'Let the accused sit.' Stumpf sat on a small black wood chair before the bench. Karfreitag dropped his wrist so his pistol kept a line on Stumpf's head. I pulled my seat up close to the bench, and touched my pen and paper, checked my ink and sand bottle. The people edged back to where they had been standing, order fell over the room and the trial began, as all trials should – quietly, formally, with the date noted in the court ledger and the charge of 'a multitude of murders' read against Stumpf. He nodded where he sat and looked up at the ceiling when Paulus asked him to make his confession before the people, the court and God almighty himself.

★ ★ ★

Paulus and I had written the charge together. Or rather Paulus had dictated the charge and I had written it out. He wanted to make it simple, so every cowhand in the village could understand precisely what was happening.

'The landowner, Peter Stumpf, of the parish town of Bideburg, is charged under statute – that is law – with a multitude of murders, carried out against innocent men, women and children, in the town of Bideburg and its hinterlands, between the years 1524 or 1525 and the summer of 1563. He is accused of these crimes as the sole party, acting alone, with no outside influence, assistance or conspirator, corporeal or incorporeal. On full and frank confession, the sentence of the court will be execution, in a manner to be decided by the court, commensurate with the crimes in question, but with no forfeiture of goods, property, land and chattel, as heirs and beneficiaries of the accused are in no way held to account for the crimes committed against the people, Empire and God by prisoner Stumpf, and there is no evidence pointing to Stumpf having profited from the murders, which are believed to have been motivated solely by lust and blood frenzy. The families of the victims of the killer – if they can be found, identified or make themselves known to the state with proof of relationship – will, however, be allowed to petition for the right to sue Stumpf's heirs and successors for blood money by way of recompense. Magistrate Paulus Melchior presiding, and the court held as final arbiter with no right to appeal.'

I read the charge. Stumpf sat impassively, and Paulus began.

'Stumpf,' said Paulus. 'You are an avowed killer. Yes or no?'

'Yes, sir,' said Stumpf. He looked at Paulus while questioned, but on answering directed himself to me.

'And you acted alone?'

'Yes.'

'With no human assistance?'

'With no-one but myself, sir.'

'And with no other assistance?'

'What other assistance could I have, sir?'

'The Devil, sir?'

'No, sir.'

Paulus addressed his audience – speaking like a father to a child. 'This is a killer before you, Bideburg. No work of the Devil. I have seen the work of men before and men can behave like the Devil, though the Devil has never touched them. In some folk, be it through a mistake in their mind, or in their experience, there is a level of hate and will to commit evil that we may often confuse for the hand of Satan. It is not – it is a lesion in the make-up of humankind that exhibits itself large in Stumpf, but hides within us all, as the Bible tells us all. For it is our shared and common sin that we have the capacity to do evil.'

The crowd shifted in their seats, those standing shuffled their feet – but there was silence, no loud talk to merit another shouting from me. Fromme watched Paulus from the front row of seats, unblinking and fixed – like he studied a mite under an eyeglass, fascinated by the hair on its legs, and the teeth and eyes in its head.

'All of us are wicked,' Paulus told the people, 'this we know from the second story God teaches us. First he made the Earth for us, and then we spoiled it with our faulty soul. We disobeyed. We acted against nature. We are all the children of Adam and Eve – perhaps Stumpf more than all. Two nights ago, I watched Stumpf eat the wafer, drink the wine, touch the book and praise the Lord Jesus Christ. Did I not Stumpf?'

Paulus shouted out his question, and Stumpf nodded. The people looked at each other and then at Stumpf and back to Paulus.

'And I did so in front of my church official.'

Paulus waved his hand in the direction of Fromme. Fromme nodded once.

'So now we accept this man is a killer – nothing else.' Paulus paused. 'Do we not?'

The room was so silent that if a mouse had put its head from a hole in the wall it would have been heard.

'Then I will ask the prisoner to make a full account of his crimes. Stumpf, I am ready to hear your full public confession.'

'Yes, sir,' said Stumpf – and the people craned to see him speak like he was a fresh oddity at a travelling fair, not the man who had spent his life among them, and was as familiar as a grain of sand to them. 'Shall I begin with the first?'

'No better place, sir,' said Paulus, and he sat back in his chair, steepled his fingers and looked to the ceiling.

'Of the crimes I confess to, however, sir – is it not the case that I can only be prosecuted for those committed in Bideburg – and its hinterlands as you say?'

I stopped writing. Paulus had been brought up short too, I saw, for he had dropped his hands to his lap and looked at Stumpf – breaking the position he always held in court while testimony was given, head back, eyes to Heaven, hands a church. But within a beat, he was back to his stride.

'Correct,' Paulus said, 'please note this, clerk.' And he tapped my cuff. 'The trial here in Bideburg can only deal with offences carried out in lands now governed by the Prince-Bishop.' He smiled at Stumpf. 'It is an administrative anomaly.'

I scribbled in the notes.

'Do continue,' he said to Stumpf – and Stumpf smiled back at the bench. Paulus resumed his contemplative pose of Solomon. 'I think your crimes in Bideburg will suffice for my judgement to be fitting,' he said, and he smiled one last time, his eyes to the ceiling.

'The first was as you found, sir, the servant and her child, that were buried in the Bideburg woods,' Stumpf said, clear and loud. 'I was fifteen, sixteen. Next, on the road, after I left Bideburg, on my way to join the army, I met and was accosted by a beggar, who tried to assault me in a way no man would bear. I killed him, but plead this in self-defence. In the war, I killed many people – men, women, children, folk of all ages – but that was war and so I can not be subject to law for those. But during my time in uniform I often killed many whores and beggars too when I was not engaged in military duties. I have the tally in my head and it stands at twenty-four killed by the time I was midway through my twenties.

When I left the army, I killed a family of three on the road to the town where I was to meet my wife. A mother and father and their child, a girl, of three. While in my wife's town, waiting to marry her, I killed another child, in the woods nearby.'

I wrote in my short-hand at a furious pace – and still have the notebook with me, under lock and key, though it is on my desk now and I am copying from it at times. Paulus stared on at the ceiling but he lifted one finger from the steeple of his hands, and the white flash, as it rose, caught the eyes of all in the room – Stumpf too and he fell silent.

'Stumpf – how did you kill these people and what did you do with them once you had killed them?'

Stumpf watched the bench, and waited for Paulus to bring his eyes down from the ceiling and look him in the face – then he turned his head to me.

'The manner of killing was often different. I used my hands, a stick, a knife, a rope. I drowned some, burned some. Most of them – I ate some of them.' The room gasped but Stumpf spoke on. 'With the ones that caught my eye, I made them my bedfellow, if you understand.'

'Were you finished killing in the home town of your wife?'

'Yes, sir.'

'Carry on.'

'Back in Bideburg, I killed many more. Though none from the town, as all people in this room know. I killed only those who travelled through, or that I found on the roads. By night. The land is lonely. Shall I recount them all?'

'You must.'

'The first was a father and daughter. I burned them. Then there was a run of lone travellers – a man, a man, then a woman, and another man – all beggars. A family of five. A man and wife. Then a family of three. An old woman in her cottage. More lone travellers – four, I believe, though if you wish to add five to the charge I will not complain. Another couple.

A family of three. A family of ten – with both sets of grandparents, mother, father, three children and an aunt, I think, or cousin.'

Stumpf and I held eyes while he spoke – and my hand crossed the page as I wrote without the need to look down – but on the mention of the family of ten, Paulus tilted his head to one side and clicked his fingers, bringing all to look on him. He raised an eyebrow.

'Ten?' asked Paulus. Stumpf returned his gaze to me.

'Once a child is in your hands,' Stumpf said, as if he was explaining how to catch a fish or train a hawk, 'a larger group is easier to subdue and deal with. A hostage.' Paulus nodded.

'After that,' Stumpf went on, 'there was a father and son – which is always more risky and violent. Then more lone travellers – for a long time – as the father and son before had fought me hard and injured me, and if people in this room remember back perhaps five years,' he looked around the meeting hall, folk cast their eyes away from his, 'I complained of being gored by a boar out hunting. It was the father's knife. So let us say, ten people over this period – all lone travellers. Then a family of three, when I was back to health and felt I could tackle a task like that again. Then a couple. One cripple next. Another family – of three, though the mother was carrying a child inside her. A lone beggar woman. A couple. A family

225

of four, and finally the family from last week, the mother and father outside the Dark Hedges, and the boy, later, after they let him loose from the keep and I found him in the woods alone.'

'Who let the boy loose?' asked Paulus.

Stumpf looked at Paulus now. 'I do not know,' he said. 'When I had him, the boy kept crying out about being taken to the woods by the men and left for the wolf. The wolf that he spoke of was me, I imagine.'

'Thank you, Stumpf,' said Paulus, and Stumpf put his head to one side and studied Paulus as you would study a painting to find the message in the art.

'Can we tally that, Lessinger?' Paulus asked me.

I counted, then recounted as the number unsettled me – I find omens in numbers often.

'Ninety-nine, your worship,' I said, addressing Paulus as he was meant to be addressed when officiating, though he never insisted upon it, as long as those before him were polite and respectful and called him no less than sir.

'Ninety-nine,' Paulus said to Stumpf, and smiled almost as if impressed. 'Are you sure you haven't forgot one, sir?'

Stumpf smiled, 'No sir. Numbers have no meaning for me.'

'How do the numbers break down, clerk?' Paulus asked me.

I looked at my jottings, fumbling and counting. After an aching moment, I said, 'The two dummies in Bideburg at the beginning of the murders, twenty-nine other murders committed elsewhere in the Empire in jurisdictions not under the authority of the Prince-Bishop, and sixty-eight murders later committed in Bideburg and its hinterlands – bringing from ninety-nine admitted crimes the total prosecutable number of offences under the authority of this court to seventy murders.'

'Seventy, yes, I can agree to that number,' said Stumpf.

Paulus laid his hands on the bench, and said, 'You accept your guilt in the seventy murders committed in this jurisdiction, Stumpf?'

'Yes, your worship,' said Stumpf.

'Very well,' said Paulus, 'the court finds you guilty by your own confession of seventy murders – each of which merit execution on their own, but together call for full destruction of the body.'

The crowd started to chatter among themselves, some even clapped at the verdict – I put down my pen to call silence, but Paulus tapped my leg and shook his head no at me. He let the hubbub rise and spoke loudly but quickly to Stumpf. The people could not hear him over their own babbling voices.

'You did not keep the hair of the dummies in your little box then, Stumpf?'

'No,' Stumpf said. 'I took their hair, but I lost their locks on my travels. That saddened me. I began my collection only when I came back to Bideburg after the war – for memory's sake.'

Paulus nudged me and said, 'Shut them up now.'

I stood and screamed, 'Silence in court or you face charge of contempt of court.'

The crowd froze like I'd set my Gorgon eyes upon them.

Paulus waited, and waited. He lifted his hand after two minutes or more had gone by – the people squirming inside themselves – and then nodded, to the crowd at large. They seemed to sigh of a one, and settled – my terrible cry forgotten by them, and me just a jumped-up boy in a gown again.

'I wish to make it clear to the public,' Paulus said, looking into the crowd – I could see him try to catch every eye to bring his words to the individual direct, and not leave one soul feeling as if they were exempt from his words – 'I want you all to know, that we – and that means both myself, the state, the court, our constabulary, and you, yourselves – will not rest until each and every one of these poor people that fell victim to Stumpf are found, and brought to a Christian burial, and remembered by their families and loved ones – if we can find them. I intend to go immediately from this court and write a letter of raising to the Prince-Bishop so a platoon can be dispatched to Bideburg to begin the search for the earthly remains of the folk we have spoken of today. You will all, according to a manner agreed by your councilmen, establish search parties comprised of all able-bodied men – and women – to begin searching the woods and fields and forests for the ones who suffered.'

Paulus rubbed his face – he was greasy and a little sweaty – and wiped the gloss between his fingers.

'One final set of questions, for the prisoner,' he said. He tightened his mouth, like regret was on his lips, and asked, 'Stumpf, why did you carry out these crimes to which you admit so readily?'

Stumpf lips ran over each other. He bit on his lower lip, and sucked on the upper – it would have seemed lascivious if it was not obvious to the eye that he was deep in some thought that he could not voice. He bit against his moustache as his eyes wandered searching for an answer, I believe he wished to give, and then he ran his tongue against the beard on his chin. If I had not spent many hours in his company I would have taken him for an idiot then – and this contortion went on for minutes, until Paulus looked to me, shocked, and I worried that Stumpf had lost his mind in front of us all.

'Stumpf?' Paulus said. 'Do you wish to answer my question?'

'I wish I could, your worship,' said Stumpf straight to Paulus – and his face reformed. 'But I do not have an answer. If I did, I do not believe I would be sitting here before you. Perhaps, I fear, I may just hate the human race.'

'But you love your wife and children?'

Stumpf put his head down, and I thought to myself – he will cry, this will be such a fitting end to the trial, the killer crying. But he did not cry. 'I said I hate the human race,' Stumpf spoke softly, 'not the people I know and love.'

Paulus nodded and pulled a face which said, I understand you, man. Then he put both his hands on the table before him and moved to call the session closed.

'May I speak,' said Stumpf – but he phrased it not as a question.

'Of course,' said Paulus.

'I hate the people of this town, though – and I know them well. And I hate myself for having at last pleased them – for they have wanted my land and my money my entire life, but have never been able to get it, now though they will scrabble for my estate and inheritance, and I ask that you honour your vow to me that all my assets will remain untouched as I gained nothing from my crimes – in fact they cost me in time and money with many preparations and concealments. Though, I am happy for my heirs to pay acceptable blood money settlements to any family that comes forward – but no family from this filthy town may come forward to chance my money as I killed not one of you. I would not have your taste in my mouth, or your dirt in my belly.'

And he sat back, looking around at the crowd who stood within hand's touch of him, with wide eyes on him, not one saying a word. I thought them shamefaced for a moment. They should have cried out against him if what he said was lies – I would have, if a criminal in chains spoke to me in such a way.

'It has already been noted,' said Paulus, calm as a Sunday, 'that your family has played no part or parcel in this case. Their asset is safe, pending the outcome of any settlements as agreed.'

'Then I am done,' Stumpf said, and turned his head to me.

'Stumpf,' Paulus said, 'I will, with my advisors, settle upon a suitable sentence of death overnight. Your punishment will be one fitting the extraordinary nature of your crimes, though I will – as should any man of justice – take your full confession into account. Have you anything else to say?'

'No, sir.'

'No contrition, or plea? Do you not wish to beg the people and God for forgiveness?'

'No, sir, I do not.'

'Very good, Stumpf,' said Paulus, and he seemed a little proud of how well his prisoner had behaved for him today – he had provided much theatre, and the drama had been quick. Folk began to move, excited at the coming of the end, and waiting to be dismissed so they could run outside and talk of their part in the great story unfolding for them in their town hall.

Karfreitag kept his pistol level with Stumpf's head as he had throughout the trial. The guards moved forward with their dogcatcher poles, to bind up Stumpf and lead him back to the keep.

'No,' said Paulus. 'Let the prisoner remain a moment.'

The guards stamped to attention and stood behind Stumpf – who rolled back his head and looked up into their faces. He smiled at Karfreitag.

'One other matter, that I wish to address to the court and town.' The court settled itself.

'We have heard multiple allegations that the child who was rescued by Greet Werren and the other washerwomen was abandoned by people in authority in this town. I tell you here, that once the sentence of execution has been carried out on the prisoner, another court of law will be drawn up to deal with this offence – of abandoning a child wantonly and deliberately to the killer Stumpf. Those found guilty will be adjudged murderers by this court. That hearing will be followed by a trial into the murders of the two Stumpf boys.'

Stumpf rolled his head to take in the eye of every man in the room – then his gaze settled on Jens, Rodinan, Kroll and Odil, sat in a row beside each other, and stayed there upon them.

Paulus nodded at me.

'Stand,' I shouted. 'Empty the court.'

Some faces in the crowd were white, and the court emptied.

★ ★ ★

It was still early in the afternoon – not much gone three – when the court rose. Paulus asked me to come to our room above the inn. Some food was brought up to us as we'd not eaten since breakfast, missed lunch, and it was still long before dinner. Paulus was beginning to shake and sweat and talk of his hunger-weakness. The maid came and went. Paulus smiled at her.

We ate and drank and when he was back to sorts and food in him, he asked me about the sentence that should be handed down.

'What alternatives do you have?' I asked.

'I am free to do as I please with him,' said Paulus. 'Anything.'

I picked the flesh off a chicken leg, and ate it with a bite of pickle and a wedge of good bread – still warm from the oven. 'I have no experience in these things, sir,' I said. Paulus was testing me, like my examiner in philosophy class. 'What do you feel would be right?'

'If I could I would behead him first thing in the morning, and leave town. But I do not think that can be done. A little more drama is required, I feel.'

'His crimes permit as cruel a sentence as can be imagined.'

'Do you think this town will benefit from more violence and blood?'

'I don't know, sir.'

'I will break him on the wheel, behead him and burn his body. That is enough.'

'That should satisfy the people.'

'I doubt it.' He sat without speaking and drank a glass of wine, then he poured another and drank again. 'I want Stumpf's family taken from the town before it is dark with a bodyguard of six. Take them to the university.'

'I can not leave, sir.'

'You can.'

And I was silent as I knew that was an order, and my celebration of the trial's end was over before it had began.

We ate on in silence.

'What do you make of the judgement, Willie?' he asked me.

I thought a moment and said, 'I believe the townsfolk will think it in accordance with God, though there will surely be some who say it should go further.'

Paulus laughed in my face – though not cruelly – and I felt stupid for my scholar's craven answer.

'Oh yes, I could disembowel him, Willie. Unman him with a scythe. Burn him alive. Flay him. Boil him. Death by a thousand cuts like the mandarins, in a jacket of razors. But I tell you what, Willie – I am not Stumpf and I am certainly not a member of this town.'

He turned his attention to eating again and we sat in silence a while longer. The sun started its decline towards the west. The sky turned pink and indigo. I went to the window and looked out onto the street below. Bideburg carried on its life of buying and selling as if the wolf had never existed.

'I will want to come back, sir, once the women are safe at the university,' I said. 'I have made a promise to someone who needs me to come back.'

'Ah,' he said. 'I will expect you back in no more than four days. You will be in trouble if you take longer.'

'Yes, sir,' I said.

'Who knows, though,' Paulus said, quietly, pouring himself another drink and settling to look at the sun through the open window, 'the maid could be going with them, and you could travel all the way to the university and stay there with her.'

'As I am commanded to go,' I said, 'I want to see the werewolf one more time. I will miss his execution, so I would like to make my peace with him the best I can, as I hope I am a good Christian,' and I got up and left the room without goodbye. I could not bear to be around him and his commands a moment longer.

'Do not be long, Christian,' he shouted after me – and I imagined his lip curl in contempt from the sound of his voice. 'You must be on the road with the women soon.'

Peter Wolf's card's were in my pocket though – and Paulus knew nothing of them, which made me glad, for I had one up on his cleverness.

The Third and Last of the Werewolf's Meditations

A discussion on fortune telling

The wolf had asked me to bring him his cards. We had talked of fortunes the day before and I had sent a guard to fetch the deck from his home. He said he could read them, so, curious, I ordered them brought. I gave them to him. He took the dry, old deck, and shuffled them in his lap, hands bound, while he talked to me of fortune telling.

'You have told me, Willie,' he said, 'that you are unsure if such things as astrology are true. I agree. I do not know. I am an Aquarius. This is the sign of peace and learning. But I am not a peaceful or learned man. You may think that if my fortune in life was to accord with the stars then I would be an Aries. I am not, but that would have been a wrong sign for me too. I am not just warlike. I should have been a Gemini. I have two souls. The soul I show in the street, and the soul I have in the forest. And yet I am an Aquarius, and that proves astrology to be a lie.

My mother – at least she taught me the cards. And I believe in them. I do not believe that they show me the future, but they do unlock the soul inside you – they let me see the soul of the sitter. I do not read the cards, I read the sitter through the cards. Take the deck,' he said, handing the pack to me. 'Now you shuffle, and cut and pick three of your choosing. They will be Past, Present and Future. Pick from anywhere in the deck.'

I drew The Magician, The Stars and The Lovers and placed them face up on the cell floor between us.

'This, Willie,' he said, 'is the most perfect hand ever drawn. The possibility of choosing at random such lucky, felicitous cards is astronomical.' He smiled – and though his teeth were broke, and his face bloody, it was a caring smile. 'Draw again,' he said.

I drew Judgement, The Devil and The Tower.

'I don't like the look of these three, Peter Wolf,' I said.

And he laughed, for he liked the nickname I had given him. It was a name just between us – no-one else knew of it. That pleased him.

'They are beyond misfortune,' Stumpf said. 'That's the most cursed hand I have ever seen. It couldn't be more ominous if you drew Death thirteen times in a row.'

'The cards scare me,' I said, and Stumpf nodded.

'Try best of three,' he said. 'Your mind is fixed and full of thoughts of your life – of only success or failure. You are a boy, that is all you can imagine. But clear your mind and this time try and not draw either Heaven or Hell; try something possible.'

I drew The Wheel, The Chariot and The Hermit.

He laughed and shook his head.

'You are choosing classic hands, dear Willie,' he explained. 'This is a life story in three cards. You're born by chance somewhere, to somebody and at some point in time; that's your starting point. Then you are whisked off from this entrance to life into the world and all its events – babies and bodies and books and being – the calendar running over, until there you are, years from now, crouched in your own little world, with the walls you've put around you, just thinking, taking no notice of what's going on outside, and what's going on outside taking no notice of you.'

Stumpf put his hand through the cages and beckoned with his fingers for the cards. I collected them together and offered them over to him. He studied the artwork on them – thick, old, yellow card, hand-painted and lettered, the drawings graven and frightening.

'They shouldn't be played with by others,' he said. 'The Questioner should only hold them to deal otherwise your essence, Willie – your manna, your miasma – will get all over them and drive my personality and aura out of them; and I need to be implanted in them for the cards to work.'

He riffled the deck and cut and shuffled them.

Sifting quickly through, he picked out three cards and threw them down, face up, on the floor before him in the cell.

'Here's the perfect three for me,' he said. Emperor. Hierophant. Fool. 'So, you see I know the cards, and think them pretty.'

Stumpf fingered through the deck, looking at the pictures on each card. We had not talked of the trial or the sentence. He wanted to talk idle.

'Many years ago,' he said, as he played with the deck, 'I was travelling the country – before I was married. There was a woman I was told of, who lived *along the road thereabouts and told fortunes. I went to her. Her house was good – not the hut of a witch – but a home with a garden and vegetable patch, and some pigs and geese. She had no husband or children though, and made her money as a wise woman, of the white sort, blessing pregnancies and crop harvests and foretelling marriages and wishing good luck – providing a warning here and there, to her neighbours, though, over the cards, telling them to be good and stop drinking, love their wives a little more, or pay some extra into the parish tithe. It was Catholic country and the priests were her friends.*

I came to her house on my travels, and knocked at her door. She looked at me, sideways.

I asked to come in, and she asked me why. I said, "Because I heard you were a wise woman of the white sort and I wish my fortune told."

"I do not do that any more," the woman said. She was younger than I thought – no more than forty, and handsome, though fat.

"I can pay," I said. I had a lot of money and offered her much more than an hour over the cards merited, so she took me in, still tossing me looks I did not like, for they said "I do not trust you. There is something wrong with you."

She offered me no food or drink, but just took me to a table and passed me her cards, telling me – draw.

I pulled the Fool first, which was good, as I respect that card and see it in me. Then I pulled the Devil and the Hanged Man.

Her face was blank. The sun flowed in the window behind her hot and heavy, and I could see her making up her lies in her head for she would not tell me what the cards said – though I could read them very well myself, and they said: I come from nothing, I bring pain and I will be sacrificed, like Christ.

"The cards," she said, "they say that you are an innocent and good man – that is the Fool. But temptation lies in your way and wishes to twist and damage your innocent soul – that is what the Devil card says. The Hanged Man – he tells you to stay away from the temptations of the world. To be lost from life. To remove yourself from life, to perhaps join a monastery. Live a quiet life. He hangs because he is waiting – that is the message of the card."

"The Hermit card," I said.

"What?" she asked.

I said, "The Hermit card is the one which would tell me to retire from life to avoid temptation. The Hanged Man card says I am a lost soul, and will be sacrificed for the crimes I have committed – even though they are no crimes at all, for the Hanged Man card is one of innocence and speaks most closely to the

235

story of *Jesus Christ himself, who tried to understand the world in which he was forced to live and bring it to some order, but was bewildered and murdered for his trouble."*

"You tricked me," she said. "You can read the cards as well as I."

"I like to see how others with the gift use it," I told her.

"Well, you have seen my way, so now you should leave, and you may keep your money," and she handed me back the fair sum I had given her.

I put the money on the table in front of me, and said, "But you lie when you read the cards. I tell the truth."

She got to her feet, but I grabbed her arm and put her back in her seat, across the table from me.

"Now deal yourself three cards, and I will tell you your fortune."

She cried now – because there comes a time in all such things when the true nature of what lies ahead is suddenly exposed, and those seeing the future can often not believe that their life will end and I will be sitting by them.

"Deal," I said.

She trembled and shook and I said to her, "You will not deal Death. I do not have the gift of second sight, but this I know full well – Death will not appear in the cards."

And nor did she deal Death. She pulled Temperance, Strength and Judgement.

"My good God," I said. "Aren't these the three most dull cards in the deck. Our aristocrats, telling us how to behave. One is bad enough in a hand, but three. You must have been an evil woman to receive so much warning throughout the three stages of your life. It seems to say you were a wicked intemperate girl in your youth, a proud bully now, and then soon judgement will call you for these failings because you judge others."

"It does not say that," she told me – angry and brave, and for that I admired her. "If you say you can read the cards then it tells you that I lived a life of almost nothing as a girl – a quiet country mouse – but I built this home on my own after my parents died, and now I stand judged in the eyes of God a good and decent Christian woman."

"But a liar, nonetheless," I said. "You lied to me in my cards. You must be judged."

"The cards said you were a Devil with an empty soul who would find execution for his crimes. I could not say those words to any man or woman. It is not allowed."

"You should have," I said. "For then I might have trusted you."

"You should let me go," she said.

"You know why you did not deal Death," I said. "Because Death means new beginnings. As a wise woman of the white sort, you surely know that."

And what I did was this: I took her outside. She had a cross-beam in her yard for drying clothes or slaughtering her pigs, one or other. I tied her hands behind her back, and her right foot to her right knee, so she was bound crook-legged – like the Hanged Man on the card. Then I hoisted her up on a rope by her left foot, tied her to the cross-beam and slit her throat, while she hung head down. She bled the yard red. Her blood rolled into the pig pen and the creatures squealed in delight at the taste and stink.

I went back to her house and ate some food and drank some milk and washed. I left the money I had paid her on the table, and then I walked out to take the road for – oh, I do not remember where it was I went next, Willie. Peter Wolf's memory is growing grey.'

Chapter Twenty-Two

And we see the creeping face of low treachery and black betrayal.

I came back to the inn and expected to find Paulus drunk with the soldiers. He wasn't – instead he was in our room, writing.

'I'm starting on my treatise right away,' he said as I came in – not even looking up at me. 'This town is a cesspit – and I will call it such.'

I poured a drink and sat down.

'You will have to leave soon with the women. I want you all over the mountain by dawn,' he said.

'Can it not wait until the morning?' I was tired and happy and wanted to go off to see Greet as we had planned when the moon came out and Paulus fell asleep.

'No. I have listened this last hour down in the inn while I drank some wine to stories of how Odil and Rodinan and Kroll were full of joy at the thought of a werewolf trial and how it would feather their beds when the church claimed the Stumpf lands and split them with the town. These folk are so stupid they do not know the import of their own idle gossip – but the butcher and his friends they talked their jaws sore to me over three bottles of wine at my expense. Stumpf vineyard, as well, which amused me. Odil is so full of rage at the trial that he is now drunk and asleep, with a broken jaw, I hope, after beating his wife in front of the inn – which is the reason I came downstairs in the first place – to have him flogged. Why else would I sit among a group of lepers such as these people of Bideburg.'

He was running at the mouth from the fizz of excitement within him, like a bubbling chemical – and his wildness made me smile wide.

'You had Odil beaten?' I laughed.

'I heard a row to wake the almighty not long after you left, and there was Odil – in his own inn – kicking his wife on the floor. Kicking her. Two guards were there. I called them, "up" – and they rose and I said, "Bring this man to order".

Oh, Willie – they gave him such a hiding. It was good to see. Then his poor, bloodied, idiot wife – she picked him up from the dust in the front yard and carried him to his bed – crying, and stroking him, shouting at our boys, calling them beasts – snot red and dripping from him and from her.

The butcher, he comes to me and says, "Oh sir," and he was laughing at his friend Odil's broken face, "oh, sir, you ruined his dreams for him and that was why he was so wild."

"What's that, my good fellow," I said to the butcher – who is short and hairy and red-faced, if you have seen him, like a Barbary baboon – and I walked him back to his table and his friends and filled them up on wine. They told me all I need to know about this town. Bideburg would soil itself in a sea of manure for money and land. Whore its own mother. Murder its own child. So I would like you on the road with those women as soon as you can.'

'Yes, sir,' I said, and I drained my cup and got up to gather my necessities. 'I'll pack what I need and go right away. I understand the situation now.' And that was apology enough for both of us.

With my kit sorted, I took a pistol and sword for my belt. I felt myself shaking a little, for I knew what I had been thinking of saying to him, what I must indeed say to him before I left, or I would drive myself mad with not knowing on the journey.

I blew a big breath of air through my lips and walked to the window. The sun was just setting and the air blue-rinsed fire. I stared out of the window as I felt too embarrassed to look at him while I spoke and feared my face would start to wobble or quake and my voice tremble like a cretin playing the pipes.

'Very well, sir, I must say something,' I said, and I spoke like my tongue was a wild horse off the rein, 'as I am going to leave this town now I need to ask your permission and assistance in helping me fulfil a vow – which I made yesterday – to Greet Werren, that I would marry her. We are pledged to each other – in body and soul now – and can not live without being married. I would ask that you speak to her people, please – though she has no parents, so that should be easy – and also to my parents, which may be more difficult,' and I laughed all lunatic, on the sudden, midway through my speech. 'But help us arrange a speedy marriage, please,' I said, continuing on as if I had not brayed like a donkey. 'You know that I am your loyal and loving servant and any favour you do me now I will repay to you over my lifetime ten, twenty, one hundred, one thousand times over.'

'I am happy to help.' His voice came like it set its hands on my shoulders.

Now, many lads would have raced around the room, and hugged the curtains, kissed the boots of Paulus and roared their love out the window to the world. Even though Paulus would have found such a performance amusing, I am not of that type of excitable show-off. And sometimes, I like to try and impress what I believe to be my great inner nobility – or so I saw my pride and haughtiness when I was young – on those who have done me good.

'I thank you, sir,' I said. But I still could not turn around, and I could not stop myself from saying – squeaking my pride to shame – 'You mean it?'

'Yes, my friend,' he said, from behind me, and I slumped my head down on the window ledge for I could not hide any more that the cold ice in the blood of excitement and fear had run through me and wrung me out.

'Good, good,' I said, 'thank you,' and I raised my head and took a deep breath of the blooming night air. I felt steady again. Bideburg – for all that Paulus told me he hated it – looked calm and pretty in the twilight to me and I was happy now, rushed in the head with delight, and the sight of the town made me feel joyous, because I had found joy here, joy – like a pretty angel had passed through me. That's how I felt back as a boy, and I have no embarrassment about the love in me then, and the green and awkward sentiment it made pour from me. There were only a few people in the street. Lights were on in the homes, and the air was clear and fresh. The night was starring up, and the moon beginning its ride through the sky.

Fromme, I saw, was walking towards our inn, two soldiers behind him who I hadn't seen before, and the town priest, Barthelme, scurrying at his side.

'Sir,' I said, without turning. 'Here comes Fromme in a hurry, with two guards I do not know.'

Paulus got up and went to the casement. The party passed quickly beneath the window, as they walked into the inn. Paulus had no chance to see them properly.

'What the hell is this?' he said, looking at me. I shrugged. Then there came the sound of running on the stairs.

Paulus looked around the room, and walked to the table by his bed where he'd left two pistols and a short sword.

'Hold the door,' he said.

I'd just touched the wooden frame and reached for the handle, when the door swung open, and Fromme strode into the room.

He pushed past me, and the two guards and the priest Barthelme stood around me, hemming me in, while Fromme walked up to Paulus. Fromme had a letter in his hand. I could see the Prince-Bishop's seal.

'Move out of my way,' I said, and shoved back the guards and priest, and walked to Paulus' side.

'What the hell is going on here, Fromme?' he asked.

'A letter of dismissal.' said Fromme. 'You are relieved as circuit magistrate. The letter from his grace instructs that I take charge of the legal affairs of the town, and preside over the trial of Stumpf as a werewolf, a heretic and an agent of Satan.'

'Fromme,' said Paulus, and he laughed. 'You are not funny.'

'I am not joking with you, friend,' said Fromme.

'Do not play,' said Paulus. 'What have you done? Why have you done this? This will end peaceably if you let me do my work.' And Paulus went to pat Fromme on the shoulders. Fromme stepped back.

'I wonder about you, Paulus,' Fromme said, and the Devil stood out in his face. 'You have worked against the church and God and the Bible for too long. You have heretic blood in you.'

'Shut your fucking mouth,' said Paulus, and he drew back his fist, and before the guards could move, had knocked Fromme to the floor. The priest lay there, dazed, a sliver chipped from his front tooth, his lip cut and mouth well bloodied up. There was a look in his face and it was like a little boy in school knocked down by the lad who is everyone's friend and then laughed at – though no-one laughed at Fromme now.

The guards dropped their hands to their swords on their hips. Paulus lifted one finger and said, 'Hold your ground. I know you and you – and have done your families favours. Step back. I will leave this room with my apprentice, and you will not accost us. We will leave town directly. I intend to return to court to speak to his grace. This will go no further until the Prince-Bishop has full understanding of affairs in this town.'

The guards looked to Fromme, who got to his feet, wiping blood from his chin. His eyes were hot and red with tears and I had to look away from him as he embarrassed me – I felt ashamed of him. He rose with a limp – and it was the first time I had seen him make such a cowardly use of his old war wound, for he strode as well as any man I knew.

Paulus also turned away from Fromme, ready to leave – and looked at the town priest, standing in his way. Paulus pushed him. 'Who or what are you?' he said to Barthelme. 'Get the fuck out of my way.'

'That is why you have no need to speak to his grace. Good Barthelme here conducted my message to his grace,' said Fromme, and his voice was hoarse and brittle. 'As a man of God, despite his affiliations, he could see what was happening in this town under your command. He returned with the instructions, and these guards, whose families you claim to know.'

'You move fast for someone more used to a life on their knees,' said Paulus to Barthelme.

'I used your man stationed at the inn in Reissen,' said Barthelme, bold for a little black crow. 'He took his horse, and rode back with this answer from court, and Brother Fromme's new soldiers.'

'All snakes and liars together then,' Paulus said. He walked up to Barthelme, till his chest touched the pastor's black gown, but he turned his eyes to the two new guards. 'They will kill you, little Protestant worm,' he said. 'I have just thought to myself, Barthelme, that it would well suit my good Catholic lord, the Prince-Bishop, to have a Lutheran town like yours known as a cesspit of witchcraft. Well done, Pastor Barthelme, you have lost your war with Rome.'

Paulus slapped the minister so hard on the back that Barthelme stumbled.

Fromme said, 'Liar. You are a liar and a danger to the state with your talk, Paulus. Be careful from this moment on. Be warned.'

Paulus grabbed my arm. 'Gather up our things,' he told me.

'Don't bother,' Fromme said. 'You are going nowhere.'

'Be careful what you threaten, Fromme,' said Paulus. 'I will see you back at our grace's court – and he will hear all of this.'

'I make no threat. Your boy may leave the village, as he is not needed. But you have work to be done here. Stumpf may have accepted his guilt under your jurisdiction, but he does not admit his guilt as a werewolf and practitioner of witchcraft, as I will lay charges against him. So, he needs an officer of the law to act in his defence. His lordship, the Prince-Bishop, has instructed that this be you. It seems fitting given your already brave efforts on the werewolf's behalf. There will be no other diversions or trials about lost boys in the woods or the werewolf's sons – these are not matters for us. We are here to deal with one matter only: an attack by Satan on the godly people of the Empire. Read the letter, Paulus. I will not waste my breath further on you.'

Paulus stood, like a dunce, in the middle of the room. Fromme pushed the letter into his hands, turned sharply and nodded to the pastor and the guards. He walked from the room, they followed at his heels. At the head of the stairs leading down to the tap room below, Fromme called over his shoulder, loud enough so the whole inn could hear, 'I will see you in court tomorrow, Brother Paulus. Have a good evening – you and your boy. I will make my way to the keep now to speak with the prisoner, and then pay his family a visit. I have words I must pass with them as I am sure you can imagine.'

Paulus sat at the edge of his bed, and looked at me.

'I am scared, Willie,' he said.

This shocked me, and I hesitated what to say. 'It will go badly for Stumpf now,' I said.

'No, Willie. When God is in command the whole world is at risk. Man has been demoted now, and that means that it is to their book and not the laws of the state that these people will now turn for all answers – and their book is wrong and full of lies and cruelty. That book is evil, Willie. It is cursed. It brings destruction.'

A look passed between us – him questioning, checking, asking with his eyes, me answering with my silence – I did not frown or denounce him. I thought of the one hundred and thirty-seventh Psalm – it had eaten at me all my life, since I first read it as a boy of eight – and now it made my blood become cold water. 'Oh blessed with joy is the one who takes up your babies and dashes them against the rocks.' So the holy song goes.

'Then I am also worried for the Stumpf women,' I said.

Paulus changed in that moment – as if I had lit a fuse under him, as if he had just a short allotted time left on Earth to stand up, take action and complete his life before the fire touched the powder.

'We'll go to their home,' he said, and he stood and walked to the table where his pistols lay. He looked at the guns a moment and then took off his jacket. He turned and went to his chest, rummaged and pulled out a long brown leather thong – a cross-hatched holster, I saw. He slipped it over his shirt, a holster under each arm. The pistols went in the holsters, and hung down over his ribs.

'Just in case,' he said. 'I mean no harm, but I will not be hurt. See, I have not lit them. Yet.'

He put his jacket back on, buckled his dagger onto his belt.

'What will we do?' I asked – dumb in the head.

'See them, speak to them, advise them to run.'

We left the room, walked down the stairs of the inn, and into the street outside. People stared, but there was no suspicion – a little laughter, maybe, as the town had learned that Paulus was no longer in charge, but people were too scared to rile or insult or accost us, they knew he still had power over them. Karfreitag stood at the gate to the inn.

'Best go back, sir,' he said to Paulus, and he tugged at the coloured sash across his chest. His sword clanked.

'Why is that?' asked Paulus.

'Not safe, sir. Lot of angry people. I've been instructed to look after you.'

'I am quite capable of taking care of myself,' Paulus said.

'Best not, sir,' Karfreitag talked over him. 'I've been instructed to instruct you to comply with my instructions, sir. For your own good.'

Paulus about-turned very slowly – said 'fair enough, goodnight' over his shoulder – and walked back into the inn. The cloud that was to come over him and make my friend Paulus a Baal, a Baphomet, had not yet settled on him for good. His rage was passing through him still – and it passed when he knew it could yet lead him into danger, and Karfreitag was danger, old, brutish danger. Though, the threat of danger, the good kind warning that danger offers, it would pass from Paulus' mind soon too, and then only rage would be left. And what does rage leave us? War. Funeral pyres on foreign beaches. A ruined city of smoke and blood. The gods gone for good, I believe – that is the true gift of rage, if we listen to the old poets, and the stories of Troy.

Chapter Twenty-Three

And I ask, how can such things happen in this world, and still this Earth claim it is governed by a god who is good.

It was late in the afternoon, and I watched from the inn window for an hour or more as a crowd grew around the keep's open door. Fromme had ordered it to remain unclosed, so Stumpf's screams could be heard – coming up the stairs from the cells, through the winding halls and out the keep's door into the summer air and Bideburg square. Paulus was drinking. He often drank, but rarely got drunk – now he was on the verge of drunkenness, his mouth cynical and eyes hard and ugly.

'Fucking animals,' he said. I looked at him. 'Not because of their station in life, Willie. Because of what they believe in. Primitives. The world is full of primitives. One percent of us are advanced, the rest savage.'

'Should we start thinking about the defence?' I asked.

He snarled a laugh at me. 'Grow up, Willie. It's already decided. I'm there as an act of humiliation to me. No-one could care if you are there or not – though maybe it makes my humiliation all the grander to have you in tow.'

'There has to be some defence of the family if they are charged,' I said. 'Please.'

He sat forward in his chair and sucked at his cheeks like he wanted to vomit or spit. Stumpf had been quiet a while – then another sharp short squeal came from the keep. 'They are dead,' he said, and he got up from his chair and walked to the window, leaning out.

Paulus cleared his throat. Before I could make sense of this most extraordinary thing that was happening he had begun to sing. Paulus singing was like rain falling upwards. I'd never seen such an event. His voice was clear and the song was over before I could take in the meaning of the words – but they are simple to recall, and he sung them out loud and strong over the crowd below, then waved to them and smiled.

I'm an angry fucking peasant
and I hate the fucking rich.
I'd kill their fucking children,
and so'd my wife – the fucking bitch.

The tune was mournful and jaunty at one and the same time – mocking and threatening.

There was no-one high enough in rank out on the street in front of the keep to challenge him. The soldiers kept their eyes on the crowd, and the crowd, after they'd chanced a look at him, stared at the ground and were quiet.

Paulus turned to me and said – loud enough, I feared, to be heard below – 'That's an old rebel song, Willie. It used to put the fear of God in the enemy and get the blood up.'

He walked over to the bed and lay down, his hand over his eyes against the hard yellow sunlight in the room. I opened our law books and started to read, searching for a direction I could give Paulus to take for the family. He woke a few hours later – and I had got nowhere in my books except lost and confused.

'Go see Greet, the girl,' he told me. 'Find out how the Stumpf women are.'

Stumpf's wife and daughters were still at the family home, under guard. We had not been told what was to happen to them – though arrest and trial seemed sure.

'Will they let me?' I asked.

'I suggest you find out,' he said. 'How can they stop you seeing the maid you are sleeping with – tell them you are fucking her, if they stop you, then they will let you pass.'

'You do not need to speak like this, sir,' I said. 'I have not spoken like that since I was a boy.'

'We are different,' he said. He took the law books from me. 'You do not need to hurry back. I'll set about working on some argument on behalf of the family – there is a chance for the wife and the daughters. Fromme is not set on their deaths, fully, I believe. He will take the issue to trial though – that I know. It would be quite a feat, committing to law the ruling that the curse of the Devil could pass from one line of the family to another. No-one would be safe.'

I left the inn, and two paces into the street, Karfreitag was on me.

'Where are you going, sir?' he asked.

'Shall I lie or tell the truth, Karfreitag?' I replied.

'Tell the truth, sir.'

'I am going to see the Stumpf's maid, Greet.'

'Why, sir?'

'Why do you think, Karfreitag?' I asked.

'You can't enter the house, sir. The woman and her two daughters are under guard inside. Tell one of the lads to call the girl for you and she can come out. I better hear of nothing which does not conform to these instructions, sir, otherwise you will live to regret it, and I would regret that.'

'What's happening, Karfreitag?' I asked.

'Sir, you know me, I do as my orders tell me, and the women are to be kept in the house until I am told otherwise, that is all I know.'

'Thank you for letting me pass,' I said.

'Anyone stops you, tell them I allowed your travel,' he said.

I bowed to him – like an idiot, out of gratitude – and as I moved off, Karfreitag said, 'I'm sure the strictures I have put on your visit are not too unkind, anyway, sir – after all, I doubt you will be much minded to sit with young Greet in the parlour. It would be more fun out in the woods when twilight comes down, I would imagine.'

I walked on – I had thanked him enough. I got to the house after the sun had set. I did as ordered, and Greet was sent out to me. The guards and constables wanted to talk to me while I waited, but I told them I did not want to talk because what was happening in this town was not right or good or decent. They would have beat me if they could but instead they turned their backs to me – and I was glad, for they were all beneath me, not because of their station in life, but because of the contents of their souls, and their wanting spirits.

Greet and I walked into the woods, under the moon, blue-veined and stark. It was a warm, heavy night. I threw my coat on the ground and we sat, and talked. There was no chance of the Stumpf women escaping from the house, she explained. Too many guards. The child was sick and could barely walk. The two women – Madame Stumpf and Divara – were terrorised with fear and grief. The horses had been confiscated for the change of guards. There was talk of them being taken under arrest to the keep within the day.

'Talk to them,' I said, and I kissed her. Her mouth was warm and red and wet. 'Tell them to think of anything they can to prove their innocence.' And then we put thoughts of Stumpf and his family and Paulus and Fromme and Bideburg and the dead from our minds and lay back together to be together.

And it fell into the deepest night. We parted our bodies later, and then touched again. And this went on for many hours – till the stars were high and blue at their zenith, the moon huge and bloated over us.

We lay together, dreamily then, on my coat – the hot night washing over us and cooling the sweat on our skin. I wished to sleep, but I wished to look at Greet as well, for such a long time. I started to tell her once again that she must come with me, and marry me, and be my wife and I would look after her. She turned to me, and nodded and smiled.

'I had a thought,' I said.

'Oh yes?' she laughed. 'Well done.'

'After we spoke and you were upset about whether we could be together – I had a thought, and I do not know why I did not think of it then. Maybe it is my own pride and self-regard.'

'And so what is the thought, Willie?' she said.

'In truth, my family is no different to yours. My father owns a tiny printing press. Imagine if we take Paulus away – pretend he does not exist – and here we are just met and in love, then I would have been a good match for you as a printer's son – and my father and mother would have spun cartwheels that I had met and fallen in love with a girl like you. Our background is the same, there is no difference, and so the question is closed and safe and done. All that we need to do is leave this town as soon as we can, and marry. Yes, Greet, my wife?' I asked, and I kissed her bare belly, and wanted to disappear inside her.

'My family, what little remains, is not like other families around here,' she said. 'We can trace our line back a long time, to before the great plague.'

She paused.

'Which was when?' she asked me. 'I do not have your learning.'

'Nearly two hundred years ago,' I said. My own family could trace itself back four generations at best, which is no more than seventy years. I knew no-one but nobility and land-owners who could recall their ancestors' names from before the great plague. The plague had caused a little Dark Age in the memories of the poor.

'So, my family – my father's father going back twelve times – they came to this town in the days or weeks after the plague ended,' she said as we lay together. 'We are told that they came from the east – Bohemia, Moravia, I know the names of these places as they have been handed down to me. The town was nearly empty, but the lord was still alive, up in his manor house – centuries before it was burned down back in the time of my own father when he was a boy and the war began, long before Stumpf built his own home up in the lord's old hunting lodge.

These ancestors of mine, they moved into the smallest little hovel they could find – all the poor homes were empty, and nearly all of the others too, but they chose the most meagre one to stay in as stealing the least is morally the best when a human has to survive. It was a few weeks more before the lord came out of his manor house to see what was left of his village – our family story has it that before the plague, Bideburg was home to maybe one hundred and fifty people, and after, about twenty, counting my own family – a man, a woman and one child of three, it is thought.

When the lord appeared, he told my family straight that they could either leave, die, or work for him – he owned the home they were in, and if they wanted to stay, then they had to get to the fields and start the workings of life again, sowing and reaping and threshing. We know that this family of mine were not peasants, and had no knowledge of country life and work. The man and woman could read. It's said he was an actor or clown or singer, that she was a lady, maybe – lots of songs are still sung in our family that only we know, and stories told that are just from us and about us, and all of us have been able to read and write, as our parents taught us and their parents taught them all the way back to the time of the plague, though none of us have risen any further than me – a maid.

For the weeks that the family had lived in the hovel, the lord charged them a sum they had no hope of paying if they lived as long as Methuselah. So they were bound to the land and work, and the people of Bideburg who were good back then, helped their new neighbours learn how to sow and reap and thresh. But the debt carried on to the child they had, a boy, and when he grew up his family worked in the fields, still bonded to the lord by debt, as did his child's family and his grandchildren's and great-grandchildren's. We have no idea when the debt was finally paid, and we doubt that even if it was paid off one day back so long ago that our family even knew – who would tell them? The lord's great-great-great-great grandson? Would he have even known of the debt? And so my family was bonded to the land until the war came. My father was one of the first young men to pick up a knife and a torch and head to the manor house – though the lord was long gone; thankfully, he was killed in one of the battles that began bursting up a few weeks later, we learned. We burned the manor house down. Though I was not born yet, of course. Like you, Willie. My grandfather – because he was respected, not many peasants can read and write, and lords do not like a clever peasant and our family suffered for our learning, and were kept down – my grandfather was put in charge of dividing up the lord's land, and whatever goods could be salvaged from the fire, among the townsfolk. Back then, the town thought for a moment to live like Paulus' people of Munster – keeping all goods in common and being the chosen poor of Christ and such – but we did not last very long on our path of righteousness and soon were back trading and swindling and living our lives like before, except, for a little while, there was no lord to give us orders, keep us beneath the heel.

For the short time that the good spirit reigned in Bideburg, though, the people chose my family as their leaders – my grandfather and his son, my father, though no-one had full command or could condemn another. It served my family nothing in the end, however. Leadership did not change our status or our riches. With command on his shoulders, my grandfather took my father who was then an oafish boy – though when he died he was a wise and lovely man – and they tip-toed their way through the remains of the manor house and its blackened timbers and scorched brick walls, once the fire had cooled to ash a few days after the burning, looking for pickings to share among their neighbours. One gutted room was more intact than the others – it was to the rear of the house where the fire had petered. A great desk was burned to black charcoal in the middle of the room. My grandfather struck it with his fist and it fell to the ground in cinders. The walls of the room had been burned out, but the fireplace and chimney breast still stood, made of solid local stone from our mountains. In the centre of the chimney breast the fire had burned so hard that bricks had fallen free – there was a little cavity behind, like a fairy hole in a tree trunk.

My grandfather knocked out the hanging bricks to look inside, and there was an urn, lidded. He took it out – the fire hadn't reached it, so it was just warm to the hand. He unstoppered it and looked inside – he could not see, it seemed like a ball of dark linen. My grandfather turned the urn to the ground and shook. From inside, came a shrivelled baby – though a baby that had not been born, that was unformed – and also malformed, for its head was big and its hands like the gills of fish, its toes webbed. The eyes looked like frogs' eyes. And it was old – ancient like old parchment. It crumbled on the ground. My grandfather tried to pick it up and put it back in its urn, but it turned to dust in his hand and mixed and blew in the wind with the black ash of the burned room.

This was magic. Old magic. Not devil worship, but the magic the people of these forests used before Christ came along. Long after my grandfather's death, my father told me this story and said that he believed the lord back in the time of the plague had placed the baby there for protection.

I asked my father where the lord would have found the baby, and my father said he remembered a story that he had forgotten – one of those tales from childhood which would have died without him, unless he'd been in that burned room and found the baby's urn with his own father. And the story had been that during the time of the plague – when the sickness first gripped the village, and so months before my family arrived from wherever they had travelled – that the peasants of Bideburg – and I rejoice that no-one calls us that any longer – the peasants of Bideburg had begged the lord's steward to let them shelter inside the manor house, where there was food and drink and warmth. They had worked for his lordship since the time of Adam, and deserved some protection, they said. The lord sent a messenger who told them those families able to raise certain monies, or offer up a higher tithe on their labour once the plague had passed, could send one child each to the manor house for protection, or one woman with a child in her belly.'

And Greet stroked her own bare belly as she talked. But the night grew a little cold, and we gathered our clothes over us like blankets, lying on my coat, and moved together, our faces close.

'It is known that none of the lord's family died,' she said, 'and of the ten children and four pregnant women from the village who were given shelter, all died. Perhaps, my father thought, this baby was a result. The women and children had been kept inside the manor house walls for near on nine months by the time the plague was gone. Anything could have happened, my father said, and my mind plays awful tricks on me and makes me wonder what might have been done to those children and women and their unborn infants.'

Greet and I stayed on my coat until dawn was up and angry – like it was shouting at us to get back to our lives, that our little secret night was done and gone for good.

'I hate you, Sun,' I said, and shook my fist up at the sky, in play.

'I love the Sun,' said Greet, and she pushed the coverings off us and lay back on my coat one final time.

'You are a bare faun, a laughing dryad,' I said, like an idiot – for I was trying to remember a verse of poetry to charm her, but could not, and only saw in my mind pictures of Greek nymphs from books I had read but forgotten.

'Is that what I am to be now?' she said.

Finally, we rose, and I walked her a little way back to the Stumpf house.

'All will be well with you for being gone for the night?' I asked.

'I am my own mistress,' she said. 'There is nothing to command me in this town any longer.'

'Good,' I said.

'Paulus will be cross with you, though, I think,' she said.

'I don't think so. He had work to do. I would have asked too many questions. He wants me to be a man.'

'Help Madame Stumpf and Divara and the little one, then, if you can,' Greet said. 'In truth, I love them, somewhat,' and she laughed. 'They are all I have. There's my sister, but she is married to an oaf. And my cousin, who is simple. And then there is me. Nothing more. There is little to keep me here.'

We walked hand in hand, in a silence that felt right, and made neither I nor her feel bashful or awkward. On the rise, through the woods, to the house, a screaming din tore up. Greet began to run and I called to her to stop.

'Be careful. Let's go up quietly together – see what is happening first.'

We walked through a little orchard that swung to the south of the house – the screaming louder and more pained – and we stopped. Karfreitag was dragging Madame Stumpf by the hair towards a cart. In the cart, Divara was on her knees, guards holding her down, with her little sister in her arms. Madame Stumpf fought like a cat. Karfreitag dragged her to her feet and knocked her unconscious with one straight blow to her jaw. He picked her up and placed her very gently into the cart before her two daughters. The little child's eyes sat open like moon flowers, but it seemed that her soul had slipped away, so blank she was, and dead of expression.

I reached for Greet's hand, beside me, under the apple trees, but she slipped from my grasp, moving forward – and then she ran.

'Greet,' I called – half-whisper, half-shout, a useless sound.

'You there,' I heard Greet shout, 'do not touch those women.'

The white and red check of her dress cut through the trees before me – ahead I saw Karfreitag turn from the foot of the cart and look around, for the voice. There was Raben beside him – he looked towards the orchard. I saw that all the guards – one, two, three, four, five, six of them – wore their arquebus pistols, long and heavy, lit and loaded on straps slung under their shoulders.

'Stop,' shouted Greet.

Raben pointed and called, 'There, sir, in the trees.'

Greet was still in the orchard, running forward – bobbing white and red. I ran to catch her up and called, 'Greet, come back. Be careful.'

She broke the line of trees a good twenty paces in front of me.

The guards swung round to the trees, pulling their guns up from the waist – each had a burning wick.

'No,' I screamed. 'Karfreitag, it's me.'

And the tree line flared up in a thunder of fire and splinters – but I was unhurt, like Jesus had thrown his cloak around me, and I ran on.

Greet lay just outside the tree line, shot to bloody red bits. I looked up and the guards were statues, they had their hands to their mouths, and Karfreitag was bent over, hands on his knees, shaking his head. Raben was crying.

I remember very little now. I was on my knees by her, holding her – and her beautiful face was blown away, like the hands of the wind had ripped her. Her heart was wounded, and her belly. Her hands were shot through.

Sentiment is a terrible failing, but what else can I say than I told her I loved her and kissed her, and tasted her blood in my mouth, like pennies and meat. She patted my hand when I told her I loved her, and though her face was broken, she said, 'Yes, yes,' like an old lady, consoling her grandson. 'I love you too,' she said, and then she died.

I looked up at the guards. Karfreitag lifted his hands and said, 'Son, now, be calm a moment, we did not know it was her. We did not know what it was.'

His face was grey and hanging, and Raben beside him had sat on the ground, his head in his hands, and he was saying, 'My God, my God, what did we do, it was an accident.' I felt sorry for them – and I hate myself for that because I question whether I loved Greet if I had pity for the men who killed her and regretted what they had done and seemed to hate themselves for it.

'She would not stop,' I said.

'You warned her, son,' said Karfreitag, coming up to me, and touching me on the shoulder.

'I have seen arrests before,' I said. Karfreitag sat beside me next to Greet, and put his arm around me.

'I know you have, son,' he said.

'I knew you might shoot if she ran out.'

'I know. She did not know though.'

'I tried to catch her.'

'I am sorry. I thought it was – I do not know what I thought it was. A wolf. The Devil. We just saw something red and white that was screaming at us. I thought I was doing my job.'

Raben walked forward. 'We are sorry,' he said, and he offered me his hand to stand. Then I heard Divara screaming. She had been screaming all along, but only now did the sound make its way to me – and my head became clear.

Raben's hand hovered there in front of me – black powder burns in the cup between his thumb and forefinger, smoke still on the knuckles. I could smell the saltpetre. I stood quick and put his nose across his face with one jab – a beautiful right that Karfreitag had taught me to use – and kicked his legs from under him, but that was pointless as he was already out by the time he hit the ground like a sack of old flour.

Then I was up and off the ground – choking. Someone had me by the neck, in a sleeping hold. Karfreitag – I could see his boots as I was bent forward and down, the blood rushing to my head. He was cutting the air off, and it was like being drugged. I was spun as I fell and I saw Greet on the ground before me, her body shredded and red.

★ ★ ★

I woke in the bed of the cart, Madame Stumpf and her daughters by me. Divara was holding me up in a sitting position, so I could breathe. I did not know if they were taking me now to be executed. I sat still, inside myself, and to my shame all I thought was, 'I am young. For Greet to die so young is wrong. I do not want to die while I am young. I want to live. I do not want to be Greet.'

My love did not have the courage of its heat in so many ways. I do not think my love has ever been as brave as it was strong. It was mercury, not iron. But I have pride too – and my sinful pride is as powerful as my love is weak. So, I did not ask any of those guards, in the cart or on horses to the side, what my fate was, whether they were going to kill me or torture me. I sat impassive at the feet of Divara, like a statue fallen from its plinth, as the cart tumbled on. My head was propped against her knees. She held her mother and her sister to her – Madame Stumpf came round, but she was bleeding from the mouth onto Divara's shoulder; the little girl, Rosa, with her head in her sister's lap, silent.

I did not want to die, but I would not die a coward and show fear. A coward's death is still a death – fight until you can fight no more and then give up and die without a word. I keep this as my path in life and have tried to live by it.

I looked about me as the cart rode down the Stumpf Path to the road for Bideburg. If I spoke quickly and spoke in a whisper none of these men would hear me. I turned myself around so I could see Divara and her mother – I tugged at their skirts.

'I swear I will help you,' I whispered. 'I will fight for you.'

The mother's jaw was swollen and her lip black with caked blood. She slurred her words, saying, 'Do not help us, young man, you are putting yourself at risk.'

'This will not be allowed to happen,' I said. 'We will stop this.'

'Get us poison, or a knife,' said Divara, in a hiss. 'Ground glass. Mushrooms.'

The child began to wail. Divara's face moved like another monstrous face lived beneath her skin. The guard driving the cart turned at the sound of the little girl.

'Keep the child quiet, please,' the guard called, almost politely. He sounded like a warden in a church asking for silence.

Madame Stumpf clasped her hand over the little girl's mouth.

'Be quiet,' she said, in such a voice that the child fell still and cried no longer.

'I will help you,' I whispered again. 'Paulus will not let this happen. No-one will let this happen.'

'It has happened,' said Madame Stumpf.

The cart and guards drew up at the crossroads to the town now. Karfreitag sat on his horse and called to me, 'Again, Willie, we are sorry for what happened. And I am sorry for having to use force to silence you, but you were a danger to yourself and others and I needed to get the prisoners here and you back to your master, as you have a job to do for him, and for the state and the Prince-Bishop. So be a good lad and jump down now from the wagon and go back to the inn.'

Even now, as an old man whom people must marvel at for the slowness and heaviness of his steps, that walk back to the room in the inn where Paulus was remains my life's greatest labour. It felt like Death was in me – that the black wings of the angel were about me and dragging me through the earth to my everlasting sleep, because that is what I craved then: sleep. My body and soul were rinsed dry, there was nothing left within me, and my mind was hung upon the waking moment, unable to think backwards, nor see forwards, stuck solely on the plod of my feet up the stairs to a place where I could sleep.

And I did sleep – Paulus said – for a day or more. He fed me, and helped me to the pot, though I remember neither eating nor toilet. He worked on his trial papers. When I woke, he told me we had been granted access to our clients – that is the word he used.

Paulus told me to stay in bed, while he fetched some spiced warm wine and a little porridge for me. I began to say, 'Please, sir, you do not need to,' but after just a few words I felt I would cry if I spoke another sound, and I lay back down.

The food was brought and Paulus said, 'Karfreitag is not a good man. Get that out of your head.'

'Why do you think I believe Karfreitag a good man?' I asked.

'You talked about him throughout the night. You told me what happened. Don't you remember?'

'No,' I said. I still do not remember telling him – and that is not the weariness of age – it was a memory that never settled in my mind, killed by whatever fever or delirium was on me.

'Karfreitag is the poison of the world,' said Paulus, 'and that is why we are dying here today – killed by the poison of men like him. Do not think of him as a good man reluctantly doing his duty. He is not.'

Karfreitag was a man of the Empire – where the Empire had gone, he had gone, what it had done, he had done. He wore its uniform, and I have never in my life met a man who wore a uniform and still could be called a human being. Putting on colours is the taking off of self.

'The world would be a better place without all Landesknecht,' said Paulus. 'Mercenary. Dogs for hire. The whores of war. They will fight on both sides of the same battle. Only money means anything to them. They are creatures of their time. As Caligula said, I would they all had one throat so I might slit it.'

I was still tired, weary – I felt ruined inside and out. Paulus had been working for hours, and was excited. He wanted to talk, it seemed, so I listened, though the story I did not like, as it made me fearful, and feel more alone than I already did. But the act of listening took my mind away from Greet, and even fear is better than the pain of grief and loss and guilt.

Paulus had first met Karfreitag in the village of Alderbrecht during the crisis, before the peace, when towns were changing hands faster than money. A village would be Catholic and a full part of the Empire one day, then overnight it would switch to Luther, and though it might still say it was loyal to the Emperor, how could it be loyal if it rejected his faith? The world was back to front, like writing in a looking glass. The village would be taken back, and reconvert to Rome, under force sometimes – though usually no violence was needed as most people by then only cared that there was bread on their table and that their lord was decent, not how he prayed to his God in Heaven. The peasants had been crushed in the war, Munster had been quelled – ordinary folk had no time for revolution now, and would not have for many years to come. The embers of the rebellion just needed stamped out like a campfire at dawn – and that was easy done, though the lords still called it The Crisis. The last time the poor had tried to stand so tall was when the Englishmen Jack Straw and Watt Tyler took on their king – and that was two hundred years or more ago. The lessons taught to the English kept the rest of Europe down till our poor rose up in the twenties. Perhaps it will take another two hundred years or more for the poor and working to take a stand against the rich again on this continent. By then they will have forgot the scourging our peasants took in their war against wealth – and be brave once more.

Alderbrecht was one of those villages and towns constantly swinging on the pendulum between Rome and Luther before the peace was settled and a little freedom returned to the world when it came to how a human being decided to speak to their own God in their own way. Alderbrecht did not vacillate from one to the other because of rebellious town leaders or insurrection – it was simply on the frontline between the lands of the Prince-Bishop and his Catholic lords, and the Lutheran lords who opposed them. So every month or so it would slip between the hands of one side or the other. This was politics, government and war – and so it remains today across the world.

Paulus was legal advisor and court liaison officer to the Prince-Bishop's field commanders. It was his job to tell the commanders when the territory they controlled had shifted back under the governance of the Prince-Bishop, or once more moved to the Lutheran side. Often, this ebb and flow of power involved no military manoeuvres, but was accomplished merely by messengers. A Lutheran lord might dispatch a letter to the Prince-Bishop informing him that the peasants in such and such a village or town were now free from Rome, or the Prince-Bishop might write to the Lutherans that town such and such was now back in the fold and acquitted of the antichrist monk. The people of these smaller towns and villages seldom knew whose command they were under until a platoon of soldiers from one side or other rode in to collect taxes or demand food and lodging. But these messages could be confused. A town could return to the Prince-Bishop before the soldiers in the field knew it had happened – letters on horseback often moving faster than men.

Paulus kept track of the political changes and made sure they were translated to the battlefield. Sometimes, he had to ride out in search of small squads of soldiers dispatched to retake towns which had already returned under control of the Prince-Bishop. Alderbrecht was such a town. A platoon under Karfreitag's command had been ordered to retake the village from the Lutheran lords, but a day later it had been ceded back to the Prince-Bishop in an exchange of territory. Karfreitag and his soldiers, however, were unaware, and Paulus left from the field headquarters to find them and discontinue their orders. Usually, such confusion was no cause for concern. The soldiers simply garrisoned themselves in the town they were ordered to take, and lived off the peasants, with little or no violence. Karfreitag, like all the old Landesknechts who had fought in the Peasant War, was not so dilettante in his duties. A village could not be taken without suppressing the peasantry, and then he and his troops looted what they pleased – not just food and lodging, but gold, livestock, women, whatever took their fancy.

Paulus rode with a small guard party to the village. Men and boys were hanged from the lintel of every home in the street. At the town crossroads, the women of the village were lined up, naked, on every side. Karfreitag and a handful of men were raping the youngest and prettiest girls in the village. The rest of the men guarded the remaining older women – who they would take in their turn later, after the more senior soldiers had finished with the best spoils. The town men who had not been hanged were herded in the meeting hall.

Paulus rode up the street, calling out, 'This town is free and has been for days. It is a loyal town. Let the people go.'

Karfreitag rose off the girl beneath him in the street, and fixed his clothing, adjusting his old Landesknecht sash, so it sat correctly across his breast and hip. The other senior officers with him were set on finishing their game, though. Karfreitag kicked at them and ordered them up.

'Release these good women,' Karfreitag said. The officers mumbled their anger but got to their feet and fixed their clothing too. Karfreitag helped the girls to their feet, saying, 'Ladies, forgive us. Let us help you back to your homes, and bring this town to peace.'

The girls rose, shambling, and looked around mad-eyed. All the women and the girls were crying now and wailing. The fear of death had silenced them before, now they gave up their horror to the sky above in screams and tears.

'Cut down the men,' said Karfreitag, and the lower ranked soldiers took their swords to the ropes around the necks of the village men and boys. 'Release the other men from the meeting hall.'

'You should have found us sooner, sir,' Karfreitag said to Paulus. 'It is not right what has happened.'

If Karfreitag had been ordered to kill a mother's baby before her eyes and then a second later to guard the mother with his life – he would have done so. Orders and the money which paid for his orders were to Karfreitag the nerves and sinews which moved his mind and body.

'This was ten years or more ago,' Paulus said. 'Karfreitag was perhaps forty, and he still wore the full peacock uniform of the Landesknecht – the wide-brimmed hat with multicoloured feathers, the slit red doublet, with the blue and white shirt pulled out through the vents, the high-heeled red knee-boots and tight black britches. The purple sash which held his sword – for a scabbard is for the weak, the Landesknecht believe.'

Karfreitag, like all the old Landesknecht, no longer wore their gaudy war clothes. Times had changed after the peace, and too much colour on a military uniform caused fear and upset among the peasants and ordinary folk. The sight of a Landesknecht in full regalia might have been for many like the rapists of their mothers and the executioners of their fathers returning to the world when it was seeming to come under order for the first time in generations and that was not good politics. All lords – Catholic and Protestant – had rolled their Landesknecht units into their wider armies and banned their motley. Older hands, though – like Karfreitag who had fought at the Sack of Rome – kept their sash, and were allowed to do so, and Karfreitag still wore his – the hilt of his sword tied in a billowing figure eight knot from the purple at his hip.

'These people who live like dogs by the orders of others – Fromme, Karfreitag – they are the agents of Satan in this town,' said Paulus. 'Their minds are filled with the thoughts of other people – whether they are their masters and captains, or prophets from the Bible. I would exterminate from the land all those who do not or can not think for themselves. Liquidate the unthinking.'

'The land would be empty, sir,' I said, and I got up from my bed now. My body was weak and my mind tired, but grief had been replaced by an anger I had never held in my heart before – and it is an anger which has still not burned itself out in me.

The table was littered with papers. I walked over and rifled through the sheets with Paulus' scribbled notes and mind-maps.

'Is this the makings of the defence?' I asked, and sat down at the table as my legs shook under me.

'Yes,' he said.

'We have to save these people,' I said.

'Young Greet is to be buried. You should go.'

I looked down at my hands on the desk and my stomach revolted against me.

'I have leave to see the Stumpf women in the keep,' he said.

'Give them my loyalty.'

Paulus smiled and came over to me, rested a hand on my shoulder.

'You are made of the right and proper materials, Willie,' he said.

'I owe everything to you,' I said.

'At the funeral, find out how the people of this town feel about what has happened. I doubt they want an insurrection, but I would care to know. Greet's life can not have meant nothing to them, and there is the matter of the child, also – the boy in the woods – that can not sit well with any decent man or woman among them.'

'I do not know any longer, Paulus,' I said. 'Raben shot Greet. If Raben is not good in this town, then who can be?'

'I do not know either, Willie,' he said. And we readied ourselves to go out – he to the keep, me to see Greet put into the earth.

'The trial starts tomorrow,' he said, and we shut the door to our room behind us and walked down the inn stairs to the street.

I nodded.

262

Chapter Twenty-Four

Time runs on twin threads for Paulus and I. Paulus constructs the damning of Stumpf, while I am taught what it is to be a man at the funeral of Greet Werren.

When I was a child, I believed that my mother and father and brothers and sisters ceased to exist when not in the same room as me. For a child, this is a sign of an advanced mind – it shows they are somehow aware of the roots of philosophy: identity, experience, perception – but for an adult to think the same indicates an intellectual weakness, a solipsistic lack of imagination. Thus, I appear to have been an advanced child who became a backward man. I still struggle to contemplate the lives of others when they are not in my company. It often happens to me when I am with a woman: she leaves my bed, goes to dress or to toilet, to cook maybe if we have worked ourselves hungry, and when the door to my bedroom shuts behind her I can not imagine her combing her hair, washing her face, putting on her gown, breaking eggs, cutting bread, laying the table. Until she walks back into my room, or I leave and go in search of her, she might as well have lain dead in the corridor. I can not fathom what kind of life another person can experience when I am not there to experience it with them – my life leading their life. That is a recipe for loneliness, I have found.

I did not have it within me to imagine what Paulus said and did at the keep with the Stumpf women – though it preyed on my mind throughout Greet's funeral. I wished to know. I wished Greet back to life, but almost as hard I wished that Madame Stumpf and her two daughters were away from this town, and safe and well – and so I could not shake from my head the whirring question of what Paulus was doing to help them, or if he was able to do anything to help them. And this felt like treachery to Greet that I should worry about her mistresses when she was dead, but to my mind, they were not quite lost yet, gone like her, not good as dead already.

I wished to be there in the keep with them to help them, but I would have been of no use unless I saw young Greet safely taken away into the earth. I could not turn my back on the dear dead just to help the helpless living.

Greet was buried in the churchyard up on Far Hill – at Barthelme's little stone chapel in the midst of the farmland and fields where the townsfolk grew their crops and kept their cattle and sheep. The service was sloppy and short, dry and without love or wailing – a Protestant goodbye. Barthelme's black robes hung on him as he stood in his wood pulpit. Only the poor were in the church. Thirty people, perhaps. I kept to the back of the pews. None saw me, until the service was over, and Greet's coffin – splintered cheap wood, the lid not nailed down properly – was lifted and taken to the lower graveyard at the bottom of the hill. The wealthy were buried up on the hill, their graves ringing the church.

It was hot summer and Greet had few family to mourn her – just her sister Erma and Erma's new husband, and her cousin Efer and Efer's new husband, neither woman had yet borne children themselves – so she was buried quickly, as most poor are. Mourning is an expense and luxury for the rich.

Funerals are hard to remember – especially the funerals of those you love. I know no-one who remembers the moments before their mother or father or child or lover was placed into the ground. The service blurs – a whoosh of grey, and mumbled words and no smell, until at the graveside, with the brown deep earth in your throat and nose, and the hole there, Death grabs you by the shoulders and says, 'Look. Remember.' Yet, Death did not grab me. I do not recall her coffin being lowered into the ground, or the dirt flung upon it. I do not remember – I have no picture in my mind – my first wife being put in the ground and covered up either, nor my second – and I loved them both as much as Greet, though because I was young, and we had known each other such a brief few days, Greet left a mark on me like a hot poker in a clasped hand. My memory returns after the earth had covered Greet, and I recall I longed to cry as I walked away from her grave, or to talk to someone of my heart and how it felt for her, but I was an intruder there, and knew no-one.

Efer and Erma's husbands – two young coltish men, still gangly, like me they were just youths – came up on either side of me. I had left the graveside first, as I thought I should not be there, though felt a traitor to Greet for walking away. I did not recognise the young men but they told me their names – Erwin was wed to Efer, and Roland to Erma.

'Our wives,' Roland said, 'would like to talk to you.'

'You were with Greet when she died and they hope you can tell them of her last moments,' Erwin said.

'Of course,' I said.

'Come to my house then with us,' said Roland. 'We will be drinking a goodbye to Greet, and you are welcome.'

I smiled then, in the graveyard – and thanked the two men. I would be able to speak of Greet to someone who loved her, and that made me feel light and alive again. And though I smiled my eyes were sticky with tears, and my mouth hot and thick.

* * *

Paulus told me that the Stumpf women could also talk only of Greet.

They were held in the second cell – away from Stumpf. Inside, their cell was split in half lengthwise, the left for guards, visitors, the right caged off and locked for the prisoners.

Paulus tried to keep them to the matter of their innocence, asking them to help him formulate their defence, but they could only talk of Greet and their grief and guilt at her death. Paulus had brought the child Rosa a board and chalk to draw, to occupy her as he spoke to Divara and her mother. The child drew star after star on the board – crosswise triangles – but kept her eyes on the adults as they spoke – her hand moving and tongue stuck out to the side.

'We may not be guilty of my husband's crimes,' said Madame Stumpf, 'but Greet died because of us.'

'I loved her like a sister,' said Divara.

'She was my sister,' said the little girl Rosa, still drawing her repeating stars.

'Then shall I leave?' asked Paulus. 'And let Fromme burn you? For he will burn you all.' And he pointed to Rosa. 'Even your little one here.'

Rosa threw down her board and chalk and came to cower between her sister and mother. Madame Stumpf said, 'Have you come to torture us too? Is that it?'

'Do not say such things before a child,' said Divara.

'Bad wicked man,' little Rosa called out, from behind her hands.

'I am not bad and I do not wish to torture you. I wish to help you. But if you will not speak of the things we need to speak of then I can not help you and you will all die.'

The women and the child were silent.

'Shall I go?' he asked.

'Do not go,' said Divara.

'I am sorry,' Madame Stumpf said – and her face was ice. Here was a woman sick of living her life for men, and listening to men.

The child wailed, 'Will he burn us?'

The women comforted the child and shushed and reassured her till she was quiet and lay down on the cot in the cell. She turned her face to the wall, and pretended to sleep but her crying could be heard, sharp and then wet and smothered.

'Prove to me your husband was evil,' said Paulus.

'My husband was not bad to us,' said Madame Stumpf, 'he was always good as a husband and father. Kind. Never cruel.'

'We told you this,' said Divara. She walked to the cot her sister lay on and sat by her, resting her hand on Rosa's back. The little girl did not turn her face from the wall, but her crying quietened and her shoulders stopped rising and falling. Divara patted her. Rosa was silent and still for a long time, now. She slept, Paulus thought – maybe.

'No wife who knows her husband believes him to be all good,' he said. 'If you go into that court telling tales of what a great man Stumpf was, what a wise provider and good shepherd, then you are vouching for an agent of the Devil, and will be judged a devil's accomplice.'

'Do you believe now he was a wolf as well?' Divara said, shrill.

'Of course I do not, but the man in charge of the new court does. I am not here to save Stumpf – he has confessed and will die. You I perhaps can save.'

Divara moaned and rocked a little. 'Do not say "perhaps,"' she whispered. 'If we are to die,' – and she hissed the word almost silently, looking at her sister as she patted the child's back – 'then I would rather leave now by my own hand than go through this all.'

'What was bad about him?' asked Paulus. 'Denounce him to me.'

'I told you he killed his dogs. Is that not evil? He beat dogs to death for amusement.'

'The court will be full of men who have beaten dogs to death. Think harder of this man you love and find me his failings.'

Madame Stumpf looked at Rosa on the cot – the child still as a painting – then turned to Divara and smiled, a wan thin fake smile. 'He had some books,' she said to Paulus.

'I have seen his books. They are not unusual.'

'No, he had other books,' she said. 'They are in our bedroom. You did not see them.'

'What books?'

'Books which I am uncomfortable to speak of,' she said.

'You should speak, Madame Stumpf. You will not embarrass me.'

She looked at her daughters again and lowered her head, and spoke low, fast and mumbling.

'These were books of pictures. Of people engaged in coupling. Men and women. Men with men. Women with women. Groups of people with animals. The people in the pictures took pleasure in hurting while they made love. People were bound and tied. The pictures were set in places like this – in cells, or in woods with masked men attacking women and raping them, some were set in an outhouse, a soldiers' latrine, which disgusted me more than anything else.'

Divara watched her mother speak, unmoved and unashamed – curious, her head cocked to one side, as if she was at a lecture on some exotic subject never before heard: the discovery of a new plant, or continent.

'Did your husband do such things to you?' Paulus asked.

'My God, no – never,' she said. 'He was a gentleman to me.'

Divara spoke, even though Paulus had neither looked at her nor spoken to her. 'My father was the perfect father to me,' she said.

'In these picture books,' Madame Stumpf continued, 'my husband had made his own drawings. The pictures in the book were rendered very well – most artistically, with great draughtsmanship and accuracy. It could have been real life, like looking through a glass at the world. But my husband's drawings were brutish and crude – done in black ink, and smudged and spidery. He had tried to copy the scenes in the book, or sometimes there was a drawing in the margins from his own imagination. I remember one: a woman sitting naked against a tree, with her head at her feet, blood was drawn on the page as if it spurted from the neck. Her hands and feet were tied.'

'Do you believe your husband was a deviant?'

'Yes now, I do.'

'Now,' said Divara. 'Not before. We knew nothing before.'

'Is this proof of deviance?' said her mother. 'To have such books? I do not know. Maybe it is. Do other men have such books? If so, then why should I have thought him a deviant. If not, then I was a fool. I am a fool. I know that now.'

'But we did not understand what was happening,' said Divara.

'I have heard of these books,' said Paulus. 'They are rare, I assure you. Expensive. Many would think them deviant. You should call them such in court and denounce them.'

'Then my husband is a deviant, sir,' said Madame Stumpf.

'Good. Did this scare you?' asked Paulus. The child roused a little but did not turn or seem to wake.

'No. I did not know what to make of it. He is rich, he is curious. I did not know then that he was sick – if that is what you are leading me to believe. If I had known he was deviant, then I would have been scared. But I did not, so I was not.'

'He had friends?'

Madame Stumpf laughed. Her mouth was still raw and cut, and she threw her hand up to her face – her laugh hurt her. Divara had stopped stroking her sister's back now. Her hand lay still across Rosa's shoulders.

'No, sir,' said Divara. 'No friends. My father did not like people.'

'That is not normal,' said Paulus. 'Does it make you think anything was strange about him?'

'It is not normal to dislike people?' asked Divara. 'Sir, tell me who you like in this town of ours?'

'It is not Christian to hate your fellow man,' said Paulus.

Paulus would never – on his word, or his life – help a witness or accused construct their statement to see them better served in court, but he wished these women would see the trajectory of his questions, so they could save their own lives, without him having to fetch Rosa's blackboard and chalk and draw their testimony for them like a teacher: Stumpf as a monster in the home, as well as in the woods.

'He was not a Christian,' said Madame Stumpf.

'Well, now we come to something,' said Paulus – and he almost sighed. 'Did he tell you this?'

'Yes,' said Madame Stumpf. 'He told me he had no faith.'

'Did you try to bring him to church and find his faith?'

'Of course.'

'And?'

'He asked me not to bully him – those were his very words. He said he would not bully me into believing something I did not believe or ask me to act in a way which I felt wrong. And he asked the same of me.'

'Did this worry you?'

'Of course. I worried for his soul after death.'

'And did you and your children attend church?'

'Of course, we love God dearly and Jesus is our saviour.'

'We pray to God each night,' said Divara. 'We have asked him to help us as we are not sinners and have done no wrong.'

'We pray to God each night,' the little girl said, her face to the wall. She brought silence to the cell.

Paulus nodded. 'Well, this is good,' he said, after a moment. Divara took to stroking Rosa again. 'Will you say in court that Stumpf was violent – that he beat his dogs to death. And say that he kept books of deviant material that was an affront to you. Also, that he wished to keep no company with others, and that he denounced Jesus Christ, the Church and God himself? And you tried to save his soul?'

'The words you use are true, but they are twisted,' said Madame Stumpf.

'I am not asking you to lie, Madame,' said Paulus. 'I am asking you to try and save your life,' and he pointed to the child lying on her cot, 'if you can find an honourable way to do it.'

Divara spoke. 'These words can be said.'

It was afternoon now, and Paulus called the guard outside the door to bring some food and wine on his expense. The little girl Rosa lay with her face to the wall still, and they did not know if she was awake or asleep. They left her alone, to give her peace, they thought. Paulus ate in the cell with the Stumpf women, and reassured them that he would fight their case hard. He spoke of the life he would help them build in a new city of their choosing.

'Set up a little inn,' he said. 'You have money. You know business. I will speak to folk about property, and tradesmen to help you get started. All will be fine. Any monies I incur helping you, I will set against the paper I will write on this case, which will, I am sure, find a ready audience. And you can repay me once you start to earn.'

'We will not die?' asked Divara.

'I will not let you,' said Paulus. He kept his eyes on the plate of food before him and did not look at the women as he spoke.

The two women wept then over the plates of beef and bread which sat on their knees, and the little girl stirred and stopped pretending to sleep, and called out, 'Why are you crying, mother? Are we to be hurt?'

And all three of them – Paulus, Divara, the child's mother – they said, 'no, my dear', and 'be still sweetheart', and 'we are safe'. The child would not settle again though.

★ ★ ★

As Paulus called for food to be brought to the candled cell, I walked down through the fields in the summer sunshine – thinking of him with the Stumpf women – Greet's little family leading me on to the allotment homes, up by the Dark Hedges, where they lived with the other poor. The two sisters lived in two cottages side by side, sharing a wall and a kitchen garden, a sty and a shack.

The allotment was home to maybe fifty families – the cottages no higher than a tall man, thatched, one window with shutters. And it was a maze, tight and close built, with dun walls to all sides, and middens on every other corner. Smoky in the sunshine, and dank too from the frothing gutters that had formed in the water runs down the lanes and alleys, that starred out to every side. The two back-to-back cottages where Erma and Efer and their husbands lived was deep in the heart of the allotments.

Ten or so people gathered outside the family cottages, sitting on stools they brought with them from their own homes, or hunkered on the ground. More arrived as the afternoon wore on. Greet, I learned, had lived with Erma and her husband Roland, when not staying at the Stumpf house. Drink appeared immediately – bitter home-made spirit, clear as glass, and jagged with buffalo grass. There was sweet bread in mounds on benches that had been taken from the two cottages and put outside.

I sat with Efer and Emer and told them that I loved Greet, that we had talked of getting married.

Emer shook her head. 'This did not happen,' she said.

Efer said, 'Why did she die?'

'Our officers and your constables shot her by mistake.'

'We know. But why?'

'They mistook her.'

'For who?' asked Emer.

'I do not know. They could not explain. Have they not told you?'

Emer said, 'They told us nothing. That she had been shot by accident while the Stumpf women were being taken away.'

'That is true,' I said.

'Did she try to save them?' asked Efer.

'I do not know what she wished to do. She saw them being taken, while we were walking in the trees, and ran shouting towards them and the soldiers. To help them, maybe. To ask the soldiers to let them be. To comfort them. I do not know.'

'Did you not try to save her?' Emer asked.

'I ran to catch her and hold her back. I knew it was dangerous. I called to her. She did not stop. I wish she had. I hate myself for not catching her and keeping her from what happened. Please believe me that I loved her very much and I am in pain now to speak of her gone.'

'As are we,' said Efer.

We drank on, and their husbands joined us, where we sat under the cottage window.

Roland said, 'You were a gentleman with Greet?'

'Yes,' I said.

'Why were you in the woods with her?' asked Erwin.

'We were walking.'

The two men drank and the women looked at me.

'These men who shot her,' Emer asked after a while, 'you are their comrade?'

'We are together in a party, but we are not friends.'

'You have no loyalty to those you work with and travel with?' asked Efer.

'I did have loyalty. Not now. They killed Greet. And they wish to do harm to the Stumpf women.'

'Good,' said Emer.

'Why do you wish to defend them?' asked Roland.

'And save the wolf from the church?' said Erwin.

'I want harm to come to them,' said Efer. 'Bitches and cunts.'

The men looked at her but said nothing and drank on. Twenty or some guests were now gathered around the cottage in the hot late afternoon. I sweated as the drink had gone to me, and made me dizzy.

'The women and the child are innocent,' I said. 'They have done nothing and should be left alone. They are destroyed by what Stumpf has done, and they have lost the two boys as well. I have pity for them.'

'Pity?' said Erma. 'Fuck your pity. You pity the wrong people.'

'You pity murderers and monsters,' said Efer. 'Are you a Christian?'

'I am,' I said, offended. And if I was the old man I am today, with the knowledge I have learned, I would have realised back then in the allotment that here was the moment when women turn on a man, with the intention of making other men beat him for their pleasure and revenge. I have not seen this often, but when it happens it is, to me, the purest crystal terror – men set on you by the women they love.

'No you're not,' said Erma, 'you are not a Christian.' And she sneered at me, and looked to her husband, Roland. 'You're a fucking traitor. You let my sister Greet die. And you lie that you loved her.'

'You backstab your own comrades,' said Efer, 'and you pity a fucking whore and her two whore children, who were probably born from fucking the devil or a wolf – which you try to defend too.'

Erma stood and pushed me in the chest. 'You should have your fucking throat cut.'

It made the very centre of me – as the man I thought I was – shrivel and still like stone.

Efer stood too and put her hands on the shoulders of the two men – their husbands. 'You are lucky we do not hang you here.'

In such a moment, the mind makes one thousand choices and takes in a thousand little clues: should I stand and shout back, run, argue logically, fight, tip the table over; has Roland moved, is Erwin armed, might Erma reach for that bottle, will Efer just keep talking? Can I appeal to anyone near by; how far is it back to town; what might I use as a weapon; could I fight both those men and survive; I can not fight all the men here and survive. No, I could not fight and survive, so I raised my hands and said, 'Ladies, I am sorry if I offended you. I shall go if you wish.'

Without looking at her husband, Erma, eyes still on me, said, 'Roland, are you going to let him talk like that to me?'

'I was trying to be polite, madam,' I said.

'Madam? Who the fuck do you think you are?' said Efer, and she put her hands in the hair of her husband Erwin, and stroked his head.

'Don't you fucking talk to our women like that,' said Erwin.

Roland stood up tall like a poker – and I was off, away from the table and running through the garden. The allotment homes were a warren of alleys and walls, and I ran blindly in twists and turns away from the family cottages in the direction of town. I was lost within a few moments and paused to look around – and then they were on me, I do not know how many, six, seven, eight men, maybe.

I was on the ground, and one man had me by the hair, beating my head off the dirt and then off the wall of a house. I freed myself – God knows how I did, I think I ripped my hair from his hands, half scalped myself, for my face ran with blood – and took to my heels, and thought I was away and safe and free again, but then fell or was tripped and they gathered around kicking me like a sack of cats being stamped to death. And the kicking went on and it went on till I saw just black and white behind my eyes and the world was gone from my comprehension.

Someone, a woman's voice, was saying, 'Don't kill him, you can't kill him. Let him alone now.'

Another woman said, 'He's got what he deserves. That's enough. Stop.'

The huddle of men around me moved back, and the sun appeared above them, bearing down on my face. I could taste my own blood, and my nose was full, it was hard to see, my eyes were swelling closed. I tried to sit up, and rose on one elbow as the crowd shifted back more and a space opened up in front of me – and there was the road to town just twenty paces away, if I could make my way through these men without being kicked again. I could not push myself up as my fingers were stamped and bloody, and so I attempted to roll on my side and get myself standing using my legs alone. But then a foot swung towards me, landing square above my heart – toe to breastbone – sending the breath and the brains out of me. I fell back, gasping but still conscious, my heart felt like it had stopped in my chest and I was suspended between life and death, my time on Earth hovering over whether my heart would beat again.

A man's voice said, 'I decide when they've had enough. He's had enough now.'

Another said, 'Let's go.'

My heart beat again and I sucked at the sky for air, then I slipped away into a dark dream that lifted all the pain from my brokenness.

It may have been a minute, it may have been an hour, but someone threw water over me, and pulled me to my feet – man, woman, child, I have no idea. They woke me and pushed me from the run of houses in the alleyway to the road outside the allotment homes. I staggered in the sun, and, with the Dark Hedges at my back, made for town, in a haze of hurt, and half-blinded by the light, and hate.

★ ★ ★

Paulus had called for a sleeping draught to be brought for the child. The child had drunk and was now truly lost to the waking world.

'May you get us both a sleeping draught also?' asked Divara. She and her mother sat up close to the bars of their cell on the floor, Paulus was perched on a stool before them.

'I can do that, gladly,' said Paulus.

'Get me ground glass, or poison,' Madame Stumpf said. 'Bring me a knife. Make the draught too strong.'

'Please, mother,' said Divara.

'He does not have to do it,' Madame Stumpf said, angry, to herself more than in answer to her daughter. 'I have clothes on my back. I can shred them and hang myself if he does not.'

'If I need to, I will bring you something,' said Paulus.

'What will you bring?' asked Divara.

'Poison or a knife,' said Paulus.

'Bring it now, before the trial,' said Madame Stumpf.

There was laughing in the hall outside the cell, and the door to the hot barred room thudded open.

One of the soldiers from our party, and a town constable, came stumbling through, drunk and sweating and grinning. The constable came first, then the guard.

'Ladies,' the constable called out, laughing. 'We have come for you.'

Paulus rose and lifted the stool from under him – he stepped forward and brought the stool hard across the face of the constable who fell like a stunned heifer to the floor of the cell.

'Oh, sir,' said the guard. 'We did not know.'

Paulus grabbed the guard – he was young, maybe eighteen, and I can not recall his name – he grabbed him by the hair and cracked his head off the wall.

The boy's skull opened up but he did not lose consciousness. Instead, he groaned and slumped, but Paulus held him still by the hair, hanging like a tousle.

Paulus dragged the young guard into the hall and called for Karfreitag. The boy was on his knees, his face dripping blood onto the floor.

'Karfreitag,' Paulus screamed, and then looked down at the boy. 'I will have you fucking hanged,' he said. 'Do not think I won't. One finger laid on those women and the man behind it dies. I will have the Prince-Bishop banish their family and confiscate their properties. They will have to pay for your execution and that will ruin them and they will die in the almshouse. You fucking dog,' and he kicked the boy between the legs. The lad went to the floor, his hair coming away in Paulus' hand. 'Karfreitag,' Paulus screamed again.

The sergeant walked down the stairs and into the hallway. 'What is going on here, sir? What have you done to these lads?'

'They were going to rape them,' said Paulus, and he walked back into the cell, and kicked the unconscious town constable now, again, hard between the legs. The kick woke the boy, who rose and screamed and held himself and brought up his breakfast on the floor of the cell.

'These women are under your protection as the head of this guard,' Paulus shouted to Karfreitag as the sergeant walked into the cell. 'If you do not keep them safe, sir, then I will hold you as responsible for what happens to them as the men that hurt them. And I will have you killed, sergeant. You know I could do it, and that I would do it.'

'That is understood, sir,' said Karfreitag.

When I was a boy I would marvel at the labourers unloading wool and wood and coal and meat at the market where my father bought his paper and ink for the press. These men could lift sacks the weight of two men onto each shoulder with a heft of their arms. Up the sacks would come and the men would hold them over their backs in their red clenched fists, veins popping, knees propped. Karfreitag lifted the young constable and guard like a docker hoisting two fat sacks of coal or cauliflowers. He heaved them by their collars and slung them over his back – one, two – then, bent only a little forward, he hauled them up the hall.

'Your boy, Willie, is outside the keep,' Karfreitag called back as he took the stairs, up to the keep's main quarters. 'He has been hurt. You will need to see to him. I was about to look after him, but now I have these boys to tend to.'

'What have you done to him?' asked Paulus.

'I saved him, sir,' said Karfreitag.

Paulus fetched a bucket of water from the hall and sluiced it over the vomit on the cell floor. He walked to the women, and rested his head against the bars between them.

'You are safe,' he said. 'I must go and see my student.'

'You should put this town on trial,' said Madame Stumpf.

'Bring us the poison and the knife you promised,' said Divara.

Paulus felt his soul empty and all sense of good and hope leave him, filled up in their place by fear – not fear and hate, he said, but just cold fear. Fear for himself, but fear most of all for what he could not do, and what he would be made to be a part of, to witness and agree to, as if the sins of others were his own work, his own will, when they were not – and that made fear a dark, black bath that swallowed the self.

Chapter Twenty-Five

The retrial of the Werewolf Stumpf under the authority of the Holy Roman Church.

And so I was patched up by Paulus again – but now pain did not hurt me and fear did not keep me shivering and quiet. It was as if I had taken a drug which turned my body into a torch of energy. I groaned when I moved but I would not sit down. My jaw felt like frozen stone, but I talked on and on to Paulus, and he knew I would not rest or let him be, so we worked on the argument on behalf of the family until nearly dawn. We slept and went into the court early, taking our breakfast with us, to prepare our wits for the case.

I had written out page upon page of notes and case law regarding complicity in murder, the withholding of information in capital crimes, a wife's right not to incriminate her husband, duress on witnesses, non-liability of heirs in criminal matters – on and on, every avenue of defence I could think of.

Stumpf was brought into the court room chained and on the dogcatcher's poles, shuffling more – tortured but not broken. He had not been racked, that I could see. His wife and daughters were taken in flanked by guards, their hands shackled. They seemed unharmed. Stumpf was placed in a chair to the far left of the bench, the women and the child on chairs to the far right. A rank of constables between them. They did not look at each other.

Before the charges were read, Fromme told the room that no torture had been used on the 'creature's women' – those were the words he used. 'If it is proved that they are consorts of Satan, and the offspring of coupling between a woman and a wolf – then they would not be classed as human and so torture should not be used against them as torture has no effect on the infernal.'

I passed Paulus a notice saying, 'Then how can he justify the torture of Stumpf who he calls a werewolf?'

Paulus turned my note over and wrote on the back, 'Challenge him and he will torture the women. He is laying traps.'

Madame Stumpf and Divara looked straight ahead at Fromme as he spoke. Rosa kept her head down – twisting her fingers together in her lap. 'Also,' said Fromme, 'if it is shown that they are indeed Satan's whore and her two wolf children, then torture before the trial would only weaken their bodies for the execution to come. That I will not have.'

The charges were read against Stumpf: witchcraft, consorting with Satan, entering into a pact with the Devil to gain wealth and power over Bideburg, for which the Devil required human sacrifice – and, in order to aid these sacrifices, Satan had given Stumpf the ability to transform into a wolf using an enchanted girdle. The wife and children were held as accomplices to all crimes – with the children moreover branded as off-spring of a werewolf, and therefore inhuman and beyond redemption and the love of the church. Madame Stumpf was additionally charged with conducting unnatural relations with an agent of Satan.

'Do you have anything to say?' Fromme asked Stumpf from his chair up at the head of the court.

'I am a werewolf and admit guilt to all crimes levelled against me, but deny the involvement of my family, or anyone else,' Stumpf replied without raising his eyes.

'Very good,' said Fromme. 'And you?' He directed his question to the wife and children.

'Sir, we are innocent of all charges against us and beg for our lives,' Madame Stumpf cried out.

'I do not beg,' said Stumpf, raising his eyes to her. 'I am guilty.'

'Sir,' Divara said to Fromme, and then turned to look at all those watching in the room, 'we knew nothing. We pray forgiveness.'

'I know nothing, sir,' her little sister said and cried into her cuffs.

'My family are innocent,' Stumpf said strong, though his eyes reached in pain and longing to his youngest child. 'Burn me.'

Fromme pursed his lips and said, 'The pleas are accepted and recorded. We have no further need of examination of the werewolf Stumpf, and hereby sentence him to death – the form of which will be destruction of the body. We will proceed with the case against the rest of the Stumpf family given their collective plea of innocence which the court does not accept. Their bodies were inspected last night and they have each witch and devil spots upon them which is proof enough to proceed – and in fact proof, almost, of overbearing guilt. None who have not compacted with the Devil have such marks on their flesh.'

Stumpf rose in his chains, like the Kraken, like Samson, and dragged the two guards on the dogcatcher poles almost off their feet. 'You liar,' he said – loud but calm. 'You promised that if I accepted what you said about me then my family were free.'

'Gag that dog,' Fromme shouted – and the guards put an iron bit into Stumpf's mouth and buckled it closed on a clasp. Stumpf neither struggled nor tried to say another word – in fact, he sat slowly back into his seat as the guards pulled and slapped at him, his mouth bleeding from the iron bit.

Madame Stumpf looked at her children and tried to smile to comfort them. The little girl seemed to curl and vanish in her own lap, and Divara trembled as if she saw the gate of life close behind her.

The people in the court chuckled and nodded and whispered approval to each other.

Paulus stood. 'If the sentence is cast against Stumpf, may I proceed to defend my clients, his wife and children?' He spoke hard and sarcastic, his head turned slightly so the words were directed more at the crowd than Fromme.

Fromme grinned a grin you'd give your oldest friend. 'Of course,' he said, and spread his palms wide.

Paulus stood with one hand on his hip, and looked at my jottings on the papers in front of him, numbering the key points of the defence. He winked at me, and pushed them away.

'I will not begin where I should begin in this case,' he said. 'Where I should begin is enumerating the many reasons why the Stumpf women – and this child,' he pointed at the little girl, 'a babe still, who you would wish to burn – why these good and decent women are all innocent, namely: they killed no-one, no-one knew of Stumpf's murders except Stumpf himself; that even if they were aware of his murders, what witness would be expected to risk their life by informing on a killer – or werewolf as you would have it; or that if they knew, were they not regularly beaten and abused and intimidated by this devil you have found in order to maintain their silence; or if they knew, and acted even to help Stumpf, that this constitutes no crime – for again, if I held a pistol to many a man's head and told him to kill his neighbour or face being killed by me, how many would not commit the murder? Murder can not be committed under duress. This is juvenile law, that even the greenest young scholar knows, so why would I waste my time tacking this path with the court today. No, I will say none of that – yet. Nor will I say, that the people of this town seek the death of the Stumpf women, so that they may prosper, taking these ladies' goods and properties as their own.'

The crowd shouted in outrage and some hisses came to their lips.

'Silence,' shouted Paulus. He turned and bowed to Fromme. 'Apologies,' he said, 'that is your job now. Force of habit.'

'Be quiet,' Fromme said and the crowd obeyed. His boy, Jodel, sat at his side, a lumpen dolt, who neither spoke nor moved.

Paulus had kept talking. 'And I won't yet say either that the end of these women will also bring an end to the charges I sought against those in this town who allowed the orphaned child to die – the child whose parents were, we know, murdered by Stumpf. For that will not happen. I will not allow those men who conspired in that crime to go free and avoid scrutiny, and punishment – and I would recommend death, if I had them before a court, for their crime in aiding and abetting the murder of the boy I talk of – for in that act they are as wicked as Stumpf.'

Paulus held the last word, with a sibilant hiss on the F. The crowd was just about to stir, when he continued, 'And I will not say that these women have denounced Stumpf and all his crimes, or that they see now and despise the evil that was in him, which he hid so well from them. Though these words should matter to you if you call yourself a judge. For you will not believe a word of truth that is spoken to you. This is what I will say to you, though: you ask me to believe that a werewolf exists. Then you ask me to believe that this werewolf lived with a human woman, and she played his succubus – she bore him unnatural children, whose veins run with blood not human? Do you take me for a fool? A lawyer defending a client before a court would usually say "us" not "me". Do you agree? I would usually say, "You take the court for a fool" or "you ask the court to believe such nonsense". But this court is full of fools of two different stripes. There are fools here who will play along with your devils and daydreams because it will make them rich to see the Stumpfs wiped off the face of the Earth – the guilty and the innocent. And believe me I think Stumpf – guilty here in front of us – should go and be sent straight to Hell for his offences against humankind. But these women,' and he pointed to Madame Stumpf and her daughters, 'and this child have done no wrong. If I walked into the inn this evening and killed the first man I laid my hands on, would my family be sent to the gallows with me?

There are people in this town who, you know as well as I do, desire the deaths of these women for their own pocket. And then there are fools like you.' And he pointed at Fromme – and I could not believe what he was doing now. 'Fools who believe in what they say. The others,' and he cast his arm behind him to the crowd, 'they will listen to you, and play the fool, and believe you because it benefits them. You, sadly, my college friend, believe your own foolish thoughts.'

Fromme's face fixed itself into a strange upside down smile. He nodded. But Paulus would not stop.

'Your folly is an act of faith. You have read as well and as wide as I have. Before you lived there were men like you who would kill the innocent because they believed Zeus or Jupiter wanted blood, before them there were men who thought the stones and rivers and trees should be worshipped and sacrificed to – these are fairy tales that you talk. You would kill these women and this child for a leap of faith? If so, I bid you now, slit their throats in front of me and tell me you do it for your God.'

Paulus sat back down in his chair beside me and looked straight into the face of Fromme.

Fromme kept nodding – over and over again, dozens of nods, for maybe a count of fifty or more. The Stumpfs were statues.

'Good,' Fromme said finally. 'Very good. Thank you for your contribution. Gentlemen,' and he looked at me too, 'you may be excused.' He nodded to the guards and two walked towards us.

'I am not finished,' said Paulus.

I got to my feet, 'Brother Fromme, please,' I said. 'Stumpf is guilty – kill him, do as you wish – but these ladies are as innocent as I. Let me give you the points of law I have considered in their defence.'

'As innocent as you?' said Fromme. 'Who sits there while your master flits like a butterfly around the petals of heresy? As innocent as you? I do not want to hear your points of law. You would be well advised to return to your chamber with your master and bide your time until we return to the court of the Prince-Bishop where you can both account for the position you have taken.' He rose to his feet, 'A position which casts infamy and disgrace on the Holy Bible and Jesus Christ and the sanctity of the Church and its teachings. You both disgust me.'

The guards grabbed us both, hard and unfriendly, by the shoulders. 'Get them safely back to their rooms,' Fromme said. They marched us to the door.

'Are you out of your mind, Paulus?' I shouted at him, and I would have surely struck him if I was not held hard by the guards around us.

'There was no point,' he said. 'So better to make a point.'

The guards bundled us on through the court towards the door. The crowd jeered and pushed at us.

'We have allowed them to die,' I said.

'They are already dead and you knew that,' he said.

Paulus was pushed along forward a little more roughly than I was, so I chanced a look back over my shoulder. Madame Stumpf and Divara and the little girl had fallen to their knees – as one, maybe, I do not know, I did not see – and were weeping and praying to Jesus and Mary and the Lord in Heaven, crossing themselves and swearing on Christ's name that they loved God and his saints and every divine word the book contained. The crowd laughed and pointed at them. The guards and constables kept the crowd back from them. Fromme sat in his chair and drummed his fingers on the table before him. Stumpf, I could see, was weeping also – his face, though, was a mask of rage and shame, and I believed I saw beneath the iced skin of Stumpf and into the real man hiding far away inside his heart, hidden from the minds of all other men and women until now – and the Stumpf I saw, he was weak.

Fromme spoke, loud, as we left the hall, loud enough so we could hear well, 'The Stumpf women and child are sentenced to death also. They too will suffer destruction of the body, but with less force and severity – forte et dure – than the werewolf, their husband and father.'

His boy Jodel called the court to rise – with a guttural grunt – and the hall shuffled and buzzed like a hive of insects rising in the heat.

'That was the fastest trial of my career, Fromme,' Paulus shouted as he was shunted forward by guards and constables. 'I salute you. Your speed has saved the state much money. Your God must be proud.'

We were outside the hall and the crowd was loud – but I hope they heard his words.

Chapter Twenty-Six

Paulus speaks of the fall of Munster, and how the books of God permit the murder of all.

It was strange to sit and listen to Paulus espouse policies of violence on a summer's afternoon with the wind through the window blowing in the scent of blossom – covering the smell of the town middens which were starting to heave now in the heat. His talk calmed my anger for him, and his behaviour at the trial. I saw now that he meant to act, and that in the courtroom there had been no chance to act out the policy in his head – the only policy we had left which was worth acting upon. And he justified his policies through the word of God. How Saul had annihilated the Amalekites and enslaved their cities. How the Israelites had destroyed the Canaanites – murdering all before them.

'It is on account of the wickedness of these nations that the Lord shall drive them out before you,' Paulus preached to me. 'Even the land was defiled and I punished it for its sin.' Flicking through his Bible and pointing out his passages.

'God is a killer,' Paulus said. 'That is the lesson of this book.' And he threw the little brown bound Bible on the floor. 'We are made in God's image.'

That afternoon filled in the missing holes in the life of Paulus for me. I knew of his past and his childhood – he'd told me stories in smatters and drabs – but I had not known that his time as a child had marked him so. For he was the creation of his childhood years in a way that I was not.

'Civilisation is the keeping down of violence,' he told me – and he walked back and forth across the room, sitting one moment to clean a pistol – I joke not – the next to whet a blade, like he needed to slip it clean into someone right at that very moment. He should have frightened me, but he did not. I was excited. 'When civilisation yields up its ghost to God, and violence walks in, then no man, or woman, or child should do any other than pick up a weapon and defend themselves. That is what God teaches us – for the creator will kill when displeased, so why not you or I kill too or all the good poor of Munster? Repay the lordly rich in the lessons of their own book.'

And he fell back on his bed and the memory of Munster swept over him as it sometimes did and he looked at me with ghost eyes that did not see me and he talked, but only to himself, I believe.

'Before the final fall of Munster,' he said – and he was crying, but only from his eyes, there were no tears in his voice, 'I had been lugging shot and stone to the defenders on the wall. That's what the boys did for the men. In my mind's eye I can see thousands of the enemy on the plain before us, among the canals beyond the city walls, camps and banners and horses and cannon, and thousands upon thousands of armoured men moving across the land, but in front of me, on the wall, there were ten or twelve of the godly poor who I was runner for, five hundred more maybe were lined along the rest of the city walls – like us, a handful of fighters in batches and a boy to keep them stocked – we were outnumbered.

I did not believe – even back then – in the thinking of my father. I did not support the executions and the tearing up of respect and love for other people. I did believe in Jesus and Francis, and his love of the poor, that would take the shepherd and blacksmith to Heaven and have them sit higher than the king or the bishop. I did not believe in the men leading us – men like van Leyden – but I believed in what they had started fighting for – which was fairness, that we are all equal in the eyes of Jesus. Not God – but Jesus. They are different beings to my mind. There is no Trinity, for Jesus would not sit in quorum with the god of the desert – and without those two in bondage with each other there can be no spirit or ghost of the divine moving among us.'

What he said was of the most black heresy, but I listened, and, in truth, I wished to believe as he did. Rebellion made my brain spin, like I was drunk or with a woman – or more truly, drunk on an endless flow of wine gushing from a woman's mouth and into mine. Its taste was good to me, and I knew why men wanted blood now.

'It ended very quickly – when it came,' he said. 'And I wonder now why they let the siege go on so long, if with a few hours of cannon fire they could take down our defences. Why let the city waste for eighteen months? I guess they read the siege manuals and found that, like the Cathars, heretics like us should starve till they ate the dead, before being sent beyond the living world. Complete destruction. Salted over like brave Carthage. When they moved against us they lost some men from the front ranks of their fusiliers and cannon-men, but not many to my reckoning. They would have lost as many if they had attacked us on Day One. The wait was the better to torture us, I believe.

The city was exhausted. The defenders of Munster had wasted all their cannon shot and mortar rounds over the many months of the siege, fighting off feints from the enemy. We were reduced to filling our cannons and mortar with tin plates and iron ingots. When fired – if the cannon or mortar did not explode and kill the crew – the shrapnel spray was useless, and the gun disabled after one round had been spent. We were down to arquebus, pistols, swords and some grenades. My section of the wall – the troop of men I was supplying – turned into brick dust and red rain with one shot from an enemy mortar cannon that had been brought up close to the wall. I was climbing up the wall steps to the section when they disappeared before my eyes. I woke, maybe a few minutes later – for the dust still floated in the air and red blood was mixed in the haze. The city gate – one hundred paces from where I lay in the mud – cracked, and a siege ram sprouted like a tooth through the wood. Soldiers poured behind it. I ran to a bent corner of the wall, and pulled my pistol from inside my coat, and readied it. We had plenty of small guns – our best soldiers strode with six strapped to their bodies and twelve smoulder-wicks lit and tied to their coats – we'd taken the whole town armoury when Munster fell to us, so even a little junior soldier like me had the power of a gun in his hand.

The soldiers scattered through the city, and more poured after them – like wine through a broken cup, and they were drunk with their win, for it was a win now and no mistake, the Kingdom of God on Earth ruled by the Christ van Leyden was over. I remember I wondered then, at that moment, where is Jan van Leyden, and I looked up into the sky to see if he would appear with the host behind him and burn the invaders to cinders with fire from his eyes while the children of Christ, like me, watched in safe composure, and rose beside him in alliance.

That did not happen, and I cowered in a corner of the wall, hidden from sight, with my pistol shaking in my hand, and I cried. An enemy soldier came around the corner I hid behind – his sword was up, and he was no more than five years my senior. He pulled back his arm, his sword stiff, and I fired. He fell on top of me. He groaned. He was alive. I pushed him off me, and he clutched at my shirt – there was a hole in his throat which was ragged and gushed with blood as black as tar. I hit him with the gun. He would not die – he grabbed at me and pulled me towards him, and there was a look in his eye that if he could kill me now, he would, because he wanted to take me to Hell with him. I hit him again with the gun yet he still pulled me down toward him, though he was weak, and I had little trouble resisting him. I hit him once more and then dropped the gun. I pushed his hands away and sat astride him like a horse – dipped my head and bit him. I bit him – on his face – and thumped his head off the ground. My thumbs dug into his neck – into the wound in his throat – as he would not stop struggling and reaching for me, and I beat his head flat against the earth.

When he was dead, I sat there like the first man on Earth – the world, the noise and the war, and the dead man, meant nothing to me. Life was a living fog. I rose and I recall reloading my pistol, making it ready again – and my hands were not shaking. I loaded it quick – quicker than the men in my troop had loaded; I was ready to fire again in less than a minute – but I walked so slow that I felt an old man by the time I reached the corner of the wall, away from my hiding place, and stood in the throng of screaming and murder that was the city square. People rushed by me – enemies, our soldiers, our women and children – and they must have seen me as a ghost that was not with them in the physical world at that moment, for none touched or spoke to me. I raised the gun to my head, and looked sideways onto it, to see if I could pull the trigger and keep it steady at my temple. I could, so I turned my eyes to the front again and watched the burning and killing for a last few moments, I thought. A soldier, in a blazing breast plate, came into my line of sight. I turned the gun towards him, but as I did, he took the pommel of his sword and struck me – one hard tap, I am told, as of course I can not remember, on the side of my head, where I'd had the gun pointed. Perhaps, at twelve, I was too young for that soldier to kill, even with a gun in my hand.

I woke in the square with hundreds of our people around me – some still flat on the ground, like me, others clinging in little groups. The Prince-Bishop's soldiers surrounded us in a square of armour and sword and gun. There were women and girls there as well as men and boys. Families were calling and looking for each other. My mother and father ran to me – the rest of our family behind – and gathered me up. I kissed my mother and oldest sister, and as my father knelt to tell me of his pride in me as a soldier of Christ, a mercenary – you could tell by the red ribbon on his arm, and the purple sash across his breast – walked towards us and kicked my father in the face. My mother screamed, sisters screamed – I sat back on the ground and all I thought was, "I have no weapons".

The mercenary called to his troop of four, and they took us away from the crowd of prisoners in the square.

"Look at his clothes and his rings," the mercenary said to his men, pointing at my father. I looked at my father and thought, he could not have been fighting with his fingers full of rings – that would stop a man holding a sword or pistol – and his clothes are too padded and rich and soft to move fast or run, or to protect him.

"Where's your house?" the mercenary asked, and my father bowed to him, and said, "I am a merchant that was trapped within this city and have done the best I can. I am no enemy of yours."

The mercenary said, "But your son wears a yellow cockade," and he flicked the feathers in my beret, "and dresses like a soldier boy?"

He hit my father then like Macedo beat his slaves before they turned on him – do you know that story, Willie, from Pliny? A fine story – and my father lay in the dirt, with his rich clothes, and cried for his life, saying, "Sir, we have longed for your arrival."

The mercenary laid off and looked at his troop. They shrugged.

I walked over to my father, and knelt. I touched his hair, then took my hand away. He looked up. I said to the mercenary, "We are not merchants. My father ran this city with van Leyden. My mother was a queen here. And I fought on the walls against you – though I wish you no harm."

The mercenary laughed – and I have often thought that if a cat could laugh as it played with a rat, then it would have sounded like this. He said, "Lead onwards then, van Leydens." And he made me march them to our home, and our printing shop.'

Chapter Twenty-Seven

Divara and her mother relate twin tales of Elfhame to the little girl Rosa in their cell at the keep in Bideburg.

I went down into the street after supper. Between Paulus and I, we had come to a choice, made up our minds. He had drunk more after we'd talked together, and fallen asleep once again on the bed. Lying on his back, snoring, as I shut the door of our room behind me, he looked much fatter and older than before – sleep had taken off whatever mask of handsomeness it was that he put on when awake.

I walked to the keep and told the constables on the door to go to Fromme and ask if I could speak with him for a moment. One left, returned, and escorted me to Fromme who was sitting alone in the main guard room. He sat straight and tall in a chair in the middle of the room – the only other furniture was a cupboard for weapons and a few benches along the walls. Fromme watched me as I entered – he was an island in the bare room.

He did not speak, so I said, 'Sir, I would like to talk to the Stumpf woman and her daughters, if I may.'

Fromme looked away from me, towards nothing in particular, and replied, 'Why?'

'To tell them goodbye.'

'You wish to say goodbye to a witch and two monsters with wolf blood in them?'

'Yes, sir, I wish to look at them and speak to them and know if they were fooling me.'

'Of course they were fooling you. Paulus was fooling you. The Devil plays tricks because he is bored in hell.'

'That is what I wish to discover for myself, sir.'

'You want proof? Understanding?'

I did not speak as I had gone far enough and wanted to go no further. I would not beg or seem desperate. If he let me see them, so be it; if he didn't then there was nothing I could do about it – for we were set on our path anyway and would travel it regardless of what tried to stand in front of us.

'You may speak to them if you wish.'

He got up and took me by the arm to the door. If he escorted me himself, and stayed by me, I would say no more than a few words to the women and leave. He called at the door for one of the guards and told him to take me to the women's cell.

'Remember,' he said, as I walked with the guard to the head of the stairs to the cells, 'you got your beating for taking their side.' My face was still black with bruises, and my walk stiff from kicks and punches.

'I was at the funeral of an innocent young woman,' I said.

'Good,' he replied. 'And Paulus is…' and he paused and waved his hand like a court dilettante, 'well?' I could see the old aristocrat was still in him, though kept mostly hidden.

'He tells me he thinks of you,' I said, and walked down the stairs, leaving the guard to catch me up.

'Be careful, young man,' Fromme called after me. 'You and your master are on the precipice and should step no further.'

On the way to the cell of Divara and her mother and sister, I passed the cell holding Stumpf. The grating to Stumpf's cell was pulled shut so I could not see him inside. The guard hurried me on – I told him to mind his manners – and he unlocked the women's cell and ushered me in.

'You creatures have been warned,' he said, 'do not interfere with this young man or I will burn you in your cell tonight.'

I walked in and he shut the door behind me, though he pulled the grating open and stood with his back to the small iron-slatted slit. The room was big enough, though, that if I sat in front of the bars at the far wall, he could not possibly hear us if we spoke quietly.

Divara and her mother rose as I walked in – the child lay on the bed sleeping. But she woke when the guard spoke loud. I smiled at her, and Rosa smiled back, bleary.

'The sleeping tincture has worn off her,' Madame Stumpf whispered. 'But we have enough left to make us all sleep too when the time comes.'

Divara looked at her mother with a streak of anger on her brow, but said nothing.

I walked down the length of the bars separating me from them, ushering them back to the far wall.

'Quietly,' I said.

They sat on a bed and I stood before them, the bars between us – keeping my eye to the grille in the door, and my voice low.

'Divara,' I said, 'go sit up by the door with little Rosa here and tell her a story, or talk. Speak loud enough so what I am going to say to your mother can not be heard, but not loud enough to anger him or bring him into the room.'

Then louder I said, 'Little Rosa, I think you should go and play for a moment, while I talk to your mother.'

The little girl had been listening intently and she looked at me now – wise in the eyes – and said, 'Yes, sir, I would like that.'

'Come, Rosa,' said Divara, and the pair of them moved down the cell and sat by the bed nearest the door. They began drawing on the board and playing a guessing game – where each had to guess what the other was drawing before the picture was complete.

I heard Rosa start guessing first. 'A cow,' she said.

'No,' said Divara.

'A sheep.'

'No.'

'A fox?'

'No.'

'I know – a deer.'

'Yes, a deer,' said Divara. 'Well done. Your turn.' And Rosa started to draw.

I spoke to Madame Stumpf as they played. 'You have the means to kill yourselves now if you wish,' I said, and pulled back my half-cape, showing two shaving blades – glint sharp – that I had in my belt.

'I came to give you these,' I said. 'You have been kind to me, and are good people. I wish you no harm – but you will not need to use them. So listen to me.'

'Give me those,' Madame Stumpf said, and without waiting she put her hands through the bars and slipped the blades from my belt. She hid them under her skirts.

'We will get you out,' I said. 'You will not need to harm yourself.'

'How?' said Madame Stumpf. 'We would all be killed in the street.'

'We would not,' I said.

Divara had put down the board and chalk, and had taken Rosa up onto her knee now. She was telling her a story and the little girl, bit at her fingernails and listened.

'I know a story,' Divara said, 'of your great-aunt – our mother's aunt. Who, when she was little, about your age – was very sick and very sad and was taken to Elfhame.'

'Is this true?' the child said, and she turned to her mother, who nodded.

Then, I told Madame Stumpf of the cave – her husband's secret hide up in the Steipplingers. 'Your daughter knows it better than I. We can get you all there.'

'It is good they had their secrets, then,' she said, and there was not anger or disappointment on her face, but a smile – fond and distant.

As I spoke to Madame Stumpf of what should be done, my ear was drawn to Divara. 'What happened was this,' she said. 'This little girl prayed at night to the elves to come and help her – for the elves are good and kind and wish to look after humans who are good and kind also – especially human children who are good and kind.'

Madame Stumpf nodded. 'Do it if you think it best. Either that, or this,' she said, and she patted her skirt, where the blades sat beneath. 'I will not be tortured in front of this town and burned with my children.' Her eyes wandered when she talked, I saw, and her voice was blank – with neither fear or excitement or despair or courage or hope colouring her words, even though there was a little hope now.

I began to lay out what should be done, but I could see she was not listening to me. She was listening to her daughter.

'Divara's story is wrong. Either it is wrong or she is lying,' Madame Stumpf said. She spoke to me, but did not look at me – her eyes over my shoulder somewhere, focussed as if on something invisible in the middle of the room. I had to turn to look for she unsettled me, but there was nothing there.

'The elves are evil – if they exist,' said Madame Stumpf, and she sat on her bed, with her back to the wall and was silent. Divara and Rosa did not hear her. I could barely hear her, for she spoke so soft and dead.

'The elves came for our great aunt,' said Divara. 'The Elf King and his Queen had sent two of their most important courtiers to her. She was sleeping in bed – late at night – when she stirred, and standing there in the middle of her room was a little man no higher than your own knee, and a little woman holding his hand. Their clothes were made from leaves and stems and stalks, moss and ferns – beautifully woven and tailored, flowing around them, like the robes of ancient Romans. They wore jewellery of holly and nightshade, and their hair was filled with all the flowers that bloom at night.'

I do not know why but I reached through the bars and took the hand of Madame Stumpf, who seemed settled to her death. She left her hand in mine but did not stir or show she knew I touched her.

'The elves took the little girl from her home and outside there was a cart, pulled by two ponies who stood no higher than your hip. The ponies glowed golden in the night. The cart was just big enough for our great aunt – then a girl of your age – to sit in. The two elf courtiers got up in the cart and flicked the reins. They rode through the night to the forest and, at the forest, a door opened up in the depths of the woods and they travelled down into Elfhame, under the earth. The passage way beneath the earth was lit with torches and the walls shimmered with silver ore and diamonds as big as your fist.

At last the passageway opened up onto a great chamber, filled with all the folk of Elfhame, dressed in their woodland clothes. They were dancing to slow sweet music, eating from long tables filled with cakes and wine, playing games of chase. When the cart drawing our great aunt rode into view, they all stopped what they were doing and bowed and then clapped. The Elf King and the Elf Queen got up from their thrones of gold and rubies at the head of the chamber and made their way forward, their courtiers parted for them like the sea before Moses. They were dressed in gowns made of leaves and stems and ferns and mosses and stalks too – but these woodland clothes were gold and purple, deep blue and scarlet. The flowers in their hair, and the holly and nightshade on their wrists and about their throats in necklaces, were made from diamonds and sapphires and emeralds and red carbuncles. The cart stopped in the centre of the chamber and the two courtiers jumped down, bowing to their King and Queen.

"This is the human child we told you of, your majesties," said the woman elf.

"The child is sick, but has a heart pure. She prayed to us," the man elf said.

"We have been looking for her over the land of humans these last two days and tracked her prayers," the woman said.

"We found her and brought her here, for she needs your help."

Our great aunt was not afraid, though she was very little and very sick. She stepped down from the cart and curtsied to the King and Queen.

The Queen walked to her and stood by her – although the Queen was only as high as her knee, still she seemed to stand shoulder to shoulder with the child, placing her hand on the little girl's head.

"You are dying, child," the Queen said.

And our great aunt was still not afraid.

The King walked up behind his Queen. "We must heal her," he said, and he clapped his hands.

Then the chamber spun as the male elves went and brought back wood for fires, and buckets of water. The water went in cauldrons and wood was lit beneath. One hundred or more giant cauldrons steamed and bubbled. The women elves had brought flowers and berries and herbs and strips of bark, they put them in the cauldrons. Then the elves stirred the pots and sang over them – their music so sweet and strange that our great aunt felt herself falling asleep.

As the cauldrons boiled, twenty or more of the strongest elves – and there in Elfhame many women elves are as strong as male elves – they dragged a great golden bath into the chamber. It seemed as tall as a man and as long as a house.

The elves broke up into parties and hauled the great boiling cauldrons over to the bath. They placed a giant sieve over the bath, wrapped in muslin, and began, slowly and careful to fill the bath to the brim. They sang all the while.

The King and Queen of Elfhame stood with our great-aunt while their subjects worked. It took so long to fill the bath that by the time the brim had been reached, the water was just right for bathing – neither too hot nor too cold.

The King called out, "Let us leave," and he and the rest of the court walked in silence from the chamber, leaving only our great-aunt and the Queen of Elfhame behind.

The Queen undressed our great-aunt – who was not scared, or shamed, but felt half-asleep and half in dream.

Then the Queen brought our aunt to the bath, and placed a golden ladder at the side for her to climb inside.

"You will not drown. You will not need to swim," the Queen said.

Our great-aunt climbed up the ladder and stepped over the edge.

Although the bath looked as tall as a man and as long as a house, once she was in and sat down, the sweet warm water rose no higher than her chest, and if she lay back then her toes just touched the far end of the bath.

"The bath is magic and the water inside is magic also," said the Queen, standing at the side of the bath, eye to eye with our great-aunt. "It is no taller than me, but as tall as you, and as tall and as long and as wide as the tallest and fattest among you humans – but also, if I cared to, and put a mouse inside, the mouse would not drown, for it would be a perfect mouse-bath also. Or a flea for that matter."

Our aunt bathed and the Queen sang to her, an elf song whose meaning she did not understand, but whose sound put her to sleep.

When she woke, she was back in her bed at home. She was hungry, she realised, and got out of bed. She no longer felt sick. She felt strong and full of life. She called out to her mother. And the family rejoiced, for the little girl had been saved. And every year, on the date of her journey to Elfhame the family left out food and wine and money and gifts for the elves, in thanks of their help in saving a child who everyone loved so very much.'

Rosa said, 'I loved that story. I wish the elves would come for us.'

'No you don't,' said her mother, Madame Stumpf. She moved her hand from mine and sat upright on her bed. 'No, you don't, Rosa.'

'Why mother?' the child said. 'It is the best story I have ever heard.' And she turned her back to her mother and said, 'Thank you, Divara. That was a lovely story. It has made me happy.'

'I wish you happy,' Madame Stumpf said, 'but I will not lie to you.'

'It is a story, mother,' said Divara.

'Firstly, it was not your great-aunt this story happened to, it was your great-uncle – and it did not happen in the way you tell it either.'

'Well, this is the story that my grandfather and grandmother have told me – your own parents. I have heard the story from no-one but them.'

'Do not fight, please,' said Rosa.

'We are not fighting,' said Divara.

'I will fight for you not to be told lies,' said Madame Stumpf and she looked at her child Rosa, with eyes like a killer. 'You will not live with lies in your head, even if it makes you happy.'

'Madame Stumpf,' I said.

But she cut me off with a raised hand, that shook as if she had palsy.

'My uncle was not a little boy when he was taken to Elfhame, if that is where he was taken – he was a baby – not even a year old,' she said. 'You do not even remember their names, Divara, so how can you tell the story?'

Divara pushed her sister, Rosa, from her lap, saying, 'Go to your mother. Hear her story.'

Rosa walked down the cell and sat by her mother on the bed – though not up close.

'My aunt, Eleanor,' said Madame Stumpf, 'told me that one night when she was no more than eight, and before her sister, my mother, was born, she shared a room with her baby brother, Arno, my uncle, and the elves came for him. Arno was a quiet and peaceful child. He had not cried since the day he was born.

Eleanor woke in the depths of the night to see Arno floating in the middle of the room – perhaps two foot off the ground. The child was still asleep and he moved through the air, across the room, the handle on the door turned of its own accord and the door opened. Arno floated out of the bedroom and into the hallway. My aunt thought she was dreaming, and decided to follow Arno in her dream. He floated through the house – still no more than a few feet off the ground. The door to their home opened – again of its own accord – and Arno went out into the night as if he rode on air.

Eleanor peeked out of the door and saw now things materialise around Arno, holding him above their heads. These creatures were not dressed like the forest and shimmering gold – they were not made of flesh, or anything living. Eleanor said that they were like wisps of black rags, billows of black smoke, that moved and changed – faces appearing then fading in the black smoke, arms here, legs there, feet walking and vanishing as they hit the ground in curls of shadow, hands raised, dissolving into rags and then rags dissolving into hands. It could have been one creature or a hundred creatures carrying Arno above them towards the gate, and on into the forest.'

'I do not like this, mother,' said Rosa, and she looked to Divara – who said nothing.

'You do not need to like it,' said Madame Stumpf, 'you just need to know the truth about elves and not to pray to them as your sister tells you.'

I did not like the story, either, or the way that Madame Stumpf told it – listless, her eyes blank and voice dead, not looking at her child now, or touching little Rosa to comfort her.

'At the gate, the whirling, twisting black smoke, with its many arms and eyes and faces and hands, moved and shivered – from amidst the rags and shadows, a gallows appeared – a travelling gallows, with wheels and handles, so that it could be pushed along while the condemned swung from the cross-bar – put on display and carted through the streets as humiliation while the victim hanged and strangled.'

Rosa got off the bed and ran to her sister. 'Your story is stupid and I do not want to hear it.'

'Do not speak to me like that, child,' said Madame Stumpf, but her tone was without menace or warning or anger.

'Mother,' said Divara, but Madame Stumpf talked on. Rosa sat facing her sister, her arms crossed before her – angry not frightened.

'The smoke and shadows and rags and black clouds hanged little Arno from the travelling gallows, and he sprung awake then as he dropped from the noose, writhing in the night, the hands from the smoke all over his body, the eyes watching him from the wisps and whorls of shadow. My aunt, Eleanor, tried to run now to her brother, though she was terrified for her life, but she could not move or call out – as if she was as a statue of herself. Her eyes could not even turn in her head, and they were fixed forward on her little brother.

Faces appeared from the smoke and rags – staying solid for a moment, then fading, and others returning in their places, with white glittering teeth against the black cloud, and yellow hard eyes. They laughed at Eleanor and waved to her from the shadows, then took her baby brother towards the path to the woods on the travelling gallows – the smoke and rags whirling about its handles and wheels, pushing it forward and running at its sides, pulling at the legs of little Arno and choking him as he kicked and his body swung, and his face bulged with the death that choking brought to him, wisps of shadow binding his hands behind him. They laughed all the way to the woods, and the child and the travelling gallows and the churning, writhing black smoke and rags vanished into the tree line. In a blink they were gone, and the scream that had been building in my aunt as she watched frozen burst from her, waking the house.

Her father and mother – my grandparents, God rest their good souls – came to her, and Eleanor garbled out her story, between sobs and screams, dragging them to her room so they could see that little Arno was gone.

When they got to the room, Arno was still there and still alive, but his skin was blue-tinged, his face fixed in a look of pain and horror, and his body stiff and unbending. By the morning, he still lived, but his brain was sour-mash in his head and his soul gone from him. He could not focus on a finger in front of him. He could not swallow or drink. In time, a week or so, he died.'

Madame Stumpf stopped her story, and the room was silent. No-one spoke. Rosa remained with her back turned to her mother, facing Divara, and played with the fringe of her sister's shawl.

I was about to speak for I could not stand the silence, when Madame Stumpf said – as if to add a full stop to her story – 'that is what the elves do, they steal the souls of babies, for God knows what purpose. For food or to breed, for magic to make them live forever?'

'That is not the story I was told,' said Divara. 'My grandparents did not tell me that story.'

'Who knows why they told you what they did, Divara,' her mother said. 'Perhaps they were lied to, perhaps they lied to you. Perhaps they heard the true story and did not like it and changed it into something that suited their souls better. I do not know. I am not to blame for the lies that other people tell to themselves. But this is the story I heard from my own grandparents, and they were alive to see it happen.'

'There are no such things as elves,' I said.

'Perhaps,' said Madame Stumpf. 'Perhaps the child was just ill. I have often thought that.'

And Madame Stumpf started to laugh. A false laugh that frightened me, for there was no feeling it in, whether good or bad. It was the sound of a laugh, but there was no laugh in the sound.

'Madame Stumpf,' I said, 'are you well?'

Rosa jumped – that is what she did – she jumped like a little savage from the bed and stood square-footed on the cell floor turned to her mother.

'Well, I am not ill,' she shouted at her mother. 'I am not ill.'

Divara rose in a panic – the room was like a madhouse now, with her mother's dead laughing and her sister screaming over and over that she was not ill – trying to quieten them.

'Help me,' Divara said to me.

I did not know what to do. The guard was looking in the grille to the cell, so I went up to the door and said through the slats to him, 'They are going mad in here. Do not worry. I will calm them. They are scared.'

'Keep them quiet,' he said.

I turned and shouted, 'Madame Stumpf – be warned, the guards will separate you if you are not quiet. Rosa you do not want to be taken to a cell by yourself away from your mother and sister.'

And it was as if a cloud had come over the sun. They stopped. The room was still. Divara took her sister and sat the two of them down by their mother, and she put her arms about them both. Rosa put her arms around Divara and her mother, and then Madame Stumpf held her daughters, so that all three were in a web of arms, circled, heads together, on the little straw bed.

I went back to the door. The guard still watched. 'All's well,' I said. 'They know to be good now.' He turned his back.

I walked to where they sat, and whispered through the bars, 'Divara, a word before I go.'

Then I said loudly, 'Madame Stumpf, you should take your child to her bed and nurse her asleep after all this upset.'

Rosa looked at me, and I winked at her. She looked very wise, her lips pursed and eyes bright, and nodded her head. She took her mother by the hand and said, 'You tell me a story now, and make it a nice one.'

Madame Stumpf smiled, and the life seemed to come back into her a little, at least I could see that her soul was returned to the shell of her body. She rose off the bed and took Rosa up the cell to her own little cot. Rosa sat on the bed, and Madame Stumpf kneeled on the floor, her skirts billowed around her. They put their heads together and whispered. Madame Stumpf spoke into Rosa's ear, and Rosa smiled and put her arms around her mother's neck and kissed her. Madame Stumpf kissed Rosa too.

I told Divara what I had told her mother. That I knew of her cave. She listened and understood, and I saw then what words of hope can do to a human being. Divara filled into a woman again, not cowering inside herself any longer. For there was a choice and a chance now, where there had been no choice or chance before. A glimmer of life amid ruin. Though it was a just a glimmer – and I could see that on her face.

'This is Greet's gift,' Divara said as I left.

Chapter Twenty-Eight

To this day, wedded to my heart, I hold dearest the words, 'None shall be left behind.'

I'm not a scout or a spy or a soldier – I am a bookworm now and I was a bookworm in Bideburg, even though I sometimes bolster myself and make myself sound more brave and daring than the pitiful boy I was in that life back then. My first wife used to say that I sneeze all the time – I sneeze several times a day, sometimes to the power of ten, usually seven sneezes minimum, and at best a record of seventeen in one go – she used to say that I sneezed all the time because my nose is always buried in books, and that it would make me sick. She is now dead, and was buried while still a young woman and I a man of forty – there is the wisdom of youth speaking to you.

But I became a scout and a soldier and spy, also, I suppose, in the last few days of Bideburg.

Paulus woke me early the next morning, as he'd said he would, and watched as I ate breakfast, ladling honey on my oats and telling me to lay off the wine, talking me through the routine and the contingencies – every contingency, until I told him that overplanning was often a tactical error and left no room for flexibility, adaptability. He nodded me a nod and said Alexander could have mocked old Aristotle with that line. I didn't fully get the joke – and still don't know if he was insulting me or praising me, all these years later.

At the keep, the constables wagged me through – I had asked permission to take the living will of each of the Stumpf women the day before they died on Fromme's agreement. He found it amusing that folk with nothing – for the church and state were to divide up their land and properties, the town fairly apportioned – should feel the need to make a will. 'Who will they bequeath their nothing to?' he asked me, smiling. I said they had relatives they wished to send their final thoughts on Earth to – and Fromme replied, 'Oh, they have relatives.'

The same guard took me down to the cells, and stood as before with his back to the door and the open grille. I gestured to the women to move down to the far wall of their cell again – they were chained to the floor now, as they were on the last passage to their death, so they shuffled, wincing at the sound of their own clanks. I spoke with them all – including little Rosa – and explained. When they were clear about what we were to do, I stood up and nodded to Madame Stumpf. She took the blade from beneath her petticoat and held it to her throat. I ran to the door, banging, calling, 'Guard – she is trying to kill herself.'

Rosa wailed as she'd been instructed, 'Mama, mama, no.'

The guard turned and looked wide-eyed through the grille. 'Who?' he said.

'The wife,' I said. 'Quick.' And I pulled on the locked door. 'Open it and stop her.'

Keys rattled like bones and the door scraped. The guard ran past me. I followed behind. He stopped at the cell and stared at Madame Stumpf, the blade drawing blood from her neck, and the red tripping onto her collar – once white now brown with dirt. The guard looked at me.

'Stop her,' I said.

He turned back to the bars of their cell, I drew the dagger from my belt, walked quickly to him and slid the blade in where Paulus had shown me – where I guessed the third rib down from his armpit would be, under his heart. It went in at the upwards diagonal, and he looked over his shoulder at me, seemed to smile and cry at the same time, and slid dead to the floor, slipping off the knife – it remained bloody and black in my hand.

'I need Paulus now,' I said, and I picked up the guard's keys and threw them to Divara through the bars of her cell. 'Get yourselves unchained. From the floor first – then your hands and feet.'

'No, no, no,' Madame Stumpf said, 'do not go.'

'I need him. I have no weapons but this,' I said, and I waved the bloody dagger at her, 'if anyone comes we are dead. Two minutes and I will be back. Start to free yourselves so you are ready to go when we return.'

Rosa said, 'Go, go, be quick.' And Divara began to unlock the chains around her own feet.

Paulus had told me the way, truly, one hundred times at least – left, right, right, right, left, left, left, right, right, left, left, right, find the door in the floor outside the armoury. I had walked the keep with him, only once, but had been busy thinking of the design of the building – not routes to and from rooms and places in it – and the passageways were just a maze. He had the position easy in his head, though, as he had walked it many more times than me – when it was his domain and the town was ours – but he had to draw maps for me and walk me through it, pacing across the floor of our room in the inn, to get the directions to the hatchway straight in my head – but the passages confused me, and my head could not take it in, until we had walked that imaginary route for hours and I was sick with the routine of it, and all the while he plotted out the contingencies till I was bubbling inside my own body and my brain buzzed like bees.

But I weaved the maze of passages expertly – all study pays off – and I pulled on the door in the floor, and the hatch came up. I was down in the tunnel, inside in the pitch black. I put my hands out to either side, they found the walls – the tunnel was no wider than two men abreast – and on I went, straight ahead in the dark one hundred paces. I hit the wall, lifted my hands, found the catch and pulled. Light poured in and Paulus dropped down – dragging the hatch closed behind him. We ran back – with two of us, the tunnel was as tall and as wide and as tight as a coffin, a casket stretching on underground in the dark until you found the afterlife.

Our eyes pinned in the light and we were out, back in the corridor of the keep's basement, and on the way to the cells. Paulus had packed himself with his pistols – two in his hand, two in his belt, two in the braces on his back – all smoking and lit at the wick. He wore a leather breastplate and a leather cod.

Divara was out of the floor chain and free from her manacles and opening the bars of their cell inside the holding room. There was a sound on the stairs, and I heard, 'Boy,' shouted in hate. 'Come up here, boy.' It was Fromme.

That word – boy – tolled through me. 'Go,' said Paulus, 'speak to him. Hold him off.'

He shook me and unfroze me. He took one of his pistols and gave it to me – the ember tip of the rope-cord match smoking in its stock like the fire in an old man's pipe.

'Lead him down here if you can and I will kill him. Or kill him if he calls you up – you can not go up. We will be separated and you will die, if we escape.'

When I was a boy, my older brother's friends would dare me to jump off the town bridge with them into the water – and I would pause when they asked and then run for fear like a kitten. But Paulus pushed me forward and I went headlong into the corridor. The door from the corridor that led to the foot of the stairs up into the guard room above was closed.

'Coming,' I shouted, and still today I can not believe how smooth the word came out, and how honest. I held the pistol behind me, opened the door and put my head around the corner of the stairs, looking up. Fromme stood in silhouette.

'Hurry up,' he said.

'I will be no more than five minutes, sir,' I said.

'What is that smoke?' Fromme said, and he took a step down the stairs. Another black shape – a guard or constable – appeared over his shoulder. Over my own shoulder, I saw the smoke from the pistol cord come wisping like old lady's hair. Fromme began walking quickly down the stairs – the shape advanced behind him. I could have shot Fromme dead at that moment – and I know that to this very day – but I chose to shoot a man I could not see, whose face I did not know, and I levelled my pistol and fired at the black shape. The stairwell lit up in flame and roar. The shape fell. I stepped back and shut the door to the cell corridor. The keep above erupted in noise and clamour. It sounded like a hundred feet were running down the stairs and Fromme at the head of them. Paulus was behind me now, a few paces. He threw the bolt on the door and barred it shut.

'Minutes,' said Paulus as we ran back to the cell, low like running soldiers, and pistol shots came whipping through the wood door behind us. Paulus fired two pistols together at the door and the men drew back. Fromme screamed – not words, but a cry of primal old hate. A crashing came, and that was the guards coming back to the door again, and ramming it with their shoulders, kicking at the hinges.

Divara shouted, 'Give me a weapon.' Paulus handed her the two fired pistols, and tore off one of the little leather munition pouches that ringed his belt. He threw it to her. Inside, there was ball, powder and wadding – enough for six loads. He told Divara to ready the guns. Paulus pulled two more pistols from the bracers on his back and fired again at the door – aiming for the grille and sight of the guards' heads, working to break through. Fromme and his men had not yet had time to reload their guns. Divara threw me the keys and I turned to Madame Stumpf. She shouted,

'No, no', and pointed to the child. I took the keys to the locks on Rosa's wrists and trembled as I tried one – the little girl kneeled as I struggled to free her – the key would not fit, I tried another – and Rosa prayed to God, quietly. Then I realised that first I should be freeing the child from the chains that kept her to the floor. I dropped the keys.

Paulus fired his last two pistols, by my count. Six shots had been fired now, I was sure. There was screaming. A man had died behind the door to the cell corridor. Paulus holstered his pistols, and turned to Divara, clapping his hands. She had the two other guns loaded already and gave them over to him. He lifted them shoulder high, moved around the doorway of the cell and fired again. I heard only chaos and more screaming from dying men, and could not see in my mind's eye what was happening. I fumbled with the little girl's floor chains and dropped the keys again and screamed as they fell to the floor.

Paulus was laughing. 'The crowd ebbed back as one, in the way that crowds have possessed-together madness,' he said. 'I could write about this.'

Paulus reloaded two guns, while Divara reloaded two others. The guards returned to the door and there were shots from them now through the grille and I could hear them start in again with their shoulders and boots, like Samson tearing down the temple.

'Run Fromme, you cowardly cunt,' Paulus called. 'Stay back,' he shouted, at the men – their banging and kicking against the door to the corridor the sound of a carnival in Hell now. He fired again – and took fresh guns from Divara. He held the pistols to the door.

There was stone silence amid the smoke. The men behind the door did not move or speak. We did not move or speak. Then, from Stumpf's cell down the corridor, there came a muffled roar, a moaning cry. He was gagged – I could tell from the sound.

'What does he say?' I said to Paulus.

'Get out,' Paulus said – he looked at me and at Divara. 'There is no time. We must run.'

Divara pulled the keys from my hands and dropped to her knees to unlock the irons on her sister. Her father's gagged roar continued.

'Which key?' Divara screamed. 'Which key?'

The soldiers and guards took up their charging and kicking at the door again – and then we heard it splinter, like time stretched to breaking point.

'Shoot,' I said.

'We have only two guns ready and no more time to reload. Not just yet, Willie,' said Paulus. The door cracked down the middle, and was ready to break.

'Get through the door on my command,' we heard Fromme shout.

Rosa looked at Divara as she tried key after key to unlock her sister's chains – and pushed her away – in love, not hate.

'Now,' called Paulus and moved into the centre of the hallway, holding the guns before him. 'We have to go now.' Stumpf's roar became a suffocated wail – exhorting, terrified.

Divara ran to her mother, and said loud, 'I love you.' Her mother waved the blade she had held to her throat. She pointed it at the little girl and at her own chest and then cut the air with it, at the men behind the door.

'I love you, Rosa,' Divara said, but she could not look at her sister. I could not either. I could not leave the cell but I could not stay in it.

We could not free them – they were chained to the floor still. If we had stayed, we all would have died. I did not want to die – and that is shameful – I wanted to win, and I could not win if I died in that keep underground. None of us wanted to die, if some could live.

I took Divara by the hand and we ran out behind Paulus. We did not look back. She did not hesitate now. The door seemed to scream as it broke in two and clattered to the floor of the corridor, but the cowards still hid to the side and waited – thank Jesus. And we ran for our lives, leaving the little girl and her mother to die behind us.

'Run,' we heard Rosa shout. 'Run and kill them.'

Fromme's men rushed then – six, I think. Paulus fired and two died. I saw him pull two blades from his belt, and I pulled out mine. We turned a corner – Stumpf's muffled roars lost to us in the corridors now. I stopped, though, and held my place, out of sight around the corner, and waited. Paulus and Divara ran on a little, then turned back and called on me. I put my dagger through the throat of the first man who came around the corner – and I knew his face, though could not remember what had passed between us in the days before. I knew his name, but I have not been able to remember it since. Then many men closed around me, and a pistol flash sent glints of knives into my eyes. The air was bloody and like fire – we moved like we were all falling off a mountain together and fighting until we hit the bottom. A man was on top of me. Paulus appeared above his shoulder and slit his throat – the blood sprayed into my mouth. He threw the man to the side.

'Look,' he said. 'There's no more here yet. They are hiding like cows, we have killed so many of them.' And he laughed and he frightened me more than Fromme or the guards, or even being burned alongside him for what we were now doing.

Divara groaned somewhere behind me in a way that sounded like death. I pulled myself to my knees and three men were dead around us. Divara had mounted another man, still living, and ground the tiny blade I had given her between his legs. His throat was cut, and he was gargling and drowning in his own blood, while his hands flapped, weak and useless, at Divara's chest.

'Let's go,' I said. 'What are you both doing?'

Paulus stood like some botanist, studying her. I pulled Divara to her feet, off the man.

'Listen for Christ's sake,' I said – and I could hear the sound of more men running down the stairs and towards the open door of the corridor behind us. 'More are coming.'

Fromme was calling like a bull – no words, just a sound of retribution and old Bible vengeance.

'Satan,' Paulus screamed.

'We go now or die,' I said, and I pulled them – they came with me, and they came back to life, for they had not been in life for those moments, maybe until the count of twenty – they had been taken and I have no wish to know to this day what they saw in their own heads when they went away for that little time.

The guards followed us and they came hot to our heels, like a master's torch, but – and I do not believe in the God of the Bible now, but I do believe in the Christ incarnate – I swear to Jesus that we rounded every corner and bend just seconds ahead of them, so all they saw were the soles of our shoes. Shots were fired but they ricocheted back, and we screamed laughter at the sound of them yelping as the lead balls came winging up the corridor toward them.

Paulus was in the lead, then Divara, then I – and as we came to the hatch Paulus opened it, threw Divara inside, pushed me after, and jumped down himself as the guards rounded the corner to the sight of his disappearing head. They banged off one last shot, and Paulus had the door above us locked before their feet hit the iron hatch.

It was a short run of one hundred paces for us, but a race of three minutes or more for them to get out of the keep and to the outdoor hatch on the green at the foot of the Steipplinger mountains – by that time, of course, we were gone like ghosts and disappeared up our little rocky, tree-hidden path to the cave high above the keep and unknown to the town – where we could stand a watch over each and every one of the people down below. And the first thing we all watched was the town beat the bracken and the thickets and fields for our hides. Then, standing on the green behind the keep, the soldiers dropped grenades into the tunnel entrance. It blew and the earth sunk, like a bad settled grave. Fromme, we could see, sat on the ground, in the dirt, outside the keep with his head in his hands. Then he stood, tall, and went inside.

'My mother better have slit my sister's throat and then her own,' said Divara.

Paulus put his arm around her, and I did the same, and we sat in the mouth of the cave and watched. Divara patted our hands. But we knew, all three of us, that Madame Stumpf and Rosa were still alive, or we would have seen their bodies on display in the town square. It would have been Fromme's way.

Chapter Twenty-Nine

A family is forged in a cave as if monkeys had human hearts.

Above the town, the air in the cave was cool and sweet like rain water. Two days and nights we stayed there, and I felt it was my home – I have fondness for it still, and would like to describe the rooms, for the cave was built, or made rather, by God or nature, as if it were a house. When I had come to the cave before with Greet, we had stayed in the mouth and not ventured further inside. We were only interested in ourselves. Now, I wanted to know the corners of my home and how it had been forged by rain and wind and time. The design was like that of a man lying on his belly with his arms and legs outstretched. It was thus: imagine you walked into the left foot of a man flat on his stomach – spread-eagled. The sole of the foot was the opening to the cave, and this chamber was big – room-sized; from there you could look down on the town below. Now walk up the left leg of that spread-eagled man, and after a slow decline of perhaps nine yards deep, you come to his belly – though Paulus joked that it was his arse. It was like black night here. This was the central chamber – deep, dry and dark. Pitch. Any light lit here could not be seen from the entrance of the cave, nor could a light at the entrance be seen down in here. Off from the central belly chamber, ran the right leg – a long low passage that ended in a bell-shaped vault. Forwards from the belly, was the trunk of the lying man. The floor of the cave rose here, and light came in from somewhere ahead, and water could be heard, though low. The trunk of the cave led on to a fork, like arms: to the left a strivulet of water cut down through the rock at a steep angle – a narrow walkway ran beside it – to the right, the water carried along a brown slope of stone and through a large hole in the rock that let on to the outside world. This back entrance here, a hand flung out to the world as I saw it, was the size of a man squared – so, it was big enough for three of us to stand in its frame and look down on the woodland below, behind the mountain we'd made our home. Divara and Paulus remained looking out on the land – hand in hand, I saw. He talked low to her and I could not hear what they said between them. I walked back a little into the cave – stood where the neck of the spread-eagled man would be, with the water running past my feet. In front of me, across the shallow, slow stream was the place in the cave where the head would have lain. A curved little shrine. The head grotto, I called it – and you could sit in the head grotto and cast your eyes to the cave's back door and look out on the sun setting on the world below. It was a place to be alone, away from the others, when time was needed for a person to sit and think and gather their soul about them.

We made a fire up by the back door of the cave – the smoke would leave through the hole and die over the woods below, and no-one would see it from there, creeping from the back of the mountain, with Bideburg on the far side oblivious. Stumpf had kept his cave well stocked – still, Paulus had left bags with supplies and weapons outside the hatch behind the keep and we had picked these up and ran with them up the mountainside, while Fromme and his men were still lumbering inside the keep. There was meat and flour and such like, and we ate the meat and cooked pancakes on hot stones – there was fresh water from the stream, and we had a few flasks of wine, and spirit, packed in our bags too. There were apples and honey as well, that Stumpf had left there, and that Greet and I had eaten together. We talked – and I was glad of talk, even if the talk was dark, for I did not want to be alone in my head.

After a little while, when we all accepted that any return to help Rosa and her mother was beyond our power, we sat in silence.

Divara said, 'My mother and I knew nothing.'

Paulus and I nodded.

'This cave is now my home and property,' she said, with artifice and formality and fear in her voice, 'and I welcome both of you to it. I am in your debt.'

'Thank you,' said Paulus. 'You owe us no debt.'

'I will live as I please here,' said Divara. 'I am alone in the world, and have no-one now to command me or limit me. I may be dead soon and my life until then is my own and no-one else's to dictate.'

'Your life is your own,' said Paulus. 'We should all live as we please.'

I asked, 'And what do we do now?'

Paulus said, 'The night is getting cold.' And it was. 'Why don't we sit in the arse chamber where it is warm.'

'Belly chamber,' said Divara.

We lit a fire and settled into the belly chamber. It was like a cannon-shell hole in a battlefield – maybe twenty paces across, six deep. When we all sat, we were close and our bodies touched. The flicker of the flame made devils dance on the walls and in our faces.

Paulus spoke of Revelation – and it frightened us.

'I do not mean figuratively, like the last book, which is a poem by a lunatic. God is not coming from Heaven, and nor is Jesus – though I wish Christ would. I am not preparing an analogy or stealing John's metaphors. I mean that Revelation is already upon man and always has been. The matter that we are – our flesh – it is about the true revelation of Christ: that man must raise up man. Those who do otherwise are not men. I have always felt like a soldier of Christ when I saw men grind down other men, and women and children. And a soldier must strike eventually if he is to be worthy of Heaven. Even Christ in his great pity knew that not all men can be saved and redeemed and forgiven – when Christ harrowed Hell he left many behind; of course, he could have saved and forgiven them all, but he did not. He chose which great Greek scholars to take and which to leave, which savage if they had been born into Christ would have made Heaven anyway and which would have burned in Hell regardless of baptism because of their irredeemable soul. Christ sees evil and lets it burn – but the righteous man must make that happen by being the agent of the will of the true Jesus – being one of the righteous poor and dispossessed as we are tonight. For we have nothing now – though I have had nothing before.'

Then he talked of books he wished to read, and I grew tired. Divara was sleeping, slumped against me. I fell asleep, listening to him talk of how he had never yet been able to devise a class in which he could teach the variation in rhetoric and versification between Chaucer's Tales of Canterbury and The Decameron, without getting bogged down in the problem of cross-translation between English, Italian and German. And he wondered on the construction of a universal language to beat the evil curse of Babel.

'Those two books are perfect reflections of a pan-culture at work in two places at once,' he was saying, 'separated by language and tradition, yet also joined by something, perhaps, akin to blood – ancient tribe?'

I tried to listen, and I was struggling to formulate some answer to his problem about how to teach the similarities of these poems without language getting in the way – if that is not a logical fallacy – but his voice slurred into a buzz of shifting sound and cadence – for he almost sang, sometimes, when he became animated on his subject – and I fell asleep.

When I woke, Divara and I were curled into one another. Paulus was not there. We joined together and her body was like wine and honey, and silk between her legs. In the dark, I saw her as Greet. We slept. I woke in the night and the fire was out, though it was still warm. She was not beside me. I slept again, and woke when a sound – like love – came from somewhere in the cave. I crawled up out of the belly chamber, just a little and listened. Paulus was back in the bell chamber – the right foot of the sleeping man – I could hear his voice, but not his words. The love sounds died. Divara spoke. I could not hear her words either. I returned to the belly chamber, and slept. I was happy for them truly, and easier in my own soul now that they were as one. Guilt was on my fingers from the touch of Divara, and betrayal on my breath – and nothing, not sex or wine or sleep, could lift the pain in my heart, the loneliness for Greet that would not leave me.

Later, Divara woke me, turning her body into mine. We did not kiss, or touch. I could not have done so, and she made no sign of wanting me in that way. We pulled the old cloaks and blankets around us and slept together – but did not sleep. I could hear from her breathing she was awake beside me, but she seemed snug, and I was snug, and though I did not sleep my mind hovered like a may-fly on the borders of sleep.

When I wake-dream, I lie in my bed, even to this day, and my dozing brain, still conscious to the world around it, plays over old memories. That night, wrapped around Divara, I felt warm and drowsed and safe. After only a little while of wake-dreaming, though, I heard Paulus come down into the belly chamber and slip under the blankets with us, on the other side of Divara. His arm came around her, and touched my own hand lying on her waist. She turned towards him and they kissed.

Our fingers touched – mine and Paulus – and squeezed each other, tired out – but it felt like my father touching my hand in love – and our fingers parted with no awkwardness or fear. I rose quietly and walked to the bell chamber – down the right leg of the sleeping cave – and lay on the skins there, where Paulus and Divara had lain. Skins Stumpf must have left. I slept well – deep and long and dark – for it was good that they were together, and the sound of them comforted me.

And so, I will allow myself the indulgence of a memory – a memory which was my dream that night in the bell chamber. A memory of Paulus that took me to sleep, wake-dreaming – and this memory, it proved something about myself that I could depend upon for the rest of my life, it wrote words into the constitution of my intellect which I still abide by, and it created me in a way that as boys we dream a great father will create something great in us, though they never do. But Paulus did, and he helped create me, with a little work on my own behalf, in that school he ran attached to the university – a small school which bore the promise that if we were smart and good boys we too would make it next door to university and become a man like Paulus, if we wanted it and worked for it.

Paulus had his study right at the top of the school house – in the attic gable. Quarters not as grand or well laid out as his offices at the university, though a slant window opened up to the night sky, so the stars could be seen from the chair at his desk. A rank of candles ran along the top of a small bookcase, behind his chair – and a globe, chest and two more bookcases were on the other side of the room. A Turkish rug lay on the floor, and all visitors had to leave their shoes at the door – not just to save the weave from muddy footprints but because, he said, the rug was a good Moslem and Moslems never wore shoes indoors, so it should be respected and not trod on by the boots of filthy boys. A chair for visitors he didn't much care for sat by the door – a couch for those he was fond of was in front of his desk.

Paulus kept religious lessons to a minimum in the school, and so when the young students had worries on their mind they would come to one of the masters, for priests were scarcely seen. Of all the masters, I favoured to come to Paulus, if he was in the college, not just because he had picked me as a scholar – he'd handpicked all the boys – nor because he knew my family, again he knew most of the families of the boys, but because he was the most approachable – though that is a weak word, 'soft' perhaps is better, and that is not meant to insult him, but he was more soft, more gentle than other masters, and knew the mood of the person he was with as if it was his own. Our religious education was taken care of with eight hours of lessons at the monastery per week. When Paulus negotiated the right to set up the school, with the Prince-Bishop's imprimatur, church officials, much disgruntled at a school being established beyond the control of the ministry, would yield to no other settlement but one hour of religious education for each day of the week, plus one extra because of the lack of God inside the college walls.

The world was afire with religious confusion then – even more than now – and what young soul never has doubts about creation and the nature of the world that surrounds them? Questions about God, that need to be asked.

I first came to talk to Paulus about my confusion just a few months after I enrolled as a scholar on my twelfth birthday – and he listened and said, 'Think of why it is you want to love God, and why you want him to love you. Think about what type of God you want to love, and to love you back in return.'

I visited his study whenever I could – often he was away on court business, that is both business of the law courts and business for the court of the Prince-Bishop – but we met at least once a fortnight in his room, if he could, and he also took my class of ten boys in rhetoric lessons, making us proclaim great political speeches, and lines from the ancient poets and playwrights. Teaching us the mathematical and musical tricks of composing words into form with a purpose – for language has its mathematics and music.

Paulus did not break my relationship with God. We simply read the Bible together, and discussed the God we found and the lessons the Bible taught. And we began at the beginning. Who were the angels in Genesis who mated with the daughters of man, and then bore children? Where did these creatures go? Why was God happy that Lot offered up his daughters to be raped? Why did God tease and lie to Abraham, trick him on so many occasions? Why did God toy with Job as with a fly? God rewarded cowardice and cheating if it was in his name, but punished cowardice or cheating if it was not done to further his glory. He delighted in blood and waste and war and lying; he would not forgive weakness, or pity the frail.

Christ was different, though – as if blending humankind with God removed the cruelty from God. Though this defied reason, as the logic forced the conclusion that humankind was purer therefore than God, that God needed redeemed by humankind. 'One can not beat the cold march of logic, Willie,' Paulus said to me. 'It is your only map.'

Paulus was gone for my thirteenth birthday – in the low countries somewhere on official business. A trade mission, maybe. But a few days later he returned. I went to his study in the evening – it was June, and the window was open. He was burning some sticky foreign resin in a little crucible to keep the stink of the city street below from his room. I asked what it was and he said pogostemon – a thick heady smell that made me feel lazy, and that I still love to this day, though in Scotland it is almost impossible to find. Their perfumers have barely heard of civit or ambergris.

I sat on the couch before his desk without asking permission. He shut the books that were open on his desk and put his pen down. He took off his eye-glasses – which made his eyes seem huge, and so he only wore them when forced to and never in public for the look embarrassed him.

'I have lost the road to God,' I said.

'Then you should best sprawl on the couch, and drink some wine,' he said, and I did, I lay back a little and put one foot up. He poured two cups of wine and walked from behind his desk to hand mine to me.

'Do you know which God it is you are talking about?' he asked, and drank as he sat again. 'Your good health,' he said. And I drank too.

I asked him how there could be more than one God, and he said there wasn't – there is only one God, but he is not the being who created this world we walk upon. This world was not the work of an all-powerful, all-knowing, all-loving God – this world was the work of some lesser being.

'How can this work – the making of the world – be anything more than the actions of the Devil?' Paulus asked.

A year before, I would have ran to the priest crying heresy, and cheered as Paulus burned. But the school never frowned on free thought and questions, and Paulus, I guessed, was posing a debate for me – and if he were not, then I still would not cry heresy. I would be interested in what he had to say, though scared – but I would stay loyal to him. If he had killed a man, I would have helped him bury the body.

'I will tell you something,' said Paulus. 'You will have heard of them, but you will not know them for what they are because of centuries now of propaganda. You know of the Gnostics? The Cathars and such?'

I nodded. Of course I knew of them.

'They were not Satanists, as told. Nor did they deal in witchcraft or the debasement of God. These are lies, carefully crafted upon the Gnostics' true love of God, and the wisdom that these people had in abundance.'

I settled back a little further in the couch. I could see he was readying himself for a lecture – and that was good. I liked to listen to him for he made me think when I was a boy.

'At last I can say this to you, for I think you are old enough and wise enough now,' he said, and I realised this would not be a lecture, but some different sort of conversation that I had never had before in my young life. That scared me.

'Do you think this world of disease and cruelty and poverty and war – was made by God? If what we mean by God is something great and good and kind. That is the immense lie we live within. We believe God created this world, when only Satan could have created it. I believe this to be true. Our God is Satan, Satan is our God.'

I gasped – truly gasped, like a schoolgirl seeing a lion – but even now I would gasp to hear a straight denunciation of God – though I may believe it true, though I do believe it true. I would still gasp today to protect myself.

'Listen and think,' he said. 'Do not speak or ask questions yet.'

Paulus sat very still in his chair as he spoke. 'Satan is not the correct term either for the being that made this world. It is not evil – not just evil – but it is not good. It is like man – it has the morality of man. That is why we are told we were made in its image: it is no better than us – perhaps, worse in many ways, though so much more powerful, and so it is a god to weak things like us, but not like the God who resides above this place of matter and flesh. That God is unknowable to us, and has no bearing on us, but we can attain this true God if we overcome the world. I hope. That I believe. Only in death can I see the true revealed face of God, and it will not be the creator of this world.

Whatever created this world was an architect – something above humankind with the power to form the universe and the world and every creature on it; it created the mathematics of the world, the pattern of seasons, tides, waves. It shaped suns and mountains but also disease and sickness and age, blindness, hunger, madness. Like humankind it feels and so created happiness and love and pity, but it also was full, like us, of hate and jealousy and cruelty. Only such a creature would fashion this living world. The Gnostics, they called this creature the Demiurge – and if you have your languages like I know you do, you know it means the godlike shaper of things, but not God. This was not a thing worth worshipping because it was cruel and fickle and had no lessons to teach the creatures it had created. Some of these Gnostics – and these are not just the French and Spaniards I speak of from back three hundreds years ago – their thought can be found going deep back in time, into the ancient world, among the Hebrews, further back to Babylon.

The Church had it that the Gnostics were saying God was evil and therefore Satan good, as Satan stands opposed to God, and so the Church burned them – all. But no – they were not saying such things, they were saying that the creator was a not a creature of good intent. The creator – Yahweh, Allah, Jehovah, Elohim – was not God, God the all-loving, all-powerful, all-knowing. That God – the God of Love – lay outside the world of matter formed by Yahweh. And so we must reject matter and the flesh. In death, is our only hope – that we may return to the true God, outside the universe, and that Yahweh can toy with us no more. But that is only hope – for, in truth, we do not know. Perhaps, there is no escape, and we can not reach God, and when we die Yahweh just has more suffering for us. I do not think it is Hell he has waiting for us – though I could be wrong. If Yahweh could think up the plague then Hell might well be a pit of fire. Something tells me though it will be cold and lonely and once he has finished with us here in the world of flesh, he just forgets us in the world of the spirit – that wherever it is he plans to send us, millions of grey cold ghosts walk across a field on a misty chill autumn twilight in silence, forever.'

'And Christ?' I asked, and I recall being conscious of making my voice not tremble.

'I think he was a man – a great man, greatest of men, and that is all. No creature sprung from the creator, the architect, could be the man that Christ was. And the true loving God would not enter the world of matter, certainly not to kill his own son. I am sure the true God, he shakes his head at the world of matter and flesh. Like the Gnostics, I follow Christ with all my heart for every word he preached was a word against Yahweh and the Allah to come and all the creator Gods that human beings have knelt before since our formation at its hands. Christ is the son in rebellion, and a human, and I am for that.'

I don't know how many boys Paulus talked to like this – it was not a subject for discussion, unless I wanted to see Paulus dragged before a religious court. I guess he only spoke to three other boys, throughout my time at the school, as he did to me – for each of us had positions with him of one kind or another when we went up to the university on his recommendation. I believe, though I may be wrong, that I was the closest to him out of all of us. It was me, after all, that he chose to take to Bideburg with him, and he must have believed that if I performed well there, it would be the making of my career, and another one of his boys would be off on the road to success, and whatever that meant for him.

And so I was pleased for Paulus, and for Divara. And I was not jealous and I did not feel tested or rejected. I could sleep well knowing these things, and I could sleep safe in the cave, and I did just that – I fell asleep on the skins Divara and Paulus had been on, and as I found sleep I listened to them quietly come together in the belly chamber, and it lulled me.

★ ★ ★

Before dawn, I woke, and I rose and went to the mouth of the cave overlooking the town. It was still dark night and quiet, but lights burned in the street below from torches and lamps. Across from the cave – across the river behind Bideburg – a bluff of rocks ran thick with trees. The light from the fires of the torches and lamps in the town played strange along the branches and leaves.

Paulus walked through the tunnel behind me, and sat down by my side. We smiled at each other and I went back to looking at the shapes forming on the trees in the dark from the light of the town's fires. A huge rustling head made itself known, shuddering and shaking in the branches – its mouth open, like God crying down to Earth. Along from the head of God, to the left of his wide open mouth, another face rose rustling from the leaves, and another beside it, and another – six in all. One had the face of a goat, one seemed a devil with horns, another a raging face of hate, one in pain, one lost and screaming in fright, the last laughing cruel, Caligula, I thought. I looked back at the green face of God, and thought, no, this must be the Devil and this is his banquet, for they seem to sit at a long bench together, and Satan is conversing with his host.

I had been lost in the shapes and faces in the trees, and turned to speak to Paulus. Divara was there now as well, sitting on the floor behind me. I had not heard her appear.

She kissed my cheek and then kissed Paulus, and moved up snug by him.

'You can scare yourself with the images trees make at night,' I said. 'Like staring into fire – but I have never stared at trees and watched them change so.'

Divara asked me what I saw and I told her, and after a while, as I pointed, she said she could make out what I saw too. Paulus moved closer and looked as well. He too said he could see what we both saw in the trees.

The night was warm.

'I could not sleep,' said Divara.

'Nor could I,' said Paulus.

'Nor I,' I said. 'I was making a story from these shapes.'

'Don't tell me what it was,' Divara said. 'I think it would frighten me and I do not want that.'

We sat in silence for a while, and the air smelt of night flowers and old grass and smoke. I did not turn to look at her but I knew Divara watched the keep. The bodies of her mother and sister had not been removed and so the only truth could be that they still lived. I knew she willed them dead and safe – and so stared at the keep and wished her thoughts to be magic that would take them quick.

'I have a story,' said Paulus. 'One my grandmother, Suzi-Anna, told me when I was small.'

We asked him to tell us it. I hunched myself against the wall and pulled my knees up to my chin. Divara turned toward him and rested her back against my legs.

'Is it frightening?' she asked.

'It depends,' said Paulus, and he began. 'It is called Sweet Briar Rose,' he said.

'Ah, I have heard it,' she said.

'Me too,' I laughed and settled down, cosy, though my back was to the cold stone wall, feeling as I did when a little boy at story-time.

'Well, my grandmother's story may be different,' he told us, and he coughed to begin. 'Sweet Briar Rose lived on the edge of the forest with her grandmother and grandfather, for her mother and father were dead, in the war, or so she had been told. Sweet Briar Rose was slim and blonde, with pale blue eyes, and wore a red drindle over a white smock, with white stockings and shoes the colour of her sky-eyes. Her grandmother and grandfather doted on the child and loved her more than any mother and father ever could – though they told her never to go away from them, especially into the forest.

One day Sweet Briar Rose was chasing butterflies in the green field behind her grandparents' home. The butterfly skipped off along the grass and into the ferns by the forest fringe, and Sweet Briar Rose followed. The butterfly flitted from plant to plant and tree to tree as the forest got deeper and Sweet Briar Rose followed. Deep and far in the forest the butterfly vanished behind a tree and Sweet Briar Rose chased after it. When she came to the tree a girl stepped out and stood before her. The girl was Sweet Briar Rose – her double, like a twin. But the girl was different too – she was dark-haired, black like pitch, with green eyes, she wore a red drindle over a black smock, she had black stockings and shoes green like the grass in her eyes.

"Who are you?" asked Sweet Briar Rose. "Are you me?"

"I am Dark Briar Rose," the girl said. "Are you me?"

Sweet Briar Rose looked around her and said, "I am lost." She began to cry.

"Don't cry," said Dark Briar Rose, "I am lost too. We can help each other."

"But we are in the middle of the forest," said Sweet Briar Rose.

"Not quite the middle," Dark Briar Rose said. "That is where I am trying to get to."

Dark Briar Rose said that if Sweet Briar Rose helped her find the very centre of the forest, its heart, where her mother and father lived, then her father would surely take Sweet Briar Rose out of the forest and back to her family.

Sweet Briar Rose agreed.

"We must walk in the opposite direction, then, to the one you came," said Dark Briar Rose.

And they walked towards what must have been the dark wooded heart of the forest.

After many hours, they came to a clearing – indeed right at the very heart of the woods – and there stood a careworn cottage, with a garden and smoking chimney. By a side wall, painted white, sat a little wood-pile – high as a child.

"I must hide," said Dark Briar Rose. "My parents do not want me. They took me to the woods and left me there. If you can make them take you back to the world outside the forest, then I can return to my house, lock the door and live there without them. Then they will be lost in the woods."

Sweet Briar Rose said this was wrong, but Dark Briar Rose told her that if she did not do as she was told then her parents would see that they were together and do nothing to help her – for they would not help a friend of Dark Briar Rose.

Sweet Briar Rose agreed at last and Dark Briar Rose ran to hide behind the woodpile. Sweet Briar Rose walked to the cottage door and knocked. The mother appeared – so pretty and soft and warm. Sweet Briar Rose said she was lost and asked if anyone could lead her out of the woods to her home, beyond.

The mother called the father and he appeared – strong and tanned and kind. He said he would lead the child home. But Sweet Briar Rose, remembering her promise to her friend, said, "No, you both must come. My family would not allow me to walk alone with a man, and they will also wish to reward you, and if there are two, then the reward will be twice as much."

The mother and father nodded their heads, and left the cottage each taking Sweet Briar Rose by the hand. After an hour, they stopped to rest and the mother said to Sweet Briar Rose, "Is it your grandmother and grandfather you live with?"

"Yes," said Sweet Briar Rose.

"And they live in a cottage, like ours, on the fringe of the woods?"

"Yes," said Sweet Briar Rose.

"And they love you very much – but never talk of your mama and papa?"

"Yes," said Sweet Briar Rose.

The butterfly that she had chased skittered onto a fern in front of Sweet Briar Rose. She put out her hand to it and it rose, hovering in the air.

"Then you are our child," said the mother. And the father advanced towards Sweet Briar Rose with a dagger in his hand which he had pulled from his wide leather belt.

Sweet Briar Rose ran, ducking through bushes and trees – much faster than the adults behind her. The butterfly skipped at her heels. Soon, she had lost them, but she had lost herself too. Sweet Briar Rose could hear the mother and father shouting through the trees far away. When she was ready to sit down and cry, she saw the butterfly – wafting close to her face. Off it darted, and she followed. She ran and ran behind the ducking and diving wings, and the sound of the grown-ups grew fainter and fainter. Soon, she popped out in a clearing behind the butterfly – right back at the little glade where the mother's and father's cottage stood. She fell to her knees crying, for now she was sure she would be found and would be killed. The butterfly floated off towards the cottage door.

Dark Briar Rose pulled open the cottage door and ran to her friend.

"Do not cry," she said. "But be quick and get to your feet and follow me, before they come back."

The girls ran to the house and bolted the door behind them. Dark Briar Rose took a key from the dresser by the hearth and locked the door shut. The room was warm and cosy, with a fire and cushions and a kettle just ready to whistle. Cakes were on the table, and the parlour was clean and bright. Lace curtains were threaded across the front window, and tied with patterned sashes.

The girls looked through the glass. The mother and father running through the glade towards them – the father's knife flashed in his hand.

"Don't fear," said Dark Briar Rose.

The parents walked around the house, shouting and screaming, demanding to be let inside, but Dark Briar Rose called out, "You may not come in – I own the house now and the door is barred against you."

The parents sat outside the door and wept and moaned now – sometimes they scrabbled with their nails against the wood.

From the back room of the cottage a baby's wail arose.

"Our brother," said Dark Briar Rose.

She got up and came back with a baby boy. "This is the one they wanted," she said. And she returned the baby to his nursery.

By the morning, the parents were crying with hunger, saying they must eat.

"There is no food for you here," called Dark Briar Rose.

"Nothing," shouted Sweet Briar Rose.

The parents were quiet, and Dark Briar Rose told Sweet Briar Rose that even if their parents left or died, the girls would never be able to leave this place for children could not find their way out of the forest alone.

"You will never see our grandparents again," said Dark Briar Rose.

Sweet Briar Rose cried and her sister comforted her.

By afternoon, their parents said that if they had no food then they would die at that moment.

The girls shut their ears to them. Come night, the parents said that if they could take their baby son then they would leave and never return.

Dark Briar Rose told them to get up and walk to the edge of the glade – if they did that, she would leave the baby on the doorstep and they could come and take it and go. They did, and she did.

Inside the cottage, the sisters heard the parents run back to the door and lift the child. The baby screamed and there was a terrible sound like pigs make at a trough or dogs fighting over a bone.

The sisters watched their parents run to the woods – there was moonlight, and they seemed to carry something, swinging, between them.

The sisters fell asleep together on the floor and woke in the morning, like it was the first day of creation. They needed no-one or nothing, and though they were sad they would never see their grandparents again, they knew that they would meet the old couple in Heaven one day, but until then they would live out their lives in happiness together here in their cottage in the heart of the forest. And they still live there till this day, or so my grandmother Suzi-Anna told me.'

Dawn was up now – and the faces of the devils had disappeared in the trees.

'We need some sleep,' said Divara. 'Your story was frightening for me.'

'I liked it,' I said.

'I am not sure what to think about it,' said Paulus, and we returned to the belly cave and all of us slept together until noon, I think.

* * *

When I woke in the cave, Paulus was reading by the light of the fire we had built in the belly chamber – he had brought a book with him, of course, some compendium of poetry. The wind was blowing from the town, through the cave, so the smoke flew out the back entrance, and none would be wiser. It made us laugh that the people of Bideburg were so blind to us, hiding above them.

I got up and covered Divara, and sat beside him. He shook his head and smiled.

'I have learned more in these last few days than I have my entire life,' I said to him.

'Good,' he said. 'But I do not want you to die for it.'

'We can escape,' I said. I looked over to Divara and she was still and quiet on the other side of the fire.

'You know what I have learned, Willie,' he said, 'throughout my entire life?'

But Divara turned on her side towards us, wide awake, and spoke, stopping him.

'Friends,' Divara said. 'You woke me. Be quiet.'

We apologised for talking so loudly. She sat up, her clothes rumpled and twisted around her. 'I have listened to you a lot,' she said, 'but you should listen to women more, ask more questions of the women you know.'

Some folk – and many women – can be petulant when they wake from sleep too soon.

'We will try to be more quiet,' said Paulus, 'so you get the sleep you need as a woman.'

She looked at Paulus, with something close to pity, I thought.

'We are in a cave, Divara,' I said. 'I fear it will be hard for us not to be heard by one another sometimes.'

'We are indeed in a cave now, Willie,' she said, 'and anything may pass that we please. There is no law in this cave – only us, and we decide what passes and how we live. It does not please me to be a woman, as you see it, any more. This little world you have created, it is a failure. You have listened to your fathers, and they listened to their grandfathers and to their great-grandfathers and great-great grandfathers and great-great-great grandfathers, all the way back to the time of Moses listening to his father in the sky. Tell me: where do you give a woman space in this world? Where does a woman have choice? I will have choice – if only in my cave.'

She came and sat between us. 'You are good men and I am sure my criticisms are not about you, but living under the minds of brothers and fathers is what women do, and I am sick to the ends of my soul with it. Neither of you have moved to stop it, or speak about it – no men have, ever, even the good ones – so perhaps my criticism is of you too, for not noticing, or if you notice, then doing nothing.' She patted us both on the arm like we were her children. I looked to Paulus, but he did not look at me, he studied Divara.

'Strong arms, boys,' she said, her hands still on us. 'Your arms are thicker than mine. Your head can take more punching than mine. But you grovel to other men, and you think the ideas they tell you to think. You go and die in a town like Bideburg because some other man says so. I do not understand men.'

'I am not like other men,' I said. 'I respect and protect women. I love women.'

'That is why I am saying these things to you. At least you might listen,' said Divara. 'And do not be angry. I am not trying to hurt you. You are my friend and I love you now. I am in debt for my life to you and would do anything to repay you and protect you in return. But telling me that some men are good does not change anything, and if you were a woman you would not think this way. We here in Europe, we fight the Moslems – and I am sure not all Moslems are wicked, but still we know they are a danger to us. We know we are not safe until the Moslems change or are no longer. So it is with men and women.'

'Divara,' Paulus said, and I heard a university lecture coming up in his voice. 'The way some ignorant foolish men treat women can not be made metaphor for the wars the Moslems have waged on Europe or us on them. This is a fallacy in the making. Although, I agree that many men are low and like beasts in the way they treat women.'

'Do not talk down to me, my love,' said Divara – and she kissed Paulus on the cheek. He looked unmanned but did not speak or move. 'I have read pamphlets telling how the Moslems raped their male Christian captives, sold them off in slave markets, forced them to covert as Muhammadins.'

'Precisely,' said Paulus.

'Yes, precisely,' I said, and I laughed a little, wickedly. 'Men can be wicked to men as well, not just women.'

'Have you ever seen a woman slapped by her father or husband or brother for laughing at them the way you just laughed at me?' Divara held my eyes hard as she spoke.

'A slap is not being forced to worship Muhammad,' I said, and looked away.

'And if they raped and enslaved the Christian men they took,' said Divara, 'then what did the Moslems do to the women? That is not told in the pamphlets – written by men.'

'Pamphlets are not histories,' said Paulus.

'What may I do that a man tells me not to?' she asked. 'Tell me that. You are men and therefore must know.'

Paulus and I did not speak.

'For a woman, if her husband says bed, it is bed,' Divara said. 'If her father says go to church, it is go to church. If I wish to read this book, speak to that person – I must ask. My men own my money. I can not leave where I am without permission of men. What women but whores are allowed to work as they please? And even whores must answer to the men who own them. For sure, I am not beneath the Moslem, but if good men were really good men then my life would fare much better. But good men are too busy just being men and enjoying all that being a man may mean today. You are forgetful of others – even you, my two friends, who I love.'

'I am sorry,' said Paulus, and he kissed her, clumsy on the ear, and they sat close.

'If anything can happen in this cave, then please,' I said, 'turn the world on its head. I am glad to see it happen. But may I still fall in love with innkeepers' daughters and ravish them,' I laughed.

'If they wish a ravishing, then ravish them,' she said, and laughed in return.

We set to making some food, for we were all coming on hungry now.

Our kitchen was the back chamber – that looked out over the woods behind the mountain, on the far side of Bideburg. I made griddle cakes of flour and apples and honey; Paulus cut dried beef and cooked it in wine with some onions and mushrooms, that were part of Stumpf's stock, and good fresh herbs plucked from the mouth of the cave.

Divara drank a cup of spirit and talked to us as we worked. 'It is my mother who makes me think these thoughts,' she said. 'Compared to her, the men who hold her down there,' and she jerked her head in the direction of Bideburg, 'those men are nothing. During the wars, back when my mother was a girl, her village turned Lutheran quick and ready. My mother was about to marry – her first husband, a schoolteacher. The war was not so brutal where my mother came from – the ordinary folk had not been pressed down so harshly by their lords and the poor not treated as animals, like in many parts – but the people were still angry, none the less. They expelled their lord – though did not kill him – and they sent a delegation to the convent in the town to tell the sisters that they must hand over some land by way of recompense for the years of exploitation. The sisters raised bees and grew flowers and were allowed to trade untaxed by the Prince-Bishop – so honey and rose oil and sunflower seeds and candles made them very rich over the years. They bought up land on bad debts, became merchants for the village traders – for trading through the nuns meant a better profit. Though the sisters were good too – they tended the sick and old for no charge, gave charity when it was needed. Some of the ranking sisters did act the high lady, but not often, and most of the nuns were decent. There was no cavorting, for sure, and they behaved according to their vows of chastity.

My mother's husband-to-be was among the delegation to the nunnery, as was her own father and grandfather. The nuns agreed to hand back some lands – for they had plenty, and knew it – and the village settled. My mother was married within a few days, for her husband was due to go to fight for the Lutheran lords. But war is a man's game, as you know – and men like chaos, I believe. There was fighting around the country, and villages which had switched sides were being burned by Catholic armies. Everyone knew of the atrocities – and it stoked a slow anger in my mother's town. A few days before my mother's first husband – the schoolteacher – left for the army, he and some other men in the village, those with voices listened to, they said the nuns should be expelled and their lands seized for the town and divided among the families equally – for the Catholic armies had gone too far and justice means revenge, so the Bible teaches us often. In fact, the nuns should be killed, the men decided.

The men went up that night to the convent. But the nuns had been told what was coming for them, by some women in the town – my mother among them. The sisters had bolted the great gates to the convent – it was square and tall, with strong brick walls high as ten men. The men were drunk and they were at the walls calling names and threatening. They surrounded the nunnery – and said they would wait for the sisters to come out, and if they were not out by dawn, they would burn the convent to the ground.

The townswomen came to the nunnery then – some men tried to chase their wives and daughters and sisters and even their mothers away, but the women would not leave, and my mother moved quick and came up to her husband and made him call the men to order, he was clever and brave and though young he was looked on as a leader by the other men.

My mother was sixteen, perhaps, but she spoke to the crowd of men, though she addressed herself to her husband. "Would you act like this if your mother or sister or daughter – or I your wife – if one of us was in there," she said, and she pointed to the nunnery.

And of course many men laughed and said frigid whores in black and white would never be mothers or wives.

"Or daughters and sisters I said," my mother shouted out to the laughing men in the crowd.

Her husband raised his hand and told the men to be quiet. "It is right the women have their say," he said to them.

"I am not asking you to be merciful because they are women," she said. "Would you act like this if your father or your brother or your son – or yourself – if one of you were in there? Our town is a good town of good people and you are shaming yourselves and the place we call home by your actions. Your women will not stand by you in this. We will stand beside the sisters of the nunnery if they come out to you and we will not let you touch them – and if you try to touch them then you will have to touch us, your mothers and sisters and daughters and your wife." She spoke directly to her husband now.

"If you try to burn the nunnery, we will stop you – we will take the torches from your hands and you will have to beat us dead to keep us back. We will open the gates to the nunnery to let the women flee the fire, and fight you if you come between us. You will not kill these women."

Still she held her husband's eye. "I am not asking you to do this because you love me or I love you – or any of you love your women here. I am telling you – and so are all your wives and sisters and mothers and daughters – that you will not do this because we say so. Come away from these women now," and she pulled her husband by the sleeve towards her.

The other women were with their own men now and talking to them, pulling at them, scolding, stamping, none were crying or begging.

My mother's husband called to the other men, "We will not kill, will we?"

None called back, yes, we will kill – most shook their heads and gave in to their women around them.

"But the nuns must go," he called out. "The town is not safe for them any more. Their lives can not be guaranteed. War is making men mad."

My mother said loudly to him – though she stood at his side, with her arm around his waist and his around her, for they were acting now their parts before the crowd and not in conversation with each other – she said loud, "The nuns will not leave – unless the nuns wish to leave. We can guarantee their safety. This is a good town, and always has been. What happened tonight is forgotten."

And women beside their men, ringed around the nunnery, said "forgiven", "forgotten", "never spoken of again". "Come home".

And the men did go home.'

So many expressions passed over Divara's face as she spoke that I could not count them – rage, joy, tranquillity. Her face was a theatre.

When she finished her story, she came to the fire where Paulus and I cooked, and helped us – for my pancakes were crumbling and his stew too watery. She salvaged what she could and we sat by the back door of the cave looking over the woods behind the mountains and we ate. The food tasted good, despite its looks, and I was glad. So was Paulus. So was Divara.

★ ★ ★

When we'd eaten, we sat around our fire by the back entrance of the cave – and watched the sun pass over the sky and listened to the birds sing. We were quiet together for a long time.

At last, Paulus spoke – and he spoke to Divara.

'There is something wrong with many men,' he said. 'I have thought this throughout my life but never spoken of it – as the thought was until now not really thought. It lay in my mind like the memory of a dream – and those memories are so faint and weak they mean nothing in waking life. I think it is lust which turns some men mad. It breaks their mind. Perhaps your father, though I do not think him mad. These men, their veins are afire with the imps of lust and it turns their minds to wild diversions, dark places. My own father, one day, came back home with a young woman, after he had been made one of the Elect of Munster. She was seventeen, I believe. Her husband had been beheaded as a traitor and heretic for refusing to take in payment a coin pressed with the likeness of Jan van Leyden on one side as the king and notary of the gold crown – on the other side there was a jagged city imprinted, Jerusalem. The husband's property had been divided among the Elect. A heretic's dependants are not considered human. They are oppositional to the coming of the Lord Jesus Christ and so must be handed out like fish and wine among the chosen people for their benefit.

This girl was brought home and decreed a handmaiden – as in the Bible, like Abraham and Sara's Hagar. My mother would have killed her if she could. But the girl was my father's property. My mother beat her half to death every day anyway – hating the heretic in her more than any usurper she saw, for she agreed that heretics were chattel and my father may as well have been fornicating with a cow.

Our Hagar tried to run – but she was caught before she could leave the city. Her punishment could have been anything – flaying alive if it was wanted – and my mother had ruled that she would decide the girl's end. She ordered her hanged, and was forever boastful about her great kindness to the filthy slave she'd taken in under her roof.'

Paulus lay back, and I could tell from his silence that just as in school and then in university he was inviting someone to speak.

Divara said, 'Poor Hagar', and we were all quiet again for a little while.

I wished to speak to them over the fire about my childhood, though I had no great stories to tell – my years until now had been ones of aching expectation and terror at my station in life, and I said so to them both, but they were the words that all boys say at one time or another, and that others listen to but do not hear or care about. Paulus listened and heard and cared, though, and so did Divara.

Paulus said to me, 'The world and everything you know is a lie, my dear friend Willie. Your parents – though they sound good people – are wrong about everything they told you. I am wrong about everything I tell you. Not one word that comes from your mouth – unless it is about how you feel in your soul – is true. It is tainted and full of lies that we do not even know we are telling because our fathers told them to us and their fathers to them and on and on back until their god created Adam in the Garden. Though I wonder if he did. Maybe Satan passed us into creation.'

Divara lay back by the fire now. Her voice came over the flames, 'Satan pissed us into creation.'

I laughed, and it shocked me to laugh at such a time and at such words, and I said, 'You dare God. What woman says such things?'

'I do now,' she said.

Paulus got up and walked the few steps to the back entrance of the cave, looking down on the valley on the far side of the Steipplinger mountains, the sun getting low in the afternoon sky.

Divara rose too and said, as if she was suggesting a walk after a meal, 'Let's piss together. I need to piss.'

Paulus shrugged, and gestured with his hand for Divara to stand at the edge of the cave mouth beside him. She turned towards me, looking back into the cave, and hoisted up her skirts and crouched. She rustled with her clothing, and the rustling to me was more shocking than seeing a pig mate with the moon.

'Come,' she said to me, and she jerked her head to the mouth of the cave as she pulled her clothing down.

I walked to them. I had the sense that I was not in the cave, because the foundations of life were upside down – and I felt debased, yet I rejoiced, and as she began to gush – the sound was horrific to my ears, but thrilled me too as it was the sound of a body letting go – I unbuttoned myself and stood to her left and gushed too, down over the mountain side, the water silvering in the orange sunlight onto the woods below.

Paulus unbuttoned himself and stood to her right, hanging. He looked at me, and I could see he was not ashamed – none of us were any more: she looking into the cave, us looking out. Then as we were gathered there, on the lip of the cave mouth, over the valley and the hot horizon, wriggling and wormed far away on the edge of the Earth, we three of us, we all pissed, long and hard, deep flashing shards, down onto the trees and the green of the land below us, the water flashing like swords from us.

Chapter Thirty

Execution and the wrath of almighty God on the Earth below.

From where the three of us sat perched in the mouth of the cave, looking down on Bideburg, the town at night was a pinprick board of lights and fire. The inn whirled with singing and dancing and drinking. The constables took a stave post, thick as a man, and knocked it into the ground at the town crossroads. It jutted up from the earth, waist high. Some townsmen carried the wheel of a hay cart up the road toward the constables. They set it atop the stave, flat, and nailed it in place, making the shape of a T, with the spokes and rim of the wheel casting black jittering shadows from the moon and the torches on the ground below.

There was fiddle playing from the inn, and singing, from the inn. We could not hear the words, and Paulus asked Divara if she knew the tune.

'I did not mix with these people and know nothing about their songs,' she said, though the air carried snatches of their words – green tree and bone, we heard, and head and hell below, and a body worn as a rags. The melody was hard and churning, low.

A group of townsmen set up a flat platform, no more than knee-high off the ground. The size and shape of a family bed. They threw straw and rushes on it, and tamped the bedding down. As they worked, two more groups of men set up three high stakes, heaped with faggots and kindling and brush. The final construction was a flag-pole, which the men and guards put up together.

Fromme walked from the keep – full priestly – with his brother Barthelme behind him. The sergeant called for silence, and the village hushed – no-one chanced a smart remark or low mocking whistle. This was naked stilling justice. People stood and shuffled forward, bowed their heads, formed ranks in the street, three deep from the keep to the crossroads and, it seemed to me, their spirits left their bodies for a while as they waited, quiet, excited.

A constable stood at the keep door, and played on a drum, a rolling, rivelling drone of summons and warning, the sound quickening in rhythm with each new flick of his wrists. The people glanced to the side, to the keep door – and a sound of running feet could be heard from within. The running grew louder, and Stumpf came pushed and flying through the keep door into the street, as the drummer reached his peak. Stumpf landed on his face, hands chained behind his back, his mouth bloody and gagged with an iron ring, the drummer stopped and the crowd came back to life roaring and screaming and leaping off the ground. The two guards who'd thrown Stumpf out onto the street, kicked and dragged him to his feet – behind them two more guards carried Stumpf's wife and child into the street and threw them on the ground before him. They were gagged and bound too, with rope and iron. Their mouths ran wet and sticky with spit. The child Rosa seemed dead from fear but the mother writhed and screamed behind her gag, kicking out. Stumpf stared at the ground.

Beside me, Divara lowered her head and looked down too, then breathed, and lifted her eyes once more. Paulus laid a hand on her arm, and left it there.

I ran my eyes over the crowd of people below us. I could see them all – Kroll, Jens and his family, Rodinan and his family, Raben, Odil. Every living soul in Bideburg had gathered to see the Stumpfs die tonight.

Fromme walked toward the prisoners and said, 'Your death warrants have already been read, there are no more proclamations to be said. You have had your last words. This is now a time of execution.'

The guards held Stumpf and his wife and child by the hair, forcing them to look at Fromme. The mother struggled and kicked more, the child hung lifeless, and Stumpf watched Fromme – like a dog would stare at a master set to kill him.

'It's time,' Fromme shouted, and raised his arms, clapping his hands. The people pushed forward, and with the guards, they lifted Stumpf and his wife and child above their heads – and the folk screamed with laughter, their teeth and tongues bright and pink in the light. Music was struck up again, and they bounced the family over their heads, passing them along – punching them, ripping at their hair, jumping up to bite them, pulling their clothes from them till they were naked – all the way up the street, hand over hand and head over head, to the crossroads, with the wheel and the stakes and the platform waiting.

Stumpf was stiff like a planed timber, his wife roared and jumped trying to escape, and little Rosa was soft as a fresh corpse, but still the crowd beat and bit and ripped at her so she became naked and bloody too.

At the end of the street, at the end of the row of people, where the crossroads stood, the crowd threw the three bodies onto the ground. The guards and constables circled the Stumpfs, drawing the crowd to a halt.

'You should not watch this, Divara,' said Paulus. 'We will all of us go back into cave and wait until this is over.'

Divara was like a woman made of ice. 'You gentlemen may leave,' she said. 'I will stay here and witness this for my family.'

She did not cry, she did not screw her hands in rage and dig her nails into her palms, or pull her hair, bite her mouth, punch the ground, cling to me or Paulus for hope, protection, comfort. She remained still, watching, breathing. Alone and within herself. I do not believe she even blinked. I feared her a little then, and I think Paulus did too.

Below, Stumpf was tied to the flagpole. His wife and daughter were picked up and placed on the low platform. The sergeant, Karfreitag, and his man-at-arms, walked forward, and knelt down between their legs. Rosa came to life then and screamed and struggled, but was slapped and punched until she was quiet. The mother seemed to have swapped spirits with her child, because now she lay still like she had died – though she hadn't as her toes and fingers curled and uncurled all the while. Soon Karfreitag and his man-at-arms were bare from the waist down, and when they finished two other uniforms took their place, and on it went until all the constables and guards were done. Then Karfreitag made a queue of townsmen. Stumpf stared, unseeing, unmoving, unblinking, at the whirling crowd around him.

I would have walked back into the cave now, away from the sight – but I feared seeming weak before Divara. Paulus, I believe, would have turned away also. Divara and her judgement kept Paulus there as well, I know. I dropped my eyes to the floor of the cave, though, and saw that Paulus did the same. Divara watched on, through her still veil of ice.

Much later, the child was bloody from head to foot, and a man on top of Madame Stumpf cried out and jumped away, as he pushed her legs far back, and her hips cracked, breaking at the joints and dislocating so they hung strange and awful from the sides of the platform.

Fromme walked to Stumpf, raised his head by the hair to look, and said, 'Enough.'

The guards stepped forward and lifted Stumpf's wife and child off the platform. The wife hung like a broken spider, and the child was tender and raw, her face like bitten meat.

They tied them then to the stakes for burning, but they were not burning living things, though they both still breathed – they looked like clots of blood nailed to two posts. The faggots and kindling and brush were piled up around them and Fromme told two guards to light the fire. The summer had been dry as dust so the woman and the child went up quick like pitch-soaked rags. And there was plenty of choking smoke to make the killing fast, thank God. Rosa screamed – and the sound still reverberates in my heart today – but soon the smoke shrouded her, the flames starting up on her body and hair, and she was quiet, at last, suffocated – and I knew her life was over. I prayed to God in thanks. Madame Stumpf gasped as the fire was lit, and screamed long and loud just once – it was the sound of pain and dying – then she gasped again and it sounded like she cried tears, but her sounds were soft and gentle and soon she too was choked quiet by the smoke and gone, as her dress burned away and her face seemed to melt as the fire took hold of her body. How a woman can die sounding gentle I do not know to this day, but no man could die in such a way.

The crowd was quiet while they burned, silently.

Divara watched on, unblinking, shaking me away when I touched her arm and begged her to come down into the belly of the cave with me and not look at such things.

'I need to see so I can act as I see fit,' she said. There were still no tears, no fear on her face, but now she throbbed with a rage that told me she would rip the men below to ribbons and throw their guts into the trees to feed the crows if she could. Her hate was more ice than fire, and I felt cold beside her, though the heat of the hot thick night, and what I saw below, made me sweat.

Paulus said to me and Divara, 'If there had been screaming and begging, they would have been happy and cheering.'

'I will kill everyone down there,' said Divara, turning to Paulus. Then she looked back to the town and said no more.

'They are animals. It would be no sin to kill them,' I said. Neither Paulus or Divara spoke or acknowledged that I had spoken.

Tied to the flagpole, Stumpf was unchanged, staring, and – I promise – mild. The townsfolk stood as the fires burned on in the night, and watched.

There was little talking among them. Fromme stepped forward again, the priest officiating – before the burning stakes – and said, 'We have dealt with a small matter. Now, we have great justice to avenge. We shall break the wolf upon the wheel.'

And the spark returned to the crowd then at these words – whatever it was that made them feel alive, it poured back into them – and they clapped again and sang and laughed and pointed at the burning mother and her burning child – now black lumps of rind disappearing in twin bonfires – and cheered.

They chanted, 'Wolf, wolf, wolf.'

* * *

I had never seen a human broke upon the wheel. What the wheel does is prove the pointlessness of the body. It reveals the body as a sack, as clothing, for the soul. Stumpf was dragged to the stave post with the wheel sat on top – and the crowd, they hurly-burlyed like all the world's festivals had come on the same night. The constables placed Stumpf on the wheel. He lay on his back and stared up at the stars and moon, and we looked down on him from the cave. I felt his eyes could see mine, and I asked, 'Can he see us do you think?'

'No,' said Divara, her voice old, an echo.

The guard spun Stumpf then. From where we watched, our eyes revolved and danced following the cartwheel, following his body round the points of the compass. And I thought, this is comical, they have placed a man upon the wheel of a cart. The crowd laughed, and I thought this makes sense, they are laughing because a man has been placed upon a wheel, and the sight is absurd – a man is spinning upon a wheel, tied, on his back, staring at the stars and we can all see how ridiculous this looks, and how ridiculous we are for watching it.

Two of the guards stepped forward with Karfreitag. The wheel was slowing now, and the blur of Stumpf was forming back into the shape of the man. The guards lifted poles – clubs – in the air. They were iron poles, for they shone in the light. The clubs came down. In military training, I had seen live pigs hung up and beaten with clubs or stabbed or shot, to show recruits the effects of weapons on a body – pigs, physicians say, have a physiognomy similar to humans. The sound of the clubs on Stumpf's body

335

was the same sound as a club against a living pig. But the pigs squealed and honked hard. Stumpf only groaned low, and the air huffed out of his body with each blow. The weight of the clubs brought the wheel to a halt – then slowly and in pattern the two guards beat Stumpf with the clubs. Have you seen the master of a boat keep time on his rowers with a drum? That was the rhythm of the guards on Stumpf with the clubs. One, two. One, two. Like marching. The crowd clapped in time, and whistled and called out support. Stumpf's arms and legs hung broken, from the wheel rim. He was a crushed father-longlegs. He began screaming, then, at last, though with no words. They beat on, down on him – though never once the head – and his body began to slip down through the spokes of the wheel. His feet hung over the rim, but his thighs dropped down inside the spokes. One blow split open his belly – and it steamed, even though the night was warm. He called out then.

'Take me, take me, take me,' he called.

And the crowd called it back at him, mocking. Some shouted, 'Beat slower.'

Stumpf was blood and white jutting bone, like broken antler horn.

Divara watched – her face emotionless, her body still, but I could feel a rage, like the wrath of God, come from her, cold, aching, endless. Neither Paulus nor I spoke to her. We knew she would not heed us, would not listen, that we had no power over her, nor should we have had power over her, for she was Lady Vengeance and Lady Vengeance has no master or mistress but herself.

They skinned Stumpf then, while he was still alive. I remember thinking – if only his body was not so broken, then it would have been easier for him, quicker, as his skin could have come off in one swift tug. But he was too jagged to be undressed in one go. The men skinning him had to duck under the wheel, navigate the spokes – cutting and slicing here, pulling and snipping there. Stumpf cried out now – high and screaming – and did not stop, a long howl of pain that would not cease. The skin from his hands was removed like gloves, and then from his arms. But taking off the sleeves was like undressing a wayward child, all gangly and awkward, as the bone poked through the skin, and pulling it off was a matter of ripping and tearing. They undressed the rest of him bit by bit – coat, britches, underwear. Then skinned his face.

He was alive, just rasping and cawing like a bird now. They took off his lips and nose, removed his tongue – and then they cut him free from the wheel. Fromme put out one hand and spun the wheel as if he was spinning a child on a merry-go-round. He did not look at Stumpf. The wheel turned slow and Stumpf slipped to the ground. To me he was a bag of jelly – living jelly. Stumpf lay on the ground in a heap of red meat and bone, and moaned. His eyes still saw, though. Fromme beckoned to a group of four women in the crowd and they came and stood over Stumpf and stitched his skin back together – gloves to sleeves, sleeves to coat, coat to legs, and then the face and hair. They thought he watched, I know – for they called to Stumpf, telling him how fine his skin was under their fingers, as they ducked and dived their darning needles, blood on their hands to their wrists.

When his skin was stitched into a red coat, the guards hoist it up the flagpole they had erected, and it fluttered there, the legs like the points of a torn battle pennant.

Some in the crowd could still entertain the idea of dancing and celebrating, but many were weary now, I could see. It was late, hot. The Skin Flag had not impressed most of them, after all that had gone on. Some wanted to go home, but they could not. Stumpf was not yet dead. Fromme clapped his hands, and we heard a sigh from the back of the crowd.

Karfreitag rolled a barrel into the crossroads square.

'Let's salt him,' called Fromme, loud and excited into the night. The crowd clapped obediently and a few cheered.

'Quieten the music,' called Fromme, and the two or three musicians still making tunes on their instruments immediately left off playing.

One or two people – maybe more, as the shadows were so deep at the edges of the town that I could not see clearly – they started to leave the crowd. I watched them walk through the dark woods back to their homes. A cracking sound brought my eyes back to the crossroads square and when I looked on Stumpf again I drew in my breath and turned away. I am not ashamed to say it. What man wouldn't? Divara kept up her silent, still watch though. Karfreitag was pouring salt onto Stumpf. Stumpf writhed a little on the ground, all twisted and twitching, like a dumb slug would under those biting white grains – raw. He chewed at his mouth and froth came from him, and he gargled like a city gutter.

Karfreitag went on pouring and the salt heaped over Stumpf like a cairn. He was covered, though the grains of the white grave ran and rivelled a little as he moved by broken inches under the mound. Then there were sobs. What remained of Stumpf was crying in the salt.

I did not turn to look at her, but from the corner of my eye, I saw Divara lift her hand to her face and seem to wipe her cheek. I could not see if there were tears on her. She did not move again.

The crowd gasped as one when Stumpf wept within the mound of salt. Let me tell you, I have never ceased my fascination with crowds – they move as one, as one physical entity. They experience hate and horror and love and adoration as one, and it frightens me more than the damnation I face for not believing in the God of Abraham, though I still honour Jesus as a saviour of humankind and the poor.

'Enough,' someone called from the crowd, and 'No', 'Just kill him', 'Put an end to it'.

'We are tired and wish to sleep,' called one woman.

'I've work in the morning,' shouted the man beside her.

Paulus looked at me and whispered, 'He can not command a crowd.'

'If there is a god then he will give them all canker in the face now,' said Divara, the first words she had spoken in a long time. She waited a moment, then said, 'They live. Their faces do not rot. There is no god.'

Fromme raised his hands, but more in defence than calling the crowd to silence.

'He must be burned,' Fromme called out, as deep and sonorous as he could.

'Just kill him and be done with it,' a man shouted.

'Kill him now,' another man called. And the crowd began clapping and chanting 'kill him, kill him' – much in the same rhythm as the guards used to measure out the beating on Stumpf, and ship masters to pattern the speed of their rowers.

'We will burn him now, then,' Fromme shouted – his voice unsteady.

But the people were not going to have that – they shouted no, and inched forward a little. They wanted it over.

'Burning will take too long,' one woman called out. 'We wish to go to our beds,' her friend beside her shouted.

Fromme pointed to the guards, ordering them to push the crowd back. Karfreitag shouted something – but the noise of the crowd now was so loud I could not hear what – the guards stood before the crowd, and Karfreitag walked up to Fromme and grabbed him by the shoulder, and spoke into his ear.

Fromme turned, bowed to the crowd, stood tall, and waved his hand at

Karfreitag. The sergeant drew his sword, as easily as he drew himself onto women's bodies, and slipped the blade into the mound of salt, like your father poking the fire on a winter's night. The crowd clapped him, civilly. He drew the bloody sword out and slipped it in once again. They clapped again. The cairn collapsed some as Stumpf died inside. A little river of blood gurgled from the white mound of salt.

'Done,' called Karfreitag.

Fromme walked behind the sergeant and set his hands on his shoulders. 'Good people of Bideburg,' he said. The folk were quiet.

'Good people of Bideburg – one of you a moment ago said they had to work tomorrow. That you need bed. Well, let me tell you that you do not. Tomorrow is a proclaimed day of celebration – a day free from work for all.'

He shouted the last words and the crowd loved him then, again – they roared and cheered, and leapt up and down on the spot, slapping each other on the back.

'Listen, listen,' Fromme shouted. 'Please, friends.'

'Yes, my lord,' called out a voice, and some in the crowd bowed to him. Others shouted 'shush' and 'be quiet, the master must speak'.

'Tonight, we celebrate the Lord God's victory over the werewolf of Bideburg. Our work is done. The state will make sure tonight that all meat and drink is paid for by us. Do as you will – that is the rule tonight, good people of Bideburg.'

The folk were dancing together now, and the music struck up again. The men and women cheered Fromme as the people's champion. Those who had left were sent for and returned to the celebration.

'So, no more speeches,' said Fromme. 'No more justice. Tonight, you must celebrate the rebirth of your village under the grace of God.'

The people went off to drink and dance. Fromme stayed with Karfreitag in the street. A few other townspeople still stood there too – to look at what remained. Fromme spoke to Karfreitag – we could not hear. Karfreitag called over two constables and pointed to the still burning stakes where Stumpf's wife and child were lumps of tar now somewhere under the embers. The constables pulled Stumpf's body out from the mound of salt and dragged it over to the fire. He was a curled pink dead snail. The two stakes were falling now, together and against each other, into one wide licking bonfire – slipping, with biting sparks and grating. A great orange and black pyre. The stake that had been erected for Stumpf sat to one side, unlit. Fromme had wrongly measured out the killing. He'd piled on pain too soon and robbed himself of the sight of Stumpf burning alive under the moon before the townspeople.

The constables swung Stumpf's body – on a count of three – and threw it – for it was an it, a heap – easy onto the fire where his wife and child burned somewhere within. The body fell down into the flame – a broken jumble – and sizzled for a moment, but then it was gone. The wild fire collapsed in on itself and sent up a shudder of red sparks and flares into the night air.

Karfreitag clapped his hands and all the men, and all the townsfolk still in the square, they jumped. 'You have orders, people,' he called, with a laugh in his voice. 'We must celebrate.'

The guards and constables and townsfolk laughed with him, and they walked off with Karfreitag to the inn, and the dancing and singing on the banks of the black river, silvered up by the moon and stars.

Karfreitag called out, 'Drink men, and sleep tomorrow – for the next day, we will find the wolf's daughter, and our old friends Paulus and Willie.'

★ ★ ★

Sometimes when I watch a play I am so transfixed and taken into the world of the characters, that I am not within my own body – I am on the stage, and part of the drama. I wince when a character falls or is hurt – and I feel echoes of the pain they feel in my own body. When Faustus is torn I feel the Devil's razors on me. Executions are like plays, and plays are of religious origin. Death and drama and God are all one.

Paulus did not watch closely, lost, like I did. He looked away often, for long moments, and he cast a low, repetitive monologue on the killings, cursing the people below, and their ignorance, and God and all the churches, and human kind, both men and women. 'We are forked monsters. Look at us, we have teeth and claws and the bodies of monkeys. Lechery and fear and hate – but most of all ignorance and greed. For that the world should burn on its stem.'

Divara kept her steady, quiet, hateful study throughout. Only at the end, when the stage was empty and Bideburg was celebrating in the inn, dancing on the patch of grass behind the inn by the river, only then did Divara cry for her family – and she also talked for the first time since we had come to the cave of what we were to do. Between us, we knew we had to leave the cave – but where and how, when, we had not resolved.

'We have these,' Divara said, and she fetched the keys to the keep, taken from the guard I had killed in the cell, from one of the bags.

'To what point?' I asked. Her family were dead. There was no-one to save. Nothing could be done in Bideburg.

'We can run tonight, tomorrow, the next day,' she said. 'but they will find us if we run. I know this. So do you. We can, then, stay here – until the food runs out. We have enough food to last us many days more still. But once the food is gone, we are finished. Or we can go to the keep.'

'There are weapons in the keep,' said Paulus. And I knew from the way he spoke, that words had passed between them which I knew nothing of – they had decided something together in the night, when they were hushed and touching in the bell chamber.

'A man should fight,' said Divara. 'So should a woman.'

'Gunpowder. Arquebus. Grenades,' Paulus said to me. 'A full armoury.'

'We need to escape,' I said. 'Not fight. Get to the Netherlands. To England. If we set foot in that town, we will be cut to pieces.'

Divara nodded.

'Yes, you are right. We need to escape,' she said. 'Perhaps escape is best. I am not thinking clearly.'

'Escape is maybe best, then,' said Paulus. 'We do not need to fight, if we can find a safe way to run.'

And a look passed between them that I did not understand – though it felt the kind of look of judgement that parents share about the children they love, but who let them down.

'Wait till Fromme and Karfreitag have left the town,' I said. 'They will not find us here. They will search and then leave in a few days. Then we can make good an escape. We can do this. I believe it.'

'Their keep is empty tonight,' said Divara, half dreamy. 'I have been watching. No-one has returned there. It is deserted and they are drunk in the inn and dancing by the river.'

We could hear them in the inn, and see them twirl each other around by the arms on the banks of the dark running river.

'Escape is best,' said Paulus, though he sounded false.

'I know,' she said. 'I am just seeing in my mind the vengeance I could have on them. I would bloody the sky. Scorch the earth.'

'If I were brave enough to die, I would do it,' I said. 'But I do not wish to die.'

We watched the town fall drunk to sleep and become quiet. Then we went back to the belly chamber and slept together on the cave floor, under blankets. I thought I would not have been able to sleep but sleep, my old friend, came over me in a few moments. Sometime later, I felt Divara and Paulus move, and they roused me a little. They were going to the bell chamber to be together, and that made me happy again. I returned to sleep but I did not dream one dream, nor hear them love, though their talk was a low murmur that lulled me through the night.

★ ★ ★

I woke – it must have been many hours later. Divara and Paulus had returned and were sat away from me, still talking together, whispering. I did not stir or show I slept no more. I listened to them.

'A soldier, a soldier – can you imagine me a soldier?' it was Paulus who was speaking. 'I had to become one, though. After the fall, when Munster hit the ground and the holy poor with it, and the Kingdom of God risen did not come to the Earth, it was then I had my little rescue. I was not strung up like some of the children who refused to put down their weapons; I was not given away as sold labour either – and that was all well and good and down to the brains in my head. The children were questioned and assessed by priests from the Prince-Bishop's court. The Prince-Bishop ordered me, and some of the other boys like me – twenty of us, maybe, the bright ones who could read and write, for few of the rebels' children were literate or numerate – to be sent for schooling in the monastery, and saved from death as repentant innocents, which we had sworn before the cross we were – and I was repentant for who would wish Munster on the world a second time. The repentant girls were sent to a convent and I heard from them never again in my life and have not asked about them to this day.

School at the monastery was good enough for a few years – our sins had been forgiven and we were not to carry the guilt of our fathers and mothers – but I knew time was running out fast for me, and I'd only be a schoolboy for a little while longer, so I worked, and when I got my shout for the army, even the monks had not much more to teach me – I'd read all the books in my father's print shop since I could remember and was far ahead of my friends in class, though they were not stupid and did not need encouragement to keep their noses in the books and work hard either. There is safety in study. My education in the monastery cost me a three-year service in the Prince-Bishop's Hunter regiment – that was the price that the Prince-Bishop had decided when he plucked me and the other boys up like flowers on the battlefield. I was not put in as a common soldier, though – thanks to my education – I was attached to an officer as his bodyguard while I trained. But it was a time of general peace and I was allowed a dispensation, a furlough, from his Grace, the Prince-Bishop, to go on to university and take my studies in law, while I was still in uniform. I got that degree in just one year, Divara – one year, I was the king of my class.'

Divara interrupted him. 'Oh, Paulus,' she said, not mocking but teasing, as lovers do with each other, 'you do not have to tell me of your great successes. This is not St Agnes Eve – you do not need to woo me with the wonders of your life. It is you I am grown fond of, not what you have done and what others think of you.'

And I heard her kiss him.

'I suppose I may have been boasting,' he said, 'and that is my vice. But that was not the purpose of my story. My story is about the army, but I do not like to talk much of those times – and it is always easier for me to talk of the university, which is my home. I am not a man made for the barracks.'

'That is good to hear,' she said. 'I do not like soldiers.'

'I wish you to learn something of me,' he said, 'so you may know me better as a man.'

'That, I would like,' Divara said. And then Paulus kissed her.

'So when I was not in training for the army, I was up at the university lost in law books. That was my life – studying and soldiering. I was like a worker bee – again, I am not boasting, simply explaining. When I took my degree, I found my time split – sometimes in uniform at my work as a soldier, and sometimes in my town clothes working for his grace, the Prince-Bishop, where he needed me – apprenticed to this magistrate, or that magistrate, working on state papers, the drudgery of a young lawyer. But the time came soon, when the peace looked unsteady once more, and I had to put my academic life on hold, and wear the badge of a soldier. I entered the army full-time and was made up to officer-adjutant.

It was a position wealthy young men, the third or fourth sons, usually acquire. As a new adjutant, I had an advantage over the other young soldiers, fresh recruited – few had seen any of the life of war like I had seen, and so I was more ready for uniform. Or if they had seen war, they'd seen it from a hilltop with a picnic basket and wine, their nursemaids or mothers beside them, watching their father move his regiment around on the field below. The other boys who had come to the monastery with me from Munster were not sent on to university as I was, and so had joined their own regiments, and gone deep into the military life ahead of me, though with positions much like mine. I saw none of them again either, and have never wished to do so.

I found I could fight – not well like the front-line men or a skirmish group – but if someone closed on me I had that thing within me which allowed me to kill. A platoon of us were sent with my officer to clean out a little squad of Black Renters up by the Flemish border. The old peasant fighters from the revolutionary war had set up in the swamps, and were extorting from what passed as lords up there – young puny boys whose fathers had been killed or lost most of their lands.

We raided their settlement at night – in the marshes and squalid as a midden – and I killed two men and a boy. Soldiers often say they never talk about the men they kill to their friends. I do not worry. Better to talk about them, so someone remembers them, than to be forgotten forever. In my heart, back then, I did not oppose what the Black Renters had done. I maybe even favoured them – for a little of Munster has always remained within me, though I have kept it buried down. Still, I was on one side and they were on another and I had a life to live. Their headman wasn't taken alive, but his brother was – and his brother was his chief lieutenant. We'd been told that the Black Renters were a mill stone around the necks of the local lords so we took the brother of the headman and hung a mill stone around his neck and made him walk into the marsh. After he drowned, the other men and all the boys above twelve were hanged, and some of the soldiers – nearly all of the soldiers – did what they pleased with the wives and daughters. It looked like a painting of Hell – again. When men put on badges and uniforms and are given power, they become the engineers of Satan. There is no God in an army, and even the good can be more wicked than the worst devil in hell. In the morning, a number of the women had been killed, and the little children were crying. One woman, who I had watched die, had her children gathered around her in her hut. I gave the children some coins – a lot of coins, all the money I had – and her oldest son, maybe ten, flew at me, to strike me. I knocked him down and he did not get up. My officer came and told me to get out of the hut – we were burning the village. I picked up the woman's two daughters, girls of six and seven maybe, and they screamed like little foxes under my arms. I gave the girls the money and pushed them away. A friend of mine, a boy called Dolphie, he burned the hut and we left.

After that I was in clearing operation after clearing operation. I fought two campaigns in the east, where I came to hate Slavs, and one in Italy, when my regiment was sold to the Papal State. During the Italian campaign, I was promoted to company officer. I had languages so was able to run intelligence for the regiment, and a decent grasp of tactics from reading the endless campaigns of Caesar – Julius also taught me how to dress up a good battle report or field report so it seemed that I was the golden child of Mars blessed with Alexandrian brains. I got promoted again, and was called back to court when my time as a soldier had all but ran out. I was young and fresh from military service, and I thought it a good time to continue my education. My lord, the Prince-Bishop, agreed and paid my scholarship, on condition I join his court once I had finished my studies in the university. One debt was paid off, and another offered to me on a plate of gold. I accepted, but I wangled it, though, as time went on and I kept getting my degrees, that I could both work for him and continue in the books at university. My lord, the Prince-Bishop, has kept me bonded to him like a little slave boy since he first plucked me off the field in front of Munster – I live because of him, I was educated because of him, I work as his servant, at what he tells me – whether killing or lawyering or running his lies and errands for him. I am my lord's awful creature. But I love him a little.

Before he let me go back up to the university, though, my lord sent me on one final errand – to go find a wife. He told me, "Take a month, son, two, three, as long as you need, come back married." The man who was to be my professor at university told the Prince-Bishop that I could not be married and attend his college, no student could. My lord changed the law, that day – for me – and he took me aside, after he'd mapped out my future the way Philip once drew his battle plans in a sand-pit in his army office in Macedon, and my lord told me that if he'd had a son like me he would have been proud – and I did love the Prince-Bishop then for all that he had done for me, and I felt in my soul that I should serve him, and do right by him, and all the thoughts of the lies of Munster and the heresy of the holy

345

poor and the destruction of the church and the state and the rule of law seemed to me like words written in the book of Hell by the smoking hand of the Satan and van Leyden and his followers, like my father. So I wanted a wife because my lord had forgiven me my past and told me I needed a wife to serve him, and I wanted to serve him because he had saved me and blessed me. So I went off to find a wife.'

* * *

I lay dog, and pretended to sleep, and listened to Paulus talk of his life to Divara.

'Back in Munster,' said Paulus. 'I thought to look for family and friends – but everyone's family was like mine, one or two at most surviving. This is how I came to know Willie – my blood aunt's husband was still alive and so was his niece. Though in blood it all means nothing, we were still some kind of distant kin – this uncle and this far cousin and I – in-laws in a way. This distant family of mine, which did not bear my blood, was the tiny spark that brought me and Willie together, years later. This uncle, he was Willie's father's oldest friend. The time when I speak of, though, this was before Willie was born, I think. It must be, though I am not sure. However, it is good to have kin, even distant kin. My uncle and his niece had not lived through the siege of Munster – and so they were not scarred or wounded in their souls. They had fled during the uprising – terrified by men like van Leyden. Though my aunt had stayed behind – as she was in the vanguard of the holy poor, and married one of the high Elect in the early days of the free city. The parents of the niece had stayed to fight with van Leyden too. My uncle snatched his niece and took her from the city when the chaos first broke out. My aunt, the niece's parents – they had all died when the siege was broken. And this is how many families were split and sundered by the war. My uncle and his niece returned to Munster after the fall, and took up the threads of their life in the city they loved. He raised her like his daughter, and she treated him as a father. They were good people.

I married the niece, as there was no family blood shared between us – we were just cousins by connection – and my wife was pretty – fresh and natural. She could read and write and was clever – sharp – and she enjoyed me talking to her about books and the world and the ideas that were changing in the world because of books. Her name was Alice.

Munster was still rebuilding, and the people were quiet – the government quiet too in how it treated them, for the folk of Munster were a whipped dog that had taken enough and needed some time to lie down and lick raw wounds clean. So our wedding was small and still, but we dressed well, as I had the money to pay for good clothes for us and a party with cakes and pies and plenty to drink for everyone. I took the smallest dowry – I wanted no money – just what custom insisted. I had spent two weeks in the city and this uncle of mine, he had taken me in, and his niece had been kind and gentle, and I believe we would have loved each other very dearly for the rest of our lives. When we married, we did say to each other that we loved one another, though I felt that the word love was still too much, yet I said it to her as I wanted her to be happy and I wanted to love her. We were coming on to love, quicker than most young couples. We were at the same stage, I believe, on our wedding day – wanting love, knowing it would come, that we were the best that we could find, just needing to grow into our love that was still unformed and soft and in want of a little tending.

We spent three nights married in Munster, growing closer by the moment – full love just there beneath the surface, waiting to sprout and flower – and then we set out back to the court. I had lodgings arranged for us, as it was still not agreed that my wife Alice and I could live together in the university. She was not fit for court – though she was a lady in her heart and mind and manners, and I saw her as a lady too. We'd live in town and I would study and do my business at court as commanded. Alice would be my boon at home and my babies' mother. I was happy and free as the birds in the sky.

If I paint a picture of Alice for you it will break my heart. She was, to me, a woman perfected. Pretty, not beautiful, womanly in her shape – not thin or fat – but a girl you wanted to touch. Brown hair, ordinary in colour, but luscious like running water, and her eyes clear and wide – a high set face, with a mouth shaped like wanton. She had grace, but was not prissy and dull or coy – and she had wit. When we left Munster, taking the road back to court, she sang and told tales, and could read the stars at night – tell their stories, which I adored as I knew them too, and we could share ideas about the first people who thought these myths up, while looking together at the sky above us. It took two days' and two nights' travel to get from Munster to court – but it was summertime, and this made the journey fine. I'd sold my army kit, bought us good travelling clothes and a little crafted tent of nine poles and two tarpaulins. I had my horse and a cheap pony for Alice, plenty of wine, bread, cheese, meat, pickles. The first night was like Heaven had fallen on top of us – by our fire, with our talk and a little drunk and kisses from one another when we grew silent. In our uncle's house, back in Munster after our wedding, we had to be quiet, but here under the moon, we had a night of love as loud as we wished. I had never experienced such a thing as love that swallows you before, and we were finally and fully in love then, and when we were together in the night we talked about the baby we were making and what it would be called – the lengths I would go to for them, and all the kindnesses and tender things Alice would shower on my baby and I.

In the morning, we said to each other, let us live exactly as yesterday. We rode, we sang, we told stories and jokes, at night we put up our tent and cooked and ate and drank and kissed, looked at the stars, and talked of the baby we were making, and our life to come, and then we slept. A sleep like I have never known again or before – a sleep as safe as knowing you are dead and all cares are gone.

Before sun up, I woke, thinking I heard a dog or wolf in woods near where we camped in an open field. Our fire was out, the stars were growing a little faint. I looked out from our tent, and I thought I saw the dog moving in the trees – black and low – and then came a whoop, like a battle cry – like the battle cry my old Hunter regiment put up when it charged, and a team of men, of state soldiers, my old comrades came running from the woods. They were maybe one hundred paces from our tent.

I came out of the tent and shouted, "Lads – brothers." Though I did not know their faces.

They were right up on me now, all armed, and the nearest to me, drew back his free hand and – he must have hit me on the chin, for I woke up later tied in my tent, my mouth bleeding. The flap was tied back, and the sun was up now. Outside six men, I counted them, were pulling Alice around like she was a doll, and naked. They had a leader – a man they called Brock and then sometimes Badger as a nickname. He did not need to coax or terrorise the other men, they were happy to take part, but he directed and commanded and made the action happen. They raped her, and when they said they were going to kill me in front of her, she pulled a knife from the belt of the man on top of her and rammed it through her throat. I can not say what then happened, but they did not let her go or be in peace, even after she was dead.

When her body was of no more use or entertainment to them, they took me from the tent and marched me past her to be hanged. First though, they said, they would have their breakfast, and they sat and ate our food and drank our wine, around the ashes of our old fire. Alice was not even covered with a coat. They stripped me naked, and tied me face first to a tree. Then they slept and said they would have more fun when they awoke. I would like to say I slipped my bonds and cut their throats – but I did not. A scout team came through, tasked to pull the separated squads together – they were hunting heretic bandits – and I knew the subaltern. We had served together in the eastern campaigns. He cut me free, and rounded up the men who had killed my wife.

What would I like to say about what happened next – I would like to say that I learned of a side of me I had not known before, even through my time in Munster. My friend, the subaltern – all the attackers had been buck soldiers without a rank amongst them and so were immediately under his command, and my witness was good enough for him to sentence them to death – my friend gave me permission to hand out any penalty I saw fit.

I told them that I was going to whip them until they begged to be gelded. And I began. I took Brock the Badger and I tied him to the tree he had lashed me to – hard, old birch bark. The subaltern – young Tenly, that was his name, and he was a decent, good man – he gave me the company whip. I whipped Brock, telling him I would not stop until he asked to be gelded, but he did not ask for a terrible long time. I whipped Brock until there was no skin on his back, and I whipped him until his ribs showed through his side and the humps of his spine were bare. Then he asked to be gelded. I cut him loose and he took down his clothes and he offered himself to me. I gelded him, and showed his meat to him and threw it in the ash of our old fire. Then I hanged him by my own hand – putting the rope around his neck, throwing the length over a tree branch, dragging him up off his feet and holding him there, both of us gasping for air, until he died and I dropped him.

I looked at the other five prisoners. It wasn't that I could not face repeating the same punishment on them as I had doled out to the Badger, Brock, it was that I knew if I began whipping them they would ask for their gelding too quick and then they'd be hanged, and that would be it over and done with. So I said to Tenly, my old friend, "Gather your guard together."

And Tenly got his men on parade, twenty in all, good veterans and no greenhorns. I pushed the five prisoners in front of them, and asked Tenly if I may address the guard as stand-in officer giving that we had served together. He said, of course.

I told Tenly's men, "In ancient times, the great Romans – or so we think of them – had a special punishment for comrades who betrayed them – decimation. This was the policy of removing one man in ten and beating him to death. We do not have ten men here, we have five, so the policy is elimination. There are five of you to every one of them. Split into squads of five and execute each prisoner. Bare hands and feet. No weapons."

The squad shrugged – almost as one – a few held back, but soon the men were on the prisoners like dogs. And kicks and stamps take a long time to kill. To really finish another man with your bare hands or with your feet, you must jump on him, stamp on him, or lift his head and break it off the ground. I told the men not to rush.

And so, that was done, and I returned to court, and asked the Prince-Bishop to excuse me from court duties for a little while – I explained my circumstance and he agreed and even kissed me – so I could involve myself more in studies and forget the world around me for a time.'

★ ★ ★

Divara spoke softly to him, of marriage, saying how as a child, and as a young woman, she had never understood the passion other girls had to be wed. 'Now, I am not so sure,' she said. 'Perhaps, it would be good to be with one other person for the rest of my life – if that other person wanted me.'

'It would,' he said. 'I believe this too.'

Divara was silent a while, and then said to Paulus, 'My mother told me in our cell, "My marriage was not perfect – what marriage is, but certainly your father and I loved each other through all our years of being a husband and a wife. I thought our life together was normal in all ways, bar one perhaps, in that he did not wish to be commanding around me, or you or your brothers and sister. At home, as you know, I was the ruler. He had his commands to give outside, I thought, and so was happy to be still and quiet and ruled over at home. I wonder now if what I was seeing was a bear or a wolf, even, coming home to its cave and cubs and mate to sleep between meals. Perhaps that does make him a shape-shifter – he was the man at home with us, and the beast outside. I know that even at the timbermill, he was feared and could be brutal. Maybe that was him with his pack and biting at their tails to keep them in their place. Out on his own, out when he went hunting – for that is where he told me he was going when he left for all those many days when he was away – that was, I think, when he was his true self.

But he loved being with us too, and he loved me and he loved all of you – you most of all, Divara. I know this in my soul. Your father had strange ways, though. When I think back, I can see those glimmers of his strangeness more clearly now – they were there to be seen if I only looked harder. We are where we are, now, you and I, and I have no shame in telling you things I would never have told you if our lives had remained safe, where they were – but they are not, so I must say, if you are woman enough to hear it, that your father had strange ways in love. He wished me to be commanding in love, if you understand, to often be strong and like a man with him.

He told me once, when we were young, when I was carrying you, in fact, that he wished to drown in me. 'Drown in me?' I asked – and we were fully in love at this time, not just used and accustomed to each other as a wedded couple, but become true lovers and friends, which is rare in marriage. He said he could only feel whole when I was with him, and not just with him but in charge of his mind and his body and his soul, he said. Inside me and so part of me.

'If I could die,' he said, 'I would like to die by being swallowed by you. Being put within you forever.'

I said I could not swallow something so huge and we laughed, but he talked on, saying, 'I do not mean that you eat me – I mean I wish to disappear inside you, to become a part of you, like the sky soaks up dew from a petal.'

He could be poetic. When you and your brothers – my poor boys – were born, and then your sister, I had less time for him when he came home to us – because of you all. Neither of us resented you children, but he was sad, and I was sad for him. I could live as a couple growing old together with children – your father, though, I think, was lost, because it was no longer just he and I alone.

He got his dogs then. I did not really care but for the noise, and what man does not beat his dogs if he is a hunter – the dogs were meant for hunting and if they were not good at hunting then they had to go, and the other dogs learned by seeing the lesser got rid of in front of them. It taught them to be strong – and that is a good lesson, no matter what anyone says. Think nothing of that, though, such behaviour is not unusual among men – they have all been soldiers most of them, and I think that means sometimes the brute must come out of them, as once discovered it can not be locked back away again forever.

But every Friday, we would dine together alone – no matter what was happening with you children. Do you remember? Even recently – two weeks ago, now, I think – we had our last Friday supper together. You children always knew to make yourself scarce, or Greet or her mother before her would keep you entertained and catered for.

We would eat in your father's dark study. I loved how dark it was after the bright whiteness of the rest of our home. We would sit at the low table in those two deep red chairs and eat and drink wine, and talk. He would tell me of the week's business and I would sculpt and shape our response to what was needed – a quick sale, maybe, sackings, hirings, setting up of accounts, loans – to others, never for us, loans are there to make you rich not poor, because you must be the banker. Then we would talk of you and your brothers and sister and our dreams for you, and soon we would drink to get drunk, because we enjoyed becoming drunk together. He was a rare husband, and I was lucky to have him – I did not know about crimes then, and his secret self or what he truly was. So, I speak now as I felt back then, not as I feel today, for I feel nothing now but despair, and betrayal, and madness sometimes, which frightens me, as I do not want to be mad, Divara."'

Divara spoke to Paulus. 'I fear she was mad and I did not know it, Paulus.'

'I can not say,' he said. 'I did not have time enough with her to come to any understanding.'

Divara was silent a little while and then continued, 'In our cell, my mother told me, "When your father and I were drunk we would sit by the fire and laugh about things I can not remember and that meant nothing at the time, nor would be funny now – mostly we would laugh at people we knew and how stupid they were for the way they lived and the things they thought. We would kiss while we laughed and soon we would be together on the floor, not worried how we looked as the door was locked and we could have been on the moon, so far were we from other people.

I would bend him to my will then, your father, in ways he loved – and I do not care if this embarrasses you: live, and go and do with your husband what you will, that is what I say to you as a young woman. I pray one day you marry, and do as I did with mine, and be a woman, free in all you do. Men call us blossom and petal and flower – but a good man is as rare as those flowers wise-women look for in woods and never find. Mine was good to me and to you, and to your brothers and sister. I never saw him hurt other people, as it is said – so how can I judge him on what I did not see when all I can see in my mind and soul is the man who walked in front of my two eyes and did me good? That is why I am here and why you are here: I did not denounce him and scream and point in his face shouting monster or call for his head on a spike.

So it is. But, in his study, after we had been together, we would sit up talking and drinking wine, and sometimes we would still be there when the sun rose and the damn cocks started their crowing and then the dogs their barking. In those hours, we would look through books together and read passages that interested us, or that we thought we could learn from.

He had banned books – Anabaptist books, books said to be written by van Leyden while in Munster, lots of heretic texts. These Munster books – I know it is dangerous to speak of, but I do not think talking about the ideas which came to my mind while I read these books will put me in much more danger than that I am already in – these Munster books, they seemed to make some sense to me.

A person could not be a Christian, they said – unless they accepted Christ. That is all the teaching amounts to – well that, and the holy poor and such, but the holy poor is mere embellishment to sell the central message: I must choose to be a Christian, and so the baptism of a child is a sin – one is forcing the love of God on a child who can not consent to loving God. A baptism is a sign of entry into adulthood and communion with Jesus – only when a child or a parent or a grandparent is ready to accept God should they be allowed to take the rites which show acceptance of God. Age is irrelevant – consent is all. And in that one lesson, the churches and teachings and the authority of the world seemed to come tumbling down for me. I felt excited and on fire.

'Would you take baptism now?' your father, Peter, asked me.

I was scared to speak, even in front of your father, about what I thought of God, but I told him the truth and said, 'Yes.'

I asked him if he would, and he replied, 'The only baptism I want is from you.'

And I took him and held his head in my lap, and I let him kiss me, and I baptised your father and I called him lover and even my god – for he called me his goddess, so why should he not be my divinity too?'"

Minutes passed – many of them – and I realised Divara and Paulus were silent. They were still too – there was no movement. Quietly, I moved so I could see them. They sat together by the fire, watching the flame flicker on the cave wall – not speaking, not touching. I felt the fear of madness too then.

★ ★ ★

It was still night, though pale night, when the shot woke me. I was alone. I stood up and left the comfort of the little fire in the belly chamber. The cave corridor was long and cold, and as I walked, hunched and stooped like an old man, to the entrance chamber, I lost the light of the fire behind, and felt my way forward blind as a mole until the faint dusting of light from the stars and moon outside appeared in the cave's mouth.

There was another shot. I looked out and around and down, the fat curled lips of the cave mouth, shielded by green, a blind to any eyes below. At two hundred paces down beneath my feet, Paulus and Divara were looking over the black battlements of the keep's roof. The town hadn't yet stirred to the sound of the shot. Paulus and Divara walked backwards and forwards across the flat black-brick disc of the roof, fifty paces wide. Divara was loading an arquebus – long as a leg, of slick red wood, the match burning above the firing pan. She handed it to Paulus. He aimed down at the street below and fired another shot – this time at the inn. The shot lodged in the lintel. I threw a stone down onto the keep roof. They turned and looked up. Both lay down on their backs so they could not be seen from the street below. Divara pulled something white from her pocket and Paulus did the same. They waved white rags at me. I threw another stone down. Lights were going on in the town now. Divara scuttled across the roof on her belly, found the stone I had thrown, turned to lie on her back again and then aimed. The stone hit the trees at the cave mouth. Paulus rose fast to his feet, looked over the battlement, and lay back down. He pointed at where he guessed I would be, looking from my perch inside the cave, and he shouted, 'Stay put.'

I could do nothing else. Once out of the cave I'd be seen. It would take me twenty minutes of climbing to reach the ground, another minute to run to the keep – and then what, if the door was locked – they must have locked it – then I would be stood in the street alone. Dead. The town would be full of people in minutes, and Fromme would be set on finishing his business tonight.

The door of the inn opened as Paulus shouted to me to stay put, and a body just stepping outside jerked back in at the command in his voice. Divara crawled up onto her knees and lifted her hands in prayer to me. Her mouth moved silently but with exaggeration. In the dark, I could not decipher what she was trying to say to me. A wolf bell began ringing – the one by the side of the inn. Divara started to load another arquebus. Lights appeared in doorways and men began to come out onto the street. Divara raised the gun in the air and shot. The folk leapt like dogs jerked on a chain, and ducked back inside.

Shadows ran around the backs of the buildings – covered from whoever it was they imagined was shooting at them from the roof of the keep. I watched, intrigued and terrified. I could see everything – beyond all the other players. Paulus, even if he looked over the battlement, would not see the running shadows at the rear of the inn as I did. The townspeople down below could not see who was on top of the keep or what weapons they had with them. When the next shot came – again from Divara, holding the gun at her shoulder – I saw them flinch and move to cover; as they began shouting instructions to each other to get guns, I saw Paulus and Divara squat together and talk. They had no panic. Divara chopped at her palm with her hand – maybe measuring something, reinforcing a point, ordering. Paulus patted the air, calming, controlling. Bells were ringing all over the town now, and lights appearing from further away, up by the poor homes in the allotments, and coming out of the woods.

A shot was fired from cover, somewhere too far away to hit the keep – the bullet petering out with a puff of dust about a hundred paces from the door. Divara handed over a loaded arquebus, and readied up her own. Paulus crawled to the battlement wall – she walked – and they aimed and fired down. A collective gasp came from the men hidden in the shadows around the houses below – it sounded as if there were twenty maybe.

Then Fromme's voice came rippling across the night. 'Who is there?'

Paulus shouted, 'Paulus Melchior.'

'And Divara Stumpf,' she called.

Divara, crouching, finished loading the pistols they had with them – four I saw – and pushed them towards Paulus. The arquebus were scorching and too hot to load again. I checked the ground behind me on the floor of the entrance chamber, where we kept our weapons. Two loaded pistols had been left for me. I put them in my belt. Paulus moved towards her, hunkered low, and patted her shoulder. She lifted her hand and touched his face, and Paulus leant forward and kissed her mouth. She took her hand away and crept toward a hatch, centred in the roof.

'Why are you here?' shouted Fromme from the shadows – though now I could see him, his profile and leg, jutting out from the corner of the inn. His hand, silhouetted, swayed backwards and forwards in the air as he talked, conducting. 'You were gone. Why have you come back? What is there for you here? You know how this will finish now. You are an enemy of the principality, and you are working for the Devil, or under his spell. You are with the Devil's whore.'

Divara lifted the hatchway. The bells clanged on. People were coming from the dark, from the woods, and along the roads, towards the centre of the town, drawn by the wolf bells. Paulus glanced over his shoulder at Divara and fired down into the street. Divara shouted, 'The Devil's whore wishes you good luck in hell.' And she then slipped into the hatch like a weevil through a wall-crack and closed it over her while the gunshot and her voice were still ringing off the moon.

Remembering it now – it was god-like to watch these characters on the board before me. I wished I could move them, like a child with his tin soldiers on the nursery floor, and take control of the story below me. Finish them all, and go west with Paulus and Divara.

'Cease shooting, so I can come out to speak to you,' Fromme shouted – and to his honour he stepped out from behind the wall of the inn before any agreement had been voiced. Paulus reloaded the gun he had just fired. 'Silence the bells,' Fromme called out, and the bells in the town stopped clanging, though those out in the countryside went on ringing for minutes longer, until the ringers realised the pealing from the heart of Bideburg had stopped, and then they stopped too, and came to see what was happening in their town – they all came to see, every last one of them came to the keep to watch.

'I have stopped shooting,' shouted Paulus. And he checked his guns.

'What is this about?' Fromme called.

'This is a siege,' Paulus shouted.

'I can see that. There will be a hundred men here in five minutes.'

'No, friend. You get me wrong. You are under siege. Not I.'

Fromme walked out onto the street, and then in Bideburg – it was like someone found a termite mound and lit a fire inside – light came from windows and doors, and down the street from torches held high in the air at the head of the town, and out of the avenues of trees, from side roads; the people came like bugs, hiving out of their homes, appearing from lanes and through the hedges, carrying fire. Walking glow-flies. Light and bodies gushing up into Bideburg from the pits and holes and cracks in the town.

'Are you threatening magic?' Fromme called up.

'I threaten everything,' Paulus shouted back.

Paulus kept hard and low against the battlement, then chanced a dashed look over the top. He turned back – looking for Divara, it seemed – with a face like Thanatos the Skeleton had just stroked his cheek and kissed him. I could see no way out for Paulus from my vantage point – and did not understand his actions. From where he was it must have looked worse – for now there were dozens of men at the foot of the keep. Some had lifted stones and rocks. Fromme was talking with Karfreitag, and to the guards and constables, issuing orders. Raben was there. The guards and constables moved amongst the crowd, pointing up at the keep, aiming their own guns at the battlements. Paulus had to be able to hear them. I risked throwing another stone down onto the roof. He looked up as it fell, and I willed him to act – not to sit passive and wait to die.

Still kneeling close to the wall, he laid the four pistols at his feet. He checked all were loaded. He lifted two and then half rose to his knees, not clearing the cover of the wall – he did this a number of times, practising, checking to see how quickly he could stand and shoot. On the fourth attempt, he cast a glance my way, then turned his gaze forward, rose to his feet and fired both guns at the same time down into the crowd. He dropped the guns and ducked down again picking up the two other pistols, rose, and fired two shots once more into the crowd. The men had barely the chance to realise the first two shots had been fired before the next two went off – sending the crowd running and diving and shouting – all four shots found a mark: one man dead – I saw the bullet take the top off his head like a bloody tonsure – three others wounded, two only slightly, in the arm and leg, one hurt badly, blinded, and carried off to the inn, as the crowd of men, now over one hundred strong, moved back around the base of the keep as Fromme shouted at them to hold their ground and not show themselves cowards in front of their women when their town was under attack by Satan. The women cheered from the rear. And I could see Odil and Kroll, Rodinan, Jens – all their children and women with them. Emer and Efer, their husbands. Their pastor Barthelme. The whole town was there, to a soul.

'Enemy of the Church,' Fromme shouted.

'You have just minutes to surrender,' Paulus called from his cover by the wall. 'Go check with your god what you should do. I am coming for you, sinner.'

Paulus was on his knees now, trying to reload his pistols, but I could see, even from the distance I was at, that he trembled and shook. Fromme was running backwards and forwards among the guards and constables – sending Karfreitag to marshal and organise the town's men.

Fromme shouted, 'Fire.' And the guards and constables sent a volley of shot up at the keep, the lead chipping away lumps and clumps of the black stone battlements. Paulus shivered up closer to the keep's wall. One guard's gun blew up in his own hand, taking off his fingers and he screamed and rolled on the ground.

Fromme shouted, 'Torches.' And around twenty men hurled burning torches up onto the roof. Some missed their trajectory and fell back on the crowd below. One man's tunic caught fire and his friends rolled him in the dust to put out the flames. But most found their mark – landing on the roof – sending showers of sparks over Paulus and across the brick tiles. One torch landed hard on Paulus as he crouched against the keep battlement, but it was the wooden stave which hit his head not the fiery tip. He patted the cinders out on his clothes and edged away from cover toward the hatch.

The roof of the keep was dotted with burning torches now though – one slip and Paulus would fall on flame and be alight – another shower of torches and he would burn like a candle for sure. He scrambled over fire to the hatch and kicked the torches away that lay across it. The iron handle was red hot from the fire, the wood of the hatch smoking. Paulus pulled his sleeve over his hand and yanked open the hatch.

'Stones,' shouted Fromme, and a hail of rocks rained down on the roof as almost every man below – Fromme included – drew back their arm and threw whatever stone they had in their hand at the top of the keep. Paulus slipped inside the hatchway and was drawing it closed after him when the rocks fell. If he had still been stood on the roof he would have been knocked to the ground atop the torches and stoned to death as he burned. Perhaps, one or two stones may have struck him as he banged the hatch shut behind him and dropped down into the closed keep. The stones fell so thickly the roof was covered with them, some of the torches were even beaten out by the power of the rocks falling. With Paulus gone, the roof was a barren and jagged, grey landscape of rocks, with fires burning in glimmers beneath the stones stoked by black charcoal from the wooden staves.

'Again,' shouted Fromme. Now all three barrages came at once – gunshot, fire and stones – the battlements ripped and broken, so that even a crouching man would have no cover, the roof piled high with fire and rock.

Then from inside the keep, the voices of Paulus and Divara sounded out. At first, no-one could make out what they were saying but Karfreitag shushed the crowd and soon I made sense of it. 'Surrender. Surrender.' They were shouting from behind the great wooden front door of the keep, set thick and reinforced with iron.

The crowd began to laugh. The whole town was gathered now – though the women and children stood back behind the men, a good hundred paces, out of range should there be any more shots from the keep. Some women shouted, 'What are they saying?'

And the men shouted back, 'Surrender. They want us to surrender.'

Karfreitag sent a group of men away, pointing to the rear of the inn, down near the river. They left, and Fromme ordered all the guards and constables to shoot at the heavy door of the keep. They shot and reloaded and shot and reloaded six times at least. The crowd cheered, and the women and children came closer to the keep, and sang a droning nonsense song, crude and jagged, which went:

A-frogging, a-frogging, a-frogging,
a-frogging we will go.
Catch him by his toes
and see how long he holds.
If you cut off his leg,
see how long he can beg.
Smack him on the head,
and play with the frog when he's dead.

The guards and constables were reloading for the seventh volley when the gang of men returned from behind the inn, down by the river. They carried the sawn trunk of a giant tree, bark still on. Karfreitag organised a battering-ram party, placing twenty men along one side of the trunk, twenty on the other and two of the biggest, strongest men at the back.

They ran at the door and the trunk pounded it, splintering the wood already shot to pieces, twisting the iron holdings. Ten times they ran at the door with their battering ram – and then I heard singing from the keep. Fromme heard it too, for he called on the battering to stop. The night air carried the tart tang of burning from the roof of the keep. Fromme shushed the crowd and ordered them to listen. A child cried out and a mother slapped it into silence. I could make out the words now of the song Divara and Paulus were singing. It was the old peasant song of rebellion.

> *Now watch the young arising*
> *from their places in the green fields of corn,*
> *turning their ploughs into weapons,*
> *casting off looks so forlorn.*
> *Watch them hang their lordships*
> *from the trees they stole from our land.*
> *Watch their battle flags flying.*
> *Walk with them, one of their band.*

'Take down that door,' Fromme roared, and the battering party went to work now like the damned in hell. I counted thirty shunts of the great trunk against the door, and then there was splintering and the screech of iron on iron, the men holding the battering ram lost their footing as the tree broke through into the keep and the party followed after it. A great cheer went up from the crowd, and the people surged forward, but I could still hear Paulus and Divara singing inside – though they were deep within the keep now, far from the door.

Fromme shouted for the crowd to get back and let his guards and constables in, but instead the town's men poured into the keep through the broken door. Thirty or more were inside before the guards and constables made their way into the keep. The singing went on, though the words were faint now – and Paulus and Divara must have been down in the cellars.

The poor children of God gave their lives for him,
they martyred themselves like his son.
For the kingdom of Heaven is there for the poor -
once the rich are all killed, it's begun.

Fifty or sixty men were in the keep now. Fromme followed Karfreitag in, screaming for the townsmen to get out of his way. Odil, Kroll, Jens, Rodinan – they were all inside. I lost the sound of Fromme's voice in the crowd as he vanished deeper into the keep. Raben went in. Barthelme stood praying by the broken door. Even some women and children were inside the keep now – the Jens children, the Rodinan children, a hundred folk at least – the rest of the town gathered around the door and walls. The old on sticks, and the sick and lame, sitting down to watch, nursing their grandchildren in their arms – the parents now running through the corridors of the keep hunting Divara and Paulus.

Then the earth rocked, and the keep seemed to lift off the ground and shudder – its bricks separating, dark orange and red flame inside, roiling in black smoke as it blew to pieces. That is what the keep was doing in front of my eyes – blowing itself to pieces in fire. A wave of heat and sound and force threw me back into the cave – a pillar of flame and stone and smoke rising into the sky. I ran back deep into the cave, fearing the fire might follow me. The roaring had stopped, but smoke, thick and heavy and black, was making its way through the cave towards the centre chamber. I ran to the back entrance and sat on the little lip of cliff there, in the night air, while the smoked rushed through, over me and past me, into the black of the valley below, and up to the ice blue stars and dead-headed moon. Something landed on me, and there was a pitter-pattering all around as stone and pumice and charcoal fell to earth. Behind me, the night glowed orange and black as the keep burned, a cloud of ash rolled over the mountain through the sky. I would have to wait for the smoke in the cave to clear before I could look down on the town. I waited, my legs hunched up to my chin, my arms around my shins, coughing. The burning of the keep seemed to lift the cool of the night air and I sweated. After an hour, I realised there was no sound. There was no moaning or crying or shouts for help or bells ringing. Everything was quiet. Silence had sat down in Bideburg.

★ ★ ★

Come dawn, the cave passages were passable, the smoke mostly cleared, though some threads still hung like ghosts in the ceiling, and the walk was acrid and stinging on my nose and lungs.

At the mouth of the cave, above Bideburg, I looked down, and the town was gone – a burst boil on the land. A deep, black crater lay where the keep had been, torn at the edges, and splattered across where there were once streets and houses. Fires burned in the pit, and along the river bank, and where the homes had once been – the inn, the butchers, the meeting hall. The town was splintered, broke and gone – posts smouldering here and there, and among the ruination, there were lost parts of people, arms and legs and jaws, ribcages, feet, blood bubbling on molten soil.

I looked along the road out of Bideburg, and the fire and wreckage stopped by the head of the town, up by the Dark Hedges, though some of the poor homes there had their straw roofs ablaze from scattered burning brick and embers in the allotments. Apart from the crackle of flames, there was not a sound.

Now, as an old man here in Glasgow, I have heard of Dutch painters, and seen some impressions of their work, where they tried to mimic hell. They played with imps and infernal machines. Hell, let me tell you, needs no artifice. Hell is human dead, displayed like toys. A devil with a fork torturing a dead soul is as nothing to a child's body split and sundered, raw and red, like a slaughtered piglet, on the ground. With a woman's body, rent to ribbons beside it, then a man's, then blood and bones and bits and pieces of things and creatures that once walked around on two hind legs, but were now midden in the mud.

I came down from the mountain, and I fashioned in my head what Paulus and Divara would have done – how this could have happened. My imagining has not changed in all these sixty years or more.

★ ★ ★

Divara had gone down into the keep first from the roof. They would have secured the keep when they first crept in while the town slept drunk – locked and double-barred the big main door. Paulus stayed on the roof, he drew the crowd to the keep, and Divara waited below, inside, behind

362

the wood door and its iron holdings. She heard Paulus on the stairs soon, when he could no longer risk the roof, as the noise and screaming outside rose to pandemonium. And then they sang their song for the town. Then down the stairs, to the powder room and armoury. They shut the door behind them. Locked. They went hand in hand – I know they did – to the cage where the barrels of black hard dust sat in five little pyramids of six – three at the bottom, two in the middle, one on top. Inside, they locked the cage behind them. Both would have had an oil lamp.

They did not speak. They kissed, embraced. And then they spoke, and Divara said, 'When they get to the door to this room – how long do we have before they are able to break it down?'

'At least until the count of one hundred,' said Paulus.

Paulus measured off a one hundred count on firing-cord, and handed the fuse to Divara. A terrible deep sound of hammering came from up above – the door to the keep shuddering. They lifted two of the top barrels and split open the lids, with knives they took from their belts, and poured the black powder around the other barrels, around their own feet, and over themselves, over their hair and clothes. The keep door had broken now and people were screaming for their blood and were inside the passages, running, coming down the stairs. They could hear picks and shovels dragging against the brick walls.

Divara shook and so did Paulus. They looked at each other and Divara forced the long thick wick of the fuse cord into a crack in an open barrel at their feet, black powder piled around them, like a coal hill.

The townsfolk and the guards and constables were in the corridor outside now – a babel of hate – and through the slit grille to the armoury door Paulus and Divara saw faces, teeth and spit and hateful eyes.

And they sang their song again then, Paulus and Divara – and Divara dipped at the waist, still singing, and lifted the end of the fuse cord, held it to the lamp's flame in her hand, and lit it. They were singing the song of joining.

Come join us now, you rebel peasants
and ride our victory flight.
The world is bowed and without its armour
Heaven opens to your might.

And the door to the armoury, it shattered open then, and the people rushed inside, screaming and clawing at the cage – mounting up around them, swords ready, the door clogged with their bodies, and the stairs jammed, the hallways full, the keep stuffed like a roast hog with people, and ringed by them too outside – the old, the frail, and the young, up close by its walls in the night, to listen.

Then Paulus and Divara took hands, I know, as the cage gave way under the weight of the townsfolk of Bideburg, their swords coming close, and Paulus dropped his oil lamp behind him, to add assurance to the cord that burned and fizzed as Divara let it fall and it touched black dust and blew to pieces the people and the place they were standing in, all before the unblinking eyes of God in a pillar of fire and stone that rained down over the mountain and town.

* * *

I came down off the mountain through the ruined village – and I walked out of Bideburg, toward the lakes, with my back to the Dark Hedges.

The way was through the cleft in the mountains, where the river cut the Steipplingers open – along the valley road and into the forest, where Stumpf had run. I looked back, when I walked under the arch carved by the river in the mountains, like a door from Bideburg into the woods and the world beyond – the village throbbed with heat haze from the fires burning in ground where the keep had stood, and fires in the embers of the houses, and in the streets and out into the burning hay and corn fields, and allotment homes. The shadow from the rock roof over my head shielded my eyes, and I turned away.

The rocky archway carved by the river runs for no more than fifty paces, and I was soon out into the air, on the other side of the mountains, with Bideburg at my back. The stink of burned village was on me – wood and hay and people. I walked to the river bank and washed myself – stepping in and going under, scrubbing at my clothes and hair. I returned to the road and walked with the sun drying me. Ahead, maybe another fifty paces, I saw a bundle of rags blow in the breeze – washing flung from a line by the wind. The rags were burned, and then they rose – suddenly filled, and rags no more, but clothes with a living body inside. But it moved strangely, upon its knees, and I thought it was a scarecrow come to life for it had the articulated movements of something that was not alive but yet was automata enough to turn and try to stand and speak. It gargled – like it was cleaning its mouth after dinner. I held back and then saw the road ahead that took me from Bideburg and I slapped at my face, like a wan boy, to ready myself and I walked on towards the thing. It was a man, or a well grown child, burned black and bald. The crust of the skin was split like hot sausage and pale cooked pink inside.

As I neared, I wondered if I knew it – if I had talked to it, or seen it, if it was Fromme's boy, Jodel. Whatever it was, or who it was, or how it got there, I slipped my knife into it as I passed and walked on from the road by the river into the forest. I left my land and have never returned.

I have read some old pamphlets telling of what is supposed to have passed in Bideburg in the summer of 1563. I am here to tell you that I did not die there, as they say, with my master Paulus Melchior, and all the rest, and that Satan did not come to destroy the village in order to rescue his creature on Earth, the werewolf Peter Stumpf, who escaped and still lives in the forest. We destroyed Bideburg, and I walked away a living man, though lost to history until today.

Epilogue

For the future, so that in years to come you may understand a little more about the author and the times in which he wrote.

History is a most peculiar thing, as I have learned from more than fifty years' teaching it as a scholarly subject. The worst scholars enforce a frame around history – this happened, and that led to this, and then the result was that. History does not work in such a way. History is jelly – or rather history is time's jelly. It is never firm, it can be scooped out, and portions of it forced into pots, but all that is in the pot is a little taste, not the whole edible dish. Humanity can not see history as a whole, for we are always within it and can not look from above on the complete, vast, unending tale. History is, of course, a story, a series of interconnected stories but no story or saga or epic ever came near to the telling of full truth. Nothing tells the full truth, save for science – but science is dead to the human soul and the human soul is what fashions history. The only lesson history can teach you, if you are a student of mine, is that humanity will never have the full truth. After fifty years' teaching that is all my lessons amount to – and I would still give good marks to a scholar who admitted their lack of knowledge rather than tried to enforce a false cage of their own human fashioning upon history. Of course, it is better to have some truth – even half formed and stunted – than no truth at all. Would you rather cling to thin air as you fell from a cliff or to a thin branch jutting from the mountainside? That is why we read our history.

And so, before I finish, I must fashion some understanding of the spirit of the times back when I was a boy. And that is the story of the Empire. It has taken me until this turn in my life to come up with a suitable metaphor for the Empire. Metaphors help students. So it is a shame I am no longer teaching as this metaphor is good to my mind – not that I ever taught the history of the Holy Roman Empire as that would have been too close to my soul, and I would have feared something might be seen to slip from beneath my gown and show that the Empire was more to me than just a lesson – that I had personal knowledge of it somehow, and that would not tally with the story of my life that I have told for decades now. I stay mostly among the Caesars.

The metaphor came to me last Sunday. I was walking on the hill above the cathedral after evening service – I go for the music and choral song which I adore. It was a fine and warm late June night, which is not common in Scotland or in Glasgow, and I stayed sitting on the hill till ten at least. The weather reminded me of the times back in Bideburg. The sky was palest violet and the clouds orange, red, pink and white. One colossal cloud came across the sky. Who knows where from – the Kingdom of Norway maybe or further back from Muscovy, from the land of the Tartars even. It rode the sky like a continent would ride the open ocean if it was cut lose from its shoring in the Earth. As it came overhead, smaller clouds were ripped from it by the wind, high in the atmosphere, and these lumps dissipated or were swallowed back into the gulf and body of the continental cloud. And as the cloud ate up these blobs and drops, it changed in turn – bulging here, thinning there, and causing more of itself to cast off in smaller clouds, which were then soon consumed themselves or died and faded to wisp beyond the mother mass of that great glowing continent. That was the Empire – a huge sprawl that lost a principality here and there, regained other territory just as rapidly, saw its borders forever changing and mutating. The Empire was a shifting thing made of princely alliances, marriages, bishoprics for second sons, failed pacts, rivalry – but it was steady and moved on. Implacable. Even a wind – like the wind which whipped up then on the hill above the cathedral – could not rip it apart. The wind was as powerless as war or revolution to the Empire. The continent just juddered and split a little but held together and soon reformed back into a wall of cloud once more that slipped red and pink and white and orange past my head and on into the west, to the islands and Ireland and the sea beyond where the new world lies. Wind and war and revolution. And so it remains, until this day of my writing. Perhaps it will never change. But Rome fell. Greece. Egypt. Babylon.

I picked my way home off the hill when night started to fall, walked back to the cathedral and onto the High Street. This is a city of many thousands of people and the street was crowded. Students were drinking at The Bull and hollered me over. I went to them and they cheered to see me come their way. I still like a free drink and the attention of the young. I realised that I had taught all their fathers. I had taught one's grandfather. They were privileged young men, and they were eager to show off their learning to me. One asked me the best approach to the discipline of history, and I said, 'Just make it up – that's what the people who made history did. Ask Caesar, he'll agree.'

And they laughed, for they thought it was amusing – that I was making a point about the lies in Caesar's essays on the Gauls – and I laughed because I did not like them and they did not know it. They paid for my drinks and I left. It was only a few minutes' walk to my door, even on old legs. Twenty or thirty steps on, and on the other side of the road, a man, well-dressed – he was a linen merchant from nearby, I knew his face – was pushing a drunk girl up a lane. I crossed the street and stood at the foot of the lane and watched. The girl had collapsed. The man kicked her – to see if she was conscious, not to hurt her, though the kick was not light. When she did not move, he knelt and pulled her legs open, lifting her skirts above her head. I walked back to my student friends, waving them toward me, and shouting to them to be quick.

'You want me to teach you lessons, boys?' I said. 'Well, here's one. Go into that alley and teach the man in there a lesson.'

The boys whooped and jumped and clapped their hands and slapped each other on the shoulder. Here was permission to offend. They raced across the road. I went inside the inn and paid the boy there to go and fetch the nightwatchman from the tollbooth near my house. I left the inn and returned to the head of the alley. The girl still lay on the ground, safe now, and the boys were kicking at the unmoving body of the linen trader.

'Enough,' I said. I didn't even need to raise my voice.

They stopped and looked at me.

'Pick up the girl and bring her to the inn.'

They fixed her skirts and lifted her up and two shouldered her back to the inn. I told the boys to order more drinks and bring some aqua vitae for the girl. She did not come round – though she was breathing well, and I told the boys to lay her on a table to recover.

'Why do you care about her?' one asked.

I turned and slapped him hard across the face.

'Is she a human being?' I asked them.

The boy I slapped apologised.

'Do what is right,' I said. 'Your position blinds you to the life of girls like this – and you should know better if you have human souls. If you were her what would you want to happen? You would want some well-reared decent soul to protect you. To understand history, boys, you need to shape history. History will flow out of control unless we put our hands on it and form it. It can be a place of death and beasts or it can be our best attempt at happiness. We shape history, not others. Use force for good in your own life, and when you use it, know when to stop, once good is done.'

The nightwatchman came, and I paid him enough to make sure the girl had a bed at the charitable hospital for the night, and then added in a little more money for him to ensure that she was safe and had somewhere to go the next day. If the girl had no home, he should contact me and I would speak to some of the charitable groups of the Kirk for help.

The money I paid out did not equal the money the student boys had spent on my drinks. So I went on my way, happy with the tally of history for me that day.

★ ★ ★

A few months ago, I finished my last academic volume in the study of my rooms here in Glasgow. The book had taken me the best part of ten years to write. A simpleton could have gained their doctorate twice over in the time it took. And it only runs to some one hundred and two pages.

My work was on euhemerism – the study of how myth becomes accepted fact, history, part of reality. I lectured on this at least twice a year for thirty years. Few of my students cared, and took the class only because they had to, or to butter me up for better marks – I could not enforce the subject into the exam system, though, I was always and only a mere professor, and had no real say in the college administration.

My lectures stayed on classical myth – was Zeus an ancient king who became a God as his legend lived on? I would quote the Phaedrus and Socrates: take Orithyia and the wind god Boreas. On a certain cliff in Arga, they say, Boreas bore the beautiful Orithyia away. Orithyia, from all we know, was human – like you or I. Boreas, he stole her for his bride as she played with her other beautiful young friends on a cliff. Now might it not be, asks Socrates, that what happened was that the most beautiful young girl in some ancient time in that place along the Ilisus was playing like a nymph with her friends on a cliff when the wind blew and she fell to her death? The loss of one so beautiful, so pointlessly, had to be explained, and so the myth was born – that a god took her as his bride. Socrates and Phaedrus talk of an altar to the wind god where the girl fell. Might it not be her funeral cairn.

And what of centaurs too, I wondered to myself – for Socrates could not explain those away. I can. I believe – as I wrote in my book – that Centaurs were the first men to take to horseback. It takes years and the skill of generations to catch and break a horse. If some ancient tribe had been the first to tame horses and ride them into war then might not the first villagers and peasants to see these men charge toward them not think that man and beast were one? The myths tell us always of the Centaurs' lust – their abductions and rapes. A band of men on horse would deal in such terms with the women of a burned village once all their men and boys were dead.

Now in my book – *Meditations on the Euhemerist Interpretation of Myth* – I did not take my thinking beyond the world of Homer and Virgil. Virgil, indeed, allowed me one of my best chapters – a study of how Aeneas, fleeing Troy, founded Rome. Strip out the gods and supernatural, and you have the simple story of a man running for his life in the wake of war, and laying down his sword to found a land in the first free space he could set his feet.

Of course – and this is why my book still languishes with the academic council – all a reader needs to do is to pick up the threads of my argument for themselves and then ask the same questions of Christ, and God, and the Bible.

No-one can read my book and not be left asking – so is Christ then a myth, born out of some misremembered past? And if so, what of God?

Good. I am proud of my sneak and craft in putting such an heretical thought into the head of every man and women who can read without making a rope from my words to hang me with, for who can damn me for believing that Zeus is not real, that centaurs are a fantasy, that maybe Aeneas did exist but he was a simple man who founded the Roman line and never heard the voice of a god throughout all his troubled life.

And who then can think on Aeneas' story, and not have their mind drawn to Abraham – and then, does the whole rickety edifice not come tumbling to the ground in sawdust and splinters?

Perhaps, Jesus was just a prophet – that is how my argument pulls the human mind. And if that is the case, perhaps then, the Moslems are more true to their God than we are to ours. They have a human prophet – they did not make Mohammed a God too, to sit alongside Allah in equality. If they chose teaching and we chose magic... that is how the book is meant to make the mind run, without one word of this written.

* * *

Only nature has any permanence – and so it is one of the few things we can understand. There is a tree that sits outside my window. I can see it now, and I measure my life by it. Today, it is in full green lush bloom. I can see its top boughs from the window in the attic of my house where I write, three floors up. It will tire in a few months and then sleep over winter, and wake again when I am a year older, and it not changed at all. I have watched this wondrous creature – for I think of it as alive – for thirty years at least. If some vandal chopped it down or if lightning hit it, I would be bereft, and believe I would mourn for it like one of the women I have loved in my life when I lost them.

No women now though. The best of my friends is a young man who comes to visit me – an Irish student of mine, who is now graduated and teaches at the university. He has picked up some of my classes for new entrants. Niall MacAoidh – an Irish boy with a Scottish name, which I find quite amusing, but then there are many Scots in Ireland now. He was one of the few students to take an interest in my lectures on euhemerism, and helped me with some research for my book, without asking anything in return. He has taken up the case for publication of the work with the academic court as I am too tired now to stand all day in a draughty hall arguing with men that I should be allowed to say what I please, as what I have said should offend no-one. I am not to blame for the thoughts in your head. I have breakfast to eat, and lunch and dinner. I have drinks to drink, and little walks to take, and this story of mine. That is plenty for me now.

Niall MacAoidh is coming to take me to dinner in an hour, and it is getting dark in my room and becoming hard to write. He is a good boy, and I know I will not be walking on this Earth for much time longer, but I have nothing of substance to give him. You have guessed, I think, that I am childless, and that is grievous to my heart. He is not as a son to me – though

I like him and wish him a good life, for the world needs more good quiet boys such as Niall MacAoidh. So, I am going to give him this – my story here in these pages. He could, if he wished, print the book, turn it into a pamphlet, and make himself some money – for I reckon if people like tales of golems and werewolves then they might wish to hear how golems and werewolves really are when you meet them face to face. If Niall MacAoidh does publish my book when I am dead, then I will be glad – for him – and for me, as I would like the world to have some memory of Willie Lessinger who died long ago in Bideburg and has been remembered by no-one since that day. And I would like the world to remember Paulus as well, and Divara – and her mother and the child Rosa – but Greet most of all.

Note

The contents of these pages are from the text of a notebook left to me in the will of my friend and former teacher, William Loos, a Dutch master at the University of Glasgow, who died in the winter of 1627, aged eighty years old.

I have read it, and with it some letters of instruction from Master Loos, as he was known to me, though if this text is true that may not be the name of his birth, nor may he be of Dutch descent, though he was a teacher of excellence and honour, and remains a dear memory to me until this day, despite the contents of this work.

I have chosen, and instructed in my own will, not to commit his writings to print, as was my right in the instructions given me. Instead, the notebook is to be placed away, in a quiet part of the university archive, where it may one day serve a purpose.

Niall MacAoidh
1665

With thanks to Adrian Searle, Rodge Glass, Robbie Guillory, Catriona Stewart, Jean Rafferty, Julie McDowall, Colin Campbell, Iain S Bruce, Harry McDonald, Jenifer Johnston, Alison Chiesa, Erin Vlack, Louise Welsh, Iain Ruxton, Jonny Jobson, Fiona Brownlee, Persephone Lock, Morven Dooner, Oliver Ninnis, David Robinson, the staff of the Sunday Herald newspaper in Scotland, all staff at Freight Books in Glasgow, and my family Nicolla, Niamh, Caitie and Moira Mackay.